PIECES OF SKY

Behind His Blue Eyes

KAKI WARNER

BERKLEY SENSATION, NEW YORK

THE BERKLEY PUBLISHING GROUP
Published by the Penguin Group
Penguin Group (USA) Inc.
375 Hudson Street, New York, New York 10014, USA

USA | Canada | UK | Ireland | Australia | New Zealand | India | South Africa | China

Penguin Books Ltd., Registered Offices: 80 Strand, London WC2R 0RL, England
For more information about the Penguin Group, visit penguin.com.

BEHIND HIS BLUE EYES

A Berkley Sensation Book / published by arrangement with the author

Berkley Sensation Books are published by The Berkley Publishing Group.
BERKLEY SENSATION® is a registered trademark of Penguin Group (USA) Inc.
The "B" design is a trademark of Penguin Group (USA) Inc.

For information, address: The Berkley Publishing Group,
a division of Penguin Group (USA) Inc.,
375 Hudson Street, New York, New York 10014.

ISBN: 978-0-425-26326-6

PUBLISHING HISTORY
Berkley Sensation mass-market edition / August 2013

PRINTED IN THE UNITED STATES OF AMERICA

10 9 8 7 6 5 4 3 2 1

Cover art by Claudio Marinesco.
Cover design by Lesley Worrell.

ALWAYS LEARNING   **PEARSON**

*To the lovely ladies of the Loose-Hipped Book Club
of Cashmere. Y'all are the best!*

One

"Another letter come today."

Audra looked up, her mind still caught on whether to use "further" or "farther"—she always confused the two no matter how many times she consulted *Butler's English Usage Manual*. "From whom?"

"That town in Colorado Territory." Winnie Abraham set a travel-worn envelope beside the stack of scribbled pages on Audra's desk, her disdain apparent in the pinch of her full lips. "Sound a right dismal place, you ask me."

Audra checked that the letter had, indeed, come from Heartbreak Creek, then dropped the unopened missive into the overflowing waste bin beside her desk. "Has Father eaten?"

Winnie nodded, the white cap pinned atop her tight gray curls bobbing with the motion. "Had a good lunch. Hardly spill a drop."

Movement drew Audra's eye to the front window. A black, closed carriage stopped before the rented house she shared with her father, Winnie, and Winnie's husband, Curtis. Four men stepped out. *Oh, no!*

She jumped to her feet. Did they know? Had they found out what she had done? Frantically, she gathered the notes piled on the desk and shoved them into the drawer. "Hurry! Help me pick up this mess."

"What's wrong?"

"It's Father's colleagues. Maybe they found out about him." Racing to the bookcase, she stuffed books and notepads into the lower cabinet.

Winnie crammed down the wads of paper in the waste bin and pushed it under the desk. "Maybe they just dropping by."

"To have me arrested, no doubt." Audra slammed the cabinet door and looked breathlessly around. Her heart pounded so hard she thought she might faint. "Where are Father and Curtis?"

"Last I seen, headed to the stable to pet the cats."

"Make sure they stay there."

They both flinched when the knocker on the front door sounded. With trembling fingers, Audra tucked a loose strand of brown hair into her bun and made a final inspection of the room for loose papers and reference books. Everything appeared in order.

She faced the stout, dark-skinned woman, who was old enough to be her mother, and since Audra's sixth birthday had served as such. In the twenty years since, Winnie had added housekeeper, cook, nurse, and benevolent tyrant to her duties, ruling the household with sharp criticisms and gentle hugs. Audra was terrified of what might become of her, and Curtis, and Father if she went to jail. "How do I look?"

"Best remove those." Winnie waggled a finger at the cloth shields tied around the cuffs of Audra's sensible at-home dress.

Quickly stripping off the protectors, Audra stuffed them into the cabinet with the papers and slammed the door shut again. "Anything else?"

"Spectacles."

She slipped those into her skirt pocket, then smoothed her hair again with trembling hands. "Better?"

"You might at least try to look pleased. Not every day you get callers."

"Especially ones who have come to accuse me of fraud."

"Smile anyway. Wouldn't kill you and might fool them."

Audra pasted on a stiff smile. "How's that?"

"Make an undertaker proud."

Another wave of panic rolled over her. "Oh, Winnie, what if they—"

"Calm yourself, child. And quit twisting your hands. I can hear your knuckles cracking from over here."

Audra struggled to breathe. Her throat was so tight she felt suffocated. Excuses and explanations and lies tumbled through her head.

She could tell them she had always transcribed Father's papers and that when he became ill and she found his notes in his desk, she had continued to do so. It was his research, not hers. She had just put it in readable form.

And signed it with his name. And forged his signature on the royalty checks. And lied to anyone who asked about him.

Another knock almost buckled her knees.

She took a deep breath, let it out, and nodded. "You may let them in, Winnie. Then go tell Curtis under no circumstances is he to allow Father to come into the house. Understand?"

"'Course I understand. I'm not a nitwit like some in this house." Muttering, she crossed the entry hall and flung open the front door. "Afternoon, gentlemens. What a fine day for visiting. I'll tell Miss Audra she got company."

"Actually," a deep voice said, "we've come to see the professor. Is he in?"

"No, suh. He off studying whatever it is he study. But Miss Audra here."

A moment later, they filed into the room. Audra recognized them all, and knew the youngest quite well. Scarcely daring to breathe, she studied their faces, but saw nothing to increase her alarm. Richard even smiled at her.

Audra's father, Professor Percival Prendergast Pearsall, had once been a revered member of the group that these men represented. He had been the driving force behind the Baltimore Society of Learned Historians for so many years he had become the yardstick by which all other members were measured. "Mind your *P*s" had become the frequently heard admonishment whenever a contributor offered his treatise or essay for consideration in the esteemed annual historians' publication. It had been her father's exacting standards that had made the society and its annual competition the final word in historical analysis.

And now all of that was in jeopardy because of her.

Fearing the worst, she positioned herself so that the callers faced the front windows rather than the buggy house and stable in back. "May I offer you refreshment, gentlemen?" she asked, nodding in welcome to misters Uxley, Beamis, and Collins, and to her onetime suitor, Richard Villars. It was a struggle to keep her smile intact and her voice steady.

Hiram Uxley, the president and most officious member of the group, shook his head. "We cannot stay long, Miss Pearsall. But it's imperative that we see the professor. Do you expect him soon?"

Heat flooded her face. "I regret not, sir. He is still visiting the ancient pueblos in New Mexico Territory and will be gone for several more months." This was the third time she had put off her father's colleagues with that excuse. Had they finally seen through her lies?

"Several more months?" Uxley's mustache trembled in agitation. "He's already been gone over two years. What on earth could he have found?"

"I ca-cannot tell you, sir. He's been very secretive about it."

"This certainly puts a twist in our plans." With a huff, he turned to the other three gentlemen and engaged in a low-voiced conversation.

Audra watched them, terror pounding through her. A familiar bark sounded, and she looked out the window behind her guests to see Winnie chasing after Curtis, who was chasing after her father, who was shuffling after Cleo, his little dog. Horrified, she glanced at the others to see if they had noticed, and found Richard Villars also watching the drama playing out beside the buggy house.

She watched puzzlement come over his face. Then recognition.

He knows.

He turned to her and started to say something, but Uxley interrupted. "Well, Richard, there's no help for it. Present the award to Miss Pearsall, and she can inform her father when next she sees him."

Award?

Richard pulled a small brass medallion and a folded piece of paper from the inside pocket of his frock coat.

"As treasurer of the Baltimore Society of Learned Historians," he said, "I am pleased to present our annual Historian of

Merit Medallion, as well as the Peabody Grant, to Professor Percival Prendergast Pearsall for his very excellent essay, *The Development of Gas Artillery Capsules and How They Might Have Altered the Outcome of the War of the Rebellion*." With a bow, he held out the paper and medallion. "Please convey to your father my congratulations, Miss Pearsall. His article was one of the most articulate and compelling I have ever read."

Audra stared at the items in his hand, her mind slow to take it all in. They didn't know? They hadn't come to have her arrested?

"Miss Pearsall?"

Looking up into Richard's worried face, she forced a smile. "Th-Thank you." With shaking fingers, she slipped the paper and medallion into her pocket. "I-I wasn't aware he had entered it in this year's competition." She certainly had not done so, and had only transcribed her father's notes on the subject in hopes of gaining another small royalty to augment their meager income.

Mr. Uxley stepped forward. "That was my doing, Miss Pearsall. With so few entries of true merit"—he sent Richard a pointed look—"I thought it wise to put the society's best work forward. Reputation is all, you know."

Color surged into Richard's face, but he didn't respond to the jab.

"It's an excellent piece," Mr. Beamis offered.

"Hear, hear," Mr. Collins seconded. "Odd, though, he didn't write about his current project. We're all most curious about what he's found."

Audra felt wretched. One of the reasons she hadn't entered the article in the contest—other than the fact it would have been even more dishonest than offering it for publication—was that she guessed Richard would be submitting his own paper on cave drawings in the southern Appalachians. He was so desperate to establish himself as a leading American historian it was almost painful to watch. Sadly, he was a much better researcher than writer.

Uxley waved the others toward the door. "We must be off, Miss Pearsall. Our congratulations again to your father." As misters Beamis and Collins filed out, he glanced back at Richard, who hadn't moved. "You coming, Villars?"

"I'll be along in a moment."

After the front door closed behind them, Richard frowned

at Audra, then at the buggy house. Thankfully, neither the Abrahams nor Father were in sight. "Was that your father I saw, Audra?"

"My father? When?"

"Just now. Out back."

She pretended confusion while her mind raced for a plausible lie. Then she smiled and shook her head. "You must have seen Uncle Edward, Father's older brother. He took ill not long after my aunt died, and has been slow to recover. We've taken him in until Father returns."

"I could have sworn he was the professor."

"They do look much alike, don't they? Although since his illness, Uncle Edward has become alarmingly weak. I'm not sure how much longer we can keep him here without proper nursing. But I would hate to put him in a home. They're so awful. I'm quite worried about him." She realized she was babbling but couldn't seem to stop herself. She was a horrid liar.

Richard's dark gaze bored into her in that intense way she had always found intrusive. "Maybe on my next visit I might meet him. Next week, perhaps?"

"That would be lovely." The muscles in her face trembled with the effort to hold her smile. "But do let us know when you plan to come, won't you, so we can be sure he's up to a visit. As I said, he's quite frail."

"Of course. Until then."

As he let himself out, Audra collapsed into the chair at the desk, tears further blurring her faulty vision. Now what was she to do?

Winnie came in, still winded from her chase out back. "What happened?"

"Richard Villars saw Father. I told him it was my uncle Edward, but I don't think he believed me. He's invited himself back next week to meet him. What should I tell him?"

"The truth."

Audra pressed fingertips against her throbbing temple. "I fear it's gone too far, Winnie. If Richard tells Uxley, he'll feel honor-bound to bring my deception to light. Father's reputation will be ruined and all his hard work will be forever shrouded in doubt. And if I go to jail for fraud, you and Curtis will be on the street and Father will be shuffled off to one of those wretched institutions for mentally impaired indigents. I can't allow that to happen."

"Mr. Villars care enough to propose to you last year. Maybe he still take you." Winnie gave Audra a critical look. "'Specially you fix up some."

Audra doubted it. Richard didn't like being thwarted and had taken her refusal hard. But how could she have accepted him—even if she'd wanted to—without revealing Father's dementia? And if he found out she'd been lying to him and had cheated him out of a coveted award, there was no telling what he might do.

"It's too big a risk, Winnie. Richard has much to gain by exposing Father, and you know he has always been ambitious."

"Then leave."

She looked up in surprise. "Leave? How? You know I have barely enough money to keep the four of us fed. And even if I could afford it, where could we go?"

Winnie dug through the waste bin, then straightened, the sealed envelope Audra had thrown away earlier in her hand. "How about here?"

"Heartbreak Creek?"

"Why not? You say your daddy inherited a cabin there. Dismal-sounding town like that be a fine place to hide. I bet nobody there care that you wrote your daddy's papers for him." She tossed the letter on the desk. "Jail, marriage to Mr. Villars, or Heartbreak Creek. You pick. Though after thirty years married to that no-talking Curtis, I had the choice, I'd pick jail or that dismal place. Be livelier, that for sure."

Audra pulled the society's letter from her pocket and unfolded it. Richard had said something about a grant. If it was enough—

She gasped when she saw the amount. With that much money, they could cover a lot of miles—assuming Father was strong enough to make the trip, and the cabin was even habitable, and she was willing to leave everything she'd ever known.

A ghastly prospect, but what other option did she have?

Pulling out her pen and a fresh sheet of paper, she began to write.

Dear Richard,

I know this comes as a surprise, but Father has asked us to join him in New Mexico. By the time this reaches you, we will already be gone, and I doubt we'll return in the near future . . .

Two

He should offer assistance. That would be the neighborly thing to do.

Instead, Ethan Hardesty crossed his arms and outstretched legs and settled back on the bench outside the Boot Creek Depot. The woman was clearly out of her depth. Yet she kept at it. He'd give her high marks for that, at least.

A gust of wind flipped up the hem of her skirt, giving him a fine view of narrow feet encased in delicate low-top shoes. City people. They never understood that in hard country like this, sturdy footwear was second only to a good jacket, no matter the season.

Hearing a ruckus toward the end of the idling train, he glanced back to see a drover lead a fractious bay down the ramp and hand the lead to an elderly African man who was obviously frightened of the animal. Sawing on the lead and stepping lively to keep his feet from beneath the prancing hooves, the man wrestled the horse over to where the woman was supervising the unloading of a closed, four-wheel, single-horse buggy in the Amish style.

It wasn't going well.

In addition to getting in the way of the freight handlers, she was busy trying to calm the horse and the old man holding him, attend questions and complaints from a cantankerous Negro woman she called Winnie, keep an eye on a mumbling old man—probably her father—and hang on to a thrashing badger-sized dog that barked continuously.

It was like watching a circus. A poorly run circus.

Ethan couldn't remember the last time he had been so entertained.

The man he assumed was her father made a shuffling escape, heading purposefully down the track toward the outskirts of town. Ethan knew there was nothing out that way but rough mountain country, so he kept him in sight, waiting for the woman to do something.

She continued to harass the freight handlers.

Twenty yards. Sixty. Was anyone watching the old fellow?

Hell. With a sigh, he rose and walked toward the woman. On the way, he stopped beside the dancing horse. Grabbing the lead close to the halter ring, he gave a hard yank to get the animal's attention then looked him hard in the eye. "Whoa."

The horse tossed its head.

Ethan yanked again, this time keeping pressure on the lead. "Whoa."

The horse blinked at him, nostrils flared. After a brief staring match, the animal slowly let his head drop enough to ease the pull on the halter.

Ethan gave his neck a friendly pat and turned to the surprised Negro. "And your name would be . . . ?"

"Curtis Abraham. How you do that?"

"Hold him closer to the halter ring, Curtis." He had to raise his voice to be heard over the barking of the dog. "Every time he moves, give him a yank and tell him, 'Whoa.' Don't yell. Talk calmly and firmly and look him in the eye. Make him pay attention to you, not what's going on around him. He's just afraid."

"Me, too," the old man muttered, but did as instructed.

Stepping around the African woman, Winnie, who looked to be near in age to Curtis—spouses, perhaps?—Ethan approached the circus ringleader.

She was surprisingly small to be generating such a fuss, and was even able to convince two hulking railroad workers to do her biding. Ethan realized why when he stopped beside her. Despite that furrow between her dark brown brows, she was uncommonly pretty . . . in a fine-boned, delicate, citified sort of way. Hardly the type of woman he normally found attractive.

"Would you like some help, ma'am?" he asked.

She gave him a distracted look, the dog squirming in her arms. "What?"

Remarkable eyes, even with the squint. A greenish hazel that he suspected would look greener if she wore something other than that drab gray dress that did little to set off her gold-streaked hair. Although why he would notice such things was beyond him. He was more partial to breasts, himself. And she had a nice pair of those, too, he was pleased to note.

She noted him noting and narrowed her eyes even more.

Removing his Stetson, he gave a slight bow. "May I help you?"

"With what?"

He tipped his head toward the old man scurrying along the tracks. "Him?"

"Oh, Lord!" Almost crushing his hat, she shoved the yapper against his chest and raced off, calling, "Father," in a high, panicky voice.

Ethan looked at the dog in his arms, which had thankfully paused for breath, realized by the cloudy eyes it was blind, and thrust it toward the Negro woman.

She backed off, pink palms upraised. "Not me, suh. I'd as soon throw it under the train, and that would upset Miss Audra, sure enough."

"Do you want the buggy unloaded, or not?"

She thought about it, then reluctantly took the dog.

By the time "Miss Audra" had returned, leading the mumbling old man by the hand, the buggy was on solid ground, Ethan had almost finished harnessing the bay into the traces, and Curtis was tying valises and boxes to the back of the buggy under the barked supervision of both the badger-dog and the Negro woman.

A forceful trio, the badger, Winnie, and Miss Audra.

Waving Ethan aside when he stepped forward to help, Miss Audra opened the door of the buggy and dropped down the mounting step. "There you are, Father," she said in a voice much gentler than the one she'd used on the freight handlers or himself.

The old man frowned at Ethan. "Come for the transcripts, have you, Mitchell? They're not yet ready. The girl has been dreadfully slow this time. You must talk to her, Mary," he added to the woman waiting for him to board.

Mary? Ethan thought her name was Audra.

"I will, Father. In you go."

Once she got him settled with a lap robe over his legs, she took the squirming dog from Winnie and set it in the old man's arms like she was presenting a precious newborn. "And here's Cleo."

The old man grinned. The dog shut up. And the show was over.

If Ethan had expected a "thank you," he didn't get it. But feeling ornery, he couldn't let the oversight pass unnoticed. "You're certainly welcome, Miss Audra. Or is it Mary?"

"Miss Pearsall. Mary was my mother's name." She turned to squint up at him. "How do you know me, sir? Have we met?"

"Alas, no. And I admire your ability to disregard those pesky social courtesies and accept my help anyway. If you have no further use of me . . . ?"

She blinked, obviously befuddled. Confusion must run in the family.

"Then I bid you good day." Hiding a smile, he tipped the Stetson and walked back to the stock car. Renny had already been unloaded. As he tossed a coin to the hostler, he saw the buggy disappearing down the road at a rapid clip. Fleeing, would be more accurate. Much too fast for a lightweight conveyance on a rocky country road. He could guess who was driving.

With a mental shrug, he put the woman and her amusing antics out of his mind and quickly saddled the big buckskin, securing his saddlebags behind the cantle with the fiddle case on top.

If he left now, he could be in Heartbreak Creek for dinner. His meeting with Tait Rylander and his wife—the two principals of the Pueblo Pacific Bridge Line through Heartbreak Creek Canyon—wasn't until morning. Apparently there were issues with both the rights-of-way and the sluice bringing water from deeper in the canyon. Ethan's employer, the Denver and Santa Fe Railroad, was leasing the Rylanders' bridge line, and had sent him ahead to deal with those issues, and to get the surveyors back to work so the graders could get started.

He figured it was a two-week job.

Being a railroad advance man wasn't the most inspiring or challenging work, but he'd been inspired and challenged before, and look where that had led.

Before he could deflect it, an image burst into his mind: three new graves lined up on the bluff beside the hospital, all dated October 21, 1868.

That familiar feeling of revulsion grabbed at his chest. He had been so brash. So stupid. The young architect, overrun with the arrogance and impatience of the untested, anxious to get started on his first solo project.

Instead, over that sultry summer at Salty Point, he had fallen in love, had his heart broken, and had seen his dreams shattered, along with the lives of two good men and the woman he had thought he loved.

A pitiful story. One with all the makings of a sensationalized dime novel.

Except it was true. And those graves atop the bluff were there because of him. So here he was, doing boring, uninspired work that carried little risk or reward. But at least he wasn't responsible for anyone, and that suited him just fine.

After arranging for his traveling trunk to be delivered to the Heartbreak Creek Hotel, he left the depot, Renny stepping out at a fast pace, obviously as happy as his rider to be off the train and on solid ground again.

It was a beautiful afternoon with the clarity that only came in early spring, before summer's dust hazed the sky. The mountains still wore caps of white, and the breeze was cool and heavy with the scent of wet earth and new grass. The freshness of it raised Ethan's spirits and helped dispel the melancholy that always plagued him after a restless, dream-filled night.

He had ridden no more than half an hour when he saw a familiar black buggy stopped in the road ahead, the back tilted at an odd angle. As he drew nearer, he saw Miss Audra seated on the mounting step beside the open door, shoulders slumped, head drooping in her hands. A sad picture, indeed. The others were some distance away, enjoying a rest under a long-limbed fir. Even from thirty yards, he could clearly hear the badger barking.

"If it isn't Miss Audra," he called cheerily as he reined in beside the disabled buggy.

Dropping her hands, she squinted up at him through red-rimmed eyes.

She must require spectacles, he decided. No one would wear that expression without good reason.

"It's you," she said in a tone as welcoming as a stepmother's kiss.

For some perverse reason, he found that amusing. "It is. I see you've broken a wheel. How unfortunate."

She stiffened. "You find that amusing?"

"Not at all."

"Then why are you grinning?"

"Actually, I was trying for a smirk."

She gave a snort that ended in a sniffle. Then another. Horrified that she was about to cry, Ethan softened his tone. "May I offer assistance? Again."

Shoving back a wad of hair that had slipped from her matronly topknot, she regarded him through eyes that were suspiciously wet. "Do you have a gun?"

Surprised, he nodded. "I do."

"Then shoot me, please. I have reached my limit. Not in the head or face, mind you. I wouldn't want to look a mess for my obituary photograph. Here in the heart will be fine." She placed a hand over the bosom he so admired.

Leaning forward, he crossed his arms over the saddle horn. "Having a bad day, are we, Miss Audra?"

Her top lip curled in a sneer, marring an otherwise lovely mouth. "Armed *and* astute. A potent combination."

Potent? How gratifying that she had noticed.

"Get on with it." Closing her eyes, she hiked her chin in a martyr's pose. "I await your pleasure."

Even better. Several pleasurable scenarios came to mind, but he knew better than to voice them. "And the others? Shall I shoot them, too? I could start with the dog, if you'd like."

She actually seemed to consider it.

"Or I could simply replace the broken wheel."

Her eyes flew open. "You can do that?"

"I can. Assuming that's a spare wheel I see strapped to the bottom of the buggy and you don't mind untying the luggage on the back."

Hopping to her feet, she bent over to peer under the vehicle, this time hiking her skirts high enough to reveal trim ankles and rounded calves. "Good heavens! I had no idea that was under there."

"Nor I," he murmured, musing on what other delights might be hidden beneath that drab gray skirt.

"Excellent." She straightened, shoved the hair back again and gave him a smile that lit up her face in an unexpectedly alluring way. "What can I do to help?"

Very little, it turned out, but that was due more to a lack of strength than a lack of enthusiasm. If the woman had been as strong physically as her personality was forceful, she could have held up the wagon with one hand while he replaced the wheel.

Instead, he used the biggest boulder he could carry, a sturdy three-foot log to brace under the axle, and a long, stout pole to lever the buggy off the ground—luckily Curtis had packed an ax. Once the vehicle was unloaded and the front wheels chalked, Ethan positioned the rock a foot behind the rear panel, slipped two feet of the long pole beneath the undercarriage and pushed down with all his strength on the part extending past the rock.

The buggy rose. Curtis slipped the brace under the axle, and from then on, it was simply a matter of exchanging the broken wheel for the spare. Thankfully the women hovered close by, poised to offer helpful tips in case he somehow lost the ability to reason or forgot what he was doing. God bless them.

Soon—even with their help—the new wheel was in place. While Winnie supervised Curtis in the reloading of the luggage, Ethan lashed the broken wheel beneath the buggy, then rose, almost bumping into Miss Audra, who had bent down beside him to inspect his knots.

"You're sure it's tight enough?"

His gaze drifted down her bowed back to the round, pear-shaped bottom pointed his way. "I have no doubt of it."

"Excellent." She straightened. "For the second time, I owe you my thanks, Mr. . . ."

"Ethan Hardesty." He touched the brim of his hat. "And you're quite welcome, Miss Audra. Both times."

"Pearsall. My proper name is—oh, dear!"

Turning to see what had captured her attention, he saw her father scolding and dunking the squirming dog in a puddle of stagnant water beside the road. "Bad Cleo. Mustn't roll in such things. No, no."

"Father, we're ready to go now," she called, rushing toward him.

Propping a hip against the rear wheel, Ethan crossed his arms over his chest and watched her tuck the dripping pooch under her arm, then gently steer her father toward the coach. He admired her patience. The woman truly did have her hands full with this scatterbrained bunch, yet she hadn't once lost her composure . . . except with him, of course, but since that had been his intent, he didn't hold it against her.

"Where are you headed, Miss Pearsall?" he asked while she loaded her father into the buggy and placed the dog, wrapped in the lap robe, into his arms. He caught a whiff of manure and swamp and was thankful to be riding outside.

"Not far." Backing out, she blew that errant lock of brownish gold hair out of her eyes and waved the two Africans to their places—Winnie in back with the old man, Curtis up front on the right side of the driver's box. "A town called Heartbreak Creek."

"Oh? What a coincidence."

"You're going there, too?" With a look of surprise, she turned to face him.

He almost choked.

She was wet from collar to waist. And cold, judging by the way the damp fabric clung to every rounded curve and puckered tip.

He owed the dog a thank-you.

"I am," he said, tearing his gaze away before she caught him again.

"Excellent. Now we can travel together."

Not excellent. He didn't want to have to rescue her at every turn. Or feel responsible for her. The last woman for whom he had harbored such feelings had died in agony. Her screams still haunted him.

But then again . . . Miss Audra Pearsall was a beautiful woman.

And twenty-nine months was a long time.

And he was weary of being awakened by the sounds of breaking glass and screams, and fighting the urge to make them stop by sending a bullet into his brain. It would be nice to feel something other than self-loathing for a change, to be near a woman and not hear those screams in his head.

Just for a while.

So he said nothing. And swinging up on Renny, he waved the woman to follow, and headed down the road to Heartbreak Creek, feeling better than he had since the walls at Salty Point had shattered around him almost three years ago.

Three

Heartbreak Creek seemed to be a town in transition, although Audra couldn't tell if it was sliding toward decay, or climbing out of it. Eyesores abounded: a tent city inhabited by idle Chinese workers along a rushing creek, a rambling multistoried structure perched on the canyon wall above the town—probably an abandoned mine—and piles of rusty metal rails, wooden kegs, tools, and railroad ties scattered beside several canvas-topped buildings and a half-constructed water tower. It gave the place a feeling of impermanence, as if half the structures and most of the inhabitants could be packed up and gone within a matter of hours.

A far cry from Baltimore.

Yet, as they followed the creek into the main part of town, Audra saw evidence of progress here and there—fresh white paint on the little church at the mouth of the canyon, clean storefront windows, a hotel that seemed to be an actual hotel rather than a brothel, a busy general store, a millinery shop, a bank, and even a sheriff's office. The signs hanging over the un-warped boardwalk appeared newly lettered, and only the one above the doors of the Red Eye Saloon next to the hotel showed bullet holes.

Less than Audra had hoped, but more than she had feared.

Mr. Hardesty dropped back beside the buggy and motioned

for her to pull to the side and stop. "Where do you go from here, Miss Audra?"

"Pearsall," she said absently, looking around. "I'm not sure. The old Prendergast cabin is all I know. I have the papers—"

"Never mind." He swung out of the saddle. "Wait here while I check. The local sheriff usually knows everyone in town." After looping his horse's reins around the hitching rail, he stepped up onto the boardwalk and entered a small stand-alone building with barred windows.

"Was that Richard?" Father demanded from the backseat. "You know I don't like him coming around, trying to get a peek at my work."

"No, Father. It was Mr. Hardesty. He changed our wheel, remember?"

"Is Mary bringing lunch? She said she would bring lunch."

"We'll eat soon, Father. I promise."

Grumbling to Cleo, he settled back.

"Like I said," Winnie muttered, "a dismal place."

"You urged me to come," Audra reminded her.

"How'd I know you'd listen to a simple black woman? Or drag us along?"

"You'd rather have stayed in Baltimore with no work and no place to live?"

"I bet there's not a single person of color in the whole town."

"'Cept for yellow," Curtis said. "Lots of yellow folks. And at least one red," he added when Mr. Hardesty stepped out of the office with a swarthy man wearing normal attire except for temple braids and the feather tucked into a strip of leather holding back the rest of his long black hair.

"Lawd help us," Winnie mumbled. "We scalped in our beds, for sure."

"This is Deputy Redstone." Mr. Hardesty nodded toward the stern-faced man at his side. "He says the Prendergast place is about two miles up the canyon. A bit rough, but still usable. He'll be glad to take you there."

His constant jibes notwithstanding, Audra would have preferred to have Mr. Hardesty take them. At least she knew and trusted him. Somewhat.

The Indian must have noted her hesitation. Tapping the

badge on his vest, he said in a flat, expressionless voice, "Do not worry. While I wear this, I am not allowed to kill white women." At Audra's gasp, he grinned, showing strong white teeth in a smile so unexpected and beautiful it took her breath away.

"He's jesting." Mr. Hardesty glanced at the Indian. "You are jesting, aren't you?"

"White people are so easy to frighten." To Audra, the deputy added with calm assurance, "I am Cheyenne. I do not kill women. You are safe with me."

She saw the sincerity in his gentle smile and let her reservations go. She liked the man despite his odd sense of humor. At least his teasing didn't make her feel awkward and bumbling the way Mr. Hardesty's did. "Thank you, sir. I must stop by the mercantile first, if you don't mind, and pick up a few supplies to get us through tonight. Do you know if there is any furniture in the cabin?"

The deputy shrugged, apparently finding furniture of little importance.

Mr. Hardesty frowned. "The sun is already starting down, Miss Audra. Perhaps you should stay the night at the hotel. Redstone says they serve hearty fare and the rooms are clean. There's even a livery on the back street where you can leave the buggy and horse."

Audra mentally counted her coins. She had a draft on her Baltimore account, but judging by the darkened windows of the bank across the street, she wouldn't be able to deposit it until tomorrow. "Does the hotel allow Africans?"

Mr. Hardesty glanced at the deputy, who nodded, a small smile tugging at his lips. "And dogs."

"Excellent." After telling Mr. Redstone she would come by in the morning once she had picked up her supplies, she left the two men talking, and drove back to the hotel.

The desk clerk, an elderly gentleman with a gummy smile and brown teeth—what few there were—happily rented her two rooms. While the freckled bellboy helped Curtis carry their valises up to the second floor, Winnie took charge of Father and Cleo, leaving Audra to attend to the buggy and horse.

The livery was only a few doors down, but once Audra made her arrangements with the liveryman—Mr. Driscoll—she took her time returning to the hotel, needing the few moments of solitude to decide what she should do next.

She had been so driven to get Father safely away before Richard knew they were leaving or discovered her deception, she hadn't given much thought to what she would do once they'd reached their destination. The small amount of money left from the grant would last them a month or two if she didn't have to buy too much furniture to replace what she had sold. Then what? There were no more of Father's research papers she could offer for publication, and without them, they had no income. Perhaps she could find employment here in Heartbreak Creek; but would she be able to earn enough to feed all four of them?

"Why so glum, Miss Audra?" a familiar voice said.

"Pearsall," she said, automatically, and looked up to see Mr. Hardesty standing on the back stoop of the hotel. He wasn't wearing his hat, and the sable hair curling over his collar showed golden streaks where it caught the light of the setting sun. Bareheaded, he looked less imposing—almost boyish— except for the weary droop around his deep-set blue eyes and the dark stubble shadowing his square jaw. "It's been a long, exhausting day."

"Yes, it has," he allowed. "What with helping unload the buggy from the train, and harnessing the horse, and changing the wheel. Was that as tiring for you, Miss Audra, as it was for me?"

"Pearsall! And I have no time for your teasing, sir. I still must get my companions settled and fed, and see that—"

"I had the dining room send up food," he cut in. "I hope you don't mind."

Audra frowned, wondering what he was up to. "Why would you do that?"

He shrugged. "Figured it would be easier. Especially for your father."

She didn't know how to respond. The man confused her at every turn—teasing one minute, doing something nice the next. She didn't know what to expect, or how to react. But this simple act of kindness after such a horrid day undid her. "Th-Thank you, Mr. Hardesty. That's very . . . very . . ." Weakness overcame her and she sagged, head down, tears burning in her eyes.

"Good God. You're not going to cry, are you?" When she

didn't answer, he bent to peer into her face. "I'll have them take the plates back, if you want."

Blinking hard, she waved the suggestion away. "Don't be absurd. I'm sure they've eaten every scrap by now, anyway."

They stood in awkward silence for a few moments, then he let go a deep breath. "Tell me what's wrong, Miss Audra."

This time, she didn't bother to correct him. It did no good anyway. With a sigh, she looked up at him. He was really quite handsome . . . when he wasn't making fun of her. "Do you reside in Heartbreak Creek, Mr. Hardesty?"

"Only temporarily. I'm here on behalf of the railroad. Why do you ask?"

She debated telling him, then thought, *Why not?* If the railroad was coming to Heartbreak Creek, perhaps there might be a need for someone with clerical skills. "I'm seeking employment, sir. Do you think the railroad would hire me?"

His dark brows rose in surprise. "In what capacity?"

"Transcribing notes, doing accounts, filing, anything clerical. I have a fine hand and I'm a proficient speller."

He smiled. "I would expect no less." This time there was no mockery in his tone, and she liked him the better for it. "I'll ask around. Perhaps the businesspeople I'm meeting with tomorrow will have suggestions."

"I would be most grateful." When he put forth the effort, Ethan Hardesty could be a very nice man. "For the second time—or is it the third?—you've come to my rescue. You've been quite the hero today, haven't you?"

His smile abruptly faded. His face went dead set. Cold. Even his blue eyes turned glacial. "Don't ever call me that, Miss Pearsall. I assure you I am no hero." And spinning on his heel, he went into the hotel, leaving her standing, dumbfounded, by the stoop.

The next morning, after another bout with night terrors and restless dreams—the latter thanks to Miss Audra and her wet dress—Ethan left his room to attend the meeting with the Rylanders. As he came down the stairs, Yancey looked up from the front desk.

"Boss is looking for you."

"Where is he?"

"She. Her usual table." Looking past Ethan, he called, "He's finally up."

Turning, Ethan saw a man coming out of the dining room. About his height and dark like him—although his hair was black, rather than brown—with intelligent gray eyes and a scar down one side of his face. "Mr. Rylander?"

"Tait." Smiling, the newcomer extended a big-knuckled hand. "Welcome to Heartbreak Creek, Mr. Hardesty. And to my wife's hotel. Lucinda and I have been looking forward to meeting you."

Ethan took the proffered hand, noting the scarring, the thickening around Rylander's eyes, and other evidence of his violent past. He had heard that Tait Rylander had once been a bareknuckle fighter, but it didn't seem to fit with the fine suit and elegant bearing. "Hope I'm not late. And please call me Ethan."

"Ethan it is. And no, you're not late." Releasing Ethan's hand, he gestured toward a striking blond woman watching them from a table beside one of the back windows. "Please join us."

Even spoken in a polite tone, it sounded more like an order than an invitation. A man of authority. Ethan respected that.

"Thank you." He could be gracious, too . . . when it suited him.

Too bad his parting words to Miss Audra hadn't reflected that. Hopefully, he would see her again before he left. But only to apologize. Nothing more. She was the sort of woman who would expect too much from a man, and he was a man who had nothing to give.

Lucinda Rylander was even more striking up close, but in such a cool, reserved way she appeared unapproachable. Ethan sensed that beneath her watchful green eyes swirled dark currents of distrust . . . except when she looked at her husband. Then her face softened and she became almost playful. Younger. He had thought Miss Audra an intelligent woman, in spite of her addlepated manner, but as he chatted with Lucinda Rylander, he saw a woman so astute it was almost off-putting. Hardly a simpering matron, but a poser of sharp questions and insightful comments, she showed a barely masked strength of will that would have made any battlefield commander proud. Ethan didn't envy her husband, but as they talked, he could see the man had no trouble keeping up with her.

"Your letter said you were having problems with both water issues and rights-of-way?" Ethan leaned back as the serving woman placed before him a plate overflowing with beaten eggs, bacon, sausage, and pan-fried potatoes with onions. While she poured coffee into a china cup on a china saucer, another server loaded the table with bowls of oatmeal, stewed apples flavored with cinnamon, a plate of flapjacks, another of toasted bread, and pots of cream, butter, honey, and jam. He wondered if this was the usual fare, or if they were trying to impress him.

His hostess must have noted his surprise. "I didn't know what you would prefer, Mr. Hardesty, so I had Cook prepare a bit of everything." She watched him try to fit his finger through the delicate handle of the china cup, and smiled. "Shall I have them bring a mug, Mr. Hardesty? Tait prefers that, too."

Relieved, Ethan carefully set the cup aside. "I'd appreciate that, ma'am."

The server brought a thick crockery mug and filled it with steaming coffee. Ethan sipped. Strong and hot. Perfect. Picking up his fork, he dug in.

"The water issues are more of an inconvenience," Rylander explained as they ate. "Vandalism and minor theft of tools. But there are other problems, too."

"Such as?"

"One of the Irish riding bosses. Seems too fond of his whip."

Ethan knew it was customary for the western railroads to use Irish bosses to manage the Chinese work gangs. For one thing, they were bigger and more intimidating. For another, they spoke English. But several years ago, during construction of the Transcontinental, when the Irish went on yet another strike for higher wages, the Central Pacific had responded by hiring Chinese laborers at half the wage. It was immediately clear that the smaller "Celestials" were stronger than they looked. They also proved to be more industrious, and worked cheaper, never went on strike, and didn't waste time in gossip or smoke breaks. Soon the CPRR was importing thousands more Chinese to work on their railroad. An insular group that provided its own food, medical men, supplies, cooks, and religion, the Chinese worked tirelessly and caused little trouble, even when assigned the most dangerous tasks, like blasting out the tunnels. They were too valuable an asset for Ethan to allow them to be brutalized by a resentful Irishman. "What's his name?"

"Tim Gallagher," Rylander replied. "I've talked to him. But you might keep an eye on him, too. Hopefully, things will settle down once we start laying track. Meanwhile, we've got another problem. One of the local men cutting lumber for the sluice died in a fall last week."

"An accident?"

"It looks that way. But his wife insists there was foul play. The man's watch was missing. A family heirloom. She says he's never without it."

Ethan felt a headache build behind his eyes. What had promised to be a two-week job now seemed much more complicated. "The Denver and Santa Fe has authorized me to compensate for loss of life or limb. If the widow wants to relocate, I can give her free passage anywhere our line goes." Considering the harsher attitudes of other railroads, it was a generous policy. "Has there been an investigation into the death?"

"Our sheriff and his deputy are checking into it," Mrs. Rylander said.

"I've met the deputy. An interesting man."

"A frightening man," Mrs. Rylander countered, not looking frightened in the least. "Especially if you threaten someone he cares about."

From the amused glance between the two, Ethan guessed the Rylanders were on the protected list.

"He was a Cheyenne Dog Soldier with Chief Black Kettle's tribe," Tait Rylander said. "After the chief died in sixty-eight and the rest of the tribe was moved to Oklahoma, he stayed behind."

"He was allowed to do that?"

"His grandfather was white. When it suits him, Thomas uses that connection. When it doesn't, he's all warrior. I'll never completely understand the man, but I trust him with my life. Right now, he's acting as deputy, so he's white. More or less. But when Brodie comes back, who knows what he'll do."

"The sheriff is gone?"

"They work in shifts," Mrs. Rylander explained. "And Declan considers himself only a temporary sheriff. His real love is ranching. But his wife, Edwina, or Ed, as he calls her, was recently delivered of their fourth son—Declan has three others and a daughter by his first marriage—so they've been staying in town until she recovers and the sluice issues are settled."

Ethan sipped from his glass. The water tasted fine to him. "Is the sluice really necessary?"

Mrs. Rylander smiled. "You've met Yancey, our desk clerk?"

Ethan nodded. Another interesting fellow.

"Then you've seen his teeth—those that remain, that is. If that's what our water does to teeth, you can imagine what it would do to a locomotive." A look of distaste crossed her face. "It's so thick with minerals you almost have to chew it."

When Ethan leaned forward to give his glass closer scrutiny, Rylander chuckled. "Don't worry. Once we learned there was a mineral hot spring bleeding into the water table, we started carting in barrels of untainted drinking water from deeper in the canyon. As I said, our problems now aren't due to the sluice design or water quality, but because of theft and vandalism."

Relieved, Ethan sat back. A little mayhem he could handle. But he didn't want anything to do with architecture or construction ever again.

Rylander pushed his empty plate aside. "But there's still the issue of the rights-of-way." He went on to explain that most of them had been bought by his wife before they married, and she had offered them to the Denver and Santa Fe on a ninety-nine-year lease in exchange for a seat on the board of the bridge line.

"Most?"

"There's one holdout." Mrs. Rylander waited for the server to clear the table before continuing. "We've written several times to the owner in Baltimore, but haven't received an answer. Our latest letter came back as undeliverable. Apparently, Mr. Pearsall is no longer at that address."

Ethan stiffened. *Pearsall?* "Does he have a daughter?"

"I couldn't say. We know little about him. Or if he's ever even been to Heartbreak Creek. The original deed was issued to Cyrus Prendergast over thirty years ago, and the only change to it has been the addition of Pearsall's name."

Prendergast. Of the old Prendergast place. *Hell.* "Where is the cabin?"

"Two miles up the left side of the canyon. Since the original owner's death in the late fifties, other than the occasional miner or prospector, no one has lived on the property."

Until now.

With a sigh, Ethan pushed back his chair. "Thank you for breakfast, ma'am. It was delicious." To Tait, he added, "If you'll excuse my abrupt departure, I think I might be able to take care of one of your problems today. I'll explain more later."

Four

Audra was glad she had decided to leave her companions behind when she came to inspect the cabin with Mr. Redstone. They would have been horrified.

As was she.

The two-room structure was little more than a log hovel, with a bird's nest in the chimney, mice in the cupboards, and a large furry creature that scuttled out of the back room when they looked in. Mr. Redstone identified it as a marmot and said it was "good eating."

Audra repressed a shudder, praying they would never be in such dire straits that they would be forced to eat rodents.

Instead of glass, the windows were covered with warped shutters spiked with rusty nails so that the pointed ends protruded on the outside. Mr. Redstone explained it was to discourage bears from pushing in the shutters and climbing through the window.

That alone would have sent Winnie scurrying back to town.

The floor was so littered with filth she thought it was made of dirt, but then she stumbled over a piece of broken crockery and saw wood showing. It sounded solid when she stomped a foot, but until she swept it, she couldn't be certain.

For furniture, there was a warped table of mismatched planks, a stool with one leg missing, and a rope-strung bed in the marmot's room, minus the rope and the mattress, which, judging by the wealth of droppings, the rodent had eaten.

The main room held a small cookstove, a counter with a rusty pump, two crooked shelves, and an alcove that could be curtained off and used as a bedroom. For decoration, there was an oil lamp with a cracked globe atop the fireplace mantle beside a regurgitated pellet of hair and tiny bones, probably left by an owl.

The whole place stank of droppings, dust, and despair.

"Rough?" Audra rounded on Mr. Redstone, who was poking at a spider's web with a stick. "You call this 'rough, but still usable'? Are you demented?"

He stopped poking and looked warily at her. "What is demented?"

"Would you live here?"

"No."

"Yet you expect me to?"

He shrugged. "You asked me to bring you. I brought you. Where you live is for you to decide."

The fight went out of her. She looked numbly around, unable to take it all in. She had uprooted her family, dragged her sick father thousands of miles, and squandered most of what little money they had getting here . . . and for what?

"I'm such a fool," she muttered. "Jail would be better."

"No. It is worse."

She looked at him in shock. "You've been there?"

Ignoring that, he looked around. "We can fix this."

"How?"

He banged a fist on one wall. Dust rained down on their heads, but the logs didn't shift. "It is a strong house. When we clean it, you will see."

"We? You'll help me?" She didn't know whether to hug him, burst into tears, or run, shrieking, back to town.

"Others will help. Even now, one comes."

"One what?" a deep voice asked.

Startled, Audra turned to see a familiar figure in the doorway. "Mr. Hardesty! What are you doing here?"

"Looking for you."

That set her back. After his abrupt departure the previous night, she hadn't expected to see him again. Yet, here he was—and looking for her. The thought brought a surprising lift to her sagging spirits.

Today, he wore denim trousers, a collarless shirt buttoned at the neck, and a brown woolen vest with a blue thread that perfectly matched his lovely blue eyes. Even dressed in work clothes, the man had presence. Audra felt a momentary regret that she hadn't worn something more fetching than her faded black work dress, then she firmly pushed the thought away. She wasn't here to flirt—even if she knew how—and certainly not with Ethan Hardesty.

The newcomer glanced around, his gaze narrowing when it came to rest on the Cheyenne. "Morning, Redstone. No deputy duties today?"

"Declan Brodie escaped his woman. He is sheriff until tomorrow." Seeing Audra's confusion, the Indian added, "His wife just birthed a new son. With the other four, she feels . . ." He made a circular motion with his hand, as if trying to conjure the correct word. "Frightened, I think. She cries too much."

"Five sons?" Audra would be crying, too. "More like over-whelmed, I'd think."

"Only four are sons. Brin is a girl child, but more trouble than all of her brothers together." The amused affection in his tone belied the harsh words. Audra guessed the girl held a special place in Thomas Redstone's heart.

Mr. Hardesty wandered the cabin, a look of distaste on his face. "You're not actually going to live here, are you?"

"I have no choice."

He stopped by the hearth, flicked the owl pellet to the floor, then, propping his right elbow on the mantle, rested a foot on the hearthstone and slipped his left hand into his trouser pocket. "Actually, you do."

An elegant pose. Lord of the manor. Audra suspected Mr. Hardesty would feel confident and at home no matter where he was. The stance also reminded her of how tall and lean he was . . . taller than Mr. Redstone by several inches, but lacking the Indian's broad sturdiness. Not that Mr. Hardesty wasn't sturdy. She had seen for herself his strength when he'd lifted the end of the buggy so Curtis could position the brace. "And what choice is that, sir?"

Mr. Redstone resumed poking at the cobwebs.

"I've just come from a meeting with the local couple working with the railroad," Hardesty said. "Mr. and Mrs. Rylander."

Audra frowned. *Rylander.* Why did that name seem familiar?

"They're ready to move forward, except for one minor detail. The last, unassigned right-of-way."

Mr. Redstone paused in his excavations. "What is this right-of-way?"

"A document that grants the railroad permission to lay tracks across a property owner's land."

Suddenly Audra remembered all those letters she had thrown away, unanswered. "Across *this* land."

"Exactly."

Redstone tossed the stick aside. "When will you ask permission to cross mine?"

Mr. Hardesty's blue eyes widened. "You own land in the canyon? Where?"

"Everywhere." The Indian made a sweeping motion with one arm. "From one mountain to the other, this land belongs to the People. It has been so since before Raven dropped down from the sky, or Coyote played his first prank, or you strangers came with your treaties and long guns." He let his arm fall back to his side. "So I ask you again, *ve'ho'e*—white man. When will you ask permission to cross my land?"

Despite the challenging words, Audra saw more sorrow than anger in the Cheyenne's dark eyes. When it was apparent Mr. Hardesty had no answer for him, he sighed and turned away. "It is as I expected." Shaking his head, he quietly left the cabin.

In the awkward silence that followed, Audra felt her anger build. High-handed railroads. Even in Baltimore, she had read of their excesses as they had pushed west—the huge tracts of land assigned to them at no cost, the outright theft of private land not covered by those government grants, gunfights over water rights, running roughshod over the Indian tribes or anyone else caught in their path.

Overexpansion, corruption, shady dealings. It was a national disgrace.

Feeling as displaced as Thomas Redstone, she allowed irritation to creep into her voice. "And now you want my land, is that it?"

Mr. Hardesty pushed away from the mantle. "Only your permission to cross a small part of it. That's all."

"But it's only a small piece of property. How can a rail line come through without destroying this cabin? My home."

He snorted. "You don't really intend to bring your ailing father here, do you?"

"For now, it's my only option." Perhaps later, if she found work, she might . . .

A thought arose. "Did you ask your business associates about available employment?"

"Not yet."

"Of course not," she said acidly, suspicions confirmed. "Why bother to act on your offer to help when your intent all along was to cheat me out of my home?"

"Cheat you?" He lifted his hands in frustration. "How am I cheating you? The right-of-way only grants the railroad permission to cross your land. It has nothing to do with your home. Such as it is."

She clapped her hands on her hips. "It may not look like much to you, you home-stealing scoundrel, but it's all I have!"

"For the love of God!" He spun away, walked a tight circle, then came back to loom over her. He took a deep breath and let it out in a rush. "Now let's be reasonable about this, Miss Pearsall."

She almost struck him.

"You need money. I need the right-of-way. How about I pay you, say . . . fifty dollars to sign the papers. That's twice the regular fee. Enough to keep you going until you find employment, don't you think?"

"And what if the tracks come within mere feet of my front door?"

"You'll still have this lovely cabin, front door and all."

"You—you—!" This time, it was she who stalked away, unspoken words clogging her throat. The man was insufferable. As high-handed as his employers.

Whirling, she charged back. "If I were to allow the rail line to pass through my front yard, Mr. Hardesty, how would I keep my father safe, when he wanders off at every opportunity?"

"Install locks?"

"Get out!" Crossing to the door, she flung it open, startling Mr. Redstone, who sat at the top of the porch steps. "Leave now, Mr. Hardesty!"

"Seventy-five, then." He sauntered toward her, apparently unmoved by her efforts to evict him. "But that's as high as I can go."

She wavered. Seventy-five dollars was a great deal of money. Enough to keep them for quite a while. If they lived *here*. But if she had to pay to live elsewhere it wouldn't be enough. If she could get him to offer more . . .

An idea burst into her mind. Devious. Unworthy. But workable.

"What's your answer?" he asked, standing over her in a pathetic attempt at intimidation.

She pasted on a smile and pretended sympathy. "Mr. Hardesty, I appreciate the fix you're in. Truly, I do. All that equipment and all those workers sitting idle. It must be costing the railroad a fortune. But I'm in a bit of a fix, as well." She paused to brush a smear of dirt off her skirt. "Even if I wanted to, it's not my right-of-way to give, is it? The property belongs to my father, and I'm afraid he's unable to sign his name to anything."

"One hundred."

"In fact, sometimes I wonder if he even *knows* his name."

"One twenty-five. And you can sign for him."

"Forge my father's signature? Wouldn't that be illegal?"

"All right! One fifty! And I swear—"

"Fine. I'll talk to my father, but that's all I can promise." She motioned toward the door. "Now leave. I have work to do."

"But—"

"Good day, Mr. Hardesty."

As the door slammed behind him, Thomas Redstone laughed.

"What's so funny?" Ethan growled, stomping down the porch steps.

"You." Still chuckling, the Cheyenne fell in beside him. "If this is what you whites call a negotiation, I think you lost."

"Cantankerous, hardheaded, shortsighted woman! Someone should beat some sense into her."

Redstone's demeanor changed from white man to warrior in an instant. Grabbing Ethan's arm, he yanked him around. "You will not harm her."

Ethan looked at him in surprise, then jerked his arm free. "Of course not. Why would you think that?"

"You just said—"

"Hell, I didn't mean it! Not literally."

He continued on to where he'd left Renny tied near Miss Audra's buggy and Redstone's spotted horse, intent on escaping before he said something foolish or acted on the emotions churning inside. "She's just . . . just so . . ."

A sudden image bounced through his head—Miss Audra glaring up at him, eyes flashing fire, her sweet lips curled in challenge and those lovely breasts rising and falling with every agitated breath.

Words failed him. Anger dissolved into grudging admiration. *Magnificent.* That's what she was. Passion and strength and beauty. Everything he had denied himself since Salty Point.

Denied . . . but couldn't stop wanting.

Laughing, he swung up on Renny. He felt invigorated and more alive than he had in three years. "Ever heard of a firecracker, Thomas?" he asked the Indian, who was staring at him like he'd lost his mind. "It's a tiny, short-fused explosive. Small enough to fit in the palm of your hand, but noisy enough to start a stampede. That's what she is. A firecracker."

He glanced at the house, then leaned down, lowering his voice so it wouldn't carry. "And just so you know, I didn't lose. I would have paid more." Grinning, he straightened. "*That's* a negotiation."

"Ho. I think you crow too soon, *ve'ho'e*. The woman still has not put her mark on your paper, has she?"

Five

Ethan was still grinning when he reined Renny back toward town. But as he rode, his grin faded when thoughts of Audra Pearsall gradually blended into memories of another woman. Another firecracker. Eunice Eckhart.

Had it been almost three years?

He had arrived at the Salty Point Marine Hospital, north of San Francisco, with a valise full of drawings, his head swimming with ideas that would revolutionize architecture, and a belief that he would soon establish his name among the great architects of his time.

He established his name, all right. But not in the way he'd hoped.

"Before you finalize your drawings," the hospital administrator had told him at their first meeting, "check with Miss Eckhart. She's head of nurses and will know better than anybody what's needed."

Ethan had a time tracking her down, and finally found her standing atop the bluff overlooking the ocean. The image still hung in his mind—her slender frame silhouetted against an endless expanse of sea and sky, blond hair flying, uniform molded to her body by the salty breeze while she took potshots at wheeling gulls with a small bore rifle. She wasn't hitting anything, he noted. But she held the heavy rifle in a firm, steady grip, and didn't flinch from the recoil after she fired.

"Good morning, Miss Eckhart," he called when she paused to reload. He knew better than approach an armed woman without letting her know he was there.

Resting the rifle barrel against her shoulder, she turned. The sun hit her straight on, highlighting one of the most arresting faces he had ever seen. High cheekbones, deep brown eyes, a sensual mouth that curved up at the corners in an ironic smile, as if she knew things—secrets—of which others could only guess. "You're the architect in charge of the renovation?"

"Yes, ma'am, I am."

"Think you know what we need, do you?"

"Not yet. But with your help, I soon hope to."

That seemed to please her. She smiled, further enhancing her beauty.

He smiled back. "You know you'd hit more birds with a shotgun."

"Of course I would. If I wanted to hit birds. I like the noise when I fire and the way they fly off, screeching in alarm. Makes me want to scream with them. Come along and I'll give you a tour of the saddest place you'll ever be."

That had been the first bright moment of what was to become the darkest period in his life.

It was near noon when Ethan rode back into Heartbreak Creek. The sun was high and intense. With the cool March breeze, what mud was left from the spring thaw had quickly dried, hardening the wagon tracks down Main Street into ruts and ridges. Soon they would be gone, too, breaking down into loamy dust laced with horse manure. Ethan could already smell the beginnings of decay.

He let Renny pick his way over the rough ground until they reached the sheriff's office. There, he dismounted, looped the reins around the rail out front, and stepped up onto the boardwalk.

After that huge breakfast with the Rylanders, he wasn't hungry, but he figured that unless the sheriff had been called away, he would be eating lunch about now, either at home, in his office, or at the hotel.

The sheriff was in. As was his wife, who had apparently

brought him a plate lunch, which remained covered and untouched on his battered oak desk. Beside it sat a ruffled bonnet and an empty picnic basket.

The tension in the room could dull a well-honed skinning knife.

As introductions were made, Ethan studied the couple, thinking they were as mismatched a pair as he had ever seen.

Sheriff Brodie was a big fellow, taller than Ethan by a couple of inches, and even broader than Deputy Redstone. He had dark brown hair and eyes, a slow smile, and a handshake that left Ethan's fingers numb.

But what struck him most about the man was his stillness. Such a lack of vitality might have been mistaken for dullness, if not for the utter confidence in Brodie's relaxed manner and the intelligence behind his probing gaze.

On the other hand, Mrs. Edwina Brodie—or Ed, as her husband had introduced her—was opposite in every way. Fair, to his dark coloring. Tall and slender, whereas he was broad as a bull. As gregarious as Brodie was subdued. But the biggest difference was her total lack of guile—or perhaps, restraint—which allowed every emotion that flitted through her mind to show on her pretty face.

And what Ethan saw now in those wide blue eyes was fear. Or, as Audra had said, the panic of an overwhelmed woman at the end of her rope.

"How long will you be staying in our little town, Mr. Hardesty?" she asked, in the drawling, up-and-down cadence of the South.

"I'm not sure, ma'am. But I'm enjoying my stay so far."

"That's wonderful. Isn't that wonderful, Declan?"

Declan nodded. Propping a hip on the corner of his desk, he rested his crossed arms on his thigh and watched his wife.

"Heartbreak Creek isn't nearly as rough as it looks," she went on. "Why, we're even getting a newspaper. Isn't that exciting?"

Both men nodded.

"And as soon as the railroad comes through, we'll have our own little depot." She prattled on for a few more minutes, then seemed to lose steam. "Well . . . I can see y'all have business to discuss, so I won't keep you. But do come by for a visit while you're here, Mr. Hardesty."

"I will, ma'am."

"Wonderful. That's just wonderful. We'll look forward to it, won't we, Declan?"

Declan nodded.

She pulled on her bonnet, tucked in a loose strand of light brown hair, tied the streamers in a bow by her cheek, undid it, and tied it by the other cheek. Satisfied, she clasped her hands at her waist . . . in a grip so tight Ethan could see the whitening of her knuckles. He supposed if he had a new baby and four stepchildren waiting at home, he might be a little tense, too.

"Well . . . I should get back." She said it without enthusiasm, as if hoping one of them would insist she stay. When neither did, she gave a brittle smile and picked up the basket. "The children are probably tearing the house apart even as we speak. I declare, there aren't enough hours in the day to keep track of them. Especially with a new baby and all."

She did look tired. Her eyes looked bruised, her shoulders drooped, and that pinched look around her mouth gave the impression that she was using what strength she had left to hold something in.

Like angry words. Accusations. Or, God forbid, tears.

Ethan had grown up with two sisters. He recognized the look and knew what that fine edge in a woman's voice meant.

Clouds on the horizon. A storm on the way.

Hoping to divert it, he said with robust joviality, "A son, I heard. Congratulations. Have you named him yet?"

She flashed the first unguarded smile he'd seen from her. It changed her face entirely, giving him a glimpse of rare beauty beneath the weariness. Ethan understood then why the sheriff had been smitten with her.

"Whitney Ladoux Brodie. I know that's a mouthful, but they're family names, you see, and it's only fitting that he should carry names from both of us, don't you agree?"

"I do."

She looked at her husband.

He smiled and nodded.

If Ethan hadn't heard the sheriff make the introductions earlier, he might have thought the man mute.

"Well," Mrs. Brodie said for the third time. "I've dallied long enough. You'll be home by five?" she asked the sheriff.

"I'll be there."

"Because Pru still has packing to do, and won't be able to stay long. And Brin keeps taking the baby out of his cradle and carting him over to show the neighbors, and no telling what mischief Joe Bill is up to. You have to speak to them, Declan. I can't—"

"I'll talk to them, Ed. I promise."

"Yes, well . . ."

In an effort to hurry the parting along, Ethan tugged on the front brim of his hat. "I've enjoyed meeting you, ma'am. Hope to see you again soon."

"I look forward to it, Mr. Hardesty. And Declan," she added with a hint of steel in her voice. "I'll see you at five."

"Five," he said.

"Good. Now eat your lunch, dear. I fixed your favorite."

As soon as the door closed behind her, the sheriff let out a deep breath. "Thanks."

"For what?"

"Talking. Every time I do, I get into trouble."

Ethan chuckled. "New mothers can be like that." He had no idea if that was true, but he'd heard it somewhere and it sounded about right. New mothers, new wives, flighty adolescents, any hardheaded, shortsighted, contentious female—they all defied logic.

A hundred and fifty dollars. It was unheard of. An outrageous amount of money for a simple right-of-way. He would probably have to pay half of it out of his own pocket, just to save face. *Hell.*

Redstone was right. She had played him like a trout.

Pushing that unsettling thought aside—along with the disturbing realization that he was more amused by the notion than angry—he explained why he had come to Heartbreak Creek.

The sheriff nodded. "Tait said the railroad was sending someone."

Brodie didn't sound upset about that, Ethan was pleased to note. A lesser man might have taken it as interference or a lack of faith in his abilities to handle the situation. "Rylander told me about the woodcutter's death," Ethan went on, "and the missing watch. Could a raven or pack rat have carried it off? They're drawn to shiny objects."

"Maybe. Or he misplaced it. Or lost it in a poker game and was afraid to tell his wife. I'm more concerned with how a man who knew these woods as well as Hendricks did got clumsy enough to fall off a bluff."

Good point. "Has there been any recent damage to the sluice?"

"A landslide took out a hundred-foot section."

Rylander hadn't mentioned that. "A natural occurrence?"

Brodie shrugged. "It happens in steep terrain."

"Mind if I take a look at it?" Ethan didn't need permission. But he also didn't want to overstep. Doing so would only make his task harder, and might put him on the bad side of a man who could do serious damage if he took offense.

Besides, Ethan liked the sheriff. He admired his easy manner and confident attitude and the patience the fellow had shown toward his high-strung wife.

"Sure." Rising, the sheriff plucked a dusty hat from a hook on the wall. "I'd like to talk to some of the workers again myself."

"No rush. Go ahead and eat your lunch."

Brodie looked down at the covered plate on his desk. With the enthusiasm of a man peeking under a shroud in an undertaker's parlor, he warily lifted the edge of the cloth, took a look, then let it drop over the plate again.

"Not your favorite," Ethan guessed.

"I was hoping her sister, Prudence, made it. My wife's not much of a cook." Then with a broad grin and more animation in his dark eyes than Ethan had seen since arriving, he added, "But she's got other compensating attributes."

"Ah." Ethan nodded in understanding. For a nice set of female attributes, a man could overlook a lot.

Other than a steep wagon track that ended at the old mine on the hillside, there were two ways into the canyon—one on either side of the creek that had given the town its name. The lower, more gently sloped route on the left was the one the railroad would take. The rougher terrain on the right was where the sluice was being constructed.

Brodie took him right.

Eye-searing sunlight gave way to spotty shade as they climbed up through tall stands of fir and pine and spruce. Noise faded. Other than the occasional scolding from a crossbill or jay, the only sound of their progress was the labored breathing of the horses and the muffled thuds of their hooves on the soft ground.

Ethan relished the solitude and resolved to come back at another time with his fiddle. It had been too long since he'd let music ease his troubles. Might help him sleep better.

The higher they rode, the lower the temperature dropped. Here and there, patches of snow still clung to shaded crevasses. Tiny rivulets of icy water, seeping from under tangles of hawthorn and mountain maple, pooled in the tracks of horses, deer, elk, and sometimes bear. The smell of pine and juniper hung in the still air.

They had ridden a couple of miles when Ethan heard the pounding of hammers echo along the canyon walls. A hundred yards farther, they came to a clearing where a group of men worked on what looked like a log flume, only much smaller. An older man, who seemed to be in charge of the workers, waved and came forward when he saw Brodie.

While the two men conversed, Ethan dismounted and looked around.

He already knew most of the particulars of the project. The design was a common one and fairly straightforward. Approximately five miles up the canyon, and a mile past the mineral spring, a simple sliding valve would divert a portion of Heartbreak Creek into the mouth of the sluice. From there, the water would flow downhill to town, where it would empty into two water towers—one near the old mine that would service the town, and the other beside the tracks, which would provide clean, mineral-free water to passing locomotives—for a monthly charge. Any excess water would be channeled back into the creek, thereby keeping the flow moving so it wouldn't freeze in the winter. A good plan.

And a costly undertaking. But once the sluice was completed and the monthly fee from the railroad started rolling in, the investment would quickly pay off. Especially for the Rylanders, who, as majority stockholders in the Heartbreak Creek Development Company, had financed the project. To their credit, they had also dedicated a substantial amount of company stock to the town, as well as a portion of the water fees. That way, once the initial investment was recouped, everyone would have ownership of the water, and any future maintenance costs on the sluice and water towers would be covered by the fees the railroad paid.

A generous arrangement, Ethan thought.

But first, they had to finish the project.

Leaving Renny tied to a sapling beside Brodie's big sorrel, Ethan wandered along the sluice—an open trough with two twenty-inch-wide boards nailed in the shape of a V, supported by regularly spaced wooden ribs with crosspieces over the top to keep the sides from spreading. It wouldn't be watertight, but once the boards swelled with moisture, it would seal well enough. Besides, with a constant water supply, leakage wasn't an issue.

He was glad to see they were using fir and cedar. Pine could be knotty and softer woods weren't as resistant to rot. The supports holding up the trough looked solid, and the cross-bracing seemed substantial enough to eliminate sway once water was running through the sluice. He noted no evidence of shoddy workmanship that would make the structure especially vulnerable in a rock slide.

Ahead, he saw a middle-aged man and an adolescent, who was probably his son, working beside a stack of logs. Both wore the ragged homespun clothing and tattered slouch hats Ethan had seen on many a prospector. Since the sluice was a town project and not part of the bridge line, most of the labor was local, rather than Chinese, who worked exclusively for the railroad. Another boost to the Heartbreak Creek economy.

But neither of these workers looked particularly happy.

"Afternoon," he said, stopping beside them.

The older fellow paused in his sawing. The younger continued skinning a thick log with a two-handled bark stripper.

Introductions were brief and without enthusiasm.

Keeping his tone friendly, Ethan asked if they knew anything about the recent landslide.

"Warn't our fault," the boy blurted out. "That's what we know."

The man, who had introduced himself as Hopewell—an apt name for a prospector, Ethan thought—doffed his hat and swiped a dirty sleeve over his brow. "Nine sections. A week's work, tangled up at the bottom of the ravine like a pile of them eating sticks the Chi-nee use."

"Do rockfalls happen often?"

Hopewell put the hat back on his head, and looked Ethan square in the eye. "With help, maybe."

"Why do you say that?"

"We send crews ahead to check for loose rocks. 'Specially ones big enough to do damage or hurt somebody. Me and the boy walked that ridge ourselves, and we didn't see nothing that could come down on its own."

Ethan digested that. "You think someone intentionally caused the slide?"

"Maybe." Anger flashed in the man's weathered face. "But it warn't us. That's all I know."

"You tell anyone about this?"

"No time. Nobody seemed interested, anyway. Too busy pointing fingers."

"Well," Ethan said with a smile, "we're interested now."

Waving an arm to get his attention, Ethan motioned Brodie over. When he arrived, Hopewell told his story again. The sheriff posed a few more questions, then nodded his thanks and let the workers get back to their tasks.

"You think what he says has merit?" Ethan asked as they headed back to where the horses were tied.

"Maybe. Maybe not. Only one way to find out."

They rode on up the canyon to the site of the destruction, and dismounting, walked the area. Not much to see—a pile of loose stones and uprooted vegetation shoveled aside so the supports could be reset, and a few broken timbers scattered in the creek running along the bottom of the ravine. All the salvageable lumber had already been hauled out and used in the repairs.

Hands braced on his hips, Ethan scanned the slope rising above him. He could clearly see the path of the rockfall. But the longer he studied it, the more it seemed that either it had split near the top or there were two points of origin. Two separate falls—in the same area—at the exact same time? Hardly.

He turned to Brodie, who was also studying the slope. "There were two slides," he said, and pointed. "Quite a coincidence, don't you think?"

"Yeah. I do."

"I'm going up for a closer look."

"Head right. I'll go left."

Moving through brush on either side of the chute, they struggled up the steep incline. It was rough going. Twice Ethan slipped on loose rocks, and once almost ripped open his hand when he grabbed a thorny shrub by mistake. By the time he reached the top, winded and sweating, he'd developed a new respect for Hopewell and his son. And a deep regret that he hadn't brought his canteen.

It didn't take long to figure out what had happened. The two slides were about thirty yards apart. The starting point for each was a deep depression in the earth near the top. The kind of depression a big boulder might make . . . before it was shoved or pried out of its resting place and sent crashing down the slope, gathering stones and brush along the way, until it finally slammed into the sluice and sent nine sections of it sliding into the ravine.

Ethan hunkered beside a long pole that had probably been used to pry the boulder loose. Picking up a small stick, he carefully lifted aside a leafy twig and studied the loose dirt. "Tracks. Human and horse. One shod, one not, although the footprints could be from a moccasin. Indian, you think?"

The sheriff bent beside him, studied the prints, then straightened. "I better get Thomas on this. If any redskins are moving through this canyon, he'll soon know how many, which tribe, and what they ate for breakfast."

Scanning the ground for more prints, he left Ethan and walked over to where the other slide had originated.

At a sound, Ethan looked across the ravine. *Speak of the devil,* he thought when he saw a man on a spotted pony heading back to Heartbreak Creek. Bouncing along behind him was a familiar boxy, black buggy.

Audra and Redstone had been at the cabin all day? Alone?

He tossed the stick aside and rose. "Let's go," he called over to the sheriff. "By the look of the sun, it's almost five. And you know what that means."

Brodie gave him a questioning look.

"Your wife?"

"Oh, hell."

Six

On that first tour with Nurse Eckhart of the structure at Salty Point, Ethan had soon realized it was more like a prison than a hospital. Built in eighteen fifty to benefit sick, infirm, or elderly sailors who had nowhere else to go, it housed several wards of men from countries all over the world.

Nurse Eckhart was right. It was a sad place. Ethan could almost feel the despair hanging over the long rows of beds.

"It must be intolerable," she said in a soft voice as they walked through the wards. "Men who have spent most of their lives surrounded by a limitless horizon, now condemned to these four walls with barely a window to look out of."

Ethan had noticed that. The gloom was almost palpable. And whenever they could, men had left their beds to stand at the windows, staring blankly at the shimmering sea stretching below them.

"Do you think more windows would help?" he asked.

"Immeasurably. And more beds. And more storage. And a gathering place with a view of the ocean. Can you do all that?"

Ethan nodded, plans and drawings already forming in his mind. "I can try."

"Indeed?" She had studied him for a moment, those remarkable eyes as full of secrets as the smile teasing her lips. "I appreciate a man with the courage to try new things. And I'll do whatever I can to help. Come to my room this evening, and we'll discuss it." Then she had walked away, taking a small part of his heart with her.

The morning after her visit to the cabin, Audra was escorting her charges into the hotel dining room for breakfast when a voice called her name. Pausing in the doorway, one hand on Father's arm, she glanced back to see a blond woman with lovely green eyes and a reserved smile walking toward her.

"I'm the owner of the hotel," the woman said, stopping beside her. "Yancey told me you had arrived."

Wondering if Curtis and Winnie were about to be refused service, Audra braced herself for a scene.

Instead, the woman held out a slim hand. "Lucinda Rylander. Welcome to the hotel and to Heartbreak Creek."

Ah. That Rylander. Warily, Audra gave the cool fingers a brief squeeze then released them. "Thank you."

"You may have received our correspondence about the right-of-way across your land?"

"I have. I also spoke to Mr. Hardesty about it yesterday."

"Did you reach an agreement?"

"We are in negotiations."

"I see." The smile started to fade. "Are there any questions I might answer for you?"

"Mr. Hardesty was very thorough and—"

A fluttery motion with one hand cut her off. "I hate to be so forward about this, Miss Pearsall. But until the issue is settled, the railroad can't proceed, and—" She must have sensed Audra's resistance, because she caught herself, then appeared to deflate when she released a deep breath. "Forgive me. I shouldn't be pressing you about this so early in the morning. It's just . . ." She hesitated, then seemed to reach a decision. "Will you join me for breakfast, Miss Pearsall? I promise not to badger you, but I would love to hear your side of the issue." This time the smile was warm and genuine.

Audra glanced at Winnie and Curtis, unsure what to do. Not all restaurants openly welcomed people of color, and without Audra there to smooth the way, it might create an unpleasant situation.

"Where's Mary?" Father asked. "She said she would bring the papers."

Winnie patted his arm in reassurance. "Not to worry, Mr. Percy. She be along soon." Turning to Audra, she said, "We fine eating with Mr. Percy upstairs, if Mrs. Rylander, here, don't mind sending up some plates?"

Mrs. Rylander nodded. "Of course. If that's what you prefer. But we have a table by the window with a lovely view of the creek that might be more pleasant, Mrs. . . . ?"

Winnie straightened, her chin coming up a notch. "Abraham. Winnie Abraham." With great dignity, she extended her hand.

Without hesitation, Mrs. Rylander took it.

"And this here's my husband, Curtis."

Mrs. Rylander shook his hand, too. "Mr. Abraham."

Any reservations Audra might have felt about the woman immediately dissipated. Slipping an arm around Father's shoulders, she concluded the introductions. "And this is my father, Percival Pearsall." Relieved to see kindness rather than pity in Mrs. Rylander's expression, she smiled. "And I think he would enjoy the window table immensely."

"Will Mary be there? She's not usually so late."

"She on her way, Mr. Percy."

Soon they were all seated—the Abrahams and Father at a corner table by the window, Audra and Mrs. Rylander at a smaller table nearby. Before their coffee had arrived, she and Lucinda Rylander were on a first name basis.

"Who is Mary?" Lucinda asked, pouring cream into her cup.

"My mother. She died twenty years ago. But Father . . . is unwell."

"I'm sorry to hear it."

"He's gotten so much worse over the last year. That's one of the reasons we came here. I'd like for his last days to be peaceful ones." Audra explained about Father's tendency to wander, and that because of it, she had grave concerns about having a rail line pass so close to the cabin. "If I were to accept Mr. Hardesty's generous offer, I would have to move to a place more suitable for Father. And with the added expense of rent, any money received from granting the right-of-way would soon run out."

Lucinda listened without interruption, her elbow propped on the armrest of her chair and one long finger gently tapping her lower lip. Audra could almost see ideas and solutions bouncing behind those intense green eyes.

"And what if he were to offer you rent-free housing, as well?"

Audra hesitated. She knew she was being prideful and hard-headed, but the idea of becoming an object of charity, or being beholden to strangers—especially Ethan Hardesty—was repugnant to her. She treasured her independence and guarded it zealously. That was the reason she had refused Richard, being unwilling to marry a man she didn't love just for the sake of security.

She had managed so far. God willing, she would continue to do so.

Buying time to consider her response, she took a sip of coffee, then returned the china cup to its saucer. "I am currently seeking employment," she said in the spirit of compromise. "If I find something that will produce enough income to support the four of us, I will be happy to consider Mr. Hardesty's offer. Until then, I have no choice but to stay at the cabin."

"Then we must find you employment. I assume you can read and write?"

And have won awards for it, Audra thought, biting back a smile. "Yes. I'm competent with sums, as well."

A sudden smile lit Lucinda's face, one so broad it left a dimple in her left cheek. "Then I have the perfect opportunity for you, although I won't know for certain if it's available for another week or so."

"That's very kind. Thank you." But wanting to make her position clear, Audra added in a firm tone, "But until the issue of employment is settled, I shall hold off on a decision about the right-of-way and do what I must to make the cabin a suitable home for the four of us."

"I understand." Lucinda laughed, apparently undeterred by Audra's gentle warning. "And I won't badger you again about signing the papers, even though I'm certain it will all work out. But be forewarned"—she gave a sly wink—"I usually get my way. Ask my husband."

She was so brazen about it, Audra had to laugh. "I'm certain you do."

Reaching across the table, Lucinda gave Audra's hand, which rested beside her plate, a squeeze. "I sense we are going to be great friends, you and I."

"I would like that." Audra meant it. Since Father's illness, she had let most of her friendships lapse, and dearly missed the companionship of women.

Chuckling, Lucinda sat back. "I can't wait for the other ladies to meet you. They'll adore you for resisting my manipulations."

"What other ladies?"

"The ladies of Heartbreak Creek. And a formidable group they are."

It took less time than Audra expected to bring the cabin up to snuff, especially after Lucinda and Yancey arrived several days later with a wagon full of household goods, including furniture, bags of bedding, and kitchen stuffs.

"Ethan said the cabin was rather Spartan," she said, climbing down from the wagon when Audra and the Abrahams came out to greet her. "After the renovations at the hotel, I find I no longer need all this and thought it might be of use to you."

Audra was so grateful, she almost burst into tears. "Thank you so much. I shall return everything as soon as I am able to purchase my own."

"Nonsense." A dismissive gesture with one elegantly gloved hand. "It takes up valuable storage space. You're doing me a favor taking it off my hands. Yancey, while I visit with Miss Pearsall, perhaps you and Mr. Abraham can carry these items inside. I'm sure Mrs. Abraham can tell you where to put them."

Winnie grinned. "Yes, ma'am, I surely can." Turning to the men, she waved a fleshy arm. "Get on with it, you two. And keep quiet. Mr. Percy and Cleo napping."

As the men began unloading, Lucinda looked around, a small crease of worry between her blond brows. "It's rather remote, isn't it?"

Audra followed her gaze. Tall trees cast the cabin in perpetual shadow. Brushy undergrowth, desperate for sun, encroached on the small clearing, and here and there, snow still showed through the tangle of leaves. The air was constantly chilled. The ground felt damp and spongy underfoot, and the wooden shingles on the roof were covered in a thick layer of moss. By summer, mosquitoes would be eating them alive.

"It's certainly not Baltimore," Audra admitted with a thin smile.

"Don't fret." Lucinda patted her arm. "While we await word on that employment opportunity I mentioned, we'll find a better place. This is horrid."

Horrid, yes. And lonely, and gloomy, and beyond rustic.

But it was also peaceful, and much safer for Father than living on a busy city street. And it was hers. Until the mosquitoes came, she could live with that.

By the end of the first week, the cabin was livable. The Abrahams took the curtained alcove off the main room. Audra and Father took the second room, which Audra furnished with two small, slightly battered hotel beds separated by a long curtain to give the illusion of privacy. It was a struggle to fit four adults and a dog into such a small house, but they managed.

Several days later, when Audra was picking up supplies at the mercantile, Lucinda popped in to invite the four of them to dinner at the hotel. Apparently, it was a tradition among the "ladies" and their families to dine together after Sunday church services.

"It will be a boisterous crowd, as always." Lucinda counted off the attendees other than her husband, herself, and Audra's four. "The sheriff and his wife—Declan and Edwina Brodie. They'll bring their five children—a new baby and four by Declan's first marriage, and a rowdy group if there ever was one. Prudence Lincoln, Edwina's half-black half sister will be there—her last gathering until she leaves for Indiana in a few days. Thomas Redstone will accompany her if he's not off tracking whoever is causing all the problems with the sluice. The Wallaces aren't back from Texas yet—Angus is a Scottish earl and Maddie is an English lady—they're on a photography expedition. What does that come to? Fifteen? Oh, and Mr. Hardesty will be joining us, too. That makes sixteen."

Audra's reservations must have shown on her face.

Lucinda chuckled. "It won't be as bad as it sounds. Especially since my guardian, Mrs. Throckmorton, and her two

companions are away in Denver until next month. That cantankerous old dear can turn any gathering upside down."

"But so many people . . ." Since Father's illness, Audra had
avoided social gatherings, and until the trip here, he had rarely
left the house except for an occasional buggy ride in the park.
"I'm not sure Father—"

"He'll be fine. Certainly less disruptive than the younger
Brodie children, who, fortunately, will be at another table."

"What about Winnie and Curtis?"

"What about them?" Lucinda's smile gave way to a frown.
"Surely you're not thinking that because they're Negros they
won't be welcome?"

"Well . . ."

Lucinda gave a derisive snort—which was unsettling, coming from such a serene-looking woman. "We're the last people
to cast stones, Audra. Heavens, you'll be sharing a meal with
an Irish orphan who lived in a brothel, a Cheyenne Dog Soldier,
several unruly children, a near-mute sheriff, a rather emotional
Southerner, her stunning mulatto half sister, and a man who
was once hanged and later fought for money. Do you truly think
the addition of a couple of Africans will make a difference?"
She laughed heartily at the notion.

Audra blinked at her. "Who lived in a brothel?"

"Never mind. Just meet us at the hotel at ten on Sunday.
We'll all walk to church together, weather permitting."

A parade of misfits off to worship the Lord. Add a muttering
old man and a woman experienced in forgery and fraud, and
the farce would be complete.

Sunday dawned clear and sunny—although Audra wasn't
entirely certain of that until the buggy broke out of the trees
and rolled into sunshine. The air grew pleasantly warm, lacking
the blustery winds that had moaned through the eaves during
the previous few days, and the chill that had seeped into her
bones since they had moved into the gloomy cabin finally began
to fade.

She was ready for an outing. Judging by the other smiling
faces in the buggy, they were all looking forward to a day away
from their cramped quarters.

Hoping to prepare them—and herself—for the day ahead, Audra related to the Abrahams what Lucinda had told her about the other guests.

Winnie was aghast. "A Southern white woman with a mixed blood sister? Laws, I wish I could have been a fly on the wall in that house, sure enough."

Curtis seemed more concerned about how the man who'd been hanged had escaped, while Audra still puzzled over the orphan from the brothel. Through the process of elimination, she guessed Lucinda. But that didn't fit with the elegant manners and reserved demeanor. Plus, there wasn't the faintest trace of Ireland in her cultured voice. Strange, the things that catch people's notice.

She found herself anticipating the day with more excitement than she had expected. But it wasn't until she stopped the buggy at the back stoop of the hotel and Ethan Hardesty came out to assist her that she realized how much she had looked forward to seeing him again, too.

He was more formally dressed today than he'd been at the cabin when they'd had that heated conversation. Hatless, clad in a dark frock coat, a burgundy brocade vest over a pressed white shirt, and a narrow black tie around his banded collar, he looked quite handsome. He was also freshly shaven. Without the dark stubble, he looked less roguish and more civilized.

Except for that teasing light in his arresting blue eyes.

"Good morning, Miss Audra," he said, reaching up to lift her down.

"Pearsall." When she felt his long fingers slide around her waist, she mentally berated herself for not wearing a corset. As soon as her toes touched ground, she tried to step back. But he continued to hold her, the heat of his broad palms radiating through the thin fabric of her Sunday-best green dimity.

"You look quite fetching today, my dear."

My dear? "Thank you," she murmured to the top button on his vest.

"You should wear that dress often. It brings out the green in your eyes."

"My eyes are hazel." Her heart hammered so hard she thought surely he could hear it. Why had he called her "my dear"?

"Hazel?" He tipped his head to see under the brim of her

bonnet. "So they are. Except when you wear green." Laughing softly, he took his hands away.

The man must have been a terrible tease as a child.

Feeling oddly light-headed, Audra turned to assist Father.

But Mr. Hardesty was already there, and before she could gather her wits, he had them all moving through the back hallway of the hotel and into the lobby where a small crowd stood talking. Apparently, they were the last to arrive.

As Lucinda made introductions, Audra put Ethan Hardesty from her mind and concentrated on connecting the names and Lucinda's descriptions to each face.

Edwina Brodie was the most obvious because of her Southern accent and the baby in her arms. Her hulking husband, Declan Brodie, was easy to remember, too, because of the badge peeking from beneath the lapel of his dark coat and the children gathered around him, the oldest of whom, R.D., was his spitting image.

Thomas Redstone she already knew, and the brown-skinned woman beside him must have been Edwina's half sister, Prudence Lincoln. Even with the discolored skin on her wrist from a long-ago scalding, she was the most beautiful woman Audra had ever seen.

The final introduction was to Tait Rylander, Lucinda's husband. An elegant man with intense gray eyes, an engaging smile, and the scar from an old rope burn just above his starched collar.

"Is it time for my lecture, Mary?" Father asked. "Is that why they're here?"

The Heartbreak Creek misfits. It promised to be an interesting day.

Seven

"Have you spoken to your father about the right-of-way, Miss Audra?"

"Pearsall."

They had left the hotel several minutes earlier, the Rylanders in the lead, followed by Mr. Redstone and Prudence Lincoln, then the Brodie children, the younger three playing kick with a pinecone, R.D. ambling in their wake, too old for childhood games. Their parents came behind them, Edwina Brodie deeply engaged in conversation, while Declan walked silently beside her, his big hand dwarfing the baby he held upright against his chest. Escorted by Mr. Hardesty, Audra and her group brought up the rear. Within moments, however, Mr. Hardesty had managed to separate Audra from her father and the Abrahams when Father stopped to study markings on a tree trunk. Now they were walking well out of hearing of the others.

"I told him of your offer," she answered. "He said something about a lost tribe and spilled his cobbler. I took that as a 'no'. Have you asked about employment?"

He didn't respond.

"I thought not. Fortunately, Mrs. Rylander is making efforts on my behalf."

They continued in strained silence, careful not to touch. But even though her vision was limited by the sides of her bonnet, she was aware of him watching her.

She found that disturbing. But also flattering.

As they approached the rail yard where the construction materials were being stored, she noticed that the water tower was nearing completion. That surprised and annoyed her, proof that the railroad was so sure of her acquiescence that they had pushed ahead, even without her signature on the right-of-way.

"How will they keep the water in the tower from freezing in winter?" she asked, in an effort to ease the tense silence.

"Enclose it in a heated building. Why do you insist on living out there?"

She looked at him, taken aback by the abrupt change in subject.

He didn't meet her gaze, but strode stiffly along, chin up, hands clasped behind his back. The breeze tugged at the lapels of his unbuttoned coat and tousled his brown hair so that strands of gold and red glinted in the sun. Instead of his normally teasing expression, he wore a deep frown.

He had an interesting mouth. Even when he wasn't smiling, his lips held a trace of amusement, as if he was holding back a laugh. It was there when he spoke, his lips opening wider on one side and tilting up at the corner. When he smiled, the slant was even more noticeable, showing most of his fine white teeth on that side. The crooked smile was boyish and roguish and intimate, all at the same time.

But his eyes were clearly his best feature. A bright, vivid blue. She remembered reading in one of Father's Hindu translations that blue eyes were associated with the sixth *chakra*, and indicative of people with great insight and observation.

He had certainly observed her frequently enough.

But sometimes, like several evenings ago, when she had called him a hero, a shadow had muddied the vibrant blue as if within his mind a curtain had fallen. Teasing one moment, guarded the next. What was he hiding? What secrets stole the light from those beautiful blue eyes?

Realizing that she was staring, she forced herself to look away. "As I have said, I have no choice."

"But you do, don't you? Even though you know it's not safe, you persist in putting yourself at risk. I have to wonder why. Is it simply to defy me?"

"If this is another attempt to intimidate me, Mr. Hardesty—"

"Intimidate you? When have you ever been intimidated by me?"

Without warning, he stopped and put his hand on her arm, forcing her to stop, too. "This has nothing to do with the right-of-way, Audra. It's your safety that concerns me. Someone orchestrated a landslide less than a mile from your cabin. Until we know why—or who his next target might be—you shouldn't be unprotected in such a remote place."

"That's absurd. Why would anyone target me? We threaten no one. Besides, I have Curtis."

"Does he have a weapon? Have either of you ever fired a gun?"

"No, but—"

"Hell." Taking his hand from her arm, he dragged his fingers through his hair, mussing it even further. "I'll talk to him. Show him how to shoot."

"That's not necessary."

"It *is* necessary!" He rounded on her, his expression fierce. "If not for your peace of mind, then for mine. Question my motives if you will, Audra, but I worry about you. With all the scrapes you get yourself into, someone should at least try to keep you from getting into more trouble. And with or without your permission, I'll do what needs to be done to ensure that. Now come along. We'll be late." And taking her arm again, he all but dragged her toward the church.

Audra was too astounded to resist.

The Come All You Sinners Church of Heartbreak Creek was a peculiar mix of different faiths and old and new architecture, decorated with garish artwork on the wainscoted walls and religious statuettes on the windowsills. It was presided over by a wild-haired, arm-waving man in his later years, accompanied by his pianist wife, Biddy, and the three most tone-deaf choir ladies Ethan had ever heard.

All of which only added to the irritation still simmering after his latest confrontation with Audra Pearsall, God bless her.

Mostly, he was mad at himself.

What had come over him? Why had he been so insistent that she leave her cabin? Because of the right-of-way?

Partially.

Because he truly thought she was in danger?

Not really—although with her penchant for getting into trouble, he did worry about her being out there in the woods in a remote cabin that was barely livable. So who was he fooling with his knight in shining armor posturing?

Only himself, he realized. Because mostly he wanted her in town so that he could see her more often. He had missed her. For some unfathomable, illogical, inexplicable reason, he liked being around her.

He scowled over at the cause of his aggravation . . . sitting demurely by his side, her eyes piously downcast, a serene expression on her face, despite the constant babbling of her father on her other side.

Probably asleep.

As he would be, if Pastor Rickman would keep his voice down.

In an effort to shift his thoughts away from his own foolishness and the scent and warmth and soft breathing of the woman next to him, Ethan looked around, mentally cataloging all the architectural oddities present in the small one-room church.

Hardly a fine example of ecclesiastical architecture. Certainly not indicative of the Victorian Gothic style popularized by Richard Hunt, or Ruskin's medievalism, or even the lofty designs of James Renwick, Jr., Ethan's mentor and the man after whom he had named his horse. No intricate cornices, marble columns, mosaics, or inlays here. Just the simple, clean lines of hand-hewn, timber frame construction, with pegged joints, open beams, and layers of furniture wax lovingly buffed to a glossy sheen.

He guessed it had once been a barn. The scuffed floor was relatively new, slightly warped, and showed gaps where it joined the walls. As far as he could tell, there was no access to the steeple, which meant it had probably been added later simply to identify the structure as a church. And judging by the mismatched molding and crooked joints, the peaked windows had also been recent renovations, crafted by a carpenter with insufficient math skills—no doubt the same one who had built the sagging front door.

Yet, despite the inconsistencies and poor craftsmanship, the

Come All You Sinners Church of Heartbreak Creek had a comfortable feel to it, like a pair of well-worn slippers at the end of the day. Homey and welcoming, with its eclectic architecture and diverse congregation, it perfectly suited a town struggling to find its purpose.

Ethan liked it. It gave him peace. So much so, that by the last "amen"—even with the raucous pulpit-pounding and off-key music—he had achieved such a state of grace he was able to turn to the exasperating, unquestionably pigheaded, and utterly captivating Miss Audra Pearsall with a smile on his face.

"What's wrong?" she asked.

His smile faded. "What do you mean?"

"Why are you grimacing like that?"

Before he could find a suitable answer, the door of the church burst open and the Hopewell boy yelled, "Fire at the sluice!"

"I wonder what's taking them so long." Edwina scarcely glanced at her card before dropping it on the pile. "You don't think anyone's hurt, do you?"

Audra drew a card. Shoving her spectacles higher on her nose, she studied it, saw she didn't need a four of clubs, and dropped it on top of Edwina's discard. "If so, we would have heard by now."

It had been hours since the men had left the church. Both the noon meal and the evening meal had passed, and after playing cards in Lucinda's office for most of the afternoon, they were all feeling restless. Thankfully, they were spared the rambunctious Brodie children—the four oldest had gone to the livery to bedevil Mr. Driscoll, and Winnie had taken the baby and Father up to a vacant room for naps awhile ago. Curtis had left with the other men.

"Perhaps they caught him," Edwina said.

"Then they should be back soon. Gin." Lucinda spread her cards on the table then sat back with a yawn, the picture of indolence in her lovely pink taffeta frock and ivory fichu, obviously as bored with the game as the others were. "You ladies are terrible card players."

Audra agreed. Relieved to have the game over, she removed her spectacles and slipped them into her skirt pocket.

"It won't be long." Prudence straightened the cards into a neat stack, then slipped them into the card case. "Even Thomas can't track in the dark."

Pru was a fusser, Audra had noticed. If she wasn't tidying the discard pile or tugging the starched white sleeve over her scarred wrist or smoothing the creases in the brown skirt that was a shade darker than her cinnamon-colored skin, she was checking the pins in her tightly bound bun.

Audra sensed she was just as tightly wound inside. The only time she had seen the beautiful mulatto completely relax was when she was with Thomas Redstone. There was a bond there that Audra didn't completely understand, but it was obvious Pru cared very deeply for the Cheyenne warrior. Which made it all the more difficult to understand why she would leave him to go all the way to Indiana to teach in a school for freed men and women. How could they look at each other the way they did, and still choose to be apart?

But then, Audra had never been in love.

"I just want it over." Edwina's blue eyes glittered. She had steadily become more frazzled as the afternoon had progressed. Earlier, before Winnie had volunteered to relieve her of the restive baby, she had seemed on the brink of tears. Now she seemed closer to hysteria.

"The children are running wild, Whit has yet to sleep through the night, and now with Declan gone all the time . . ." The petulant note became a quaver. "I can't do it all. I need him at home. Especially with you leaving tomorrow, Pru."

"Oh, dear. You're getting yourself worked up again."

"Don't 'oh, dear' me, Pru. I have a right to be upset. And not about you leaving me—I know teaching has been your dream forever. But sometimes I feel it takes every ounce of my strength just to climb out of bed in the morning."

"Are you certain you're fully recovered?" Lucinda asked. "After all, it's only been two months."

"Two months and ten days."

"What does Doctor Boyce say?"

Fearing they were about to launch into a grisly recounting of the entire birthing process, Audra looked out the window and wondered if it would be rude to excuse herself. Already the sun was sinking toward the mountains. If they didn't leave soon, it would be dark before they reached the cabin.

"He says I'm healthy as a horse." Edwina sounded disgusted, although Audra couldn't fathom why. "It's embarrassing—having a giant baby with hardly any trouble at all. It's not as if I'm a field hand."

Pru gave her a look.

"Field hands can be white."

"Not where we're from."

"Have you talked to Declan about all this?" Lucinda interrupted.

An even less desirable subject. Audra envied the candor and closeness shared by these women—something that had been missing from her life of late—but she wasn't quite ready to be thrown into an intimate discussion of marital relations, which she knew even less about than childbearing.

Edwina sniffed. "I've tried, but you know how he is. I declare, it would be easier to put dancing pumps on a cat than get words out of that man."

Reaching across the table, Pru took her sister's hand in her own. "I know how difficult it's been since Whit was born. You've worked so hard. But you can't handle the household chores, four rowdy children, and a new baby all on your own. Ask R.D. to pitch in. Talk to Declan. Perhaps once this vandal is apprehended, he can take the older children out to the ranch for a few days."

"Oh, I'm sure he'd like that." Pulling her hands free, Edwina dabbed at her damp cheeks. "Anything to get away from me."

"I'm confused." Lucinda glanced from one sister to the other, her brow puckered in a frown. "Are you upset because you're feeling overwhelmed, Edwina? Or because you're mad at Declan?"

"Neither. Both. I don't want to talk about it anymore."

Seeing that as her opening, Audra pushed back her chair. "It's been a wonderful afternoon, ladies, but—"

"You're not leaving?" Lucinda looked shocked. "You can't go back to that cabin tonight. Not with that miscreant lurking about. What if he attacked you?"

"I doubt he has any interest in us. Besides, with Cleo—oh my goodness! Cleo!" Audra shot to her feet.

"Who's Cleo?"

"Father's dog. She's been locked inside all day." Audra grabbed her bonnet and reticule from a nearby table. "Poor thing. She's probably frantic."

"I'll send Yancey to fetch her."

"You don't understand. She's blind. She would be terrified if he approached her. Maybe even run off."

Audra couldn't bear to think of the little dog lost in the woods, unable to see or protect herself. It would be the end of her. Which would probably mean the end of Father, too, since Cleo was the only thing he seemed to recognize lately.

"Audra, be sensible." Lucinda rose, her alarm apparent. "It's not safe. If I let you go and anything happened to you, I would never forgive myself."

Ethan Hardesty's words just before he ran from the church echoed through Audra's mind. *Stay here until we get back. No telling where he'll strike next.* She thought he had been trying to frighten her. But what if he was right?

She might be hardheaded, but she didn't consider herself foolish.

"All right. We'll stay the night. But first, I must get Cleo. I can't leave her locked up all night in a place she's not yet accustomed to. Please tell Winnie to watch over Father until either Curtis or I come back."

"Of course. But you're not going out there alone. I'll send Yancey with you."

"What do you think, Thomas?" Sheriff Brodie asked. "White? Indian? White man trying to make it look like an Indian? A trapper?"

"Could be one of those yellow folks," Curtis suggested. "They wear funny shoes that might leave a track like that."

Ethan watched the Cheyenne study the trail, his blunt-tipped fingers lightly playing over the dips and ridges in the dirt. It was the third time they'd covered this area. He was starting to lose hope as daylight faded. And he was hungry.

"Not Indian." Redstone pointed at several broken twigs on a nearby bush. "Too sloppy." He continued along the trail, carefully keeping to the side so he wouldn't muss what prints there were. "Do the yellowskins have horses?"

"Not usually," Ethan answered. "The railroad ships them by train wherever they're needed. Although I guess it wouldn't be too difficult to get a horse. Anyone report one missing, Sheriff?"

Brodie shook his head. "The Chinese around here aren't known for thievery, anyway. They may have some odd practices, and dress funny with that long pigtail, but I've never had trouble with any of them."

Ethan sighed. Then who was doing this? And why? Who would benefit most by keeping the bridge line from coming through? Another railroad?

It wasn't inconceivable. Friction between competing railroads often erupted in violence. He also knew that a route through the southern Rockies could be worth a fortune over the years. Had their rival, the Southern Utah and Atlantic, sent someone to impede the project?

Wearily, he rubbed a hand over his stinging eyes. The stink of scorched wood and lamp oil hung in the air, and thin wisps of smoke still coiled above the smoldering boards scattered down the slope into the ravine. Whoever had done this wanted the lumber totally destroyed this time, and had doused it with lamp oil before setting it afire. Fortunately, most of the wood was still green and didn't burn well, or they might have lost more than three sections. As it was, the damage was more of a nuisance than a major setback—but Ethan would now have to report another delay to his employers.

Redstone looked up, eyes focused on the other side of the ravine.

Ethan turned to follow his gaze. Squinting through trees and fading light, he saw movement along the lower road. A black buggy. *Hell.* What was Audra doing out here? Hadn't he told her to stay in town until they returned?

Stubborn, willful, pigheaded—

"That Miss Audra?" Curtis asked, frowning into the gloom.

"Ho, *ve'ho'e.* Has your firecracker gone off without you?"

Heat flooded Ethan's face. "I don't know what you're talking about." He stalked over to where he'd tied Renny, wondering where Redstone had gotten the ridiculous notion that Audra Pearsall was *his* anything.

"Firecracker?" Brodie looked around, then caught sight of the buggy moving on the other side of the ravine. "Who's that?"

Scowling, Ethan swung up on Renny. "Never mind. I'll take care of it." And before they could question him further, he backtracked to an easy cross, turned Renny off the trail, and headed down the slope to the other side of the ravine.

Eight

As Ethan rode into the clearing surrounding the cabin, something green darted through the trees—something a shade paler than the surrounding vegetation, with yellow markings.

Audra. What was she doing? Who was she running from?

Alarmed, he spurred Renny. "Audra," he called, coming up behind her.

She whirled, bonnet askew, long, light brown curls tumbling around her shoulders. When she saw him dismounting, she rushed forward, spooking Renny into a side step that almost caught his foot.

"Ethan, help me! Cleo ran off, and we can't find her anywhere."

"The dog?" Ethan let out a relieved breath. Just like the woman to get hysterical over a lost dog.

Hearing footsteps behind him, he turned to see Yancey charging through the brush. When he saw Ethan, he stopped, breathing hard. "What are you doing here?"

"What are you?"

"The boss sent us to fetch Miss Audra's dog. Danged thing ran out when we opened the door. Don't find her soon, she'll be somebody's dinner."

At Audra's gasp, Ethan gave him a scolding look. "We'll find her," he said, tying Renny to a tree. "You look along the other side of the clearing, Yancey. We'll check here." After taking his pistol from his saddlebag and slipping it into his belt, he motioned Audra to fall in behind him. "Stay close," he said, and led off into the brush.

Daylight was fading fast and made footing treacherous as they picked their way over downed limbs and through heavy undergrowth. Audra kept calling, her voice wobbly and high, but there was no answering bark.

Fine time for the yapper to fall silent. Ethan shoved choke-cherry branches out of his way, then almost fell over a rotten log. But at least by keeping quiet, the dog wasn't alerting predators to her whereabouts. Unless it was already too late.

Minutes passed. The gloom deepened. Audra's voice grew hoarse, but still she plowed on, bonnet gone now, several rips in her skirt. Ethan feared Yancey was right; if they didn't find the dog before full dark, they wouldn't find her at all.

"Ethan," Audra said a few minutes later.

He turned to see her stopped behind him, head down, shoulders slumped. He could tell she was crying. "It's no use. She's g-gone. Maybe in the m-morning—"

"There's still light left. If you want, I'll take you back to the cabin and—"

In the distance, a faint bark.

He froze, head cocked. When he heard nothing more, he told Audra to call again.

She called.

Another bark. Off to the right.

"It's Cleo," Audra cried.

Flinging aside low limbs and prickly hawthorn, Ethan followed the barks to a tangle of brambles low to the ground. From beneath it came a familiar low growl. Shoving the branches aside, he scooped up the trembling animal.

"Cleo," Audra cried, grabbing the dog from his arms. "You naughty girl. I ought to shake you good." Instead, she gave the dog's furry head a resounding kiss and received several in return.

Smiling, Ethan watched the joyful reunion. Seemed like a big fuss over a little dog, but it pleased him to see Audra happy again. "Let's get her back to the cabin and see if she's all right."

It was dark by the time they retrieved Renny and worked their way back to the clearing. Yancey met them as they came out of the trees, a lamp in his hand. "Thought you got lost, too. The dog all right?"

"I think so. If you'll give me the lamp, I'll take her inside to check more thoroughly."

As Audra went up the porch steps, Ethan turned to the old man. "I assume you intended to take her back to town."

"Boss's orders, until things settle down."

Ethan was gratified to know the stubborn woman would listen to somebody, even if it wasn't him.

"Catch the fellow who burned the sluice?" Yancey asked.

"Not yet. Can you ride?"

"Since 'fore you were born."

He handed him Renny's reins. "You can ride my horse back to the livery. I'll bring the buggy." He didn't want Audra out of his sight, plus, he was the only one with a gun. "Wait here. I'll get Miss Pearsall, and we can go together."

When he stepped inside the cabin, he found Audra bent beside the dog, feeding the wiggling animal a bowl of what appeared to be leftover stew. Ethan's stomach rumbled, reminding him again that he hadn't eaten since before church services that morning. "Apparently she survived her ordeal."

Audra wiped her hands on her ruined skirt and rose.

She was a mess. Hair hanging loose, leaves caught in the flyaway curls. A small scratch on her cheek, dirt smudges on her dress—his favorite so far—and her eyes red from crying. Yet all he wanted to do was take down the rest of her hair and check under the dress for other scratches.

Stopping before him, she rested her hands on his arms, just above his elbows. "Thank you, Ethan."

Her use of his name, and the grip of her small hands on his arm, sent a rush of heat into his chest.

"I was about to give up. If you hadn't insisted . . ." Words trailed off as her eyes brimmed. "Thank you."

Uneasy with all this gushing over something so trivial, and unable to deal with the confusing emotions her nearness generated in him, he retreated into the safety of humor. "You're not going to kiss me, are you?"

She blinked. "What?"

"I wouldn't mind. Truly. Although it's a little demeaning to be second in line after your dog."

Her smile faltered.

He felt her grip on his arms loosen. Realizing he had only made an awkward situation worse, he retreated further. "No. You're right. It's a bad idea."

Her hands dropped to her sides. The tears were gone, but the squint was back. "Why is it a bad idea?" She didn't ask it in a flirtatious way, but with genuine curiosity.

Leave it to Audra to pin him down. The woman was too clever to let him get away with even the slightest slip. He took a deep breath, and when he let it go, the playfulness went with it. "I'm not your hero, Audra. I never will be."

"No?"

He watched a small smile tug at the corners of her lips and felt as if something had shifted beneath his feet.

"And yet," she went on, amusement dancing in her beautiful eyes, "you continue to do heroic things. How confusing that must be for you."

He couldn't respond, couldn't look away. The glib words that usually came so easily had deserted him.

At his silence, a change came over her face—confusion, disappointment, hurt—he couldn't tell which. But the distance he had sought was suddenly there between them. And although he knew that was best, he was sorry for it.

"It's late," she said, turning away. "We should get back." Lifting a shawl and bonnet from a peg, she put them on, then picked up a bundle of clothing from the table and a dog basket from the hearth. "Come, Cleo."

A few minutes later, they were climbing into the buggy. The pooch was exhausted after her big adventure, and as soon as Audra made a bed for her in the basket behind the seat, she curled into a tight ball, tucked her nose under her bushy tail, and went to sleep.

"What kind of dog is she?" Ethan asked as he steered the buggy in behind Yancey and Renny.

"Part everything, but mostly hair. Father found her digging through refuse behind a butcher shop. They've been inseparable ever since. Lately, she's the only thing he seems to recognize." She gave a brittle laugh. "Certainly not me."

Ethan had heard of that happening to older folks. A form of forgetfulness that grew worse as time passed. "Dementia?"

She nodded. "It wasn't bad at first, although he seemed to forget what he was doing sometimes. His work suffered the most."

"What work did he do?"

She took a long time to answer. Ethan sensed she was carefully picking her words, and that bothered him, even though he was just as guarded around her. But, unlike him, what could she possibly have to be ashamed of?

"He was a historian." She reached up to brush her fingertips over her cheek, and he realized she was crying. "He rarely speaks of his work anymore. Mostly he calls for my mother, who's been gone for two decades, or tells Cleo the same stories over and over. It's all very sad."

He reached over and put his hand over hers. "I'm sorry, Audra."

She turned toward him. A shaft of moonlight cut through the trees and for a moment highlighted the fierce gleam in her eyes. "I won't put him in an asylum," she said, gently pulling her hand from under his. "He's my father and I'll take care of him. I've managed so far and I will continue to do so."

And finally he saw the reason for her truculence over the right-of-way. What he had thought of as a simple battle of wills was much more to her—an attempt to provide for her dying father by finding a safe and affordable home for him through his last years, where she could manage him, and protect him, and keep him isolated from prying eyes. Having a train running through the clearing didn't fit into that.

Ethan understood. Since the disaster at Salty Point, he had tried to do the same thing—although in his case he was doing it to protect himself, rather than someone else. Perhaps he had more in common with Audra's father than he had realized. They were both cripples, of a sort.

They rode in silence for a time, the clop of the horses' hooves on the rocky track the only sound in the darkness, other than an occasional night bird and the sough of the wind through the branches overhead. The temperature had dropped with the sun. Guessing by the way Audra rubbed her hands over her arms that she was cold, Ethan looped the reins loosely around the brake, slipped off his jacket and draped it over her shoulders. It hung on her slender frame.

"Thank you." She shot him a grateful smile and pulled it closer.

Ethan nodded and studied the road ahead, ignoring the chill that cut through his thin shirt and pondering what he should do about this confounding woman.

What had started out as a mild dalliance had become much more—to him, at least—and now with the complication of the right-of-way hanging between them, it was liable to get messy.

He couldn't force her off her land. But he couldn't keep the railroad from coming through, either. They could build around her, skirting her property by putting a trestle over the creek to the other side of the ravine. But that wouldn't be any safer for her father, and she would be out the fee for the right-of-way.

The only other solution would be to locate a safer place for them to live.

Or build them a house himself.

If he could find the courage to pick up a drafting pen again.

Strangely, the thought of that didn't bring on the throat-seizing panic it might have a year ago. In fact, the prospect of building a home for Audra had an odd appeal.

"If you could design it yourself," he asked on a whim, "what would you want in a house of your own?"

She chuckled. "What every woman wants. An indoor water closet."

He smiled, enjoying her laughter. He hadn't heard it before, and liked the bubbly sound of it—low and musical rather than shrill—like water burbling over rocks in a stream. It was the kind of laugh that made him want to smile back. "That's all?"

"Well," she mused, "as long as we're dreaming, I'd want a real tub with hot and cold water, and a big kitchen lined with cupboards and counters. There would have to be windows in every room—with glass, mind you—I don't like closed spaces—and porches front and back. The parlor would have bookcases built into the walls, and a comfortable chair by a cozy fire where I could read, and a fine, wide desk by the window where I could write."

"Write what?" he asked, amused by her grandiose plans.

"Letters. And such like."

"Only letters? No dreams of penning maudlin poetry or lurid novels of romance and adventure?"

"Why do you call them lurid?"

"You do!" Ethan delighted in this new insight into this complicated woman. "Why, Miss Audra, you bluestocking, you."

"Pearsall!"

He didn't need light to see the hackles had come up. "Back to that, are we?"

When she didn't respond, he glanced over at her dark silhouette against the night sky. Even in the dim moonlight, he could see the rigidity of her posture. If her chin rose any higher, the brim of her bonnet would brush the roof. "I see I have offended you, Miss Pearsall."

"Not at all, Mr. Hardesty. Disappointed me, perhaps. But to be offended by your mockery, I would have to value your opinion. Which I do not."

"Nonetheless, you have my apology. I'm sorry, Miss Audra. And I wasn't mocking you. I was just . . . surprised, is all."

"Why? Am I so dull, then, that I'm not allowed to indulge in whimsy?"

He tried to think up a quip that would ease the tension, then realized she deserved his honesty. "Never dull, I assure you. But burdened. With all the tasks put before you, I wonder that you would have time for such fanciful pursuits."

She didn't respond, but a glance at her profile told him the stiffness was gone. Yet the strength of her reaction intrigued him. Had he touched a nerve? Did the prickly Miss Audra dream of being an author?

But dreams were easily crushed. He knew that firsthand.

A few minutes later, the track leveled out at the edge of town, near a small Chinese camp. Mandarin, mostly. The larger, more diverse camp was over by the rail yards. Smoke from their cooking fires rose above the tents, and strange spices scented the air. Somewhere, a woman laughed. There were few Chinese women here. Perhaps someone had brought in a whore from San Francisco.

As they rolled by, several dark-clothed men engaged in a game of fan-tan looked up. But no greetings were exchanged. Ethan knew if they weren't put to work soon, boredom would lead to increased pipe-smoking, a debilitating habit among many of their countrymen. Another reason to get Audra's right-of-way settled.

At the edge of the camp, a lone figure leaned against an aspen trunk, the red tip of his cheroot glowing in the dark. Ethan made out the darker shape of a Western-style hat, rather than the woven dishpan-shaped hats favored by the Chinese, and the glint of moonlight off the silver handle of a whip tied to his belt. Tim Gallagher. Even though he couldn't see the Irishman's face, Ethan felt the menace in the stare that followed them as they rolled by.

"Are they sorry they came here, do you think?" Audra asked, pulling his attention away from the man watching from the shadows. "I've read how the tracks of the Central Pacific are laid in their blood. One death for every mile."

"It's a dangerous undertaking," Ethan admitted. "But I've never met harder-working people. Unlike many other railroads, at least we pay them a decent wage."

"Have you always worked for the railroad?"

"Only the last two years."

"And before that?"

"I was in California."

"Why did you leave? I've heard it is beautiful country."

"It can be. Here we are." Relieved to avoid further questioning, he pulled the horse to a stop in front of the hotel, set the brake, and hopped down. "I'll take the buggy around to the livery," he said, lifting the dog basket from behind the seat and setting it on the ground. "If we haven't caught the arsonist by tomorrow afternoon, I'll check by the cabin to make sure everything is all right." He slid his hands around her narrow waist and swung her down, taking more care in the task than he probably needed to.

"In that case," she said, avoiding his eyes, "I should probably go with you. If we stay in town much longer, we'll need more clothing."

Ethan smiled at the prospect. "After dinner then?"

"I'll be ready." Picking up her bundle of clothing and the basket holding Cleo, she gave her "good nights" and went inside.

Still grinning, Ethan climbed back into the buggy and headed around to the livery. Another evening with Audra. It was almost like courting.

Nine

A wall of glass.

That's how Ethan envisioned the back of the hospital at Salty Point. Windows overlooking the Pacific, stretching all the way to the ceiling, forming a fragile barrier between the sick sailors and the sea they loved.

Since the existing structure faced more northwest than due west, there would be plenty of light, but without the intense glare of the evening sun. In winter, when the sun dropped lower to the horizon, it would partially warm the wards with heat radiating off the expanse of glass. But in summer—if he designed the lower panes so that they were open to the breeze off the water—the sound of the surf pounding against the rocks below would be a soothing rhythm to men trapped in their beds.

But when Ethan presented his drawings to the board of architects overseeing the renovation, there was grave doubt that it could be done.

"How will you support and stabilize all that glass?"

"We have gales here," another protested. "What assurances do you have that the wind won't blow the glass inward?"

"Too risky," a third decided. "We need a solid stone structure, not one made of glass."

"It's just one wall," Ethan had argued. "The rest will be of stone."

"This is a hospital, Mr. Hardesty. Not a hilltop retreat."

But Ethan couldn't let the idea go. It became his obsession. A revolutionary idea, never before attempted, that would stand as a monument to the fallen sailors and a trademark of his expertise.

Because of her compassionate nature, he sought out Nurse Eckhart. "Think of the patients," he had implored her. "And how much they will benefit, being able to watch the sea they love so much. Please, Miss Eckhart. Help me convince the board."

She did.

And construction began in the summer of 1868.

It seemed the whole town gathered outside the Heartbreak Creek Hotel several days later to see Pru off to Indiana and her new teaching position at the Hilltop Christian Academy for People of Color. It was an emotional leave-taking, and although Edwina struggled to be brave, tears overcame her when Yancey pulled up in Lucinda's fine buggy to take her sister to the train stop at Boot Creek—the same one where Audra and her charges had arrived only a short while ago.

Another round of hugs, more tears, then Pru took her seat. Audra was surprised to see Thomas Redstone climb into the buggy behind her. "I didn't realize Mr. Redstone was going with her," she whispered to Lucinda, who stood with her husband beside her.

"Only to see her safely there, then he'll return. These mountains are his home. I can't imagine him living anywhere else." Shaking her head, she dabbed at her eyes. "This is wrong. So wrong."

"Now, sweetheart," her husband murmured.

"She belongs here, Tait. With us. And you know it."

When Tait dipped his dark head to whisper in his wife's ear, Audra turned back to watch the leave-takers—the warrior, stoic and unsmiling, staring straight ahead—Pru, weeping and waving a tear-sodden hanky. She could sense the tension between them, but just as the buggy pulled away, she saw Thomas slip his arm around Pru's shoulders and pull her close against his chest, and she knew he wasn't so stoic, after all.

Turning to go back inside the hotel, she almost bumped into

Ethan Hardesty, who stood directly behind her. Had he been there all along?

"Good morning, Miss Audra. I trust you slept well?"

It was apparent he hadn't. Dark shadows circled his deep-set eyes, and there was a weary cast to his beard-stubbled face. "Exceedingly well. And you?"

He gave that crooked grin that foretold teasing. "I was beset with regrets, I'm sad to say. Mostly about you, fair lady."

Refusing to be drawn into his game, she pretended disinterest. "I'm not surprised, sir. You do aim high."

A laugh burst out of him, drawing a glance from a man entering the hotel. It was the first honest, open expression of amusement Ethan had ever shown her, and it pleased her to have caught him off guard.

Ethan. How easily she had begun to think of him by his Christian name.

"Audra, you do lift my spirits." Taking her elbow, he moved her to the side as an older couple walked by. "But the regrets are because I must renege on my offer to take you out to the cabin this evening. With Thomas gone, Brodie is shorthanded, and I'm as intent as he is to stop whoever is responsible for the vandalism. Perhaps tomorrow?"

Audra hid her disappointment behind a bland smile. "Perhaps." But if they didn't catch the perpetrator soon, what was she to do? She couldn't stay at the hotel forever. Besides, why would the vandal pose a threat to her? It seemed his main target was the sluice. "Will you be taking Curtis with you again?"

"If you don't have need of him. Plus"—that crooked smile was becoming addictive—"riding with us is helping him overcome his fear of your horse."

Audra reared back in surprise. "Curtis is afraid of Cricket?"

"Cricket?" He chuckled. "What kind of name is that for such a fine horse?"

"What kind of name is Renny?" she countered.

"Actually, Renny was named after a famous man, James Renwick, Jr."

"Famous for what?"

A shadow moved behind his eyes. "Architecture. And Curtis is more wary than afraid," he went on quickly. "But he's improving. I'll keep an eye on him."

Apparently he thought they were all as helpless as Father. Yet it was nice to be looked after for a change. And he was so good at it.

After the men rode off, she went in search of Lucinda. She found her in her office, commiserating with Edwina, who was still in a state over her sister's departure and heaven knows what else. Not wanting to become involved in another tearful discourse on the trials of childbirth and the state of Edwina's marriage, Audra excused herself and sought out Lucinda's husband, Tait, instead.

He was at the usual Rylander table in the deserted dining room, a satchel stuffed with papers by his feet and designs for the new Heartbreak Creek depot spread across the tabletop.

"Mr. Rylander, if I might interrupt for a moment?"

"Of course." Setting aside his pen, he rose and pulled out a chair. "May I offer you coffee or tea?" he asked, returning to his chair after she was seated.

Such lovely manners. But then, Southerners were known for their chivalry.

"Thank you, no. I only stopped by to ask if you might recommend someone to teach me to shoot?"

He blinked.

"I would ask Sheriff Brodie," she went on, when he didn't respond, "but he just left to hunt down the person doing damage to the sluice, so I thought I'd check with you." She smiled.

He didn't smile back.

She liked his eyes, too. Pewter gray. Not as striking as Ethan's vibrant blue, but still compelling. A shade darker than those of the Brodies' daughter, Brin, and certainly less lively. In fact, they could be disturbingly direct. Like now.

"You want to learn to shoot a gun?" he finally asked.

What else would one shoot? "Precisely."

"Good Lord."

Not the reaction she had hoped for. "Living as we do in back of beyond, it's sensible that we know how to protect ourselves, don't you think? From bears, and marmots, and . . . suchlike."

He pressed the fingertips of his right hand against his temple just above a long scar. Winnie had learned through kitchen gossip that he had sustained it in the same fall that had also left him with a slight limp. From a train, no less.

"You've been talking to Lucinda, haven't you?" he asked.

"Of course. But not about this—wait! Does she have a gun? Could she teach me to shoot?" Audra would much prefer taking lessons from another woman. Men took such things so seriously.

A deep sigh. "I wish Ash were here. He's our gun expert." He must have seen her disappointment. "But all right," he went on. "I'll talk to Declan. As long as you ladies are armed, you should at least know how to handle your weapons."

"Would he also be able to advise me on what kind of gun I should have? I'd like something that could easily fit into my pocket. Nothing too big or heavy."

"Selecting a firearm isn't like shopping for shoes, Miss Pearsall."

"Of course not." Did he think her a complete nitwit? Realizing she would get no shooting lessons that day, she thanked him for his help and went to take Father and Cleo for a walk.

Spring had definitely arrived. The poplars and cottonwoods along the creek behind the hotel were green with budding leaves, and already the first early wildflowers were pushing up through the damp soil. The sky was a crystal blue—almost the same color as Ethan's eyes—and not hazed with soot like in the city, and the air was filled with birdsong, rather than the constant clatter of metal-rimmed wheels over paving stones.

She might grow to like this little mountain town.

It seemed Father already did.

Slipping her arm through his, she smiled over at him. The daily walks had brought a glow to his cheeks and a bounce to his step, even though his mind continued to deteriorate: before they'd even reached the livery, she had heard the same recitation of President Lincoln's accomplishments two times.

But she didn't mind. He had practiced his lectures on her for as long as she could remember, and the sound of his voice was as comforting and familiar to her as her own heartbeat. The thought of it soon being silenced forever was too dreadful to contemplate.

"Is that a scarlet tanager?" she asked, nodding toward a bright red bird flitting through the branches of a mountain maple.

"More likely a cardinal. Tanagers are rarely seen here in Baltimore."

While he launched into a discourse on the migratory habits of birds, and Cleo strained against her leash, searching out every scent that reached her nose, Audra wondered what she would do with her life when she no longer had Father to tend. She could always transcribe notes for other lecturers and researchers. But how boring it would be to live in the shadow of other people's creations when her dream was to craft her own.

She smiled, remembering how dangerously close to the truth Ethan had come when he'd accused her of wanting to become an author. Years of transcribing Father's notes had honed her skills, and loneliness had fueled her imagination. So why not give it a try? She could start with *The Lost Mine of Heartbreak Creek*. Or better yet, *Murder in the Lost Mine of Heartbreak Creek*. Or even, *I Lost my Love in the Lost Mine of Heartbreak Creek*.

That would teach Ethan Hardesty not to mock her again.

Ahead, she saw Tait Rylander speaking to Mr. Driscoll outside the livery. A moment later, he rode out toward the canyon. He seemed in a hurry.

"Have I told you how lovely you look today, my dear?"

Startled out of her reverie, Audra glanced at her father. He rarely spoke directly to her anymore. More often, his remarks were directed to her mother, the ghost that drifted between them. Sadly, Audra recalled little about her, and had only a faded tintype image to remember her by.

"That dress is most becoming on you, Mary. I especially like the way you're wearing your hair. Perhaps later," he added, leaning close to her ear, "you will let me brush it out for you." Laughing softly he patted her hand where it rested in the crook of his elbow. "That'll put you in the mood, eh, wife?"

Dear Lord. Audra wasn't sure which disturbed her more—the idea that he still didn't recognize her, or the image of her father brushing out her mother's hair as a prelude to . . . whatever.

From Main, one street over, came shouts and the sound of racing horses. No doubt those idlers from the Red Eye Saloon. Without Sheriff Brodie to keep them in line, they were obviously in high spirits. Now they were clanging what sounded like a dinner bell. Resolved to ignore them, she and Father continued to the livery near the mouth of the canyon.

But it was suddenly in an uproar, too. Alarmed, Audra sought out Mr. Driscoll and asked what was amiss.

"Another fire," the harried man said, tossing a long canvas pipe with a portable hand pump into the back of a wagon filled with axes, shovels, rakes, and leaking water barrels. "A big one. Better be ready to run if the wind pushes it down the canyon into town."

"Run where?"

"The church should be safe enough. Nothing much out that way but grass, and two boys are scything it now. I'd hitch your buggy, but—"

"That's all right," she assured him. "Do you know if Yancey is back?"

"Just came in."

"Sheriff Brodie and the others?"

"Still out. Best stay close to the hotel, miss. We'll send word if you need to clear out."

Picking up Cleo and guiding Father out of the way, she watched anxiously as wagons rushed by, water spilling out of the barrels in back as they tore down the street. When the last wagon clattered up the slope into the canyon, the clanging stopped and an eerie stillness settled over the town. For the first time, Audra saw the smoke rising out of the trees in the canyon, and realized the danger was very real.

By the time they reached the hotel, Audra's eyes were burning and the sun had become an orange ball suspended in a pall of smoke. They found Lucinda in the lobby, directing Yancey to box up her papers, and the kitchen staff to make ready for those driven into town by the fire. "Do you mind if Yancey readies your buggy?" she asked when she caught sight of Audra. "We'll need every conveyance we have should we need to move everyone to the church."

"Of course. What would you like for me to do?"

"If Winnie can keep an eye on your father and Cleo, we can use help in the kitchen. We're preparing food for when the men return."

"Winnie's a better cook."

"We don't need cooks. We need helpers."

"Then I'll help," Audra said, grateful for the distraction from her fears.

Time passed. The smoke thickened. Working in the stuffy kitchen, Audra found it harder and harder to take a full breath without coughing. Lucinda was contemplating sending the children and older folks on to the church where the air would be better when Curtis stumbled through the back door. He was covered in soot, his eyes red-rimmed, his shirt dotted with burn holes from drifting sparks.

Setting down her bowl, Audra rushed to him. "Are you hurt?"

"No, Miss Audra. Tired and dirty, is all."

Lucinda handed him a glass of water. While he gulped it down, she asked if they needed to start moving people to the church.

"Wouldn't hurt, ma'am." He returned the empty glass, then dragged a dirty sleeve over his sweating brow. "With the wind coming up, it spreading fast."

Lucinda left to direct the evacuation. With a weary sigh, Curtis turned to Audra. "Got a wagon full of our things parked out back. Where you want me to unload it?"

"Our things? You were at the cabin?"

"That's where the fire started. When we come up, Mistuh Ethan already there, carrying our things out and stacking them in the yard."

Audra gaped at him as the full impact of his words registered. Then another thought sent panic through her. "Did you get Father's notes? His medallion?"

"In the box with his papers. They all safe. So's our clothes and the furniture Miss Lucinda give us. All 'cept the beds. Somebody done doused the mattresses with lamp oil."

"And the cabin?"

Curtis shook his head. "Gone. All we got is what's in the wagon yonder. Without Mistuh Ethan getting there so quick, we wouldn't even have that. We lucky."

Lucky? Without the cabin, where would they live?

"So where you want me to put it?" Curtis asked again.

She struggled to think. "Do you need to take the wagon back?"

"Mistuh Ethan say maybe later I could bring out food and fresh water."

"Then we'll take it to the church and unload it there. But first, help me gather our belongings from upstairs."

Within an hour, the town was in the throes of a mass exodus. Most of the men were out fighting the fire, so it was left to their wives to collect what they wanted to save and find a way to transport it to the church. Dust added to the foulness of the air as wagons tore down Main Street, either carrying supplies to the firefighters, or headed out toward the church on the flats outside of town.

Lucinda took charge, the calm voice amid the chaos. With Yancey and Curtis driving their buggies, she started with the elderly and children, and those unable to walk to the church at the mouth of the canyon. "Be patient," she called to those anxiously crowding the lobby. "We will get everyone out safely. When you arrive at the church, Edwina Brodie and Pastor Rickman will see to your needs." To Audra, she added, "Poor woman is beside herself. First Pru leaving and now Declan out fighting the fire. But people love her and if she can keep her spirits up, it'll help them keep theirs up, too."

And still the wind blew.

Along Main Street, pandemonium ruled—Cal Bagley shouting orders to two Chinese helpers carrying crates of canned goods from his general store to a buckboard—Mr. Gebbers, rushing in and out of his bank, loading boxes into his buggy—the Mandarin Chinese, fleeing their little tent city like a flock of dark startled birds, their cloth-bound belongings hanging from their shoulders or balanced on their heads—Driscoll, emptying every wagon and horse from his livery to help shopkeepers clear the goods from their stores.

And the smoke grew thicker.

Just after noon, several sluice workers staggered out of the canyon, coughing and covered in soot. But instead of running for the church, they set up a bucket brigade and began dousing the lower walls of the buildings with water hauled from the creek. Others joined in, grim-faced and determined.

As the town emptied, animals came in—first horses, then cattle, pouring out of the canyon, wild-eyed and terrified, chased by boys waving sticks. Audra gaped in shock as a bear cub ran down the boardwalk, its fur smoking.

By the time she had helped Lucinda stow the last boxes of business papers and personal belongings in her buggy, the smoke was so dense she could scarcely see the treetops. Looking back as she climbed onto the seat, she saw black clouds billowing into the sky, turning the sun into a brown orb scarcely visible through the layers of smoke. The wind gusted, peppering her face with hot ash. And faintly, like the sound of a distant waterfall, she heard the roar of the flames.

"Heavens, Lucinda. I can't believe this," she cried climbing into the buggy. "Do you think the town is doomed?"

Lucinda snapped the reins and the buggy lurched forward. "As long as the wind keeps blowing out of the west, there's nothing to save it. I've never seen a fire move so fast."

Audra was appalled. "But what of the hotel? All your hard work?"

"I'll rebuild." Lucinda looked over, her eyes reddened by smoke and tears, but her voice resolved. "This is my home, Audra. I'll not abandon it."

A deer bounded by, its belly distended with the foal she would soon drop, one ear badly damaged, the hair on her hind legs singed.

"Curtis told me about the cabin," Lucinda said. "I'm so sorry."

Tearing her gaze from the deer, Audra nodded. She had been so distracted trying to get everyone to safety, she hadn't considered what to do next. If the fire engulfed Heartbreak Creek, she knew she wouldn't be the only one needing a place to live. She looked out at the freshly painted storefronts, the picturesque creek, and the tall, stately trees. That it could all be gone by nightfall was too horrible to imagine. And only this morning she had contemplated a life here.

"How fortunate that Ethan arrived in time to save your belongings."

"Yes. Fortunate, indeed."

And convenient.

The thought startled her, popping into her head without warning. But once there, it wouldn't be ignored. From what

Curtis had indicated, the fire had been deliberately set . . . at her cabin. A random act by the same vile creature causing mischief throughout the canyon? Or by someone closer— someone she trusted—someone who had targeted her for a specific reason? Like a right-of-way?

Ethan Hardesty.

The notion was so abhorrent she reacted physically to it, gasping as if someone had punched her. She didn't want to believe it. But who else would gain if she were forced off her property? Without the cabin, what other option would she have but to sell the right-of-way and use the money to cover rent elsewhere?

Would Ethan do that to her? Was he that duplicitous?

She prayed not.

But why then, when the others arrived at the cabin, was he already there? And how had he managed to salvage their personal items and Father's papers, even though the mattresses in the room where they had been stored were already aflame? It didn't seem plausible. And yet . . .

She pressed a hand to her stomach, feeling half-sick. The only way to know for certain that he was innocent would be to confront him as soon as he came back. Ask him outright if he had anything to do with the fire, and look into those guarded blue eyes when he gave his answer.

She hated the thought of it.

But throughout the afternoon, as she passed out packets of food at the church, and invented games for fussy children, and tried to offer comfort to the fearful, she played it through in her mind, preparing herself for exactly what she would say, and how he might react.

She hoped he would laugh at her suspicions.

Or try to tease her out of them.

But she expected he would be furious. If guilty, to hide his perfidy. If not, at being accused of something he didn't do.

What she didn't expect was for him to return, disoriented and half-conscious, lying in the back of a wagon.

Ten

"Drink," said a voice Ethan didn't know.

He opened his eyes, blinked to ease the stinging, and finally cleared the blurriness. Then the smell hit him.

Smoke. And beneath it, chemicals, unguents, salves—odors that sent his mind spiraling back to Salty Point, and the screams, and the sound of falling glass, and Eunice Eckhart twisting in a pool of blood at his feet.

He lurched up, gasping.

A hand pushed him back down. "Take it easy, son. You're all right."

It was a moment before his heart slowed and he could think. He looked wildly around, expecting to see the long rows of hospital beds. Instead, he saw an older man with a head full of white hair and faded brown eyes distorted by smudged spectacles, sitting on the edge of his bed.

"Who—?" Ethan began, then fell into a coughing fit.

"Doctor Boyce," the old man said when Ethan sagged back, his head reeling. "But most call me Doc. You're in the infirmary at my house. Drink."

When he held out a glass of water, Ethan eagerly reached for it, then froze when he saw the huge gauze bandage at the end of his arm. For one terrifying moment he thought his hand was gone. Then a searing pain shot up his wrist, making him gasp.

"Your hands are burned," the old man said in a gravelly voice. "But not ruined. With proper care, they'll heal."

They? Ethan looked down, saw a wet cloth covering his bare chest, a sheet over his hips and legs, and his other hand resting atop the sheet—also bandaged. With that awareness, the pain in his fingers exploded into an intense, burning throb that seemed to reach inside his head. He winced. "My head . . ."

"Hurts, I'm guessing. That's what happens when people get too hot and don't drink enough water. Saw a lot of it during the war. Lift up."

Ethan tilted his head off the pillow and the man put the glass to his lips.

Water. He gulped at it, felt the cool slide of it down his parched throat, and thought he'd never tasted anything so good. When the glass was empty, he slumped back, still groggy, his thoughts slow to form. Even after the water, his mouth felt chalky and dry. He remembered that bitter taste. "Laudanum?"

The doctor nodded. "A small dose. So I could clean your hands. You don't remember?"

Ethan shook his head, then instantly regretted it. It felt like someone was hammering on his skull. He recalled helping Curtis load a wagon with the items they'd removed from Audra's cabin. Curtis driving away. Trying to find Brodie and Rylander. Heat. Smoke. Not being able to breathe. Just the memory of that suffocating feeling made his throat constrict. "Where's my horse?" he asked in panic, realizing he hadn't seen Renny since Brodie had dumped him in a wagon.

"The big buckskin? In my paddock out back."

"Is he all right?"

"Better than you."

Ethan looked down at his bandaged hands, a feeling of dread moving through him. So how bad was it? Would he ever play the fiddle again?

Doc must have seen his fear. "The damage is only two thicknesses deep. And mostly on your palms. But the blisters will need watching. How'd you burn them?"

Ethan struggled to remember. "Stuffing a burning mattress out a window. I held them in cool water. Seemed to help. Then wrapped them in a cloth."

"Not just a cloth. A woman's silk underthing." Doc chuckled

and nodded toward a pile of soot-smeared fabric in a basket beside the nightstand. "You should have come in then. Folks don't understand what heat and lack of water can do to a body. Or how easily blisters can turn septic." Removing his spectacles, the doctor pulled a kerchief from his pocket and began rubbing the smudges from the lenses as he spoke. "You were lucky. If they hadn't brought you in when they did, you likely wouldn't have made it." He held up the spectacles to the dim light coming from the window across from the foot of the bed, then polished again. "What are your scars from?"

Surprised by the sudden change in subject, Ethan was slow to answer. "A knife." Then, not wanting to discuss it further, he looked around and saw he was in a long, thin room with three beds separated by privacy curtains. Since the other two beds were empty, the curtains were pulled back. The only window was on the wall opposite the beds, flanked by two straight chairs. Not much light came through the thin window curtain, but he didn't know if that was because it was late, or because of smoke. He remembered the wagon driving past the hotel and on to a rambling house at the edge of town. There had been a lot of noise. Shouts. Other wagons racing by. But now everything seemed eerily quiet. "Where is everybody?"

Satisfied with the lenses, Doc put the spectacles back on. "At the church until we see what the wind does."

Ethan was relieved. That meant Audra and her father were safe. "Has the fire reached town?"

"Not yet. Wind died about an hour ago. If it starts up again out of the east, it'll send it back on itself, and the fire will probably run out of fuel by morning. If not . . ." With a weary sigh, the old man rose.

Ethan saw he was a tall, thin fellow with a bow in his shoulders that spoke of long hours bent over a desk . . . or his patients. Not the usual small-town bone-cutter, but a man who seemed to care.

"My wife, Janet, will be in later with food. Eat it whether you like it or not. I'll not have you hurt her feelings. And don't dislodge that wet cloth on your chest. It'll help cool you down. I'll be back to give you more water after I check on my other patients."

"Are there many?" Ethan remembered helping Thomas and

Rylander clear a fire line and cut down saplings to limit fuel for the flames. He was afraid to ask if they were here, too, maybe in beds in another room.

"Other than you, two scorched dogs and a singed horse. I doubt they'll be as much trouble as you." The doctor turned toward the door. "Rest while you can. When the laudanum wears off you're liable to feel some pain."

Supper was a tasteless barley soup with meat and vegetables, and two more glasses of water. Janet Boyce was a likeable woman, with a ready smile and gentle manner, but it was still humiliating to be spoon-fed like an infant.

During the night, Ethan awoke when two more men were brought in, both suffering heat exhaustion and dehydration. But so far, no fatalities or severe burns. Each time, Doc made him take more water, and while he drank, Ethan noticed the air smelled less like smoke and more like the chemicals and ointments usually associated with infirmaries or hospitals. He remembered them well.

It was daylight when Doc woke him up with two more glasses of water. Did the man never sleep? When Ethan complained, he said, "Until you're passing at least half the liquid you're taking in, it'll continue. So drink."

Ethan drank. But as he finished the second glass, the urge came on him. He wondered how he would manage with his bandages; it wasn't a hands-free process. But the thought of another man helping him piss didn't sit well, especially with two other men watching. "Okay. It's time. Where's the water closet?"

"No need." Doc opened the lower door on the nightstand and brought out a long-necked male urinal. "Use this." He plunked it on the bed beside Ethan's hip.

Ethan looked at it in aversion, wondering who had used it last. He remembered battling a similar device during his hospital stay in California. Because of all the stitches, it hadn't always gone well. "How am I supposed to manage that with these hands?"

"I'll hold it."

"Hold what?" he asked in alarm, ignoring the snickers from the other beds.

Doc pulled the curtain, then turned back to Ethan with a

wink. "Guess you'd prefer the help of that pretty little sandy-haired gal who came by."

"Audra came by?"

"Didn't leave a name."

"When?"

"Yesterday evening. You were asleep."

"What did she say?"

"That she'd be by another time. Now let's get this done."

Thankfully, Doc only held the urinal. Still, it was an ordeal.

When the doctor left, Ethan called through the curtain to the man in the next bed, who had come in just before dawn, "What's it look like out there?"

"Hell," came the hoarse answer, followed by a bout of coughing. Once the man caught his breath, he continued. "Midnight, the wind shifted. Drove the fire toward the ravine. With the creek there, we were able to get enough water on it to keep it from getting to the sluice. A near thing."

"So the town's all right?" Surely Doc would have told him if it wasn't.

"Except for the Chinese camp and a couple of abandoned prospector shacks by the creek."

"Nobody was hurt?"

"Nobody but us and Big Swede, who was so drunk he fell off his horse and cracked his head. But he does that pretty near once a week, so nothing new there. Who's the sandy-haired gal?"

"None of your business."

Doc returned with the cleaned urinal and a box filled with gauze, sticking plaster, medicine bottles, and surgical implements. He set the box on the nightstand and the urinal in the cabinet below. "Rimmick," he said to the man on the other side of the curtain, "your wife's here to get you."

Ethan heard movement beyond the curtain, then a man walking from the room.

"Varney," Doc called. "You can go, too."

"I don't want to."

"They're serving food at the church." Retrieving one of the chairs by the window, Doc carried it back to the bed, then sat down and began sorting through the surgical instruments.

Ethan watched, his unease growing.

"I ain't going to no church," Varney called.

"Fresh venison with all the trimmings."

Silence. Then, "No preaching?"

"No preaching."

In less than a minute, the room was empty except for Ethan and the doctor.

"Can you sit up without getting dizzy?" Doc asked.

Ethan sat up. A momentary spin, then everything settled.

Doc picked up a pair of scissors. "Let's check those hands."

This was the moment Ethan had feared. He had seen hands that had been burned, and how they had curled inward as they had healed, until they looked like claws. He dreaded the prospect of living the rest of his life that way—never to play his fiddle again, or stroke a horse's sleek neck, or feel the softness of a woman's skin against his palm.

Another regret to add to those that already plagued him.

As the last wrapping came off, he braced himself, expecting bloated, blackened fingers and seared flesh. Instead, he saw a thickly padded splint that kept his fingers in a nearly straight position, and when it was removed, a red palm covered with puffy blisters. It shocked him that such a mild-appearing injury could have caused so much pain.

"Flex your fingers."

Ethan did. It hurt, but they moved.

"Now straighten them, spreading your fingers as wide as you can."

He did.

"Again."

Flex, straighten, spread. Over and over, until his hand was shaking and the blisters burned. But everything worked as it should, thank God.

After wiping his hand with a saline solution that stung like a son of a bitch, Doc smeared on a greasy salve, put the splint back in place and rewrapped. "Now the left."

After putting him through the same exercises, he replaced the splint and bandaged Ethan's trembling hand. "How long will I need to do this?" Ethan asked.

"The exercises? Four or five times a day until you can do it without pain. You have good mobility. I want to keep it that way. By tomorrow, if everything still looks good, you can leave off the splints except at night. The main thing now is to keep the blisters from becoming infected. Two, maybe three weeks, you'll be good as new. You can lie down now."

Gratefully, Ethan did. He wasn't dizzy, but he was beginning to feel wobbly. "When can I leave?"

Doc chuckled. "Not enjoying my wife's cooking?"

"The food's fine," he lied. "But I've got things I need to attend to."

"Maybe tomorrow. That soon enough?"

A commotion in the hall drew Doc's attention. A moment later, the door opened and a man Ethan didn't recognize looked in. "Doc, we need you. Got a dead coolie, but we don't think it was the fire that got him."

After a late-morning feeding of watery oatmeal and stewed prunes—Ethan was desperate for food that didn't have to be eaten with a spoon—Doc came in to take off the splint and put him through another round of exercises.

"So?" Ethan snapped, peeved at being stuck all morning in a back room with no news. The Chinese worked for the people he represented. Someone should have kept him apprised. "What killed him?"

"The Chinaman? A slit throat."

"They needed you to figure that out?"

Doc gave him a warning look, then resumed unwrapping. "He was burned."

"Before or after?"

"After."

So the arsonist had moved to murder. Ethan wondered what had sent him in that direction. "Got any idea who did it?"

"Some say an Indian." Doc bent closer to study Ethan's palms.

Ethan did, too. Most of the blisters looked smaller, but some had burst. He quickly looked away when Doc got out a scalpel and set to work, cutting away the loose, dead skin. It hurt like hell.

"Why an Indian?"

"They like to take hair. But I don't think it was a scalping. This might sting a bit."

Liquid splashed on Ethan's palm. He refrained from

gasping. A cool salve soothed away the burn, then Doc was wrapping his hand again, this time with an intricate crisscross weave that protected his palm and fingers, but still allowed some movement. "I'm doing this so that tomorrow, when you take off the splint during the day to do your exercises, your hands will still be protected. It's important to keep these bandages clean. Blisters are as vulnerable as open wounds and can easily get infected. That happens, you could lose your hands. Or worse. Next."

Ethan held out his left hand. He was starting to feel a little dizzy. Probably the fumes from that stinking salve. "Why don't you believe it was an Indian?"

"When an Indian takes hair, he takes scalp with it. The Chinaman only lost his pigtail."

Only? Apparently Doc didn't know that a Chinaman's queue, or pigtail, was a symbol of his national identity. To have it cut off was an affront that could easily lead to bloodshed. "So who do you think killed him?"

Doc shrugged. "Maybe the same man who set the fire. Maybe another Chinaman. Hell if I know."

The Chinese had their own rules and ways of doing things. It wasn't unheard of for rivalries between families to explode in violence. Last thing Ethan needed was a blood feud. "How are the others taking it?"

"Not well." Doc tied off the last strip of gauze and began repacking the box he'd brought his torture supplies in. "They're demanding Sheriff Brodie find the man who took the pigtail so they can return it to the dead fellow's family. Seem more concerned about losing the hair than losing the man. Strange folks."

"The man who killed him took it?"

"Appears so."

"Then a Chinaman didn't do it." When one Chinaman cut off another Chinaman's queue, it was about the insult, not about the hair. He would have no reason to keep the pigtail.

So if it wasn't an Indian or a Chinaman, then who was the killer?

That evening, Ethan was staring at the ceiling, listening to his stomach beg for something other than a cup of unflavored soup—no wonder Doc stayed so lean—when Tait Rylander walked in, a bundle of clothing under one arm.

Delighted for the company, Ethan grinned in welcome. "Bring any food?"

"They're not feeding you?"

"Not enough. Those my clothes?" he asked when Tait dumped the bundle on a chair by the window.

"Doc asked me to bring them. Said your others were ruined."

"Thanks. I heard about the Chinaman."

Tait dropped his hat on the foot of the bed, then leaned forward, arms straight, hands braced on the foot rail. His scarred knuckles rose like fresh bee stings. "That's one of the reasons I'm here."

Ethan knew him well enough now not to take that probing stare personally. The man was damned intense. "There's news?"

"There's talk. Some think the killer might be one of the Chinese railroad workers. I've worked more with the Irish on the Eastern lines, so I'm not as familiar with the habits of the Chinese. Do you think one of them did it?"

"No, I don't." Ethan gave his reasons, adding, "I think the killer is more likely someone who resents the Chinese, and when he caught one alone, saw it as his chance to rid the world of another yellow devil. Sad to say, it happens."

"Someone local?"

"Seen any strangers around lately?"

Tait shook his head. "Nor have I noticed any problems between the whites and Chinese. They usually stay out of each other's way. And anyway, it's not like they're taking away jobs from the townspeople. Every able-bodied local who wants to work is already on the sluice."

"Then what about another railroad?" Ethan suggested. "If this bridge line gets built, it will bring in a fortune over time."

Pushing off the foot rail, Tait walked over to the window, nudged aside the curtain, and looked out. After a moment, he let the curtain drop, and turned. "You could be right. Brodie said a local prospector named Weems saw a surveyor with the Southern Utah and Atlantic near the other end of the canyon last month."

"You think a competitor did it, hoping to scare off our Chinese laborers?"

"It worked near San Francisco last year."

Ethan remembered. What had started as sabotage had ended in a bloody railroad war, the Chinese getting the worst of it. "How are our workers taking it?"

"There's definitely some unrest. Nothing overt yet."

"Then we'd best get them busy laying tracks."

Tait looked surprised. "You've gotten Miss Pearsall's signature?"

"Not yet. But we don't need it." Ethan explained how they could avoid her property by looping to the other side of the ravine. "It'll cost more, and we'll have to make sure the curves aren't too sharp. But it's doable." Although now that the cabin was gone, why would Audra not want to sell the right-of-way?

"By the way," he added casually, "have you seen her since the fire?"

"Miss Pearsall? Several times. She and Lucinda and Edwina handled the evacuation to the church. They're still there, even though folks are starting to straggle back to town now that it looks like the fire is burning itself out."

"She say anything?"

Tait raised his brows in innocence. "About the right-of-way?" Then seeing Ethan's expression, he laughed. It sounded odd, coming from a man so reserved. "She was worried. We all were. If I had known you were injured, I would have sent you back earlier."

"*Sent* me? You're in charge of me, now, Pa?" Even though Tait was probably no more than seven or eight years older than Ethan's twenty-seven, Ethan owed him for tweaking him about Audra.

Tait let it ride. "Doc says you can leave tomorrow. If you do, find me in the dining room at the hotel. We can discuss that alternate route."

"Maybe Brodie can join us. I'd like to hear more about that prospector, Weems, and the surveyor he saw."

Eleven

That night, sleep didn't come.

But Eunice did. Drifting in and out of his thoughts, filling him with longing and horror and that vague sense of shame he had often felt when he was around her.

He had been at the hospital at Salty Point less than a month when he made love to her for the first time. It was late. All the workers had left and he was standing in the dark in the new addition. The glass wasn't in place yet. Only a skeletal timber framework stood between him and the sea. Wind tore at his hair, his shirt. A bright moon left a silvery slash across the heaving swells a hundred feet below and the muffled sound of waves breaking against the rocks was as steady as his own heartbeat.

"Ethan."

Startled, he turned to see her standing a foot behind him. She wore nightclothes. Her untied robe whipped in the wind, billowing out behind her like unfurled wings, and the thin fabric of her gown clung to her lush form. She was even more beautiful than the woman who had haunted his dreams since the day he'd seen her on the bluff.

He drew in air, smelled her perfume, felt the hot rush of blood through his body. "What are you doing out here?"

Reaching out, she laid her palm on his chest.

He wondered if she could feel the drumming of his heart.

By her smile, she did. "Looking for you."

It was all the invitation he needed. Pulling her closer, he lowered his head.

She slapped him. Playfully. But there was still sting in it. Surprised, he lifted his head.

Now her hand soothed, fingertips circling his cheek. "No kissing on the lips. That's how disease is spread."

He chuckled. "Then the world is doomed." He brought his head down again.

She slapped him. Harder. "I said no kissing, Ethan."

Confused, he released her. "Don't do that."

"Did I hurt you?" She smiled. "Relax. You'll get used to it." As she spoke, she raked her pointed nails down his chest. Gently. Turning the sting into a shiver of desire. "Take off your shirt. I want to see you. Touch you."

He looked around. "But—"

"Now, Ethan." Her nails dug in so hard he flinched. "I want to feel you inside me. Take off your shirt."

He took off his shirt.

That's how it began. She was cold passion and a fire in his belly. She found that forbidden place in every man's mind that hovered below thought, where pain and ecstasy dissolved into exquisite sensation and obsession corrupted the soul.

He never got used to it. But he allowed it. Because he sensed her need to be in control of them—of him—and because he had convinced himself that he loved her.

When he awoke the next morning, it was to the distant sound of a rooster crowing, a ravenous appetite, and the welcome sight of Miss Audra Pearsall sitting on the chair beside his bed, reading. He took a deep breath and let it out, releasing the tormented memories with it. "Spectacles," he said, yawning. "I knew it."

She startled, turned her head and looked at him.

Today her eyes seemed more brown than green—no doubt because of the drab brown dress she wore—and they looked even bigger through the lenses. Every dark lash stood out like a fine pen stroke. Beneath the lingering scent of wood smoke, he caught a drift of scented soap. Something flowery. Roses, maybe. He could tell by the smudges beneath her eyes and the weary slope of her shoulders that she was tired.

Still, she might have dredged up a smile.

"How do you feel?" she asked.

"Better."

And a bit embarrassed to be caught wearing only his small clothes beneath the sheet, especially when she looked as prim as a preacher's daughter. "You're up early." By the slant of light coming through the window, he figured it couldn't be much past dawn.

"Mr. Rylander said Doctor Boyce was releasing you today. I wanted to speak to you before you returned to the hotel." After a moment of awkward silence, she added, "I'm very pleased to see you so much improved."

She didn't look pleased. In fact, she looked like she would rather be anywhere but here with him. "How long have you been sitting here?"

"A while. I came in the back so I wouldn't disturb the doctor and his wife."

Another awkward silence. He wondered what had driven her back behind her shield of reserve. Only a few evenings ago, they had chatted amicably. She had even laughed with him. Now she was as distant as she had ever been. "You needed to speak to me?" he prodded.

"Yes. I have a question."

He watched her carefully close the book and set it on the night table, remove her spectacles and place them atop the book. She turned toward him, and in doing so, her foot tipped over the waste bin between the chair and the bed. She righted it, then hesitated. "What's that?" she asked, bending to peer intently at the torn strips of soot-stained cloth. "Is that my . . . chemise?"

Hearing the word spoken in her voice sent images flashing through his mind. Arousing images. More arousing than those that had plagued him through the night. "I doubt Winnie could fit into it."

She snapped upright. "What are you doing with it?"

"I used it to wrap my hands. I'll buy you another. Something green to match your eyes."

She jumped to her feet and began to pace at the foot of the bed.

A strong reaction to a torn chemise. Yet she hadn't corrected him about the color of her eyes, or chastised him for his boldness.

Something was wrong. He could see it in the tight line of her mouth and the stiffness of her back. He was beginning to know all her signals, what each tiny mannerism and expression meant. Odd, how quickly that had happened. And what he was reading now was that she was angry. With him, it seemed. He had no idea why, so he tossed out a line. "You're upset."

She shot him one of those sarcastic eye rolls that women do so well, made two more loops, then stopped beside the window, gripping her hands tightly at her waist. "As I said, I have a question. Your answer is of utmost importance, so please do not prevaricate."

Prevaricate? About what? "Okay," he said warily.

"I abhor confrontation," she went on as if she hadn't heard him. "And I've fretted endlessly about how to put this. I think it best to simply come out with it." She took a deep breath, then said in a rush, "Did you set fire to my cabin?"

The words were slow to penetrate. When they did, he still couldn't accept that she'd said them, or that he had heard them correctly. "What did you ask me?"

"Did you set fire to my cabin?"

Emotion slammed through him—astonishment, outrage, disbelief. It was a moment before he could regain his balance. "Why would you ask me that?"

"Curtis told me you were already at the cabin when he arrived. Why?"

"I was checking on it, as I told you I would."

She began pacing again. "He also said someone had doused the mattresses with lamp oil before setting them on fire."

"They had."

"And yet you were still able to remove our belongings from the bedroom despite two burning mattresses. How did you manage that?"

"With difficulty." Every word out of her mouth sent his outrage soaring higher. Did she actually believe what she was saying? What had he done to warrant such distrust? "But do ask Curtis," he ground out. "Apparently I'm already condemned in your eyes. Perhaps you'll believe him."

She seemed to falter, then collected herself. Moving to the

foot of the bed, she stared intently into his eyes. "And if the fire was deliberately set, and I was the target, who would gain most if I was forced to move elsewhere?"

"I would. Assuming you were the target and gain was the motive. Hell, Audra! Look out there!" He waved a bandaged hand toward the window. "Do you actually think all that destruction is because of some piddling right-of-way?"

"No—yes." Her rigid composure cracked. "Just tell me you didn't do it, Ethan. That's all I need to know."

Anger boiled over. "Why would I set fire to your home, Audra? To what purpose? Just to injure myself trying to put it out? Does that make sense to you?"

Her face twisted. He saw her chin quiver and knew what was coming. "No! Don't you dare cry. You can't come in here with these wild accusations and think tears will absolve you. You'll tell me why you think me capable of such an act. Especially against you!"

"I didn't want to believe it. But what other explanation—"

The door flew open. Curtis stood in the opening, his face frantic. "Miss Audra, you gotta come! Mistuh Percy run off and we can't find him."

Ethan was sitting on the edge of the bed tearing at the wrappings with his teeth when Doc rushed in, wearing a nightshirt, his white hair in wild disarray. "What was all the yelling about?"

"Miss Pearsall thinks I started the fire."

"Did you?"

"Hell, no." He held up his bandaged hands. "Can you help me here? I need the splints off so I can dress."

Grumbling, Doc grabbed a pair of scissors from a drawer. "First good night's sleep I've had in three days. Who was that running through the house?"

"The African who works for her. Said her father had wandered off."

"Man can't take a stroll without permission?"

"He's suffering dementia."

Doc considered that as he cut through the wrappings. "How long?"

"Long enough. But she won't put him in an institution."

"Good for her."

As soon as Doc removed the splints, Ethan shoved past him to get the clean clothing Tait had left on the chair by the window. "If you see an elderly fellow with gray hair and a bald spot on top, and a little dog that barks all the time, send word to the hotel." He was able to pull on the shirt and trousers, but couldn't manage the buttons. Frustrated, he turned again to the doctor for help.

"You keep those bandages clean." Doc finished buttoning, then helped him into the jacket Tait had brought. "Wear gloves if you have them. Drink lots of water and come by tomorrow so I can check those blisters. You'll find your boots on the porch. I don't think you had a hat."

"Thanks, Doc." Ethan rushed into the hall. "I'll settle my charges later."

"Cash. I've got enough chickens."

Ethan went straight to the paddock and shed behind the infirmary. Renny greeted him with a nicker—probably hungry, too—but Ethan didn't have time to stop. Opening the shed door, he saw his tack, and went inside.

Not knowing where his search would take him, and figuring Audra's father couldn't have gotten far, he decided not to take the time to saddle Renny, even if he could have managed it with his bandaged hands. But he did want his canteen. After retrieving his gun belt, pistol, the canteen, and a pair of gloves from his saddlebag, he gave Renny a pat, and set out on foot.

It felt good to be up and moving again, even though he was aware of a faint, lingering weakness. Probably lack of real food. The smoke was gone, although the smell of it lingered in the air, and other than a puffy cloud bank hanging over the peaks to the west, the sky was clear.

It was still early enough that there wasn't a lot of activity along Main, except for shop owners sweeping the boardwalks in front of their stores and scrubbing soot and ash from their doors and windows. At the end of the street, scorched trees stood over what remained of the small Chinese camp, and higher in the canyon, wisps of smoke curled lazily into the morning sky.

He stopped at the hotel to fill up his canteen and see if they had found Mr. Pearsall. Yancey said no, and that the dog was missing, too. "Miss Audra and Curtis are checking in town.

Sheriff went up toward the mine, and Tait and Miss Lucinda took her buggy out toward Mulberry Creek."

"Then I'll head up the left fork into the burned area."

At the mouth of the canyon many of the pines were green on top, even though their trunks were burned black. Still usable if they were harvested before rot set in. He'd seen lumber milled from scorched wood, and a lot of it showed dark streaks in the grain that gave it a faint blue tint. Not unattractive. He wouldn't mind having it in his own house someday.

The deeper into the ruined forest he hiked, the worse the devastation became. A stark, ash-powdered landscape, dotted with tall, skeletal trees. He stopped often to drink from the canteen and look around, but heard nothing and saw no movement other than swirls of ash when the breeze swept by. Footprints crisscrossed the track. Too many to count. Probably left by the men fighting the fire. Occasionally, he saw the charred carcass of some poor woodland creature that had perished in the flames.

Silence settled around him. No birdsong, no scurrying footfalls through the underbrush, only the faint murmur of the creek in the ravine below. Even the breeze moved unheard through the twisted limbs.

And Audra thought he had done this? That he had engineered this holocaust simply to force her to sign a right-of-way? He still couldn't believe it. He might have been at fault in one disaster, but this time, he was innocent. Yet how could he convince her of that? If his actions thus far hadn't shown her the kind of man he was, or that he cared about her too much to hurt her this way, what good would mere words do?

He stopped abruptly, his own words circling in his head.

He cared about her.

The notion shocked him, instantly sent up his defenses. Of course, he cared about her. He cared about a lot of people. He wasn't an unfeeling man. But . . .

He continued walking, his steps kicking up little puffs of ash.

Audra was different. Nothing like Eunice. She challenged him, amused him, gave him a reason to greet the day with anticipation, rather than dread. She also drove him to distraction. But that didn't mean anything. Did it?

He laughed, the mocking sound of it alien in this lifeless place. When had he added liar to his list of sins?

A noise across the ravine caught his attention. He stopped, head cocked.

Up high. Somewhere above the sluice. A voice, barely audible over the gentle splashing of the creek. Weeping.

Relieved to put thoughts of Audra aside, he started down into the ravine.

Audra was beside herself. She and Curtis had knocked on every door, accosted strangers walking by, searched each vacant building. Curtis had even crawled up into the loft of Mr. Driscoll's barn. Father couldn't be found anywhere.

The Rylanders had ridden along Mulberry Creek Road at least a mile past the Brodie house, but had seen no sign of him. The sheriff had searched the deserted buildings up at the old mine, and his son, R.D., who knew several of the younger Chinese laborers, was asking around at the encampment near the rail yards. The only place they hadn't searched was deep in the canyon where the fire had swept through. But why would Father go there?

Cleo was missing, too, which gave Audra hope that they were simply out on a stroll. But after several hours with no sign of either of them, she was beginning to fear the worst. And the odd thing was that Cleo's basket was missing, too. Why would Father take that along?

Now, after a fruitless morning, the searchers had gathered for lunch in the hotel dining room, although Winnie was too upset to eat. Despite Audra's assurances, she blamed herself for Father's disappearance, since he had been left in her care when Audra had gone to talk to Ethan.

Ethan. What must he be thinking after her accusations? He had been more upset than she had expected him to be—that flash of emotion startling and seemingly heartfelt. In fact, he had actually appeared more hurt than angry, which had surprised her.

And yet . . . despite the anger, the hurt, the heated rebuttals . . . he still had not answered her question, had he?

But he wasn't the issue now. Father was.

"I don't know where else to look," she said, listlessly pushing the food around on her plate.

"We won't give up," Lucinda promised.

"We'll find him," Tait added.

"He'll probably come back when he gets hungry," Yancey offered through a mouthful of mashed potatoes. "I always do."

"I check on him right after you leave," Winnie said, blinking hard against a fresh onslaught of tears. "He sound asleep. Cleo curled up in her basket, same as always. If I hadn't gone down to the water closet . . ."

"You not at fault, Win." Curtis patted her hand. "We all got to go. 'Specially first thing in the morning."

Lucinda cleared her throat. "Tait and I stopped at every house along Mulberry Creek Road. No one had seen a thing. And by the way, Declan," she added, turning to the sheriff, "Brin put Whit in one of the feed boxes in the stable. I think she was re-creating the church's live manger scene she had been so enthralled with over Christmas. It's a wonder she got that milk cow in there with all those squawking chickens. But not to worry," she rushed on at his look of alarm. "Everyone is fine. I just thought I'd prepare you." She gave him a look of commiseration. "Edwina is a bit upset."

He muttered something under his breath.

"Heard anything from R.D.?" Tait inquired.

The sheriff shook his head. "Still at the Chinese camp. But he'd have sent word if he'd heard anything. I rode a ways up the sluice, but no one there had seen Mr. Pearsall, either. After lunch I'll ride up the burned side."

"No need," Yancey said, grabbing more bread. "Mr. Ethan headed that way earlier."

Audra looked at him in surprise. Ethan had joined the search, too? Even with his hands in such poor condition?

She puzzled over that throughout the rest of the meal, then decided as soon as they finished here, she and Curtis would get another horse from Mr. Driscoll and a saddle for Cricket, then ride up the unburned side of the ravine where the water sluice was. The sheriff had been in a hurry. Perhaps he had missed something.

Twelve

Ethan crawled out of the ravine, winded and a bit light-headed. While he caught his breath, he sipped from the canteen and tried to get his bearings.

He'd walked farther than he thought—almost five miles, if that was the mouth of the sluice he saw through the trees up ahead. Could an old man have hiked all the way up here?

Surprisingly, other than scorched grass and a charred bush here and there, this side of the ravine was untouched by flames. He realized why when he saw that the ground around the supports was muddy and the boards inside the sluice were damp. Apparently, someone had opened the gate to let in water, and the resulting leakage had kept everything wet enough not to catch fire. Impressive. If he knew who the enterprising fellow was, he'd give him a bonus.

A voice from the ridge brought his head up. He scanned the slope and saw no one, but did note a narrow game trail slanting up. On it were footprints and bits of mud that might have dropped off a wet shoe. Pearsall's or someone else's?

He capped the canteen and slung the strap over his shoulder. Not knowing what—or who—he would find up there, he checked the load in his Colt as best he could with his bandaged fingers, returned it to the holster, then began to climb.

More mud on the way up. Drag marks. But not the kind a body might have made. He looked closer, saw the imprint of a weave in the powdery dirt. A basket? At the top, he paused to catch his breath, then followed the trail through brush and tall evergreens until he came to open ground ringed by poplars.

Pearsall sat on a downed log in the middle of the clearing, a basket at his feet. Ethan recognized it as the one the dog slept in. Before stepping into the clearing, he looked around. Audra's father appeared to be alone, but Ethan didn't want to rush in until he was sure what he might find.

The old fellow was a mess. He wore a nightshirt and untied robe. Both were wet. Mud caked his unlaced boots. There was a bloody scrape on his neck and scratches on the thin, mud-spattered legs showing beneath the robe. He was crying.

Ethan stepped into the clearing, his right hand on the butt of his pistol—although with the thick glove and bandages, he didn't know if he would be able to get his finger through the trigger guard to fire it. "Hello, Mr. Pearsall."

The old man looked up, blinking watery eyes in confusion. "Is that you, Richard?"

"No, sir. It's Ethan Hardesty."

"I don't know . . . have we met?"

Warily scanning the trees, Ethan approached. "I know your daughter."

Pearsall still looked puzzled.

"Audra."

It was obvious the old man didn't know who Ethan was talking about. He doubted the poor fellow even knew where he was, or why he had trekked all the way out here wearing his nightclothes.

"May I sit down?" When Pearsall didn't answer, Ethan eased onto the log beside him, his gaze sweeping the clearing once more before swinging back to Audra's father.

He looked worse up close. In addition to the wet, muddy clothing and scratches, the old man's hands wouldn't stop shaking, and there was a wild, frightened look in his eyes.

Saddened, Ethan looked away. Something was deeply wrong in the scheme of things that such a brilliant mind could be reduced to this. But Ethan knew bad things happened to the innocent and guilty alike. He had seen it. Suffered it.

"Are you here alone?" He eyed the basket. If the little dog was under the blanket, why wasn't it barking as it usually did?

"Alone? I don't . . . there was a man . . ." The words trailed off. The old man looked around, muttering softly to himself.

Skin prickling, Ethan followed his gaze but saw no one in the trees. "What did he want?"

"Who?"

"The man who was here with you."

"I don't . . . I can't . . ." Palsied fingers plucked at the fabric of the robe. "I need Mary. She'll know what to do."

"About what?"

"I d-don't know. Cleo. I think something's wrong with Cleo. She wouldn't wake up this morning. I think . . . I think . . ."

"May I look?" Ethan reached for the blanket in the basket.

"Mary will know. Why isn't she here? We should ask Mary."

Ethan lifted the blanket. The dog was curled tight as if asleep. But the cloudy eyes were open and there was a stillness that told Ethan she was dead. He eased the blanket back over the small form.

"Is she gone, Richard? Is my Cleo gone?"

Ethan nodded. "I'm sorry, sir."

New tears rose in the faded eyes. "She was a good dog. Barked a lot. But she . . ." He moved restlessly. "Where's Mary? I have to tell Mary."

The afternoon breeze kicked up, making the poplar leaves murmur like cascading water. When Ethan saw Pearsall shiver, he took off his jacket and draped it over the old man's bony shoulders. "We should go back now."

"Back?"

"To town."

"Baltimore? What about Cleo?"

"I think she should stay here."

"But . . ." Tears spilled down the wrinkled cheeks.

"I'll come back," Ethan promised. "I'll take care of her." With these hands, he wasn't sure how he could bury the animal, but right now he was more concerned with getting the old man back to his daughter and into dry clothes.

Pearsall looked up at the ring of trees, smiling despite the tears. "It's a pretty place, isn't it?"

"It is."

"I think she'll like it here."

"I'm sure she will. Here, let me help you up."

The old man felt as brittle as dry sticks in his grip. Ethan figured he'd end up carrying him most of the way and regretted he hadn't brought Renny.

"You've been very kind, Mr. . . ."

"Hardesty. Watch your step, sir. Hold on to my arm."

"Mr. Hardesty. Yes, of course. You're acquainted with Mary?"

"Audra."

Pearsall stopped and peered up at him. "Who's Audra?"

"Your daughter, sir."

"Daughter?"

At a muffled sound, Ethan looked over to see Audra standing in the shadows of the trees, a hand clamped over her mouth. What was she doing here? How had she known where to find them?

"No." Mr. Pearsall shook his head. "You must be mistaken."

Even from yards away, Ethan could feel her anguish. To have her existence denied by her own father, the man who had been the cornerstone of her whole life, must tear a hole in her heart. He could feel the pain of it, see it in her eyes when she looked at her father, then at him. It unraveled something deep inside him.

Oblivious, Pearsall shuffled along. "I don't have a daughter. Do I?"

"Yes, sir, you do." Ethan's gaze never left hers. "And you would be proud of her, I think."

For the space of a heartbeat, she went utterly still. Then taking her hand from her mouth, she brushed it across her cheeks, took a deep breath and stepped out of the shadows. "There you are," she said with forced cheer. "I've been looking everywhere."

Her father looked up, a smile breaking over his weary face. "Look, it's Mary. Isn't she beautiful, Richard?"

"She is. And stubborn."

"Who's that man behind her?"

On reflex, Ethan reached for his pistol, then saw Curtis coming up the trail. He was relieved she hadn't come alone. "That's Curtis Abraham. Do you remember him?"

"No. No . . . I . . ."

"Hidy, Mistuh Percy," Curtis called as he approached. "You sure enough set us on a merry chase. Yes, suh, you did."

Pearsall moved restlessly, his hands plucking at his robe again. "Mary, who are these people? You know I don't like strangers coming around."

Audra stepped forward and put her arms around her father. "We were looking for you. We didn't know where you were. You shouldn't leave without telling me."

"There, there." Pearsall pulled out of her embrace and patted her cheek. "No need for tears, old girl. I'm right here. Did you bring Cleo with you?"

Audra caught Ethan's warning look and followed his gaze to the basket by the log. Understanding dawned when he shook his head. For a moment, her face twisted in renewed grief, but she collected herself and took her father's arm. "Come along, dearest. Let's get you home."

"I'm hungry, Mary. Did you bring lunch? I had something . . . a basket . . ."

"It's all right," she said gently, leading him toward the trail. "We'll get it later."

"Don't go far," Ethan cautioned her. "Stay where I can see you. I'll catch up in a minute."

As Audra and her father moved into the trees, he motioned Curtis closer. "The dog's dead," he said in a voice that wouldn't carry. "In her basket over there. I don't want to leave her here, but—"

"Don't worry, Mistuh Ethan. I'll cover her good with rocks 'til I can get back with a shovel. You go on with Miss Audra."

"I'd rather we stay together." Ethan glanced over at the Pearsalls, who were almost out of sight. "Wait there, Audra," he called, then turned back to Curtis. "Her father mentioned a man. He might have been confused, but I don't want to take any chances. I'll wait with them by that big spruce while you take care of the dog. That way I can keep an eye on them and the clearing, too."

Curtis looked around, eyes wide in his dark face.

"Did you walk all the way from town?" Ethan asked, regaining his attention.

"No, suh. We come on horseback. Cricket, and one Miss Audra borrowed from the livery man. They down yonder by the sluice."

Relieved, Ethan patted his shoulder, then winced at the sting in his palms. "Hurry, then. Pearsall's wet and we need to get him back as soon as we can."

It was an ordeal getting the old man down the steep slope. After his long hike that morning, he was so weary his knees kept buckling. But with Curtis holding on to him from behind, and Ethan half-carrying him on his back, they managed to get him down to where the horses were tied.

Ethan was a little wobbly himself. He passed around the canteen, letting the others drink their fill, then finished off what was left. It helped some, but if he didn't get food in his belly soon, he'd be as weak as the old man.

They put Pearsall in front of Curtis on the horse Audra had gotten from Driscoll, and Audra in front of Ethan on Cricket. She took the reins, which was fine with him—his hands were hurting like a son of a bitch—and let Curtis go ahead, so she could keep an eye on her father.

To give her more room, Ethan rode on the rear skirt of the saddle, but since the track was all downhill, she was soon leaning back, her shoulder blades brushing against his chest with every lurching step.

He didn't mind.

She wasn't wearing a bonnet and was small enough that he had a fair view over her head—and down her front. Her hair was silky fine. It tickled his nose, caught in his three-day stubble. It smelled like roses. Long golden-streaked tresses swept down to breasts that swayed and bounced and jiggled with the motion of the horse. Wondrous things, breasts. Hers, especially so.

But his pleasant musings ended abruptly when he realized she was crying.

He couldn't see her face, but he heard the sniffle, saw the quick swipe of a sleeve over her eyes. And he knew Audra.

Resting a hand on her waist, he leaned down and said in her ear, "He knows you. Somewhere in his heart, he knows you."

She didn't respond with words, but the tension in her spine seemed to ease.

They rode for a time without speaking. It was that watchful kind of silence that hangs between two people who had last parted on a bad note, and who were unsure of how to proceed. He stood it as long as he could, but being impatient by nature, he spoke first. "Who's Richard? Your father kept calling me that. Since he was using the man's first name, I'm assuming the two of you know him well."

Ethan hoped she wouldn't lie to him or try to evade his inquiry. One of the things he appreciated most about Audra was her willingness to go at an issue head-on. Her accusations earlier at the infirmary were proof of that, even though she had been wrong in her assumptions. She might say she abhorred confrontation, but she certainly didn't shy away from it when something was important to her. But he sensed that if she did lie to him, he would know it. Somehow, in some way he didn't question or fully understand, he'd just know.

"Richard Villars," she finally said. "A colleague of Father's. And a suitor."

"You refused him."

"Yes."

"Because of your father?"

"That, and because I didn't want to marry him."

"Why not?"

"That's none of your business, Mr. Hardesty."

But he heard the smile in her voice, and that made him smile, too.

They didn't speak for a while. Yet this time, there was no awkwardness in the silence, and Ethan was able to forget the pain in his hands, and the gnawing emptiness in his belly, and his uncertainty about where all this would lead, and simply enjoy the nearness of the woman in front of him—a woman he had come to care about, despite all the reasons he shouldn't.

Like water on stone, hope—and Audra—were slowly eroding his resolve.

It was dangerous. Potentially devastating. But he was beginning to envision a future beyond the curse of the past. Maybe a future with her.

Word traveled faster than they did. By the time they started down Main Street, Ethan saw a small crowd of people waiting on the boardwalk outside of the hotel. Realizing his time alone with Audra would soon end, he broached the subject they had both avoided. "It occurs to me, I haven't answered your question."

She stiffened, then turned in the saddle to look over her shoulder at him.

A provocative pose, one that opened a gap in her dress where a button had come undone. He glimpsed lace and creamy flesh, and responded instantly, his heart kicking against his ribs.

Just a tilt of his head . . . a few inches . . . and his lips would brush hers.

The idea of it sent blood pumping through his veins.

He wanted it. One kiss. Wanted it more than he'd wanted anything in a long time. More even than he'd ever wanted Eunice Eckhart.

Instead, he curbed the impulse and gave her the answer she needed. "I didn't set fire to your cabin, Audra."

She didn't react—no relief, surprise, confusion, nothing—but continued to stare into his face, as if all the answers she sought were hidden behind his eyes.

Had she heard him? Did she believe him? Did she even care?

Then she gave him a slow smile that reached all the way into his chest. "I know, Ethan. You're too honorable a man to cause such needless harm."

At one time, he had thought so, too.

Thirteen

While Audra and Winnie hurried Mr. Pearsall upstairs and Curtis took the horses to the livery, Ethan remained behind to answer questions. Even though they had only been in Heartbreak Creek a short time, the Pearsalls had gained quite a few friends—probably due to Audra's efforts during the fire. After his assurances that the old man was all right, the crowd dispersed, and he went with the sheriff and the Rylanders into the hotel.

"The kitchen open? I haven't eaten decent food since Sunday morning."

Tait Rylander's dark brows rose in surprise. "No one fed you at the infirmary?"

"Doc's wife did."

"Ah." Lucinda nodded in understanding. "Janet's such a dear, bless her heart, but her cooking will never win a ribbon at the fair. Come into the dining room. It's early yet for supper, but I'll see if Cook can fix you something."

Careful of his bandaged hands, Ethan toweled off most of the dirt and ash in the washroom off the back hall, then went into the deserted dining room, where he found Tait and Brodie standing over a table, studying construction drawings. Thinking they might relate to the bridge line, Ethan wandered over.

"Luce wants to put it where the old assay office is," Tait was telling the sheriff when Ethan stopped behind them. "But I'm not sure we want tracks cutting through the middle of town. What do you think, Hardesty?" He turned the papers so Ethan could see them. "This is a rough plan of the Heartbreak Creek Station."

Ethan made himself look at the crude drawings, when what he wanted to do was turn around and walk back out the door. "You drew these?"

"I did."

It was a simple floor plan: down one side of the building, two ticket windows, a railroad office, and a men's lavatory—on the other, an open alcove that housed two small shops and a women's retiring room and lavatory. The center of the structure was an open thirty-six-square-foot waiting area. Beside the wall facing the tracks was written one word: glass.

Ethan's throat grew tight. "How tall is that window wall?"

"About twenty-four feet at the peak."

"How do you plan on stabilizing it? Glass is fragile. Without a sturdy foundation, a strong wind can bring it down. And where are the support posts in the open area? You can't span thirty-six feet without them. Have you factored in the snow load in the roof pitch? And if your peak runs front to back, where will the snow slide?" Realizing he had revealed too much, he shoved the drawings away. "Designing a building isn't as simple as it looks."

"Apparently not."

Aware that the two men were staring at him, he put on a smile. "But what do I know? Best hire an architect. And hope he knows what he's doing. Food," he added with forced enthusiasm when a server came out of the kitchen with a loaded tray.

While Ethan ate, Tait and Sheriff Brodie drank coffee and discussed the Chinaman's murder and what Brodie's son, R. D., had learned in the encampment by the rail yard—which was nothing more than Ethan had suspected: no one believed the murderer was Chinese.

"R.D. said there's a lot of distrust and resentment toward Tim Gallagher, one of the Irish foremen," Brodie said. "But no one is accusing him outright. I met the fellow. Didn't much like him. Or that silver-handled whip of his. But his drinking buddies at the Red Eye have vouched for his whereabouts up until the fire alarm sounded."

"I've already wired the home office to send out a replacement overseer," Ethan told them. "Should be here in a week or two. Meanwhile, I'll keep an eye on him."

Tait nodded. "Good. Hopefully everything will settle down once we start laying tracks. While you were laid up, Hardesty, the man in charge of the graders asked when his men could start. I told him tomorrow they could begin work on the stretch between the Boot Creek terminal and the rail yard here. I hope that's all right with you. I didn't want to overstep, but his men are getting restless."

Ethan flashed him a grateful smile. "You did the right thing, Tait. I appreciate the help. Meanwhile, I'll send work gangs into the canyon to start felling trees."

They discussed a few supply issues, and how the owner of the mercantile, Cal Bagley, was upset because the Chinese were bringing in their own food, rather than buying from him. "I'll throw business his way when I can," Ethan said. "But that's the way the Chinese operate. They have their own cooks and their own food supplies, and since the railroad doesn't pay their board, there's nothing I can do about it."

"He's a whiner, anyway," Brodie muttered. "Pay him no mind."

Tait refilled his coffee mug. "I'll let Miss Pearsall know we have an alternate route, so she needn't worry about the right-of-way. But now that her cabin is gone, she'll need a place to stay. Declan, you have any ideas?"

"Someplace close," Ethan suggested. "I don't want her out of town until we find the Chinaman's killer and whoever is sabotaging the sluice."

Both men turned to look at him.

"You really think she's in danger?" Brodie asked.

"Probably not. But why take the risk?"

"I'll ask around," Brodie said. "The Arlan place was empty. I'll take a look at it."

Ethan turned to Rylander. "Audra told me your wife was looking into employment for her. You know anything about that?" Perhaps now that construction on the bridge line would soon start, Mrs. Rylander might need help here at the hotel. Audra would be good at that. And she would be safer here with a lot of people around. Her father was already a handful. It wouldn't get any easier, no matter where they lived, but at least here she would have other eyes watching over him.

"Lucinda is expecting to hear on that this week. I'll let you know."

Brodie leaned over to retrieve his hat from a nearby table. After shoving back a fall of dark hair, he put it on, then rose. "And I'll let you know about the Arlan place and if that prospector shows up, Hardesty. Tait said you wanted to talk to him."

"I do, Sheriff. If there's another surveyor working the canyon, I'd like to know about it."

After the sheriff left, Tait slouched in his chair, one arm hooked over the back, and studied Ethan in that probing way he had. Ethan could guess what was coming, but continued to eat as best he could with his bandaged hands. When he finally shoved his empty plate away, Rylander spoke.

"You were an architect." A statement, not a question.

Ethan didn't try to evade it. This man was too smart to fool, and Ethan respected him too much to lie to him. "In California." Suddenly finding it hard to breathe, he stood.

"I could use your help," Rylander said before he could escape.

"I don't do that anymore. Find somebody else." Then before more questions came, he said, "Give my thanks to your wife," then he turned and left the room.

Out on the boardwalk, he paused to let his nerves settle, then headed to the infirmary to get Renny and have Doc check his hands. They weren't hurting as bad as they had earlier, but he must have done damage getting Pearsall down that slope; when he pulled off his gloves, blood spots showed through the gauze wrappings.

"Mr. Hardesty."

Recognizing the voice, he turned to see Audra hurrying up behind him, that worried furrow between her brows.

"How's your father?" he asked as she drew near.

"Resting. I wanted to thank you for finding him. You were very kind and patient with him. Oh, and I brushed your jacket and had the bellboy put it in your room. Thank you for loaning it to him."

She'd washed and changed. Her hair was still wet, and damp curls fanned her face in a wispy halo. The smell of soap wafted up to him when she stopped beside him. It sent a rush of desire surging through him.

"I'm glad he's all right," he said, struggling to block the image of water beading on the creamy flesh he had glimpsed earlier through that gap in her blouse.

"I spoke to Mr. Rylander a moment ago. He said you've come up with an alternate route that avoids our property."

He nodded, expecting gratitude.

Instead, he got a finger-poke in his chest. "How could you do such a thing?"

"I thought that's what you wanted. Now you won't have to worry about granting us the right-of-way. We can proceed without it."

"I've changed my mind. With the cabin gone, I'll have to pay rent elsewhere, and I need the money you promised."

Ethan lifted his hands in frustration. "So now you *want* to grant the right-of-way?" After all the arguing and plotting another route, they were back where they had started?

"Heavens! What have you done to your hands?" Before he could answer, she grabbed his wrist, which surprised him so much he lost his train of thought.

"You're bleeding. You foolish man. What were you thinking?"

Still addled, he looked down where she cradled his hand within touching distance of her breasts. "It's . . . ah . . . not that bad." If he straightened his fingers just so—

Abruptly, she whirled and began towing him down the street. "Let's get you to Doctor Boyce."

Happily he followed behind her, enjoying the way her hips whipped from side to side as she hurried along. The woman had a way of moving that awakened all sorts of untoward thoughts. But as soon as he was seated in the office, with Audra hovering at his side and the doctor sorting through torture tools, his amusement faded.

Most of the blisters had burst. "What did you do?" Doc asked irritably as he began to cut away the torn skin. "Run a race on your hands?"

Swallowing hard, Ethan looked away. "I tried to be careful."

"It wasn't entirely his fault," Audra put in.

"Did you do your exercises?"

"I meant to."

"He was helping my father."

If what Doc was doing didn't hurt so much, Ethan might have enjoyed her staunch defense. Although it was a bit unsettling that she thought he couldn't defend himself if need be.

Doc wasn't mollified. "Might have guessed a man foolish enough to stuff a burning mattress out a window wouldn't be smart enough to do what I told him. Hold still."

Audra scowled at him. "That's how you burned your hands?"

Ethan shrugged.

"Why didn't you tell me?"

"You didn't ask."

Doc finished with one hand and started on the other. Ethan started to sweat. And bleed.

Audra worried her thumbnail and watched the doctor cut and blot. "What else haven't you told me?" she asked in a strained voice.

Ethan looked at her, glad for the distraction. She had that squint going that told him she was fretting. When had he been added to her list of people to manage? "Don't you have enough to worry about, Miss Audra?"

Color bloomed on her cheeks. "Pearsall," she muttered, and looked away.

Doc glanced at Ethan, a smile twitching at the corner of his lips. "Heard your cabin burned, Miss Pearsall. Guess you'll be needing another place to stay."

"Do you happen to know of any places to rent? Preferably in town?"

"Not offhand. But I'll ask around."

"And perhaps while you're at it, you could see if anyone needs a horse and buggy."

Ethan looked at her in surprise. "You're selling Cricket?"

"If I'm living in town, I'll have no need of him, or a buggy."

"You'll still require transportation."

"I can walk. Besides, I can't afford to board him at the livery forever."

"You're not selling your horse."

That brought those hackles up. "Oh?"

Aware that Doc was watching, Ethan pasted on a smile. "I'll buy him."

She started to argue, then saw Doc's grin. "We'll discuss it later."

"How is your father, Miss Pearsall?" Doc asked, when it was apparent the show was over.

She heaved a great sigh. "Not well. Ever since the fire, he's been coughing, and after getting wet this morning, I'm concerned he'll come down with a chill."

Doc finished his cutting and fitted the splints back on Ethan's hands. "Is he running a fever?"

"Not when I left."

"Does he wander off often?"

"Lately, yes."

While Doc re-bandaged, Audra told him about her father's condition.

Ethan admired her concern for her ailing parent. His own parents had passed long ago, and it had been years since he'd heard from either of his sisters. But he could see the toll the constant fretting was taking on her. She was starting to get the pinched look of a woman with too many worries and not enough joy. He was glad she had the Abrahams there to help her. But they were aging, too, and before long, she might have two more elderly folks to tend. He doubted even a woman with Audra's energy could carry that kind of burden for long.

Doc tied off the last strip of gauze. "Give him a hot foot-bath this evening, and a good, strong dose of ginger tea before retiring. You're staying at the hotel?"

Audra nodded. "For now."

"I'll come by to see him in the morning. You, too," he added to Ethan. "Leave these splints on until then. And get your horse on your way out. I'm not running a stable here."

"I'll take him back to the livery." Ethan held up his splinted hands. "But I'm not sure I'll be able to saddle him."

"You don't mind helping him, do you, Miss Pearsall?" Doc sent Audra a crafty grin. "I've got another patient due."

"I'd be happy to." But she didn't look happy as she went with Ethan to the small shed where Renny's tack was stored.

"My offer to buy Cricket and the buggy is sincere," Ethan said a few minutes later as he slipped the bridle over the horse's head.

"You have no need of another horse, much less a buggy."

She buckled the throatlatch, tossed the saddle blanket over Renny's back, then turned, hands on hips. "And I have no need of charity, either."

Hell. Ignoring the strain on his splinted hands, Ethan set the saddle in place. Resting his arms across the pommel, he frowned down at her. "It's not charity, Audra. It's concern."

"It's pity!"

Something snapped. Flinging his arm around her waist, he pulled her body against his and lowered his head. Her gasped breath mingled with his when his mouth found hers. But what started in frustration quickly changed to need when she didn't push him away. He felt her hands move to his shoulders and relaxed his hold, stroking his bandaged hand up her back to pull her closer, desperate to feel the softness of her breasts against his chest.

She tasted of tooth powder and smelled like the flowery soap from her bath, and horses, and woman. She fit so perfectly in his arms he couldn't imagine holding anyone else. "Does that feel like pity to you, Audra?" he demanded when he finally drew back, his heart thundering in his ears and his body ready.

She looked up at him, her hazel eyes wide with confusion, her lips swollen from his kiss. "Wh-Why did you do that?"

He gave a shaky smile. "Because you're beautiful, and desirable, and I've wanted to ever since I saw you standing by the train."

She didn't smile back.

But he knew by her quickened breathing, and the flush on her cheeks, and the way she stared at his mouth that she was as moved by the kiss as he was, despite her shock. It occurred to him that she probably hadn't been kissed often—or maybe at all—and that realization lodged like a warm knot of joy deep in his chest.

He could love this stubborn, gentle woman. With her, he could regain the peace that had eluded him for so long, and maybe even find his redemption. With her, he might find the will to put the past behind him.

If such a thing was possible.

"It's late," he said. "We should go." After securing the saddle girth, he looped Renny's reins over his right arm, and hooked his left hand beneath her elbow to guide her from the stable. She didn't resist, but moved stiffly at his side.

The sun had set, leaving behind an orange wash across the last of the snow on the peaks. The air smelled of spring and was brisk enough to cool the rush of desire still coursing through his body.

For most of the way, they didn't talk. Ethan appreciated that she didn't feel the need to fill the silence with idle chatter. And strangely, for the first time in a long while, he didn't feel driven to throw up a screen of quips and teasing remarks to keep her at a distance. The kiss had changed something between them. He wasn't sure what, or where it would lead. He still had his secrets and she still had her doubts. Not a great foundation.

They were angling onto the backstreet that led to the livery when she finally broke the long silence. "I'm sorry I misjudged you. About the fire."

He smiled down at her to show he had no hard feelings. "I accept your apology."

"I didn't ask you to accept anything," she said in a tone of exasperation. "I simply needed to say it, and for you to hear it."

"Oh. Well. Okay, I heard it."

"It's not that I distrust you. Not really."

"I'm pleased to hear it."

"But sometimes," she went on as if she hadn't heard his muttered comment, "I feel a bit overwhelmed. And anxious. And fearful."

"Fearful of what?" He couldn't imagine her being afraid of anything.

She made a helpless gesture. "Failing. Making a wrong decision. Not being able to provide for the people who depend on me. I tend to overreact and do foolish things."

Like harbor distrust? Yet he understood. At least she was willing to admit to her fear. He couldn't even face his. "I've never met anyone less foolish or a woman more fearless," he said in all seriousness. "Or one more stubbornly independent."

She looked up in surprise.

"You carry the burden of providing for three people who can't fend for themselves. You've unselfishly uprooted your life and traveled over a thousand miles to make a better life for your father. I admire you for that."

"You do?"

"I do. Even though you refuse my help at every turn."

She smiled. It sent that hot rush through him again. "Not at *every* turn. I did let you change my wheel, as I recall."

"So you did. Most generous of you."

She laughed out loud, and the joyful sound of it was a wondrous thing.

They walked a bit, then he said, "We'll be laying tracks between here and the Boot Creek Station, so I'll be gone for a few days. Can I count on you to stay close to town?"

At her look of irritation, he put on a cajoling smile. "At least until they catch the Chinaman's killer. It's a reasonable request, I think."

She opened her mouth—to argue with him, no doubt—then sighed. "All right. But I'm not a child who needs constant watching."

He chuckled. "I don't consider you a child. I think I just proved that. But I can prove it again, if you'd like."

He was gratified to see a blush rise above her prim collar, and wondered how far it extended the other way. It was odd, really. For most of his adult life—except for that summer with Eunice Eckhart at Salty Point—he had contented himself with the companionship of women of negotiable virtue. But now, all he could think about was Audra . . . a small, hardheaded, nearsighted woman who challenged him at every opportunity.

When they reached the back stoop of the hotel, he stopped. "You go on in. Driscoll can help me unsaddle. And if I don't see you before I leave, I'll leave payment for the right-of-way with Tait."

"Thank you." She gave him a tentative smile and stepped up on the stoop. "Mind your hands."

"I will. And Audra . . ." He waited for her to face him. "I would never do anything to harm you. You know that, don't you?"

She studied him, the smile still playing along her lips. "Yes, Ethan. I know."

Fourteen

Several days later, Audra and Lucinda were enjoying a quiet lunch by one of the rear windows in the hotel dining room when a wagon piled high with canvas-covered crates stopped by the back stoop. A man climbed down, stretched, dusted his jacket, adjusted the wire-frame spectacles perched on his nose, then walked into the hotel.

"He's here!" Rising abruptly, Lucinda excused herself and went into the lobby to intercept him.

Watching from the dining room, Audra studied the man as he spoke to Lucinda. He was neither young nor old. Slim, wearing a checkered suit, a bowler hat over curly red hair, and an earnest expression on his clean-shaven face. He glanced at Audra, gave a half smile, then turned back to Lucinda, who was still talking. Nice smile, too. After a moment, Lucinda woke Yancey from his doze behind the front desk, then sent both men back out to the wagon. As they drove off toward the livery, she returned to the dining room.

"Who was that?" Audra asked.

"Peter Bonet." She said it with a big grin and in the French pronunciation—*Bo-nay*—despite the fact that the man looked more Irish than French. "I put an advertisement in the Denver paper and fortunately he was in the area and responded almost immediately. He's the new editor of the *Heartbreak Creek*

Herald, and your new employer. If you still want employment, of course."

Audra blinked at her in astonishment.

"Meet him before you decide. He seems very nice. But after you speak with him, if he—or the position—doesn't suit, we'll find something else."

Audra finally got her wits about her. "Doesn't suit? It sounds perfect! Thank you." When Audra started to rise, Lucinda laughed and waved her back into her chair.

"There's no rush. Let them unload his printing equipment first. I asked him to join Tait and me and you for dinner this evening. That will give us all a chance to look him over before you commit to anything."

Audra's mind whirled. Working for a newspaper! It was the next best thing to writing her own novels. Plus, she would finally be earning an income again.

"Tait said you signed over the right-of-way grant. Thank you, Audra. I'm convinced we'll all prosper when the bridge line is complete. Oh, and I forgot to tell you," Lucinda added with a smile. "Declan said the Arlan place is available. It needs repair, but if you approve, he and Tait will attend to that over the next few days. You and your family should be able to move in by the end of next week."

The generosity of these people was astounding. "What's the rent?"

Lucinda grinned. "That's the best part. Nothing." Seeing Audra's confusion, she explained. "As you probably noticed, Heartbreak Creek is in a temporary decline. There are almost as many deserted dwellings as inhabited ones. Once the bridge line is complete, all that will change. If the Arlans return someday, you may need to relocate, but until then, if you want it, the house is yours."

Audra's euphoria faded. "But now that I've signed the right-of-way, I can pay." She had already deposited the draft Ethan had left before leaving for Boot Creek. Oddly, it had been signed by him, rather than the railroad, but perhaps that's the way rights-of-way worked. "There's no need for charity."

"Don't be silly. You'll be doing them a favor. Houses don't do well if left vacant. And it's not charity, Audra. It's practi-

cality. The Arlan house is prominently situated, and it would
be a poor reflection on the town to have it boarded up and
falling into decay."

"Well . . ."

"Then it's settled. If you're finished with your lunch, we can
walk over now and take a look. It's quite spacious, and although
it doesn't have an indoor necessary, there's a large washroom
on the ground floor."

Audra's disappointment must have shown. She had hated
that nasty outhouse at the cabin even more than the gloom.

Lucinda patted her arm as she rose. "I know. But if you're so
intent on repaying the absentee Arlans, perhaps you can add an
indoor water closet now that you'll be making an income."

When they walked toward the end of town that opened onto
the flats where the church was situated, they saw Yancey and
Mr. Bonet moving printing equipment inside a boarded-up
storefront beside Hattie's Millinery Shoppe. Lucinda waved,
but didn't cross the street to interrupt them. Mr. Bonet waved
back, and gave Audra a polite nod.

He did seem nice. And nice-looking, too.

The Arlan house was situated in a sunny clearing between a
stand of aspens and Heartbreak Creek. It was a boxy two-level
wooden structure made from planks, rather than logs, with a tall
rock chimney running up the outside of the house, and across
the front, a wide covered porch with a broken railing. Around
back, beside a small lean-to shed, was a small fenced area for a
horse or milk cow. The windows were glass and intact.

The inside showed wear. But despite the scuffed plank
floors, the soot-darkened hearth, stained kitchen countertops,
sagging cabinet doors, and cracked plaster walls, there was a
sturdy simplicity of construction that added a touch of charm.

The downstairs was divided into three rooms—a washroom
and butler's pantry, a large open room with the kitchen at one
end, space for a dining table in the middle, a sitting area around
the hearth by the front door, and a small bedroom behind the
fireplace wall that would suit the Abrahams nicely. Upstairs
were two more bedrooms, each with windows on two sides,
and separated by a small room that could serve as storage, or
perhaps, someday, a necessary.

It was perfect. Audra couldn't wait to move in all their

things and the furniture Lucinda had loaned them, which had been stored in the attic of the hotel since the fire. The hotel was lovely, but she longed to have her own place again, and this would be much more pleasant for Father, who had loved to sit in the garden back home.

"It will do beautifully," she told Lucinda as they headed back to the hotel. "I can't thank you enough."

"I'm glad to have another woman to talk to. With Maddie and Pru gone, and Edwina always in such a state, I've felt rather at odds. You're going to be a lovely addition to our group."

Audra dressed carefully for dinner that evening, intent on making a good impression. Remembering what Ethan had said about color complementing her eyes, she chose a green muslin with a gathered peach underskirt and sash, and green stitching around the high peach collar. She put her hair up in a topknot to make herself look taller, and used the heating iron to put ringlets around her face. Remembering that Mr. Bonet also wore spectacles, she attached a peach ribbon to hers and hung them around her neck, hoping it might create some commonality between them and make her look more professional. Finally finished, she studied herself in the mirror.

Ethan was right. When she wore green, her hazel eyes did look more green than brown.

Ethan. She couldn't seem to stop thinking about him. And that kiss. Richard had kissed her once, but it certainly hadn't caused the breathless, shivery feeling that Ethan's kiss had.

He thought she was beautiful. And desirable. How amazing was that?

A knock on the door of the hotel suite she shared with Father wrenched her out of her pleasant reverie. A final check, then she left her bedroom and crossed the sitting area to open the door.

Winnie grinned from the hallway. "Oh, my! You look plumb beautiful, Miss Audra." She made a careful inspection, then nodded in approval. "You liable to get that job *and* the boss, you don't be careful, child. And I know how you hate suitors."

"I don't *hate* them. I just find all the posturing tiresome. I'll see if Father is awake." As she spoke, Audra crossed to the other bedroom, peeked inside, then quietly closed the door.

"Still asleep, but he should be up soon. He was coughing

most of the night and awoke with a slight fever. Doctor Boyce sent a bottle of cough syrup that has a sleeping draught in it. I left it on the dresser, but don't use it without first checking with me." After leaving instructions for Winnie to call her if his cough was worse, Audra said she'd have the kitchen send up a tray, thanked her for staying with him, and left the suite.

That summer of 1868 had been unseasonably hot along the Pacific coast. The wind off the ocean never stopped and brought little relief. It moaned through the eaves of the hospital like a living thing, flayed the stunted trees along the bluff, and sucked every bit of moisture from the earth. Every day, clouds built up over the blue horizon to the west, but rain never came. Every evening, dry lightning crackled over the inland hills, catching brush and withered grass afire. The air was often so thick with smoke it hurt to breathe. And tempers grew short.

Progress on the renovation slowed. Workers squabbled with each other, railed at the heat, drank too much and grew careless. Even the hospital staff suffered, run ragged by patients who lay sweating in their beds, stinking of infection and despair, calling out to the harried nurses as they hurried by. The grave diggers stayed busy, adding new markers in the little graveyard on the bluff.

But Ethan was scarcely aware of it. He spent his days watching his dream take shape, pane by pane, and his nights trapped in Eunice's dark, sensual fantasies.

She knew how to touch him. How to make him moan and want more. How to make him hate her one moment and love her the next. She was like the drugs she gave her patients, promising release, an escape into ecstasy. She was addictive and insatiable. The dark heart of the sun.

She almost broke him.

Because sometime during that hot summer of 1868, between the first time he saw her, standing on the bluff, and the last time, when she lay bleeding at his feet, he realized she would never love him back. She was incapable of it. She was damaged in a way he didn't understand—could never understand—and every night he spent under her spell, she stole a little more of his soul.

But still, he tried. Because he was the sort of man who wanted to make things right. To look after people. To fix things.

And because he thought he loved her.

Until he realized it wasn't the heat or sickness or despair that was killing the patients.

It was Eunice.

Ethan paced restlessly on the platform, watching the afternoon train from Pueblo roll slowly into the station at Boot Creek. All he had left to do was check the vouchers against the supplies he'd ordered, then he could head back to Heartbreak Creek.

And Audra.

Had she missed him? Had she thought about him as much as he'd thought about her? He sighed in disgust. It was disturbing how often his thoughts drifted her way. But at least when he was thinking about Audra, he wasn't suffering night terrors. She was like a balm to all those dark, haunting memories in his mind.

Brakes squealed and steam billowed from the locomotive as the train shuddered to a stop. Ethan hurried past the lone passenger car to the flatcars behind it, which were loaded with railroad supplies.

He'd been here almost a week and things were progressing well. Work had finally started on the run between the Boot Creek Station and Heartbreak Creek. The graders were in full swing, and by the end of the week, the straighteners would be setting the rails in place for the spikers. Everyone seemed glad to be working, and any lingering unrest caused by the Chinese worker's death had settled into a watchful wariness. He'd temporarily reassigned Gallagher, the whip-wielding Irishman, to handle the graders, who were mostly white or Irish, so he expected no more trouble on that score. His work here was done.

"Ho," a voice said behind him, startling Ethan so badly he almost dropped his papers. Whipping around, he saw Thomas Redstone standing a foot behind him. "Damnit, Redstone. Don't you know better than to sneak up on a man? You scared the living daylights out of me."

"What are living daylights? And I did not sneak."

"Hell you say. I could have shot you."

A slow smile split the usually somber face. "No. I do not think so."

Despite the smile, the Indian looked tired. And discouraged. There was weariness in his dark eyes and the planes of his face sagged into deep brackets around his wide mouth. Ethan guessed things hadn't gone well with Miss Lincoln in Indiana. "You come in on the train?"

The Cheyenne nodded.

"Going on to Heartbreak Creek?"

Another nod.

"You have a horse?"

"I will steal yours. It is what we Indians do."

"So I hear." Ethan looked around and spotted the horse the railroad had assigned to Gallagher tied outside one of the tents. "Wait here." Walking over, he pushed back the untied flap to find Gallagher slouched on a rumpled cot, flipping cards in a game of solitaire. "I need your horse," Ethan told him. "I'll send it back tomorrow."

Gallagher gave him a sour look, but said nothing. Ethan let the flap fall and took the horse back to Thomas. "Give me a minute, and I'll ride with you."

After checking the shipment, he signed the vouchers, then went to saddle Renny. "Glad you're back," he said to Thomas a few minutes later when they started down the road to Heartbreak Creek. "A lot's happened while you were gone. We need your help."

He told the Cheyenne about the fire and the Chinese worker's death. "The fire was set on purpose, and the Chinaman's death wasn't an accident. Some think an Indian did it because the man's long braid was taken. But I figure if an Indian had done it, he would have taken scalp with it. Right?"

Thomas shrugged. "I am not French so I do not take scalps. They stink."

"And I doubt it was another Chinaman," Ethan went on. "He'd have no need of the pigtail. It could have been someone from another railroad, trying to stop work on the bridge line. Or someone who didn't like the Chinese. Or maybe a prospector or trapper."

"White people. You cause trouble wherever you go."

"Know anything about prospectors living in the canyon?"

Thomas looked over at him. "I know everything that happens in the canyon. It has been my home for many years." He faced forward again. "There were two."

"Were?"

"One died."

"How?"

"Rocks fell on him."

"You saw him? Where?"

"Three miles past your wooden trough."

"What about the other one? Weems, I think he's called."

"He wanders still. I think there is something wrong in his head. Why else would he dig holes like a mole, searching for yellow rocks?"

They rode in silence as Ethan mulled over this new information. The remaining prospector had to be the same man who had reported seeing another surveyor at the other end of the canyon. Ethan definitely needed to talk to this Weems fellow. "You should have told somebody when you found the body."

Thomas gave him a derisive look. "Why? He was just another dead *ve'ho'e*. I have seen many. Almost as many as dead Cheyenne."

"Do you think the landslide was deliberate, or an accident?"

"It was hard to tell. But the pouches in his long pants had been pulled out."

"You mean his pockets were turned inside out?"

Thomas nodded.

Had the dead man's pockets been searched before his fall or after? The ground in the canyon was rocky and unstable. Maybe the prospector had been looking for something in his own pockets. A compass. A penknife. Something to eat. Maybe he had accidentally triggered the slide. Or maybe he had been pushed to his death, and someone had tried to make it look like a rockfall. "Was he buried?"

Redstone shrugged. "If so, coyotes had dug him up."

So it could have been murder or an accident. "We need to talk to that fellow Weems. Brodie was supposed to locate him. If he hasn't been able to, do you think you could find him?"

"Of course. I am Cheyenne."

Fifteen

It was dusk when Thomas and Ethan reached Heartbreak
Creek. Although he was anxious to see Audra, Ethan wanted
to check with Brodie first, to see if he had found the miner he
wanted to question.

Reining in before the sheriff's office, he looked through the
barred window and saw it was empty. "Where you headed?"
he asked the Cheyenne.

"The Brodie house. I have a message from Prudence Lincoln for her sister."

"If the sheriff is there, tell him what you told me about the
dead prospector. If he wants to discuss it, he can find me at the
hotel."

Redstone nodded and turned toward the bridge that crossed
Mulberry Creek. Ethan cut through to the backstreet and the
livery.

His hands were much better now, and he was no longer wearing the splints, so he was able to tend Renny without Driscoll's
help. It was dark when he headed to the hotel. As he stepped up
onto the stoop, he glanced through the dining room window
and saw Audra at a table with the Rylanders and a man he didn't
know. A slim redheaded man, wearing spectacles, and talking
as much with his hands as his mouth. The way Audra was smiling at him brought a twist in Ethan's chest.

Forgoing a stop by the water closet, he went through the

hotel's back door, down the short hallway to the dining room, and straight to their table.

"Evening," he said pleasantly, removing his hat.

Everyone but the newcomer smiled in welcome.

"When did you get back?" Tait asked, rising to offer a handshake.

"Just now. Thomas Redstone came with me. He's headed over to the Brodies' house." He glanced at Audra and was gratified that she seemed pleased to see him. She was wearing a dress he hadn't seen before. The color made her eyes look greener and her flush pinker. She had never looked more beautiful.

"Miss Pearsall," he said with a nod. "Mrs. Rylander." Then his gaze settled on the newcomer, who hadn't risen, but had stopped eating to regard Ethan with a puzzled look.

"Peter," Rylander said to the newcomer, "this is Ethan Hardesty. He's with the railroad. Ethan, this is Peter Bonet, the new editor of the *Heartbreak Creek Herald*. He arrived this morning."

The newcomer remained seated, and didn't offer his hand. Puzzlement gave way to speculation. "Hardesty? From California?"

Ethan froze, too addled to respond. A buzzing began in his ears.

The man smiled. It wasn't a friendly smile and it didn't reach his eyes. "You were the architect, weren't you? On that hospital renovation north of San Francisco."

The buzzing grew louder. Ethan struggled to think. Aware of the others listening, he turned to Rylander. "We have another dead man," he said through tight lips. "If you want to discuss it, or if Brodie comes, I'll be in the Red Eye next door." Then he spun on his heel and left the room.

He was on his second drink and his nerves were finally beginning to settle when Brodie and Redstone came through the saloon door. He waved them over. Before they'd reached his table, Rylander came in behind them. Even though there was an entry into the saloon from the lobby of the hotel, Lucinda Rylander kept the door locked. Ethan suspected that in some future renovation, she'd get rid of it altogether.

Pushing the incident in the dining room to the back of his

mind, Ethan signaled the bartender to bring three more glasses. As soon as the three men were seated, he asked Redstone to repeat for Tait what he'd told him earlier.

The Cheyenne recounted finding the dead prospector, where the body was, and how long he thought the man had been dead—by now, at least a month.

"I hope you buried him," Brodie said.

Redstone shrugged.

"Hell."

"That's about when that other miner, Weems, reported seeing the surveyor in the far end of the canyon," Rylander said. "Which means the surveyor was in the area when the prospector was killed."

Ethan nodded. "Opportunity and motive, assuming he had been sent to stir up trouble."

At the bar, three sluice workers got into an argument. Brodie looked over. When the voices grew louder, he said, "Hey."

A single word, spoken in a calm tone, yet it brought instant results. It was apparent to Ethan that even though the sheriff considered his position only temporary, he had a firm grip on the town. In fact, judging by the respectful looks and deferential greetings sent their way, the three men sharing his table were the power of Heartbreak Creek.

The barkeep brought their glasses.

Brodie and Rylander each took one. Redstone asked for ginger beer instead.

After pouring whiskey into his glass, the sheriff took a sip, shuddered, then looked in disgust at the amber liquid in the bottle. "I miss Wallace."

Rylander snorted. "You miss his whiskey." To Ethan, he explained that the earl kept a private store of Scotch whiskey behind the bar. "Tasty stuff."

"Every time I drink this," Brodie complained, "my eyesight seems worse."

"That is because you are old," Redstone said.

The sheriff reared back to glare at him. "No older than you."

"Why do you think this death is related to the Chinaman's?" Rylander asked, bringing the conversation back on track.

"A hunch. But if I could question the miner, Weems, I'd know for sure. Have you located him yet?"

Brodie shook his head. "Haven't seen him or his partner."

"He had a partner? Could that be the dead prospector you found, Redstone?"

"Maybe. I have seen the two of them together."

"Then we've got to locate Weems as soon as possible, because he could be a target, too." Ethan pushed his glass away. Folding his arms on top of the stained table, he looked at the other men. "How many deaths have there been since we started this project?"

Brodie thought about it. "Three. The tree-cutter, the Chinaman, and this prospector."

"What do they have in common?" Ethan didn't wait for an answer. "They're all missing something. The tree-cutter's watch. The Chinaman's pigtail. I don't know if anything was taken from the prospector, but Redstone said his pockets were turned inside out. Which probably means they were searched. Which might mean something was taken from him, too."

"So?"

Ethan had a sudden memory—

—standing at her dresser, the box of stolen trinkets in his shaking hand. Looking up into the mirror. Seeing her behind him and watching her face change when she realized what he held.

"They were dying anyway." Leaning into him, she rubbed her bare breasts against his back. He could feel the hard nubs of her nipples and knew she was aroused. Hungry. "I just helped them along."

"You killed them, Eunice! They were your patients. They trusted you."

"And I gave them what they needed." She laughed, her breath hot on his neck. In the mirror, her eyes were as soulless as a viper's. "Think of me as an angel of mercy."

Then he saw the blade—

With effort, he pushed the image away. "I've heard that some killers like to take mementoes of their kills."

Rylander glanced at Redstone. "Like scalps?"

"Those are trophies of war," the Cheyenne said defensively.

"I'm talking about people who kill randomly for the fun of it," Ethan explained. "Or because they have some warped urge that drives them to do it. The trinkets they take from each victim help them relive the murder."

And fuel the need to do it again.

"But these deaths don't seem that random," Tait argued. "If the murderer is the same person who set the fires and vandalized the sluice, then he's got a purpose. To stop the railroad from coming through the canyon."

"If that was the sole reason, then why take a keepsake from each victim?"

"We don't know if he took anything from the dead prospector," Brodie reminded them.

"That's why we need to talk to his partner. As soon as possible. These killers don't stop. Not until they're caught."

Or killed.

Redstone rose. "I will find him."

"Need help?"

"From a white man?" Laughing, Thomas left the saloon.

Brodie pushed back his chair. "I better go, too. Brin tried her hand at cooking again, and I promised Ed I'd scrape the ceiling."

After the sheriff left, Rylander remained. Anticipating questions, Ethan prepared himself. A part of him was almost relieved to have it all out in the open. But another part of him dreaded the reactions. He liked and admired this man. And the others he had met in Heartbreak Creek. And Audra. He'd been reviled for his failure once, and it had cost him his career. What would he lose this time?

"I don't much like him, either," Tait said.

Ethan frowned, confused. "Who?"

"Bonet. He's officious and arrogant. Plus, he doesn't like railroads."

"How do you know?"

Tait swirled the whiskey in his glass. "I have friends at the Pinkerton Agency. They sent me a file."

Ethan watched a greasy skin rise on the inside of the glass and waited.

"Apparently, he had a brother who worked for one of the Eastern lines. Died in a tunnel explosion. If I'd known, I wouldn't have encouraged him to come. Or let Luce encourage Miss Pearsall to work for him."

Audra was working for him? Ethan didn't like that idea. "So why did you?"

He gave a crooked smile. "Luce wanted the town to have a newspaper." Tait took a sip, returned the glass to the exact spot on the stained table, then leveled those probing gray eyes at Ethan. "They sent me a file on you, too."

And there it comes.

But oddly, now that the moment of truth was finally at hand, Ethan was more relieved than apprehensive. "What did it say?"

"That you're an architect. That you designed a glass wall at the Salty Point Marine Hospital. And nearly three years ago, on October twenty-first, an earth tremor brought it down, killing three people. Two construction workers and a nurse."

"They call them earthquakes."

"No criminal charges were brought against you," Tait went on. "Yet you were blamed. Why?"

"Because I insisted on putting glass where stone should have been. It was my first commission. I wanted to design something no one else had ever dared." He gave a bitter laugh. "And with good reason, it turned out."

"What happened?"

More memories burst into Ethan's mind—

Eunice laughing, her arm rising and falling. A searing pain in his back. Another across his shoulder. His shoes slipping on blood as he stumbled from her bedroom into the work area. Yelling at the two workers to run. The ground shaking. Then a thunderous explosion as eight hundred panes of glass shattered and rained death down on top of them—

He closed his eyes to block the images, took a breath, and opened them to find Rylander studying him. "Glass isn't stable," he said. "The panes I insisted on using were too big. When the tremors started, they cracked. It was like twenty cannons going off all at once. Then they fell."

"An act of nature," Ryland said.

"An error in judgment," Ethan countered, "that cost three lives."

Rylander stared silently into his glass. The sluice workers left and the barkeep began wiping down the empty tables. "The report also said you settled money on the families of the two workers who died. Out of your own pocket."

"They were good men. They had children depending on them."

"And the nurse?"

"Ethan . . . help me . . ."

He could have saved her. When the tremors started, he could have pulled her with him under the workbench. Or later, after the shaking stopped, when he saw the shard of glass sticking out of her chest, he could have tried to stop the bleeding.

"Please . . . Ethan . . . help me . . ."

Instead, because they were worth saving and she wasn't, he had gone to help the two workers who hadn't escaped before the glass fell. Of all the poor decisions that led to that tragic day, leaving Eunice Eckhart to die was the only one he didn't regret.

"She left no family behind."

"It was rather strange the way he stormed out," Lucinda said, studying Audra over the rim of her coffee cup.

The men had left an hour ago—Tait to meet with Ethan in the saloon, and Mr. Bonet to return to his unpacking. Audra knew she should go upstairs to relieve Winnie, but it was so pleasant to share a few quiet minutes with Lucinda in the nearly empty dining room. "It did seem odd," Audra admitted.

"Almost as if he was jealous of Peter."

Audra forced a laugh. "Oh, I doubt that." In fact, she thought Ethan's abrupt departure was more likely due to Mr. Bonet's mention of the hospital in California, rather than any feelings of jealousy. Still, it had been surprising. And uncharacteristic. Despite his teasing, Ethan wasn't a rude man.

"So what do you think of him?"

"Of Mr. Hardesty?"

Lucinda laughed. "Oh, I know what you think of Mr. Hardesty. But what about Mr. Bonet?"

"An interesting man," Audra hedged. In truth, she found Peter Bonet rather confusing. He seemed friendly enough, but there was an intensity about him that was a bit off-putting. Granted, both of the Rylanders were rather intense, too, but they didn't seem so . . . pushy about it.

Or perhaps it wasn't that at all. Perhaps what bothered her most was that Peter Bonet reminded her so much of Richard Villars.

"Well, it's apparent he's interested in having you work for him," Lucinda said. "Will you accept the position he offered?"

"How can I not? It's a wonderful opportunity." Being a small-town newspaper clerk might not have been her dream, but it would certainly pay the bills and keep her skills honed in case she ever got the courage—or the time—to begin writing on her own.

Lucinda's face brightened when a tall figure crossed the lobby. "There's Tait. Maybe now we can find out who this new dead person is."

After pausing by the serving station to pour a mug of coffee, he continued on to their table. Settling into the chair he had occupied earlier, he sat back and regarded his wife with a knowing smile. "Let the interrogation begin."

Lucinda swatted at his shoulder. "So? Who died?"

"A prospector."

"When?"

"Maybe a month ago."

"And you think it's related to the other deaths?"

"We're trying to determine that. How is your father, Miss Pearsall?"

"What? Oh." Rattled by the abrupt change in subject, Audra made an offhand gesture. "Fine. His cough is much better, thank you."

"I'm pleased to hear it." Mr. Rylander continued to look at her, a bland expression in his gray eyes.

Audra finally got the message. "Well. I should go. Winnie is probably wondering where I am." She started to rise.

"And what was that about a hospital in California?" Lucinda asked him.

Audra sank back down.

"Ethan looked stricken when Peter mentioned it," Lucinda went on. "Horrified, almost."

Tait smiled innocently at his wife. "Did he?"

"Surely you noticed. His face turned as pale as parchment, didn't it, Audra?"

Audra shrugged.

Tait continued to smile.

"Honestly!" Lucinda threw her hands up in exasperation. "You're keeping something from me, aren't you, Tait?"

The smile broadened. "I am, sweetheart. And if you'll come with me to our room, I'll be delighted to give it to you."

"Tait!"

Audra felt her cheeks burn.

Tait threw back his head and laughed, which shocked Audra almost as much as his ribald comment had. She had rarely even heard him chuckle. "That was poorly done of me." Turning to Audra with a grin that looked anything but contrite, he said, "My apologies, Miss Pearsall. But she makes it so easy."

"Oh, hush." His wife swatted his shoulder again. "Mrs. Throckmorton is right. You're a rogue and a scoundrel." But the look in her eyes indicated she didn't mind in the least.

It wasn't until Audra was halfway up the stairs that she recognized how deftly Tait Rylander had avoided his wife's question.

So what secret was Ethan hiding behind those haunted blue eyes?

Sixteen

Audra wasn't able to pose that question to Ethan, because over the next week she scarcely saw him.

She felt like she was being pulled in a dozen directions at once. Father's cold persisted, and he seemed to grow weaker every day. He was confused most of the time now, and when he wasn't calling for Mary, he was looking for Cleo. It terrified her how quickly he was failing.

She spent most of her day at the *Herald*, helping Mr. Bonet get the newspaper up and running. The printing press took up at least a third of the small space and supplies took up another third, which left little room for other furniture. Still, Audra had her own small desk, which made her feel quite proficient.

The press was a cylinder-type printer, which, although not as efficient as the newer offset presses that could print on both sides at once, was still quite innovative for a small-town newspaper. Audra wondered how, with such limited readership, Mr. Bonet hoped to defray the cost of the press and all the supplies needed, then learned through Lucinda that her husband had set up a grant for the newspaper at the bank.

"Every town should have its own paper," she had told Audra. "It can't be considered a real town until it does." And that was that.

Audra was glad. Putting out a newspaper was a complicated

process, and she relished the distraction from her worries. Although she felt guilty leaving Father so much, she delighted in doing something creative again. It invigorated her, lifted her spirits, and gave her a much needed respite from the exhausting and heartbreaking task of caring for Father. She didn't know how she would have managed without the Abrahams.

But the nights were hard. After working at the newspaper all day then tending Father through the evening, she was so exhausted she fell into bed before it was full dark, only to be awakened by Father weeping and calling out for her mother. She comforted him as best she could, but there was little she could do. She was losing him. And that realization was a constant ache in her heart.

Thank God for dear friends. In addition to Winnie and Curtis helping out with Father, she learned Mr. Rylander and Sheriff Brodie had been putting in an hour or two each day bringing the Arlan house up to snuff. Lucinda told her Thomas Redstone and Ethan also helped out after they returned from Boot Creek, and Mr. Gebbers, the town's banker and mayor, donated money for paint, lumber, and mortar to shore up the rock chimney and foundation.

She resolved to pay them all back someday.

Peter Bonet was an exacting employer with set ways of doing things. He had been in the newspaper business for a dozen years, and seemed quite knowledgeable, although she thought he lacked journalistic objectivity. His harsh attitude toward railroads put him at odds with many of the locals, whose livelihoods depended on the success of the bridge line venture. He had shared with her the sad tale of his brother's death in a tunnel mishap, but Audra felt his resentments against the railroad might be misplaced. Railroad construction was dangerous work and any man who chose such an occupation had to be aware of the risks.

But Mr. Bonet couldn't see it that way. His anger over his brother's accident was a festering wound he wouldn't allow to heal. She felt sad for him.

Work on the bridge line and sluice continued. Even though Lucinda reported little progress in apprehending the murderer, Thomas Redstone continued to prowl the canyon, searching for clues. After a week without incident, Audra's concerns about moving away from the safety of the hotel to the more remote Arlan house began to fade. Perhaps the danger was past. Perhaps the murderer had moved on, or Thomas had scared him off. Determined to be prepared, she decided when she had time, she would talk to Lucinda or Sheriff Brodie about those shooting lessons.

The first edition of the *Heartbreak Creek Herald* hit the streets exactly one week after Peter Bonet set up his printing press. It was cause for jubilation. Heartbreak Creek was a real town now, with a newspaper, a bank, a hotel, and soon, a train depot. A town with prospects and a glowing future.

Lucinda Rylander was almost giddy with delight. "I thought it would never happen," she told Edwina and Audra over a celebratory afternoon tea in her office the day the tracks reached the water tower at the edge of town. "Can you believe how much has happened, Edwina, since we arrived in Heartbreak Creek a year ago? Maddie is reunited with her Angus, Pru has found her calling, you've had a baby, I've gotten married, and now Heartbreak Creek is becoming a true home."

Edwina carefully set her delicate china cup on the tray atop the table beside the couch. "I just wish Maddie and Pru were here to celebrate with us." It was apparent by the wobble in her voice that she was on the verge of tears.

Again.

Audra had never met a woman who cried so much, although Lucinda told her such had not always been the case. "Before she had Whit," she had confided several days earlier, "Edwina was the most cheerful of us all. Her vivacious nature made everyone want to be around her. When she smiled, we smiled. When she laughed, we laughed with her."

So what had happened? From what Audra had observed, the sandy-haired Southerner was constantly one frayed thread away from hysteria.

Today, Lucinda looked worried, too. Setting her cup aside, she leaned forward and rested a hand on Edwina's arm. "Are you still not feeling any better?"

"Stop fussing. I'm fine." But as soon as the words were out, Edwina's face twisted. "No, I'm not, Lucinda. I think something is terribly wrong with me."

"Oh, dear." Moving from her chair to sit on the couch next

to Edwina, she put an arm around the crying woman's shoulders. "Tell me what's worrying you."

Between the sniffing and dabbing and shaking voice, Audra could scarcely make out Edwina's complaints.

"I have no energy. I'm exhausted, no matter how much I sleep. I can scarcely tend the children, much less take care of the house. Declan never smiles anymore, and Whit . . ." Edwina blinked tearfully down at the baby sleeping peacefully in a basket by her chair. "If I didn't have Whit, I don't know how I would go on at all. I'm a terrible mother."

"Don't be silly. Have you talked to Dr. Boyce again?"

Edwina waved her hanky in dismissal. "For what good it did. 'This sometimes happens to women after childbirth,'" she mimicked in a deep voice. "'It will eventually pass,' so on and so on. As if he would know, never having actually gone through that ordeal. But it isn't passing, Luce. And I'm sick of it."

"He offered no help at all?"

Edwina blew her reddened nose, then searched out a dry corner to dab at her eyes. "He gave me a tonic. It smells like a hog wallow and tastes worse than my cooking. But I dutifully choked it down. For a few days, I felt better, then I started to sink again. It's like the world has lost all its color. Ridiculous, I know, but I feel like I'm going through life with blinders on and cotton in my ears. I can't blame Declan for avoiding me. I just want things to be the way they were. For *me* to be the way I was. Do you have a dry hanky? This one is a mess."

While Lucinda went into the adjoining bedroom for a fresh linen, Audra studied Edwina, an idea circling in her mind. An unorthodox idea. But if it brought ease to this suffering woman, why not give it a try?

Lucinda came back with a dry hanky and gave it to Edwina, then returned to her seat on the couch. "We'll think of something to cheer you."

"Have you ever considered a Chinese cure?" Audra blurted out.

Both women looked at her as if she had lost her mind.

She went on anyway. "Mr. Bonet is doing an article on the encampment at the edge of town. I've been transcribing his notes, and I'm amazed at how self-sufficient the Chinese workers are. They even have their own medical people. Can you believe that?

And their treatments go back thousands of years. They mostly use plants and herbs and such, but it seems to work."

They continued to stare.

"Perhaps you should give it a try."

Edwina found her voice first. "You mean go to the coolie camp and have one of their medicine men *examine* me?"

"I'd go with you," Audra offered halfheartedly, wishing she had never brought up the idea. "Or you could take your husband."

"Declan? Declan doesn't even believe in water witching."

Audra wasn't sure how that signified, but before she could ask, Lucinda rose. "Let's all go. Now. Today. Before we lose our nerve. I'll even bring my pepperbox pistol, just in case."

Edwina blinked up at her. "In case of what?"

"Never mind that. Come along. At this point, you have nothing to lose."

The encampment was bustling with activity, and had doubled in size since the fire burned down the other camp and the tracks from the terminal at Boot Creek had reached town. The noise was almost constant—sledgehammers pounding against spikes—the huff and puff of the locomotive that ferried men and supplies to the forward work areas—the chatter of Chinese workers calling to each other in their native language.

Audra found it immensely exciting.

As she followed Lucinda and Edwina toward the maze of tents along the creek, she scanned the milling crowd of dark-clothed workers, hoping for a glimpse of Ethan. She had heard he was often at the construction site, and he was tall enough that she could have easily spotted him above the woven reed hats the Chinamen wore. She did see several men wearing Western-style clothing and dark Stetsons, but none was Ethan.

"How are we supposed to find this medicine person?" Edwina asked, dodging around a worker pulling a cart full of railroad spikes.

"We'll ask. Surely there's someone here who speaks English." Lucinda glanced around, seemingly unperturbed by the men gawking at her. Audra suspected many of them had never seen a blond woman before.

"We should have brought R.D. He understands some of the words."

"And have him tell your husband what you're up to?"

"Look for an Irishman," Audra suggested. "Mr. Bonet said that because of language issues, many of the bosses on the work gangs are Irish. There's one." She pointed to a stout man wearing a cloth hat, instead of one made of reed or beaver felt, who was directing men positioning cross ties for the rails.

"Wait here." Lucinda headed toward him. "Sir?"

"This is embarrassing," Edwina muttered. "I hate the way they're all staring at us. Especially that one."

Audra followed the direction of her gaze and saw a tall man with hard, dark eyes studying them. Not Chinese. Probably Irish. With a coiled, silver-handled whip tied to his gun belt. Why would he need a whip?

"If Declan ever finds out—"

"Over here," Lucinda called, waving a gloved hand.

Ignoring the starer, but acutely aware of those cold eyes tracking them, Audra hurried Edwina toward Lucinda. As soon as they joined her, Lucinda told them there was a medical person in the next row of tents. "I believe his name is Kim. Follow me."

They did. As closely as they could without tripping on her heels.

The tent looked like any of the dozens of other campaign-style canvas tents issued by the railroad, except for a series of vertical symbols painted on the flaps.

Lucinda stood for a moment, undecided where to knock, then called out, "Hello? Is anyone home?"

It was absurd, really, the spectacle they were making of themselves—three unescorted, apprehensive women, surrounded by foreign men in a rough railroad encampment, paying a call on a male Chinese person who lived in a tent.

But Audra was far from laughing.

A moment later, a face appeared in the flap. Old and wrinkled, looking as surprised to see them as they were to see him. Words burst out of him. They sounded accusatory and angry, despite the nodding of his pigtailed head and a wide smile that showed an impressive number of big teeth.

Lucinda raised a hand for silence. When he complied, she asked with careful enunciation, "Are you Mister Kim?"

More smiling and bobbing, but this time, accompanied by

words they could understand. "Kim. Yes, yes. Okay. What missy want?"

"My friend is ill and needs your help."

"I'm not ill, I—"

"Kim help. You come." Beaming broadly, he held open the flap and waved them inside.

The interior was scrupulously clean and smelled faintly of spices and dried herbs. Not surprising, since small bundles of them hung from the pole over which the canvas was draped. A low pad lay along one wall. Across from it stood chests of different sizes, many intricately carved or painted with symbols and delicate drawings. A curtain separated the front receiving area from what Audra assumed was Mr. Kim's private quarters. Other than the chests, there was no furniture.

"What missy want?"

What transpired next was even more absurd. But somehow, with exaggerated gestures and dramatic playacting, they were able to convey that Edwina had recently given birth and was now very sad and listless, and wanted Mr. Kim to give her something to make her happy again.

It was rather like that game charades, but without all the riddles and rules.

Luckily, Mr. Kim was able to get the gist of it, if his head bobbing was any indication. Motioning Lucinda and Audra aside, he stepped up to Edwina.

"See tongue," he said, and pointed at her mouth.

With some reluctance, Edwina held out her tongue, her whole body flinching when he leaned closer to peer at it, muttering to himself.

After a moment, he stepped back. This time, instead of nodding, he shook his head. "No good. Spleen *qi*, heart blood, bad. Need harmony."

Edwina looked from him to Audra and Lucinda, then back at him. "Harmony?"

"Harmony. Yes, yes." Back to nodding, and with such vigor, his pigtail bounced against his back. "Spirit-mind need help. I do. You wait."

Muttering again, he disappeared behind his curtain.

"This is insane," Edwina whispered to Lucinda and Audra. "What if he comes back with a live snake for me to eat?"

"Why would he do that?"

"There's no need to whisper," Lucinda said. "He doesn't understand you."

"R.D. says they eat all sorts of strange things."

"Like what?"

"Dried-up things. Seaweed, animal parts, even bugs. And they stick themselves with long needles."

"Why?"

Before Edwina could answer, Mr. Kim returned. Instead of a snake, he held a brown vial in one hand and a small paper packet in the other. "Ginseng," he said, holding up the bottle. Liquid sloshed. "Astragalus. You smell." Uncorking the bottle, he thrust it toward Edwina.

Hesitantly, she sniffed. Then Lucinda wanted a turn, so of course Audra had to do it, too. It smelled earthy and a bit like licorice or dried grass. Strong, but not unpleasant.

He put a stopper in the bottle and gave it to Edwina. "You take."

"Thank you." She carefully slipped it into her pocket.

"Five days. One time. Okay?" Kim held up a hand, fingers splayed wide. "Five days you drink. Okay?"

Edwina nodded. "I understand."

"Okay." Next, he carefully opened the paper packet to reveal a dried lumpy substance. "Rhemannia and Lycium berries. Good for heart-blood. You cook." He pinched a small amount of the herbs between his thumb and forefinger and showed it to Edwina. "This much. Two times. Five days. Okay?"

"Cook it in what?"

"Pot."

"I mean . . . in water, or . . ."

"Yes, yes. Water. Then drink. Okay?"

"Okay." Taking the packet, she folded it tightly and slipped it into the pocket with the tonic. "Thank you, Mr. Kim."

"More. You wait." Turning to the chest, he pulled out a brightly painted box, lined with silk and holding a selection of long, thin needles. "Acupuncture."

Edwina's eyes widened. Her mouth opened.

Fearing an eruption, Audra stepped forward.

Lucinda reached her first. Grabbing Edwina's arm, she tugged her toward the tent flap. "Perhaps another time, Mr.

Kim. Thank you so much." As she spoke, she pulled a coin from her pocket and set it on the chest. "You've been most helpful, but we really must—"

Voices rose outside. Shouts, cursing. An explosive crack. Then another.

Edwina's eyes went wide. "Is that a gun?"

"A whip." Audra threw open the flap.

A dark-clad Chinese worker crouched in the dirt. Blood leaked through crisscrossed rips in the cloth over his shoulder and back. The tall man who had been watching them earlier stood over him, swinging his silver-handled whip.

"Stop!" Audra cried. "What are you doing?"

Another crack. Another cut into the bowed back. "Butt out!"

A crowd had gathered. All Chinese. The other Irish bosses had disappeared. The agitated chattering of the workers rose and fell with the whip, but no one tried to intervene.

Audra ran toward the figure on the ground. He was only a boy. "Go!"

"I said butt out!" Another crack. A jolt on her shoulder. Then a searing pain that took her breath away. She stumbled, went down on one knee.

Behind her, Lucinda's and Edwina's voices rose in panicky shouts.

Gasping, Audra crawled over and touched the boy's arm. "Go . . . run . . ." From the corner of her eye, she saw the whip draw back.

Something flew through the air.

She ducked.

But the blow never came.

The wounded boy's arm shook beneath her hand. Tear tracks cut through the dust on his cheeks. "Go . . . run!"

He seemed not to hear her. The shouts and chattering had risen to a deafening din. But one voice stood out.

Pain shooting down her back, she turned. Saw Ethan standing over a man on the ground, fists flying. Declan, trying to pull him off. The workers surging forward, arms waving.

Suddenly, Lucinda was kneeling beside her. "Get up. We have to go. Now!"

"Oh, God, Audra," Edwina cried, bending at her other side. "You're bleeding!"

With their help, Audra made it to her feet. The pain was a constant burn, but it wasn't unbearable. She turned back to help the Chinese boy, then saw that Mr. Kim was already leading him away.

Lucinda tugged on her arm. "Hurry! We have to get out of here. Move!" she cried, motioning aside the workers crowded around the men scuffling in the dirt.

"Where's Edwina?"

"I'm here."

Audra looked back to see the Southerner crowded behind her, her face slack with terror. "Are you hurt?"

"Not yet. But when Declan finds out—oh, Lord—"

Realizing the chattering had stopped, Audra turned to see Declan jerk the bloodied man from the ground by his shirtfront and shout in his face. Ethan was already headed their way.

There was blood on his mouth. A scrape under his eye.

She had never seen him so angry.

Seventeen

"Go with the sheriff," Ethan told Lucinda and Edwina, his voice vibrating with fury, his gaze still locked on Audra. "I'll take her to Dr. Boyce."

Edwina glanced at her husband, who was coming toward them, a scowl on his face and one big hand clamped around the back of the battered Irishman's neck. "I'd rather stay with you, I think."

Ethan turned his head and looked at her.

She edged back. "All right. We'll go with Declan. Audra, you'll be okay?"

"She'll be fine." Taking her elbow, Ethan steered her through the crowd at such a rapid pace she had to scramble to keep up with him.

They were well away from the encampment before he spoke again. "Are you insane?"

"Can we slow down?"

"What were you thinking, going out there by yourselves?"

"Edwina hasn't been feeling well and we thought a Chinese cure might help. Please, you're hurting my arm."

He loosened his grip, but didn't let her go. "How did you get between Gallagher and the Chinese boy?"

"No one else would help him."

"So you threw yourself in front of a whip? Jesus, Audra!"

"I couldn't simply stand by."

He muttered something under his breath. They walked a bit farther before he spoke again. "It's my fault."

She shot him a look, but he was staring straight ahead, his face grim, his mouth so pinched his lips were white except where the blood had dried.

"I should have fired him right off. Instead, I decide to wait for his replacement. Damn stupid—"

Abruptly he bent over and sucked in several deep breaths.

Alarmed, Audra watched him, wondering what was wrong. He was still holding on to her arm and his face was quite pale and he was shaking even more than she was. "Are you well, Ethan?"

"Hell, no, I'm not well!" He pulled himself upright and glared at her. Some of the color was back in his face . . . as was the anger. "He could have killed you!"

"I doubt it. Lucinda brought her pistol."

"Good God." He bent over again.

She refrained from patting his back in sympathy—after all, she was the one who was hurt. Yet his heartfelt and surprisingly strong reaction was flattering. It had been a long time since anyone had made such a fuss over her.

"I'm fine, Ethan. You stopped him before he did any real damage."

This time when he straightened, the shaking was gone. But he still looked pale. "You're not fine! You're bleeding."

"So are you." She eyed the cut on his lip that had already crusted over, and the bruise darkening below his eye. He had suffered that for her. As sorry as she was that he was hurt, the idea that he would willingly put himself in harm's way on her account almost made her cry. "Thank you for coming to my aid, Ethan."

Finally releasing her arm, he rubbed his hands over his face. His chest was still pumping and he seemed unsteady. Fearing he might become light-headed again, she slipped her arm through his and started him walking again. "As usual, you were very heroic. And I greatly appreciate it. But if it'll make you feel better, we'll have Doc Boyce take a look at both of us."

"I don't like your tone."

"What tone?"

"You're patronizing me."

"I don't mean to."

"And I have a right to be worried."

"Do you?"

"I care about you." He stopped. This time, he took her face in his hands. He was shaking again—she could feel it in his arms—hear it in his voice. "Don't mock me, Audra. If something had happened to you . . . if because of me you were hurt . . . I don't think . . . I couldn't . . ."

Rising on tiptoe, she gently kissed the corner of his mouth that wasn't injured. She tasted coffee, dust, the salty-sweet tang of blood. Ethan. Pulling back, she looked up into eyes as clear and fathomless as a hot summer sky. "And I care about you, Ethan. Very much."

"You do?"

"Of course I do."

An odd look crossed his face, like a shadow had moved between them. Or an unwelcome thought had entered his mind. He took his hands away and gave a strained smile, wincing a little at the pull on his split lip. "You'd be a fool not to."

She could feel him retreating from her, pulling back behind the shield of humor. She didn't know why, or what she had said or done to send him away. Yet for that one instant, before he had masked it, she had seen the truth behind his blue eyes, and knew that her words had broken through his armor and touched him in an unexpected way.

"What's wrong with you people?" Dr. Boyce complained when he saw them standing at his door. "Never knew anyone so hell-bent on self-destruction as you two. What happened this time?"

Feeling unfairly criticized, insomuch as this was the first time she had come to the doctor for help, Audra left the explanations to Ethan.

"One of the gang bosses used a whip on her," he said as Doc ushered them into his examination room.

"Only the once," Audra qualified. "And Ethan—Mr. Hardesty, that is—knocked him down for it."

Doc frowned at Ethan. "That how you got banged up?"

Ethan started to grin, then winced. "Not as banged up as the other fellow."

"At least you had sense enough to wear gloves."

"He was magnificent," Audra said stoutly. "Sheriff Brodie had to pull him off before he hurt him too badly. Hurt the other man, that is."

"Hmm." Lips twitching, Doc motioned Ethan toward the door. "Ladies first, then."

"I'm staying."

"I have to take off her blouse, son."

"Then I'm staying for sure."

"Ethan!"

"It's my fault you're hurt. I need to make sure you're all right."

"You married to her?" Doc asked when Audra started to object again.

"What? No. But—"

"Then you can't stay in here. Go."

After assuring her he'd be right outside, he eventually left the room.

"Hardheaded fellow, isn't he?" Doc said, getting out his medical supplies while Audra removed her blouse.

"He worries."

"Worry? Is that what that is?"

Fortunately, the cut was a clean one, barely three inches long, and not deep enough to require stitches. It had already stopped bleeding. Doc smeared it with a salve that took some of the sting out of it, then covered it with a bandage held in place with sticking plaster.

"You'll be sore for a couple of days, but it should heal fine. I'm not sure about that fellow in the hall."

Audra looked at him in alarm. "Ethan—I mean, Mr. Hardesty? What do you mean? What's wrong with him?"

"He's smitten, that's what's wrong with him. How about you?"

"Wh-What?"

"You have objections to him?"

"Well, no, but—"

"Then work it out. I can't have the two of you running in here all the time. I've got real patients to tend." He opened the door. "Your turn, Ethan—I mean, Mr. Hardesty."

* * *

The day they opened the sluice for the first time, it seemed the whole town had gathered by the finished water tower near the tracks. It was a bright, sunny morning and, despite the thin crust of frost on the grass, unseasonably warm for early May. By afternoon it would be shirtsleeve weather, and in another few weeks, the robins and swallows would be nesting along the creek.

Having accomplished the most pressing part of their task, the sluice workers were in high spirits. Assuming all went well today, tomorrow they would begin work on the second, shorter sluice, which would empty into the completed town water tower up by the old mine. Hopefully, by the end of the month, Heartbreak Creek would have all the untainted water it needed.

"It's a bit of an eyesore," Lucinda remarked, frowning up at the trough running overhead to the open top of the water tower. "Tait said it wouldn't be watertight, so it's liable to leak on anything below it."

"A good place for a garden, then," Audra suggested.

"Oh, yes!" Edwina clapped her gloved hands together. "I love flower gardens. We had them everywhere back home. I'll be glad to help."

Audra smiled at the Southerner's exuberance. It had been only a few days since she'd begun the Chinese cure, but she seemed better already. Audra didn't know if that was due to the herbs and tonic prescribed by Mr. Kim, or if the poor woman's melancholy was lifting naturally, as Doctor Boyce had said it would, given enough time. She was simply happy to see her new friend smiling again.

And happy for another reason, too.

She glanced over to where Ethan stood with Tait and the sheriff and Thomas Redstone near the stacks of lumber that would be used to construct the heated building around the water tower. He looked especially fine today in his dark coat and hat and with that broad smile on his handsome face. He had been so busy with the work crews she hadn't seen him since the day of that horrid scene at the Chinese camp. And afterward, when he had walked her from the clinic back to the hotel, he had been in such a thoughtful mood he had scarcely spoken. She had missed talking to him, laughing with him.

Even missed his teasing. And now, after a week of his absence, just having him within sight made the day a little brighter.

"It's almost time," Lucinda said, consulting the watch pinned to the inside of her coat pocket. "Tait said they would open the valve at precisely nine o'clock, and it should take no more than a few minutes for the water to reach town."

"Perhaps we should step back a ways," Edwina suggested. "I just finished hemming this dress and I don't want it getting wet."

"You sewed that?" Audra studied the dress in surprise. The lilac dress was beautifully made and in the latest spring fashion. "That stitching around the collar and cuffs is exquisite. I didn't realize you were so gifted."

Edwina laughed. "I can also find water with willow switches and play a piano blindfolded. I'm a gold mine of talent. If only I could cook."

"You're doing better all the time." Lucinda explained to Audra that sewing was how Edwina had supported herself and Pru back in Louisiana after the war. "Perhaps you should have her make you something." Her gaze dropped to the brown skirt showing below Audra's coat. "Something not brown."

"Or gray," Edwina put in. "What do you think, Luce? Yellow? Green?"

"Ethan likes me in green," Audra blurted without thinking. "I mean, Mr. Hardesty does. Or so he said. Once."

"Indeed?" Lucinda sent a knowing glance to Edwina. "Then green it shall be. After we leave here, we should stop by the mercantile. See what Mr. Bagley has on hand. We'll want her to look her best for the church's Spring Social."

"What Spring Social?"

"Don't you read your own newspaper? The notice was in two days ago."

"I scarcely have time to read my own notes."

"It's always the first Saturday in May." Edwina's bright blue eyes glowed with enthusiasm. "The whole town is invited. There'll be box lunches for sale and music and Declan even promised he'd dance. R.D. and Joe Bill and some other boys are charged with clearing an area on the other side of the cemetery to make a playing field and archery range. There will even be a turkey shoot if they can catch a turkey. I can scarcely wait."

"Here she comes!"

Audra looked over to see people pointing up the slope where the sluice snaked down through the trees. She could hear a faint whooshing sound now, growing louder by the second. Laughing, she stepped out of dripping range as water rushed by overhead. A man peering down into the water tower from a narrow walk-way that circled the open top raised a fist in triumph when water poured out of the sluice and into the wooden reservoir. A cheer rose from the crowd.

"It's happened." With an unsteady smile, Lucinda dabbed gloved fingertips to her watery eyes. "We've finally brought good water to Heartbreak Creek."

As the crowd dispersed, Ethan looked around for Audra, and saw her walking back to town with Lucinda and Edwina. He debated going after her—he had hardly seen her for a week— but Rylander snagged his arm.

"We're going to the Red Eye. You coming?"

"Sure." With a last glance at the three women, he fell into step behind Brodie and Thomas Redstone. "Celebratory drink?" he asked Rylander.

"I figure we earned it."

When they reached the saloon, all the tables were already full, so they lined up at the bar. Rylander had the bartender deliver a bottle to each table, then raising his own glass high, he called out, "To the scruffiest, stinkingest, most foulmouthed workers this side of the Mississippi. I'm proud of you, boys. Thank you for a fine job."

A chorus of "hear, hears," a few good-natured jibes about know-it-all, sissified, tea-sipping, suit-wearing city slickers, and the celebration launched into full swing.

Ethan signaled to the harried barkeep. "Such a grand accomplishment calls for the good stuff." A moment later the bartender plunked down on the counter a bottle of fine Scotch whiskey.

Ethan uncorked. "Any takers?"

"Of Wallace's private cache? Hell, yes." Grinning, Tait held out his glass. "How'd you manage to get it?"

"Charm."

"Theft," Brodie countered.

But Ethan noticed his glass was right there beside Tait's. Redstone pushed his aside and asked the bartender for ginger beer instead. "Maybe he can't count and won't know it's gone."

Brodie laughed. "Oh, he can count. He's a wizard with numbers. He can do them in his head faster than you can write them down."

"And he likes to fight," Thomas added.

"Helluva shot, too," Tait put in.

Ethan wondered when this paragon he'd relieved of a bottle of whiskey was expected back in town, but he didn't ask, not wanting to appear cowardly.

They drank in silence for a time, unwilling to allow idle chatter to detract from the enjoyment of fine whiskey. When Ethan poured a second round, Tait asked if they were going to the church's Spring Social on May fourth.

"I tried to get out of it," Brodie said glumly. "But Ed caught me on it. Expects me to dance, too. I hate to dance."

Thomas grinned. "But you are fun to watch."

"I notice you're not going."

"I am a Cheyenne Dog Soldier. We prefer war dances. And someone must take the sheriff duties while you lope in circles with your wife."

"Go to hell."

Ethan started to laugh, then saw a familiar face reflected in the mirror behind the bar. Setting his glass down with a *thunk*, he whirled to glare at the auburn-haired man sitting at a back table with two other Irishmen. "What's Gallagher doing here? I thought he was in jail."

"Can't keep him forever on a simple assault."

"There was nothing simple about taking a whip to a woman." Pushing away from the bar, Ethan stalked over to Gallagher's table. "I've already given your job to a better man," he said tersely. "So you can clear out anytime."

The other two men stared into their drinks, signaling this fight wasn't theirs.

But the big Irishman sat back, a sneer on his still-bruised face, the fingers of his right hand resting on the silver handle of the whip tied at his belt. "I can stay if I want. I've done my time, so I have."

"Then hear this." Ethan leaned down until his face was a foot from the other man's. "Use that whip on anyone again—white, Chinese, man, woman, horse, your mother—you'll have to answer to me. And next time, the sheriff won't be around to save you." Then grabbing the bottle Rylander had paid for, he stomped back to plunk it on the bar.

"Feel better?" Rylander asked.

"I might if I'd been allowed to finish the job I started two days ago."

Brodie sighed. "Then you'd be the one in jail. Let it go, Hardesty. I'll keep an eye on him."

Redstone gave a chilling smile. "And if he does not, I will."

Ethan started to argue when a voice called to the sheriff. Turning, he saw a man approach. Dirty, bearded, blackened stubs for teeth, almost as big as Brodie, wearing fur boots and a slouch hat that had more holes in it than fabric.

"Hidey. Ezra Weems. Heard you and the redskin was looking for me. Been looking for you, too. My partner's missing. Left a couple of months ago and I ain't seen him since. Whatcha got there?" He eyed the bottle of Scotch whiskey.

Ethan shoved it out of his reach and substituted the rye he'd taken from Gallagher's table. Grinning, the prospector filled the glass Redstone wasn't using.

"We found him," Brodie said. "In a slide up in the canyon. Dead."

"Damn." The man seemed sincerely mournful, but Ethan noticed it didn't stop him from emptying his glass in a single gulp and pouring more. "He always was a clumsy son of a bitch."

"His pockets were turned inside out," Brodie said. "Know if he was carrying anything of value?"

"I'll say. A nugget big as my thumb. He was on his way to get it assayed."

Ethan looked at the other men. "So something was taken from him, too."

"Could be coincidence," Brodie said. "Other than the Chinaman, we've got no proof any of them were murdered."

"I don't believe in coincidences," Ethan said. "I think they're connected."

"Seen that surveyor lately?" Rylander asked Weems. "The one you reported spotting at the other end of the canyon?"

"Naw. He's long gone." The filthy man frowned. "Think he's dead, too?"

"Damn." Ethan pushed his glass away. "I better warn Audra."

"About what?"

"She's moving to the Arlan place. If these deaths are connected, the killer is still loose. She won't be safe out there alone."

"Why would he come after her? Besides, she's got the Abrahams."

"Faint good that'll do, since none of them can shoot."

Eighteen

"Why do you keep closing your eyes?" Ethan asked.
Ears ringing, her nose stinging from the acrid smell of spent powder, Audra squinted through the haze to see that the can on the stump remained untouched. Disheartened, she handed the heavy Colt Army back. "It's loud."

"And closing your eyes will make it less so?"

"Don't badger."

There were in the side yard at the Arlan house and Ethan was giving her and Curtis their first shooting lesson while Winnie and Father watched from the porch. It wasn't going well. Audra heartily regretted that she had allowed Ethan to teach them, rather than Lucinda. How was she supposed to manage a gun that was over a foot long, weighed almost three pounds, and sounded like a cannon? She would have been much happier to learn on something smaller, like Lucinda's four-shot pepperbox pistol. She wasn't hunting buffalo, for heaven's sake.

"I'm not badgering. But you'll never hit anything if you can't see it."

"Maybe I don't want to hit anything. Maybe I just want to scare it off."

"Then say '*boo*.'"

She could almost hear his teeth grinding in frustration.

"Audra, you don't fire a gun to frighten an assailant. You fire it to stop him."

"You mean kill him."

"So what do you intend to do if an intruder comes into your home? Wave a gun in his face? Fire with your eyes closed? You'll miss. I guarantee it. And by the time you load a fresh cartridge, seat it, and cock the hammer, he'll be on you. Then it'll be too late."

"I'll still have five more shots. And there's no need to yell."

"I'm not yelling! I'm trying to explain—"

"At the top of your lungs?"

"I'm wasting my time here. Curtis, it's up to you then."

"Yessuh."

Muttering, Audra went to sit with Winnie and Father on the porch.

"Where's Cleo?" Father asked.

"Gone to Oregon," Audra snapped, having heard the question at least a dozen times that day. But as soon as the words were out, she wanted to call them back.

"What's got you huffing and puffing?" Winnie asked.

"Ethan's being unreasonable."

"Because you can't hit the can?"

"Because he's a poor teacher."

"Maybe you a poor learner."

"How can you take his side?"

"Who taking sides?" Leaning over, Winnie turned the book Father held right-side-up. "That better, Mr. Percy?"

But he was already distracted by a butterfly flitting through the rafters.

In the yard, the gun exploded.

Audra flinched.

The rusty can flew off the stump, flipped twice, and tumbled to the ground. Grinning broadly, Ethan whacked Curtis's back.

Men.

Lips pursed, Audra studied them. Curtis, short and broad. Ethan, tall and lean, with a long back and long legs and the kind of grace displayed by a man comfortable with himself. He had left his hat on the porch, and the late afternoon sunlight caught glints of gold in the tousled brown hair. He stood with his weight on one leg, hands braced low on his hips. Relaxed. Confident.

Insufferable.

Curtis fired. Audra flinched. The can jumped again. Laughing, Ethan walked over to set it back on the stump.

She liked the way he walked. A long stride with a slight spring in his step, the sway of his shoulders just short of being a swagger, his posture upright and energetic, as if he was eager to meet whatever lay ahead.

What would she do if someone threatened her or Father or the Abrahams, or even Ethan? Wouldn't she want to save them?

With a sigh, she pushed herself out of the chair. "Guess I'd best see to supper. After killing that can all afternoon, I'm sure they'll be hungry."

This was the third time Ethan would be joining them at the slightly battered pine table in the kitchen. Now that the tracks had reached town, he was no longer needed at Boot Creek, and spent his days in Heartbreak Creek, consulting with graders and tunnelers and surveyors charting the route through the canyon. He had tried to convince her not to move from the hotel until the killer was caught, but she wanted her own place again, and more room for all of them, especially Father.

Eventually, he had stopped arguing with her, and had even helped Curtis move their belongings and the furniture Lucinda had given them out of storage. Every day since—to Mr. Bonet's irritation, which amused Ethan no end—he had arrived at the newspaper office just before closing, insisting on escorting her home.

And now, the shooting lessons.

It was apparent he thought her incapable of looking after herself, even though she had done so ever since Father had taken ill. Still, she didn't argue with him. It would do no good, and besides, those quiet walks with him after a long, tiring day had become a treasured time for Audra.

Tonight she was trying her hand at Winnie's recipe for venison stew—from the venison haunch Ethan had brought earlier in the week—with onions and the fresh vegetables she had found on the porch that morning. Yesterday, it had been a packet of spices. The day before, a dried fish. Audra assumed the items had been left by someone from the Chinese camp, perhaps to repay her for trying to protect the boy from the Irishman. She felt such offerings were unnecessary, but since she never saw who left the gifts, she was unable to confront the person leaving them.

She had never cooked before moving into the Arlan house. The kitchen had always been Winnie's domain, and Audra had been too busy helping Father to take the time to learn. But nowadays, Winnie had enough to do tending Father all day, so Audra took over the cooking chores whenever she had time. She enjoyed it, and was very proud of her efforts, but in truth, with Winnie there to instruct her, she could hardly have gone wrong.

Ethan was a delightful guest, and took pains to help Father when he could. He often regaled them with stories of the many places he had been and the people he had met, although Audra noticed he never mentioned California. Her own life seemed quite dull in comparison.

She was dishing up bowls of stew when he and Curtis came in, their faces still damp from their wash at the trough beside the small paddock where Cricket was kept.

"Smells great," Ethan said, waiting until she'd taken her seat before taking the chair next to Father. "How's that venison holding up? Shall I try to get some grouse later this week?"

It was heartening the way he looked after them—walking her home, helping with Father, bringing meat to the table. But her growing dependence on him was troubling. He wouldn't be here forever. Soon the railroad would send him to the next construction site, and she would be left alone to fend for herself again. She didn't want to think of that time coming. Or of him being gone from her life forever. "Grouse would be wonderful."

He smiled at her, those blue eyes she'd once thought cold warming the air between them. "Then grouse it is."

As the others began eating, she broached the subject that had been nagging her while she cooked. "Ethan, I've been thinking about what you said earlier. You're right. I can't afford to be squeamish about this shooting thing. So, if you've the patience for it, I'll take another lesson whenever it's convenient for you. And I promise I'll work hard to keep my eyes open." She gave him a wry look. "That still doesn't mean I'll hit anything, of course, but at least I can try."

He studied her, his cheeks bunching as he chewed. Then he swallowed and said, "How about a dog instead?"

"A dog?"

"One of the surveyors found a stray wandering in the canyon. Singed a bit and half-starved. Might have been abused, too."

She sat back, astounded. "You're offering me a dog on the brink of death?"

"I didn't say she was dying. Just hurt. But if you want, I'll have Doc check her over to be sure." His smile cajoled, which, for some odd reason, made the tips of her breasts tingle. "She really needs a home, Audra. And you could use a dog."

Did the man feel responsible for *every* creature that crossed his path?

An unwelcome thought arose. Was that the reason for his attentions? Was she simply another stray for him to take care of? The notion was so insulting, she almost threw her stew in his face.

Then she remembered she loved dogs.

"All right, you may bring her. But I'm not promising she can stay."

Of course she fell in love with the poor creature the moment she looked into those sad brown eyes. Ethan must have carried her all the way from Doc's—Audra doubted the emaciated dog would have had the strength to make it on her own. Or the inclination. The moment he set her down, the frightened animal scurried under the table, tail tucked tight.

Kneeling, Audra bent low to peer under the tablecloth. The poor dog was shivering, her eyes darting at every movement and sound. "Does she bite?" When she received no answer, she looked back over her shoulder to find Ethan staring at her behind. "Ethan, stop that!"

His gaze flew to hers. "Stop what?"

"Does she bite?"

He cleared his throat. "If she didn't bite me, she probably won't bite you. It's men she's afraid of."

"Stop ogling," she scolded, and peered under the cloth again. "Here, pup," she said softly, extending a hand.

The dog didn't move.

But she didn't growl or show her teeth, either.

She was young, nearly full-sized, but hadn't yet grown into her feet. Mostly hound, judging by the long drooping ears and jowly muzzle. Her ribs showed, as well as singed hair along one side. A fresh bandage was taped around one front leg. Her tail was long and thin, and there was speckled skin showing beneath the singed black-and-white coat. A scar cut through the fur by one soulful eye.

A sad, pitiful excuse for a dog. No doubt crawling with fleas and carrying all sorts of diseases. Untrained, distrustful, and liable to run off at the first opportunity.

With a sigh, Audra let the drape fall and straightened.

"Well?" Ethan said, reaching down to help her to her feet.

"We'll call her Phoenix. An apt name, I think, considering what the poor dear has been through."

"Will you be going to the social this weekend, Miss Pearsall?" Peter Bonet asked over the rumble and clang of the press.

It was printing day. The office smelled of ink and the chemicals used in the print process. Lint from the rolls of paper hung in the still air, irritating her eyes and making her sneeze. She had already gone through one hanky.

"Yes. We all are. It sounds like a wonderful gathering."

"I would be happy to escort you. And your family, of course."

She dabbed the hanky at her runny nose. "Thank you for the offer, Mr. Bonet, but Mr. Hardesty is already planning to take us."

"Of course."

He went back to typesetting.

Audra laid out the pages already printed and cut. Working with Mr. Bonet was becoming steadily more awkward. He was gentlemanly enough, but she felt him watching her as if waiting for her to make a mistake, and his unspoken disapproval every time Ethan came to escort her home was almost palpable. She needed employment, and didn't want to do anything to jeopardize her position here. But she sensed a confrontation of some sort was imminent.

"That was an excellent piece you did on the latest spring fashions, Miss Pearsall," he said after a long silence. "And on Mr. Rylander's ideas for the Heartbreak Creek Depot."

"Thank you." There wasn't much to either article. Fillers, for the most part. But at least she was writing again.

"But I'm not sure what you wrote about the coolie encampment would be of interest to our readers."

Behind His Blue Eyes ✦ 163

Audra paused to look at him.

He gave one of his rare smiles. "After all, they're Celestials. Very different from us. Little more than slaves owned by the railroad."

Audra was surprised. "Granted, the working conditions are harsh. As harsh as they were for the Irish on the Eastern lines. But they're here by their own choice. And as hard as the work is, it must be better than what they left behind if they were willing to come all this way to do it."

"Beasts of burden, Miss Pearsall. That's all they are to their employers. Someday the railroads will be held accountable for the way they've treated all their workers. And for the deaths they've caused."

Hoping he wasn't about to launch into another mournful retelling of his brother's death, Audra didn't respond, and resumed her tasks.

"How long have you known Mr. Hardesty?" he asked after a while.

Another sore subject. Looking up from the papers she was folding, she saw by the clock on the wall that she still had an hour before she could escape for lunch. Edwina was meeting her in Lucinda's office for a final fitting of the new dress she was sewing for the social. The green silk had cost her most of a week's wages, but Audra didn't care. It had been ages since she'd had a new dress, and especially one so beautifully made. "I met him the day we came to town."

"Has he told you about the hospital in California?"

She didn't respond.

"He was the architect on the renovation, you know."

"How many pages in today's edition?" She didn't like gossip. Nor did she want to discuss Ethan with Mr. Bonet.

"Two sheets, four pages. He killed three people, they say."

She couldn't ignore that. "If that's true, he would be in prison, I'd think."

"They ruled it an accident."

"Then he was acquitted of any wrongdoing."

"There were many who didn't agree with the inquiry findings."

No longer able to hide her irritation, she rounded on him. "Were you there?"

"I worked for one of the San Francisco papers at the time. The story was front-page copy for several days. My editor felt the tragedy was due to Hardesty's arrogance and his ignorance of design. I saw nothing to dispute that."

Arrogance, she might believe. But ignorance? Never. Along with Tait Rylander and Father, Ethan was one of the most intelligent men she knew.

"But do ask Mr. Hardesty," Bonet snapped. "Perhaps he can explain why he put a glass wall beside the beds of men too sick to protect themselves when it fell."

He must have seen her building anger. In a kindlier tone, he added, "I say this because I feel we're friends, Miss Pearsall. With your generous nature, I fear you mightn't see the kind of man he is. I meant no offense."

Fearing if she opened her mouth, she might say something that would get her dismissed, she simply nodded and continued folding the sheets of newsprint.

But the seeds of doubt Bonet had planted flourished in the back of her mind. Had Ethan been negligent? Was he somehow to blame for the tragedy?

The notion continued to prey on her, making her such poor company at lunch that even Edwina and Lucinda commented on it.

"Are you feeling unwell?" Edwina mumbled through a mouthful of pins as she hemmed Audra's new silk. "I've never seen you so droopy."

"Just tired, I guess. We're printing tomorrow's edition."

Mr. Bonet's revelations had upset her more than she wanted to admit. It was apparent now why Ethan seemed so melancholy at times. So haunted. And being Ethan, whether the tragedy was his doing or not, he would take responsibility for it, just as he seemed to take responsibility for everything else . . . including her. But she didn't believe it was his doing. A man like Ethan wouldn't be so careless.

"Perhaps she needs some of your tonic," Lucinda suggested.

"Oh, that's long gone. I would go for more, but Declan has forbidden me to go to the coolie camp again."

Lucinda's blond brows rose. "*Forbidden* you?"

"Strongly advised." Edwina smiled, pins poking out between her teeth. "I doubt he would *forbid* me anything right now. The tonic and those herbs are both quite . . . invigorating . . . if you know what I mean."

"So the trip to the coolie camp was worth it?"

Pulling the pins from her mouth, Edwina sat back on her heels. "Not in the way I anticipated. Declan and I had a terrible row when we got home. I've never seen him so upset. I said some awful things. He yelled like he never has before. And then I realized he wasn't as angry as he was afraid. Can you imagine that? Declan Brodie afraid? And over me. I was astounded."

Audra could believe it. Hadn't Ethan had an equally strong reaction?

"But you were able to talk it out?" Lucinda pressed.

"Yes, and that's another astounding thing. We stayed up for hours talking. Declan talking! I'll warrant he used up a year's worth of words in a single night." That impish grin. "Or, most of the night. He even told me to hire someone to help out at least one day a week. Audra, if Winnie ever runs out of things to do, I'd love to have her. The children fear her. Plus, she's a good cook. I'd pay, of course."

"With me working, she's got her hands full right now. But maybe Curtis could watch Father and free her for a day now and then. I'll see what he says."

"I'm just pleased the Chinese cure worked," Lucinda said. "I was worried."

Audra had noticed that Lucinda was the proverbial mother hen, clucking and fussing over her friends as if they were new hatchlings. The ultimate manager—of the hotel, the town, all the people in her life—she wanted everything to be right and everyone to be happy. It was endearing, rather than annoying. But then, Audra hadn't been pulled under her wing yet.

Edwina returned to her pinning. "I still tire easily and sometimes get frazzled and overwhelmed, but I no longer feel like I'm trapped in a Louisiana fog. I don't know if that's because of Mr. Kim's tonic, or the passage of time like Doctor Boyce said, or clearing the air with Declan, but I'm definitely getting back to my old self." She smiled at the baby dozing in his basket. "Or maybe it's because Whit is finally sleeping at night. There. All done." She rose and stood back to study her work. "Luce, what do you think?"

"I think it's beautiful. That green does wonders for your

coloring, Audra. Mark my words, you'll be the belle of the social."

By the time Ethan showed up at the office that afternoon, Audra had decided to put Mr. Bonet's vicious gossip out of her mind. If there was anything Ethan wanted to tell her about his past, she would be happy to listen. Otherwise, she would go on as if she hadn't heard a thing.

Of course, that was easier said than done. Apparently, Ethan knew her well enough to sense her mood.

"Something is troubling you," he said before they'd even stepped off the boardwalk at the end of the street. "Is Bonet being difficult? Shall I speak to him?"

She turned, prepared to dress him down for interfering, then saw he was teasing. "Yes, please. Tell him I want double my salary and half the hours."

Instead of being amused, he took her hand and threaded his long fingers through hers. His hand felt warm and strong, his palm slightly rough against hers.

"I wish you didn't have to earn your way, Audra. I wish you had someone to take care of you, and give you a house full of children, and make sure you had all the time you needed to write your lurid novels of romance and adventure."

She looked up at him in surprise, expecting to find him teasing her again. But he wasn't smiling, and the look in his eyes was almost . . . sad.

"You're a rare creature, Audra Pearsall. A woman who gives more than she takes, and brings happiness, rather than pain, to those around her."

It was a remarkably odd thing to say, and made her wonder what he might have suffered to leave him with such a jaded view of women. But before she could question him, he leaned down and kissed her.

A short, sweet kiss. Restrained.

But beneath it, she sensed more than friendship. Or even ardor.

She sensed regret.

Nineteen

Phoenix—or Phe, as Audra had begun to call her—improved rapidly, both mentally and physically, probably due to the enormous amounts of food she consumed, as well as the burn ointment Doc had sent with Ethan.

She still hid under the table whenever Curtis or Ethan came around, but didn't seem bothered by Father. After Ethan left in the evening and the Abrahams and Father had retired, she would sit beside Audra's rocker on the porch, careful to stay out of kicking range, but still close by. Within a few days, she no longer cringed when Audra reached out to pet her, and once even gave a quick lick to her hand.

Noting the dog's instinct to hide when frightened, Audra had Ethan and Curtis construct a roomy crate for her that was closed on three sides. Not wanting the animal to feel trapped, she hung a piece of toweling over the open side, so that Phe could come and go as she wished, but was still able to hide in her safe place when she felt threatened.

She took to it immediately. Audra tucked the crate in a corner by the storage room—out of the way, but still near enough to the family and work areas that the dog wouldn't feel ostracized. Gaining the battered animal's trust would be a long undertaking, but Audra already loved Phe, so it wouldn't be a chore.

The day of the social dawned clear and cool. Audra had slept poorly, partly because of excitement—it had been years since she had attended a festive gathering—and also because of all the rags tied in her hair. But when she took them out and anchored the curly mass on the back of her head with a ribbon that matched her dress, she was well pleased with the fluffy ringlets dangling down past her collar in back, and the few wispy curls framing her face.

Once dressed, she studied her reflection in the mirror over the bureau. Motion in the upstairs window behind her drew her attention. She turned, but saw only blue sky and the woods bordering the side yard. Perhaps a bird had flown past the window and she had caught the reflection in the mirror.

That had been happening a lot lately. Glimpsing furtive movement just beyond the corner of her eye, or feeling she was being watched. But whenever she looked around, she saw nothing to arouse suspicion. With all the vandalism to the sluice and the recent deaths, everyone was jumpy, she supposed.

"Child, you outdone yourself," Winnie said from the doorway. "If this don't bring that man to his knees, nothing will."

Bending over to hide her blush, Audra brushed a speck of dust off the green silk skirt. "I'm sure I don't know what you're talking about."

Winnie snorted. "I'm sure you do. No more friendly back pats, that what I'm talking about. Maybe even some kissing out there on the porch when you send him home. Strong, healthy man like Mistuh Ethan hold himself back only so long. So watch out. This could be the day he finally cut loose."

"Don't be silly." But Audra had to smile at the prospect. Even in her own estimation, she looked prettier than she ever had. But would Ethan see her any differently? Would he finally find her alluring enough to push aside all the barriers of his past and reveal his true feelings—whatever his true feelings were?

"Come on, then," Winnie called, heading down the stairs. "Curtis already got the buggy hitched, our box lunches be packed and ready, and Mistuh Percy getting fidgety."

Ethan rode up just as Audra stepped out of the house. Reining his horse to a stop, he sat motionless in the middle of the lane, staring. His hat shaded his face, so she couldn't read his expression, but he seemed quite taken with her appearance. When finally he dismounted, she held her breath, wondering if this would be the moment he fell to his knees.

Alas, he remained upright.

Throwing his horse's reins over the rail out front, he walked toward her.

He looked magnificent. Freshly shaved, trimmed, and pressed. Even his hat and boots had been brushed. And those eyes . . .

Stopping at the bottom of the single porch step, he gave a slight bow and offered his hand. "Miss Pearsall," he said, his gaze never leaving hers.

"Mr. Hardesty." She slipped her hand in his much larger one, felt the heat of his fingers through the thin lace of her glove, and wondered if he could feel the tremble in hers.

"You look . . . so . . . beautiful."

Embarrassed by the way he was looking at her, she gave a nervous laugh. "You needn't sound so surprised."

"I'm not surprised. Only regretful."

"Why?"

Tucking her hand into the crook of his elbow, he walked her toward his horse and the waiting buggy. "Because I'll be so busy today."

"Doing what?"

"Keeping the other men away."

An unlikely prospect, but Audra delighted in hearing it anyway.

The buggy wasn't large enough to accommodate all five of them, so after handing her into the driver's box, Ethan walked back to his horse. As he stepped into the stirrup, Audra noticed a long rectangular box tied behind his saddle.

"What's that?" she asked.

He gave a sheepish grin. "My fiddle."

"You play the fiddle?"

"I did." He looked ruefully down at his hands. "But I haven't played since the fire. Let's hope I still can."

"I have no doubt of it. You're a most determined man." Laughing, she unwound the reins from the brake lever. "My, my. Playing the fiddle *and* keeping the men away. You certainly will be busy today."

He looked over at her. What she saw in his eyes left her slightly breathless. "It'll be worth it."

The crowd outside the church was even larger than the one

that had gathered two weeks earlier beside the water tower. Tables had been improvised with boards laid atop barrels and crates, and several were already laden with lunches in boxes and baskets and calico sacks. Later that afternoon, men would bid on the parcels, with the proceeds going into a church fund for those who had suffered losses from the fire, then the winning bidder would share the meal with the woman who had prepared it. It was supposed to be secret. But part of the fun was speculating on which woman had made which lunch, and which man would spend the most to buy it. Naturally, Audra hoped Ethan would bid on hers.

Throughout the early afternoon, games, archery contests, and shooting matches were held in the open field on the other side of the cemetery. Audra was glad they used paper targets rather than a live turkey. Closer to the church, tables displayed items that would be raffled later—quilts, baskets, bonnets, toys, and various hand tools. Audra regretted there were no Chinese in attendance, but Ethan told her that Saturday was a workday for them, and when they did have their Sunday off, they preferred their own entertainments, mostly gambling, playing fan-tan, or relaxing with their opium pipes.

The only thing that marred Audra's enjoyment of the early afternoon was the way Mr. Bonet watched her, and the resentful sneers directed at her by that red Irishman, Gallagher. Luckily, Edwina and Lucinda stayed by her side, and with their husbands and Ethan nearby, talking at the men's "punch" table, Audra was able to put the two men out of her mind.

Until that awkward moment during the bidding for her box lunch.

Audra didn't know how they found out which box was hers—unless they guessed it from Ethan's interest—but both Peter Bonet and Gallagher entered the bidding. At first, onlookers found it amusing, but as the price went higher and higher, they began to whisper.

Gallagher snickered at her discomfiture. Ethan looked thunderous. Finally realizing he was drawing glares from both the sheriff and Tait Rylander, Mr. Bonet graciously bowed out. But Gallagher continued to drive up the bid until Thomas Redstone, who had dropped by on his sheriff rounds, walked over and spoke quietly to him.

Color faded from the Irishman's face. Abruptly, he spun and walked away. And the bidding was over.

"I'm sorry," she murmured when Ethan came to claim both her and his exorbitantly priced lunch.

That crooked smile. "That you'll be dining with me, rather than Mr. Bonet?"

"Of course," she teased back. "And that it only cost you a week's pay."

Dropping his face close to hers, he whispered, "Again, it was worth it."

"But you haven't tasted it yet."

"I've tasted enough." When he saw her shock, a laugh burst out of him, ruffling the curls by her flushed cheek. He straightened, and with his broad, warm hand against her back, steered her toward the trees where Thomas Redstone and the Rylanders, Brodies, and Abrahams were settling on a blanket in the shade.

"Besides," he went on, "now that I've staked my claim, all the men will know to stay away, so I won't be as busy today as I feared."

"What a relief for you."

"You have no idea."

As they approached, several knowing looks came her way, but Audra pretended she didn't see them.

"What did you say to Gallagher?" Tait Rylander asked the Cheyenne.

"That I have no red hair hanging from my lodge pole."

"I thought you didn't take scalps," Ethan said.

The Indian smiled but said nothing.

"Have you noticed any unusual activity in the canyon, Redstone?" Tait Rylander asked.

Thomas shook his head. "The same people—Weems, the prospector we spoke to, a trapper now and then, a few hunting parties. Nothing new."

"I'm rethinking the idea that all three deaths are connected," Brodie said. "Or that the woodcutter and prospector died by foul play. People fall off bluffs or get caught in rock slides. Accidents happen."

"The Chinaman's slit throat was no accident," Rylander put in.

"Maybe the killer was interrupted," Ethan suggested.

"Maybe he intended to make it look accidental, but was scared off by the people coming to fight the fire."

"Or, maybe," Tait added, "he expected the body to be burned so badly you couldn't tell if it was an accident or not."

Edwina heaved a great sigh. "Must we talk about slit throats and burned bodies and murderers? This is supposed to be a festive occasion." Picking up the box she had prepared, she set it in front of her husband. "For you."

Somewhat warily, he opened it and peered inside. After a slight hesitation, he lifted out a packet of jerky, a tin of peaches, and two hardboiled eggs. His strained smile didn't mask his obvious disappointment. "Thanks, Ed."

His wife gave him a playful nudge. "Read the note in the bottom."

He pulled out a piece of paper, read it, then stared at his wife, a deep flush spreading up his neck.

"Well?" she asked, fighting a smile.

"Ah . . . sure." Looking addled, he wadded up the paper and thrust it into his pocket. Seeing the faces staring at him, he smiled weakly. "Just a reminder to save room for dessert."

"That must be some tonic," Lucinda murmured to Audra.

"What tonic?" her husband asked.

"Never mind." Opening the huge box her husband had bought, Lucinda pushed it to the middle of the blanket. "Cook made enough for five people. I do hope you'll share with us."

With Redstone and Brodie happily digging in, the box was empty in no time.

Occasionally, the Brodie children ran over from the cleared field where the three elderly choir ladies were supervising games, stole a snack, then darted off again, shouting and laughing. Their high spirits seemed to rattle Father. He scarcely touched his food and appeared quite bewildered by the goings-on, although he did show great interest in Whit, who was being entertained by Winnie, sitting on his left.

"This here the cutest child, Miss Edwina." Winnie bounced the baby in her arms and was rewarded with a gurgle. "Never seen such a happy one."

"That's because he's with you. You're very good with him, Winnie. In fact, you're good with all the children. Even Brin and Joe Bill. I wish I had your knack."

"They good young'uns. Just gotta be firm with them."

Edwina laughed. "I try. Truly, I do. But as soon as one of them gets me laughing, they know they've won."

Reaching out a pudgy arm, Whit poked at Father's nose.

Father laughed and poked back with a palsied finger. "Mary always wanted a son. Where is she? Isn't she coming?"

"She'll be along later, Father."

He looked up, his smile giving way to a frown of confusion. Audra stiffened, but before Father could ask who she was, Edwina cut in.

"Now that we'll all together, I have wonderful news! I received a letter from Pru!" Reaching into her skirt pocket, she pulled out a wrinkled envelope and opened it. "She's settling in quite nicely, she says. And everyone has been so welcoming. Shall I read it?"

Before anyone could answer, Thomas Redstone rose and walked away.

Edwina's smile faded. "Oh, dear."

Reaching over, her husband rested his big hand over hers. "It's okay, Ed. It's just his way."

"I'd like to read it," Lucinda said. "Perhaps later, after the gathering?"

Blinking hard, Edwina handed her the letter.

There followed a moment of awkward silence, then Ethan pushed himself to his feet. "I better go. Looks like the musicians are gathering by the church steps."

Lucinda looked up at him in confusion.

"He's a fiddler," Audra explained.

"Is he? I didn't know." Lucinda winked at Edwina. "Be sure to play something we can dance to. A waltz, perhaps. Wouldn't that be nice, Declan?"

"Sure," he said without enthusiasm.

Ethan dusted grass from his trousers, then gave the other men meaningful looks. "You'll keep an eye on Audra for me."

Brodie nodded.

"It would be my pleasure," Mr. Rylander said with a gracious smile.

Did he think her a complete nitwit? Audra was about to be offended, when the sheriff added, "Gallagher won't be allowed anywhere near her."

Gallagher? She looked around and didn't see him, but did notice Peter Bonet approaching. Pasting on a smile, she braced herself.

"Miss Pearsall, if I might have a word?"

"Of course." Ignoring Ethan's glare, she rose. "If you'll excuse me," she murmured, then followed Mr. Bonet out of hearing range of the others.

"I find I have a pressing matter back at the office, Miss Pearsall," he said tersely. "And I will be unable to write my column on the social. Can I count on you to pen something for the next edition?"

"Certainly. When shall I have it on your desk?"

"Tomorrow morning, if you please."

Tomorrow? The paper only came out once a week and wasn't due for another five days. Now she would have to leave early, or stay up half the night putting the column together.

"Any questions, Miss Pearsall?"

"No, Mr. Bonet."

"Then I leave you to your friends."

As soon as he walked away, Ethan approached. "What did he want?" he asked, his gaze pinned on the back of the man hurrying toward town.

"To remind me I'm here to work, not have fun. He wants an article about the social on his desk in the morning."

A look of impatience crossed Ethan's face. But before he could speak, Audra rested a hand on his arm. "It's fine, Ethan. It's why he hired me."

"You know he's only doing this because he lost the bid."

"Perhaps. But I wouldn't be able to stay much longer anyway. Father is tiring."

"Have Curtis and Winnie take him home."

His petulance was both amusing and flattering. "I don't want to ruin their good time, too. But I shan't leave until I've heard you play. And seen our overgrown sheriff dance with his wife." Smiling at the notion, she slipped her arm through his and pointed him toward the church where the musicians were setting up their instruments. "Come along. Let's not waste what time we have."

Twenty

Ethan was a more than credible musician. He made the fiddle sing through the lively dances, and sigh through the mournful ballads. Onlookers clapped the tempo and tapped their toes while dancers whirled and dipped, dust flying. And when he began a polka, and Edwina dragged her husband into the middle of the dance area, Audra saw the sheriff truly did lope around in a circle, yet she had never seen Edwina so happy.

"Aren't they adorable?" Lucinda whispered, her eyes suspiciously bright. "I love watching them together. He holds her like she's the most precious thing in the world and he's afraid he'll drop her."

It was true, Audra thought, watching them go around and around, laughing. It was like seeing love in motion. "Why aren't you dancing?"

"Tait went to have a word with that Irishman."

Audra looked past her to see Tait Rylander speaking earnestly to Gallagher. A moment later, the Irishman turned and stalked toward town, his shoulders stiff with anger. She was relieved. Ever since the music had started, he had been watching her with that sneer on his face. But now with him gone, she could allow herself to relax.

The polka ended, and a spirited rendition of "O Green Grow the Rashes" began, with the choir ladies harmonizing on the choruses. The Rylanders danced that one, and despite Tait's slight limp, they did so with the graceful precision of people so finely tuned to each other there were no missteps, and no need to take their eyes off each other through the spins and dips.

When that song ended, dancers moved toward the punch tables for refreshments. Audra hoped Ethan would come join her, but saw that he and the man with a homemade flute continued to play, seemingly lost in their music. It wasn't until she saw Father walking toward them that she realized the song they played was one of her childhood favorites—"The Water is Wide"—and as sweetly done as she had ever heard. Fearing Father would disturb them, she hurried over.

He stopped in front of the two musicians, his chin quivering with emotion and tears glistening in his faded eyes. "Mary used to sing that," he said in a shaky voice when she stopped at his side. "Do you remember?"

"Yes," she said, her own voice unsteady.

Ethan saw Father's distress, but she signaled it was all right and for him to continue. These were happy memories. Not sad ones. And even if they helped Father reconnect with the past only for a moment, she didn't want to interfere.

Ethan continued to play, the soulful melody rising and falling in harmony with the soft, clear notes of the flute.

"She used to sing that to you every night. Do you remember, Audie?"

Audie. How long it had been since she had heard him call her by that name.

She felt something give inside. *He remembers me.* Warmth spread through her, and she smiled at Ethan through a haze of tears. *He knows me.*

As if he'd heard her thought, Ethan nodded and smiled back.

"Now, now, dearest," Father said, slipping his arm around her shoulders. "We mustn't cry. Mary wouldn't like that, you know."

"I know." Pressing her damp cheek against his frail chest, she heard the flutter of his heart beneath her ear and for just a moment let herself drift back into that safe, happy time when Father was the center of her world and she thought he would go on forever.

After a while, he said softly, "She's gone, isn't she, Audie?"

"Yes, Father. I'm afraid she is."

There was a long silence. Then Winnie came up behind them and he took his arm from her shoulders. "I want to go home now. Cleo will be hungry."

Audra started to follow him, but Winnie put out a hand. "Me and Curtis take Mr. Percy back in the buggy. You stay and enjoy yourself, child."

"I can't. I have a column due tomorrow."

"Give us a minute, Winnie," Ethan said. Only then did Audra realize the music had stopped. Taking her hand, he led her away from the others and toward the late-afternoon gloom of the trees along the creek. "I told you," he said, giving her fingers a gentle squeeze. "In his heart, he remembers you."

"For a while, anyway. And I'm grateful for it." Fearing another bout of tears, she put on a smile. "You're very talented, Ethan. I'm so glad the burns weren't severe enough to keep you from playing."

"Me, too." Smiling, he leaned against an aspen trunk, her hand still laced through his. "I had forgotten how much music means to me."

"I'm sure if he knew of your gift, Pastor Rickman would be begging you to play at the services."

"Some gifts aren't for sharing."

He must have seen her confusion. "My music is a private thing. More of a solace than a gift."

"Why would you need solace?"

He didn't answer.

She could feel him drifting away again, and didn't know how to stop it. Or if she should even try. Being with Ethan was like dancing a quadrille. One step forward, two steps back. It kept her off balance, not knowing when to move or what the next step would be.

Overhead, the budding aspens were not yet full enough to make that watery sound when the breeze blew through the leaves. But the creek was overflowing with snowmelt from the high slopes, and the rush of water over the rocks drowned out everything but the distant sound of music and Ethan's breathing beside her.

She should leave. The Abrahams and Father were waiting. But she didn't want to go without voicing the thoughts that had troubled her for the last several days. Troubled her now. "Ethan, what are we doing?"

He looked at her.

"You and me. I know I'm inexperienced in these matters. Normally a mother advises a daughter about these things, or girlfriends . . . but . . . I only want to know where I stand. What I'm supposed to do. You keep me so off balance." Pulling free of his grip, she made a broad gesture and was surprised to see her hand was shaking. Where had this surge of emotion come from? She had only meant to broach the subject, but now words were bursting out of her before she could stop them. "You kiss me, then disappear for days. A week later, you show up with food for my table and act as if we're simply friendly acquaintances. Today, you've said things that make me think you're pursuing me, but I have a feeling by tomorrow, you'll fade away again. Why?"

He smiled. "Are you asking what my intentions are, Miss Pearsall?"

She threw her hands up in exasperation. "See? You're doing it now. Holding my hand one minute, retreating into humor the next." She felt she was begging for something he couldn't give. But this day—her father, Ethan, Gallagher's sneers, and Bonet's innuendoes—it was all too much. "I just want you to talk to me."

"About what?"

"Anything. Everything. California."

His posture stiffened. "Who told you about California?"

"Mr. Bonet."

"That figures." Shoving away from the tree, he went to stand at the edge of the creek.

"But I'd rather hear it from you," she said to his back. "Will you tell me?"

He faced her, his expression bleak. "It's complicated, Audra. There are things . . . things I did . . . that aren't easy to talk about."

"Even to me?"

"Maybe later. The musicians are waiting."

The fight went out of her. Already he seemed miles away, hidden behind an unbreachable wall. Defeated, she turned away. "Good night, Ethan."

He didn't try to stop her, which told her more than any of his words had. He didn't trust her. Or feel the connection she did.

How sad. A dalliance, that's all this was to him. And being the proverbial wallflower bluestocking, she had seen in it more than was there. But at least now she knew if he ever came around again, she would need to guard herself more carefully.

And maybe after a while, this hurt would go away.

Within minutes of leaving the church, Father's brief return to reality ended in a sudden, shocking tumble into confusion and rage. He became as fractious as a spoiled child, convinced the buggy ride home was an attempt to kidnap him, that Winnie was trying to keep him from Mary, and Audra was stealing his papers. His tantrum continued even after they reached the house, when he slammed around his room, shouting and throwing his chamber pot. It upset Phe. But when she tried to help by licking his hand, Father pushed her away, too.

They reasoned, they cajoled, they bribed with toast and marmalade, but in the end they had to bully him into his nightclothes. Only after Winnie administered the last of the cough syrup with the sleeping draught was he able to calm down enough to sleep.

It was heartbreaking for Audra. What had begun as a day full of promise ended with her scrubbing urine off the floor and jam off the walls. She tried not to think of the harder times yet to come. Or the empty relief she would feel when Father was finally at peace. Or the aching loss of Ethan that even now clogged her throat with unshed tears. She had a home now. She had more friends than she had ever had in Baltimore. She was writing again. This heartache would pass.

It was well after dark when she went back downstairs. The Abrahams were already abed. Phe was tucked into her crate. Pulling paper, ink, and a pen from the hutch drawer, she set them on the kitchen table, turned up the oil lamp, put on her spectacles, and took a seat.

But words wouldn't come, and the longer she stared into the flickering flame of the lamp, the less inspired she felt. How was she to wax eloquent over a church social when her father was dying, a brute blamed her for losing his position, and the man she cared for wouldn't talk to her?

Finally, the silence and her own dismal thoughts proved too

much. Tossing her spectacles onto the table, she grabbed her shawl and fled to the porch. Settling into her rocker, she tipped her head back and let the pain come.

When had her orderly life gotten so out of control?

Tim Gallagher was halfway through his fourth drink when the newspaper man who had bid against him and Hardesty at the social—Bonet, his name was—sidled up to the bar beside him. *Bastard.*

"It wasn't you I was bidding against," Bonet said. "I just didn't want Hardesty to win."

Gallagher didn't respond.

Bonet motioned the bartender over. "And to show there are no hard feelings, I'd like to buy you a drink."

Gallagher was surprised. It had been a bad few weeks—losing his job, that earlier humiliation at the coolie camp, then the one today at the church social—and he was running low on coin. Hell, he didn't even have enough for an hour with one of the coolie whores who had arrived today from San Francisco. So with a shrug, he emptied his glass and shoved it toward the barkeep. "Fill it."

The bartender poured, then moved down the bar to where three gold-seekers were commiserating over the poor diggings in the area.

"Fancy whip." Bonet looked down at his belt. "Mexican?"

Gallagher didn't answer.

"I heard you used it on a coolie and it cost you your job."

"You looking for a taste of it?"

Bonet ignored the threat. "These railroads think they own the world. Especially Ethan Hardesty. He's got his nerve after what happened in California."

That caught Gallagher's attention. "What happened in California?"

"He killed three people. Bet if his employers knew that, he'd be out of a job, too. Another drink?"

Gallagher studied him, wondering what he was up to with his loose talk and free liquor. "Man starts buying me drinks, makes me curious why."

Bonet smiled. "It's simple, Mr. Gallagher. I plan to expose

the railroads for the corrupt institutions they are—how they treat their workers—the way they run roughshod over property owners, Indian tribes, or anyone who gets in their way—their total disregard of those killed doing their work. They think they're above the law. I intend to show they're not. And I could use your help."

"Doing what?"

"I want to start with Ethan Hardesty. You worked for him. We can show the kind of man he is, how he puts foreigners above his own race. Maybe he set the fire to clear the way for his railroad. Anything you can tell me might help."

Gallagher tried to concentrate. The alcohol was starting to muddle his thinking, but he seemed to remember something about Hardesty being at the cabin where the fire started. Maybe he did set it. Maybe he really was a killer like Bonet said. Maybe if he played his cards right, he could bring down Ethan Hardesty and get his job back, all at the same time. Worth a try. "It'll cost you, so it will."

"Here's a start." Bonet set a half eagle on the bar. "Finish your drink, then come to the newspaper office." He saw that the miners were watching and lowered his voice. "I'll show you what I already have on Hardesty, then we can talk."

"Tonight?"

"No time like the present. I'll be waiting."

Ethan sat on Renny and studied the house. No light showed upstairs. The downstairs was dark except for a faint glow from the kitchen. Probably a fire in the hearth. He knew he hadn't a single good reason why he should be here, and a dozen why he shouldn't.

He should let it go. His work in Heartbreak Creek was nearly finished—he could leave and never look back. A woman like Audra deserved more than a broken man with blood on his hands. It would be best for both of them if he just rode on.

Instead, he dismounted, tied Renny to the post out front, and walked toward the house. His legs felt shaky. His hands were sweating and his mouth was so dry he could hardly swallow. Stepping up onto the porch, he lifted a hand to knock, then drew back, startled, when he saw her sitting in the rocker.

She was asleep, her head tipped back, her lips parted. She looked so small, curled tight and wrapped in her shawl. Too small to cause such a ruckus in his life.

In the gloom of the porch, he listened to her breathe. Smelled her flowery soap. Knew by the tear tracks on her cheeks that she had been crying.

This could be bad. Worse than California. Worse than anything he'd suffered so far. This could be the end of hope and the beginning of long, lonely years.

He took a deep breath, bent, and cupped her cheek. "Audra."

Her eyes fluttered open.

He took his hand away and straightened, fists clenched at his sides. When he knew she was fully awake, he said, "I caused the deaths of three people."

She sat so still he wasn't sure she heard him. "How?" she finally asked.

He told her about his design for a glass wall at the marine hospital, and how the board thought it was too risky, but he had insisted it would be safe—he was a certified architect, after all, and who would know better than he? "It took several weeks to get their approval, but eventually, I wore them down."

"Go on."

Memories buffeted him, but he held them off and stripped his voice of emotion so he could get the words out. "We were almost done when an earth tremor struck. The force of it shattered the panes. They fell. Three were killed."

"Three patients."

He shook his head, wondering what Bonet had told her. "Two workers and a nurse. There was damage in the hospital wards, too, but no patients were hurt."

"What's an earth tremor?"

She was still listening, so he allowed himself to hope. After what he had gone through three years ago with the hospital administration, the architectural board, inquiries from various legal groups and newspapers, he wasn't sure how she would react. But she was hearing him out, which was more than most had. More than he'd expected. Or deserved.

"Tremors happen frequently in California. I'm not sure why. Some sort of upheaval deep in the earth makes the ground shake. This time it shook hard enough to destroy the top of a government building in San Mateo, as well as damage the marine hospital."

"Did you do something to cause it?"

"The tremor? No, but—"

"Could you have prevented it?"

"No. I'd never been through a tremor, but I'd heard of them, and I should have taken the possibility of one occurring into consideration. I should have altered the design."

"Why didn't you?"

Her interrogation was relentless. Each question coming on the heels of the previous one, and all drawing blood. "I was arrogant and headstrong. I wanted to build something revolutionary. Something that would be my legacy."

"Why glass?"

"I thought it would bring comfort to the patients if they could see the ocean."

She didn't respond. Other than when he'd awakened her, she hadn't moved since she began her questions. He couldn't read her expression, so he had no sense of what she was thinking, and her silence grew heavier with each heartbeat.

The breeze died and the crickets started. In the lane, Renny snorted, and farther in the canyon, a coyote called up his pack to hunt under the full moon.

He debated leaving. Walking away like he should have in the first place. He'd bared the deepest, darkest part of himself—she owed him some sort of response, didn't she? Still, he waited. Hoping. He didn't know what else to do.

Finally, when he'd about given up, she pushed aside her shawl and rose from the chair. Stepping close, she put her arms around him.

He was so shocked, he couldn't move.

"I'm sorry, Ethan," she said against his neck. "Sorry for the people who died, and for what you've suffered because of a youthful mistake."

"I was twenty-five. Old enough to know better."

"And I'm sorry you felt you couldn't tell me," she went on as if he hadn't spoken. As if she didn't notice how rigidly he held himself. "But you've tormented yourself long enough.

Blame it on God. Blame it on the blindness of youth, or bad luck. But be done with it, Ethan. Put it behind you before it ruins your life."

If only he could. Drawing back, he brushed a loose curl from her cheek so he could see her better. "And you, Audra? Can you put it behind you? Can you say what I've told you hasn't altered the way you see me?"

New tears glistened in the moonlight, but she was smiling. "Of course. Between us, nothing has changed. Except now, I know you a little better."

Gratitude weakened him. Wrapping his arms around her, he pulled her close, his relief so profound he felt the sting of tears in his own eyes. "Thank you," he said, and kissed her. Then kissed her again, his mouth open, his heart pounding, his body trembling like a school boy's.

When finally he lifted his head, they were both breathing hard.

"And anyway," she said in a weak voice, "it's not as if we don't all have secrets or things in our pasts we're ashamed of."

He had to laugh. "You? A shameful secret?"

"Why not? You think I can't do bad things?" She actually sounded offended that he might think otherwise.

"I can't even imagine it."

With a huff, she pulled out of his arms and whipped open the door. "Wait here. I'll show you." As she went inside, Phe rushed out, saw Ethan, and veered away to crouch by the rocker.

Ethan looked down at the wary dog. "How can you protect her if you're afraid of every man you see?" Hunkering on his heels, he held out a hand. "You'd best accept me," he murmured. "I'll be coming around even more now."

Eyes wary, Phe stretched her neck to sniff his fingers.

"That's a girl. Maybe if I win you, I can win her. What do you think?"

The door opened and Audra came out. "I couldn't find it. Probably misplaced it in the move. Would you like some coffee? I started a fresh pot."

"Sure." Ethan stood. "Couldn't find what?"

"Father's medallion. Come inside and I'll tell you how I cheated Richard Villars out of it."

Twenty-one

Because he didn't like being ordered around, Gallagher took his time finishing his drink. Then ordered another. As he sipped, he contemplated using the money the newspaper man had given him to buy a coolie whore for the night, but decided he was too drunk to get his money's worth.

"Finish up," the barkeep said. "We're closing."

Gallagher looked around and saw that the miners were gone and he was the only one left in the saloon. Muttering under his breath, he plunked his coins down on the counter and left, weaving slightly as he stepped out on the boardwalk.

The temperature had sunk with the sun, and the cool midnight air chased away some of the alcohol haze in his mind. He stood for a moment, vaguely remembering he was supposed to be going somewhere, then remembered Bonet told him to come to the newspaper office. But first, he needed to piss.

He stepped off the boardwalk, almost tripped, then stumbled into the narrow walkway between two buildings. Bracing a hand against the plank siding, he undid his trousers.

With a shiver of relief, he watched the steaming stream spatter against the wood then run down to soak into the dirt. It smelled rank and glinted like silver in the light of the full moon. Hell, maybe he should mine it. The thought made him laugh, until a sound by the boardwalk distracted him. He looked back.

A figure stood in the shadows, watching. A man, judging by the size of his bulky form. "Faith. Can't a fella take a piss?"

The man walked toward him.

Something hung from his hand. Something bulky that clinked. A chain?

"What do you want?" Gallagher stuffed himself back into his trousers.

The man kept coming, footfalls heavy. Unhurried. The chain clinking.

A sense of unease penetrated Gallagher's sluggish brain. He fumbled with the buttons, but it was too dark to see what he was doing. "*Feis ort.* Can't you see I'm busy here?" He turned.

Something struck the side of his head, slammed him against the wall. Pain stole his breath. Gasping, he slid down, hands clawing the planks for a handhold. Another blow across his back cracked ribs and drove the air from his lungs. He fell to his knees, moaning, blood running down his face. "Jaysus . . . *Cé thusa?*"

The man stepped closer.

Blindly, Gallagher threw his arm up to push him away.

A foot kicked out, smashing his teeth. Blood filled his mouth. Fingers gripped his hair, jerked his head back and stuffed a stinking rag so far into his mouth Gallagher gagged.

His hands moving so fast Gallagher couldn't get a hold on them, the man wrapped the chain around Gallagher's head and across the cloth prying open his mouth.

His mind splintering, Gallagher flailed, kicked, grabbed for the chain as it snaked around his shoulders, his arms, pinning his elbows to his sides. Then it was around his neck, the cold, hard links sticky with blood, crushing his throat as the man dragged him from between the buildings and into the street.

Gallagher arched, heels drumming, his lungs screaming for air. Hot, white light exploded behind his eyes.

Then faded . . .

When next he opened his eyes, it was dark. Cold. The full moon had dipped behind the trees, casting strange shadows across the ground. He tried to stop the slow spin, but couldn't move. Couldn't stop the pain. Didn't know why the world was off-kilter.

Then a burst of panic brought terrifying awareness. He was

hanging by his feet, his arms tied behind his back. The rag was gone from his mouth, and every breath of cold air made the exposed nerves in his shattered teeth shriek in agony.

Twisting, he looked wildly around, and saw a man sitting on his haunches beside a smoldering fire, watching him.

Gallagher knew him. But it made no sense. Why was he smiling? Then he saw the knife in the man's hand and another burst of panic sent him into frenzied struggles.

His captor laughed.

Weakened by pain and loss of blood, Gallagher stopped fighting. "Why are you doing this?"

"Because I can." The man rose, walked toward him, the knife glinting in the firelight.

Fueled by terror, Gallagher bucked against the ropes. "Jaysus! Don't do this!"

The man stopped in front of him, stuck out a hand to stop the spinning. He bent down so their eyes were almost on the same level, and Gallagher saw madness in the dark gaze. Why had he never noticed it before?

"Man with a whip likes to give pain. Can you take it, too, I wonder?"

It took a moment for the threat to penetrate Gallagher's fogged brain. "No!" He twisted, tried to kick, bounced at the end of the rope. "They were lazy. They needed a push, is all. It was my job to keep them working!"

"Did you enjoy it, Irishman? Did you like to hear them cry and beg?" He laughed. "I'll admit, I do." He made a sweeping motion with his free hand. "That's why I brought you way out here. So you can scream and cry and beg all you want, and nobody will hear you but me." He raised the knife.

"They'll know it was you! They saw you in the Red Eye!"

"I left before you did."

"Wait! Listen to me! I'll do whatever you want!" Weeping now, tears mingling with blood. "You want money? Someone killed? What? Tell me and I'll do it!"

The man hesitated, knife poised. "Can you stop the railroad? Send away their surveyors and woodcutters and yellow-bellied Celestials?"

"Oh, Jaysus . . . *le do thoil* . . . please . . ."

"I thought not. They don't belong here. I keep telling them

but they don't listen. Maybe they'll get the message when they see this." The knife sliced down.

Gallagher screamed. And kept screaming for a long time.

Ethan reared back on one arm, heart pumping, his body thrumming with desire. "No."

"Wh-What?"

"I can't do this."

Audra blinked up at him through dazed eyes, her mouth swollen from his kisses. Her glorious hair spilled over the arm of the couch like a silky waterfall, showing glints of red and gold in the flickering light from the hearth, and the skin of her bared breasts was flushed to a rosy blush.

She was the most beautiful thing he had ever seen. Sensuality put in human form. Everything a woman should be.

He was desperate to have her.

Here. Now. Forever.

"No," he said again. With shaking fingers he pulled her lacy shift over her breasts and closed the placket on her blouse. Then he slumped back against the couch, an arm thrown over his eyes, his fists clenched as he struggled for control. He tried to focus his mind away from the scent and warmth of the woman beside him, the rapid sound of her breathing. Tried to think about snowstorms, cold baths, the nuns who had tried to beat the lessons of the catechism into him.

It didn't seem to help.

How had it gotten this far? It seemed only moments ago he had come in for a cup of coffee and her confession of her dark, shameful secret—which was little more than forging her father's signature so she could put food on the table—hardly on a par with causing the deaths of three people. Then suddenly, he was sprawled on top of her on the couch, fumbling with the buttons on his trousers.

The woman drove him senseless.

He felt movement beside him, but didn't open his eyes.

"No?" Audra said in a breathy whisper that almost undid him. "No . . . what?"

"No this. Now. Here. It's not right, Audra. You're a good woman."

Another long pause. "I believe that's what I'm supposed to say."

More movement, then her hand cupped his cheek, pulled his head around.

He opened his eyes to find her studying him, one dark brow arched, a smile teasing those swollen lips. "Are you a virgin, Ethan?"

"God, no."

"Good. Perhaps I'm not, either."

She didn't look it, not with her blouse gaping open and those round, soft breasts pushing against her thin shift. But her kisses had shown innocence, and her response had been tentative, then trusting, then eager. Just thinking about the way she'd risen to meet him made his pulse hammer. Maybe not all that experienced . . . but definitely a fast learner, God love her.

"That's not the point," he said.

"Then what is the point?" Looking down, she began to button her blouse, that furrow he adored wrinkling her brow. "What's stopping you . . . us?"

"I don't want to be that man. The one who slips through your back door under cover of darkness and sneaks like a thief into your bed. You deserve better. And I want more."

"From me?"

"Only from you."

She laughed. It shocked him. Aroused him. Made him want to lay her down again. Prove something to both of them. He just wasn't sure what.

"Are you proposing marriage to me, Mr. Hardesty?"

Marriage? "I . . . ah . . ." His throat closed up and he coughed to clear it.

She laughed again. "Relax, Ethan. I don't need marriage. Especially to an unproven man."

Unproven? Now he was offended. "What do you mean, 'unproven'? I've proven lots of times."

"Of course you have. I didn't mean it that way. But what if we . . . don't suit?"

How could she doubt it? "We'll suit. I'll make sure of it." He was too well-mannered to point at evidence of how well she suited him.

"But how will we know for certain if I even like it if we don't . . . you know . . . give it a go?"

He was too shocked to respond.

"There's a saying about it, I think." Tilting back her head, she stared thoughtfully up at the ceiling. "Something about riding a horse. Or maybe putting a pig in a poke. I don't recall."

"Give it a go? Are you jesting?"

"Shh. You'll wake up the Abrahams. And if you give it some thought, you'll realize it's not an unreasonable idea. After all, I had to pass muster to secure a position at the *Herald*, didn't I?"

"That's not the same."

"You're correct, of course." Rolling her head toward him, she smiled. It was one of those "aha" smiles and instantly put him on guard. "I can always walk away from the *Herald*. But a marriage . . ."

He sat up. "Am I hearing you correctly? You want me to try out as your lover? Just to make certain you like it and to prove to you that we'd be *compatible* enough for marriage?"

"You're yelling again." She waved a graceful hand that only minutes ago had nearly driven him to the brink by sliding up the back of his neck to tangle in his hair.

He tugged at the knees of his trousers. "I am not yelling."

"I'll grant you the idea is rather forward-thinking," she went on. "But certainly promising enough to warrant further examination, don't you think? And if the experiment proves we don't suit, we can simply dissolve the association."

"But you showed me your breasts!" Surely that meant something.

That laugh again. He was beginning to hate it. "Don't be absurd. They're just breasts. I'm sure you've seen dozens. Maybe hundreds. And I didn't *show* them to you. It was you who unbuttoned my blouse. Although I'm not complaining, mind you. For such a big man, you're quite gentle."

"You're insane."

"No, Ethan." Her smile faded. She faced him again, and this time there was no laughter in her hazel eyes. "I'm practical. I'm a woman who has ordered her own destiny for several years now. I have an infirm father and two dear friends who are like family to me. Whoever marries me will have to accept the added responsibility for them. It's a heavy burden, and although

I take it on gladly, it is not something I would thrust on someone else, especially a man I have come to admire as I do you."

He didn't know how to respond to that.

"Besides," she went on, stretching her arms over her head, drawing his gaze to those wondrous mounds she called "just breasts," "I'm reconciled to the independent life I have chosen. I thrive on it. But that doesn't mean I wish to live without companionship." Letting her arms fall back to her sides, she gave him a sweet smile. "In that respect, I feel we do suit. I enjoy your company. Your fine mind. Your honesty and humor. Given the chance, I might even enjoy your amorous attentions, too."

Might even? He was dumbfounded, unsure if he'd been complimented or insulted. It was a moment before he could gather wits enough to respond. "So you want me to-to . . ." he stammered, searching the proper word . . . "audition, as it were. And if I pass muster you'll consider marriage."

"Exactly." Resting a hand on his arm, she gave him a dazzling smile. "I'm sure you'll do wonderfully."

He almost choked. "And how long will this audition last?"

She gave it some thought, one tapered finger tapping her now less-swollen bottom lip. "A month? Would that be enough time?"

"I wouldn't know. I've never done this. Audition, that is."

"A month, then." She finished buttoning her blouse and tucked it into the sashed waist of her skirt. "I'll leave the details to you—where, when, and so forth. And you'll be sure to get some of those things Dr. Power sells, won't you? I wouldn't want either of us forced into a marriage we might later regret."

Ethan gaped. How did she know about Dr. Power's French Preventatives?

"Heavens, look." She pointed toward the window, where the sky was brightening to a predawn gray. "It seems we've talked the night away."

Taking that as his signal, he stood, still not sure what had happened. The woman confused the hell out of him.

She stood, too, and after fluffing her skirts, she checked her buttons and smoothed a hand over her tangled hair. "I must look a fright."

In truth, she looked sexy as hell, all tousled and flushed like a woman who had just enjoyed a satisfying roll on a couch. This was a side of Audra he hadn't seen before. He didn't know what to make of it. Or her.

And in that respect, he was a bit frightened of her. And intrigued. Certainly confounded, and captivated in a way he had never been before.

He had definitely met his match.

A few minutes later, he swung up on Renny and headed toward his room at the hotel, wondering how and where he would begin his audition, and if Cal Bagley at the mercantile had enough French preventatives to get him through a very busy month.

Yet despite the obvious appeal of such an idea, and her unfettered enthusiasm toward it, there was something about the whole thing that just seemed . . . wrong.

It felt like he had barely closed his eyes when a pounding on his door dragged Ethan out of deep sleep. "Who is it?" he yelled, thinking if it was Yancey, he was going to wring his scrawny neck.

"Brodie. Need to talk to you."

Something in the sheriff's voice brought Ethan instantly awake. Rising, he pulled on his trousers and a shirt. Still fumbling with the buttons, he opened the door.

Tait Rylander stood in the hall behind the sheriff. Thomas Redstone was there, too. None looked happy. Swinging the door wide, Ethan stepped back to let them through. "What's happened?"

"Gallagher's dead. Murdered. Butchered, in fact."

As the men filed into the room, Ethan wondered why it took all three of them to impart that bit of news. Did they think he had something to do with it?

Redstone positioned himself against the wall by the window, his elbow resting atop the bureau. Rylander took the only chair, sitting back, relaxed, one knee crossed over the other. The sheriff seemed to take up all the remaining space, planted like a tree in the center of the room.

"Who did it?" Ethan asked, closing the door. "The same man who killed the others?"

Brodie's craggy face showed nothing, but his dark gaze never wavered. "That's what we're trying to find out."

"Well, I didn't do it."

"Glad to hear it." Brodie's expression didn't change, although Ethan detected a slight easing across his heavy shoulders. "But there are others who might need more than your word."

"Like who?"

"Bonet, for one. A couple of Irish gang bosses."

"Hell." Ethan sat on the edge of the bed to pull on his boots. "When did it happen?"

"Late last night. Gallagher left the Red Eye after closing. Around midnight. Probably died a couple of hours later. When the graders found him this morning, he'd already bled out."

Ethan lifted his head. "Bled out?"

"He'd been gutted and left hanging so the blood could drain."

"Damn." Ethan was shocked that anyone would think him capable of that.

"We can put wagging tongues to rest right now." Rylander uncrossed his legs and leaned forward, hands clasped, elbows resting on his bent knees. "Do you have anyone who can vouch for your whereabouts last night?"

Ethan met those probing gray eyes without hesitation. "No."

"You're certain? Yancey heard someone come in early this morning. He thought maybe it was you."

"He's mistaken."

Rylander nodded and sat back. But Ethan could see he wasn't entirely convinced. The man missed nothing, it seemed.

Then a thought hit Ethan so hard it sent him rushing toward the door. "I have to go to the Pearsalls'. They're unprotected."

"Thomas will keep an eye on the house," Brodie said.

Prepared to argue, Ethan turned impatiently.

But the sheriff cut him off. "The circuit judge came this morning. Kelvin Witherspoon. A son of a bitch if there ever was one. Doesn't much like Heartbreak Creek and wants this settled as soon as possible so he can leave."

"A simple preliminary inquiry," Rylander said, rising to his feet. "Since your name has been mentioned, the judge is expecting you to be there."

Memories swirled through Ethan's mind—other inquiries, other fingers pointed his way, other stern-faced judges glaring down at him. "But I didn't do it."

"We know that." Smiling, Rylander rested a hand on Ethan's shoulder. "And we'll prove it. But meanwhile, ask me before these witnesses to represent you." Seeing Ethan's confusion, he added, "I'm a solicitor, remember."

After Ethan complied, Brodie waved them all toward the door. "Come on, then. The judge is waiting. Oh, and try not to look at his teeth. Or laugh."

Twenty-two

Audra rushed along the boardwalk, her heels clicking on the weathered wood. She noticed a crowd milling about outside the sheriff's office, but didn't stop to see what was going on. She was frightfully late as it was. Mr. Bonet would make some comment about her tardiness, then raise his brows in disappointment when she admitted she didn't have the report on the social ready.

She knew all his games—his innuendoes, condescending remarks, and expressions of pained disappointment. She knew they were designed to keep her in her place, and they irritated her no end.

Yet she couldn't fault him today. She had told him she would have the piece ready, but instead of writing the promised article, she had spent the evening rolling around on the couch with Ethan Hardesty. She smiled at the memory of it, tiny shivers running through her body to places for which she had no name.

Had her gamble worked? By taking marriage out of the picture, had she pushed him closer to revealing his true feelings? He had certainly been aroused. She wasn't that much of an innocent. But by sending him away, would that interest be heightened, or diminished?

She would have to wait and see.

When she stepped through the doorway of the *Herald*, she was surprised to find Mr. Bonet absent from his desk, and only

Roger Tilly, a newly hired apprentice photographer, in the office. "Good morning, Mr. Tilly," she said, untying her bonnet and hanging it on a peg by the door. "Where is Mr. Bonet?"

"At the inquiry," he said, riffling through boxes of photography supplies stacked in the corner by his desk. "Have you seen the folder of albumenized paper?"

"By the window. What inquiry?"

"The one about the Irishman who was killed. Tim Gallagher. Murdered, actually."

Audra sagged into her chair. "Murdered?"

"Gutted. I had to take photographs before he was cut down." A blush darkened the young man's freckled cheeks. "I'm ashamed to say I cast up my accounts. But I assure you I wasn't the only one."

Audra stared at him, stunned. She heartily disliked Gallagher, but to be killed in such a foul manner . . . it sickened her. "Have they any suspects?"

"Only one. A friend of yours, I believe. Mr. Hardesty."

"What?" Audra shot to her feet, startling Mr. Tilly into dropping his folder. "That's absurd! Mr. Hardesty would never do such a thing!"

"But Mr. Bonet said he's killed people before. In California. He showed me the clippings."

"That's a lie! Those people were killed during an earth tremor." Leaving the surprised young man staring after her, she stormed out of the office.

The crowd was still clustered at the door to the sheriff's office when Audra neared—obviously gawking at the inquiry proceedings inside. The short walk from the *Herald* had calmed her enough that she was able to think. If she just rushed in, shouting Ethan's innocence, people might question her sincerity—after all, even the newly arrived Mr. Tilly knew they were friends. She would have to take a more subtle approach.

Pausing, she donned her spectacles and grabbed the tablet and pencil she always carried in her skirt pocket when working, then pushed her way through the men crowded in the doorway.

Things must not be going well. Ethan sat in a chair beside the sheriff's desk, his face a scowl of fury. Even Tait Rylander, standing beside him, was grim-faced, and Sheriff Brodie looked positively thunderous.

Mr. Bonet stood before the desk, flanked by two Irish railroad workers wearing tams. Across from him, a small, dandified older man sat in the sheriff's chair, wearing the pinched expression of a person suffering chronic dyspepsia. Probably from the ill-fitting, brightly white, overlarge porcelain false teeth that moved and clicked every time he spoke.

"You're certain of that, are you, Bonet?" he barked, as Audra moved into position at the front of the onlookers.

"Yes, sir. I have the newspaper articles if you'd care to see them. A tragedy, to be sure."

"Yet he wasn't charged in the deaths?"

"No sir. In that instance"—Bonet emphasized *that*—"there wasn't enough evidence to proceed to a trial."

"The deaths were caused by earth tremors," Mr. Rylander cut in. "I also have reports on the incident which will completely exonerate Mr. Hardesty, should you care to see them, Your Honor. Although, I don't see how any of that relates to the current inquiry."

The judge sent him a glare. "I like to know the kind of man I'm dealing with. That's how it relates, Mr. Fancy-Pants Lawyer."

Unruffled, Rylander smiled pleasantly. "The report can enlighten you in that regard, as well, sir. Mr. Hardesty is a well-respected employee of the Denver and Santa Fe Railroad, and has established strong ties to the Heartbreak Creek community."

The judge pounced, teeth clicking. "But he hasn't yet established his whereabouts last night, has he?"

Audra cleared her throat. "If I may, Your Honor."

The judge whipped his head around. "And who might you be?"

Audra gave her best smile. "Miss Audra Pearsall, Your Imminence. An employee of Mr. Bonet's most excellent newspaper."

"What do you want?"

Audra blinked and simpered, a woman obviously overwhelmed by all this male attention. "Just to say that Mr.

Hardesty couldn't have done this terrible murder, since he was at my house last night. In fact, he didn't leave until dawn."

"Oh, hell," Ethan muttered.

A gasp rose from the onlookers. Mr. Bonet looked shocked. Ethan dropped his head into his hand. Mr. Rylander frowned and Sheriff Brodie might have muttered something, but it was hard to hear over the murmuring of the crowd.

"Shut up!" the judge shouted, so vehemently his upper plate almost flew out of his mouth.

The crowd quieted. The judge righted his dentures, then fixed his gaze on Audra. His lids were heavy, on both top and bottom, so that the dark irises seemed sunken behind narrow slits in the puffy flesh. That, and the redness in his nose, proclaimed him a drinker. "You were with Mr. Hardesty? All night? Is that what you're telling us, Miss . . ."

Audra beamed and blinked. "Pearsall. Yes, sir, I was." Then, as if suddenly realizing the import of her words, she put on a shocked face and blurted, "But not *that* way, Your Imminence! He wasn't *with* me. He was simply at my house."

"Your Honor," Ethan cut in.

"Quiet!" the judge ordered then turned back to Audra. "If he wasn't *with* you, then what was he doing there?"

"Answering questions."

"About what?"

"That unfortunate incident in California you were just talking about. My employer, Mr. Bonet, has a keen interest in the event, and I thought I might impress him with a firsthand interview with the man who was blamed—wrongly, it seems—for the tragedy."

Bonet rounded on her, his face almost as red as his hair. "You spent the entire night with him? Talking? You expect us to believe that?"

Ethan shot to his feet. Brodie and Rylander shoved him back down.

"Yes, sir," Audra said to Bonet. "I know how it sounds, but you needn't worry. I was quite safe. My father was there, and my servants, Mr. and Mrs. Abraham, were in the next room. It was most proper, I assure you." Beaming like a simpleton, she thrust out her tablet. "And I got a wonderful interview! I think you'll be pleased. At least, I hope so. It's my first one," she added to the judge.

"Well, hell." With a deep sigh, Witherspoon sat back. "Is this man the only suspect you have, Sheriff?"

"We're still investigating."

Bonet wasn't ready to give up. "But Hardesty has a history of violence toward the dead man," he insisted, his voice shaking with emotion. "You heard the other foremen, Judge. He threatened Gallagher right there in the saloon."

Rylander stepped up. "Gallagher used a whip on railroad employees, Your Honor. Because of his predilection for violence toward the men under him, he had already been relieved of his position. Mr. Hardesty was simply pointing out there was no need for him to remain in Heartbreak Creek." Turning smoothly, he aimed that piercing stare at the two Irish gang bosses behind Bonet. "Isn't that right, gentlemen?"

They might be Irish, but they weren't stupid. Both smiled and nodded. "Yes, sir. That's how it happened."

"No threats?"

"No, sir. Hardesty just told him he better not use that whip again."

Turning back to the judge, Rylander smiled. "In view of what we've just heard, Your Honor, I ask that no charges be brought against Mr. Hardesty."

"Well, hell. This has been a waste of my morning, Sheriff. When I come back in three weeks, you better have this straightened out and someone lined up to hang. You got that?"

Brodie nodded.

Witherspoon slapped a hand on the desk. "Inquiry over. Now everybody get the hell out of my way. I need a drink."

"I'll see you at the office," Bonet snapped to Audra as he stomped past.

After the door closed behind him, only Ethan, Tait Rylander, and Declan Brodie remained behind with Audra. Neither the sheriff nor Ethan seemed pleased, but Tait Rylander was grinning. "Clever girl. You not only provided an alibi, but you defused the whole California issue. You would have made a fine lawyer."

"Was any of that true?" the sheriff asked.

Audra blinked innocently. "That Mr. Hardesty was at my house for an interview? Of course. Although, in the strictest sense, the interview wasn't solely about California."

"Gentlemen." Rising abruptly, Ethan swung open the door. "If you'll excuse us, I'd like to speak to Miss Pearsall."

"It's my office," Brodie complained.

"Stop whining." Tait Rylander shoved the mumbling sheriff through the doorway. "Go easy, Ethan," he warned, with a wink at Audra. "She saved your neck."

Ethan closed the door, took off Audra's spectacles, set them on the desk, and kissed her. "You're amazing." Another kiss, his mouth open and demanding. "Magnificent." His tongue brushed along hers then he drew back. "A consummate liar. And if you ever do that again, I'll wring your neck."

Audra sighed, all those shivery feelings racing through her again.

He chuckled, his breath fanning her lashes. "But I'll still let you marry me."

"Will you? How generous." She rose on tiptoe to kiss him again, but he pulled out of reach.

"No, Audra. I mean it. Anyone who knows you will see right through that simpering nitwit act. 'Your Imminence,' hell. They'll know you were lying, and that I wasn't there on some interview. I won't let you risk your reputation."

"So you're willing to marry me to protect my reputation?" She laughed. "Oh, Ethan. This isn't the eighteen-thirties anymore. And Heartbreak Creek isn't high society. No one cares."

"I do. Your friends do. You should, too."

"Don't be silly." Planting a quick kiss on his stern mouth, she picked up her spectacles and slipped them into her pocket. "Come by for dinner and we'll discuss it if you want. But meanwhile, I'd best get back to the newspaper before Mr. Bonet locks me out." She opened the door.

"Oh, I'll definitely be there," he warned. "Whether you like it or not, Audra, I won't leave you unprotected. Not as long as that murderer is lurking about."

"Excellent." She grinned back at him just before she closed the door. "Don't forget the preventatives."

He's right. I must be insane, Audra mused as she hurried down to the newspaper office. Twice now, Ethan had offered marriage. But each time for the wrong reason—first, because he had seen her breasts, and now, because he wanted to protect her reputation. Noble sentiments, to be sure, but hardly romantic declarations. And at heart—as evidenced by her penchant for lurid novels of adventure and romance—she was a true romantic. She needed love. The kind her father and mother had shared, a love so strong it still lingered twenty years after they had been parted. With Ethan, she could have that. But she wasn't yet certain he felt the same way, and she wasn't so desperate for security, or companionship, or children to marry a man who didn't love her back.

Unless, of course, Peter Bonet truly did lock her out. Then she might have to reevaluate. One must be practical, after all, even in matters of the heart.

He didn't lock her out. In fact, he wasn't even there, although Mr. Tilly, who was making adjustments to his box camera, said he had come in earlier, then immediately rushed out again. "Some foreign dignitary has arrived at the hotel and Mr. Bonet is hoping to get an interview with him. Wants me to get my equipment and come along. Seemed upset."

"About the dignitary?" Audra asked, settling at her desk.

"The inquiry."

"Oh? What did he say?"

"Something about blind fools, and how there would be more killings before this was over. Didn't make much sense to me." The young man shot her a guarded look. "Also said to tell you not to leave until he comes back. Says he needs to talk to you. You do something wrong?"

Mr. Tilly had only been in town and at the *Herald* for a few days, but already Audra could tell he was easily cowed by Mr. Bonet. She knew his concern now was less for her than in keeping himself out of the fray if she and Mr. Bonet had a falling out.

"I defended an innocent man," she told him. "Mr. Hardesty is not a killer, no matter what Mr. Bonet thinks."

"I don't know anything about that." Avoiding her gaze, he hoisted the bulky camera and tripod to his shoulder. "Another fellow came by to see you, too. A prospector or miner, by the looks of him. Said he was poking around that house of yours that burned and found something you might want."

Audra immediately thought of the medallion she'd wanted to show Ethan last night. But she was sure she'd seen it since the fire. "Did he leave it with you?"

Shaking his head, Tilly opened the door. "Said he wanted to give it to you in person. Probably wants a reward. I better go. I don't want to get into trouble, too."

Audra waved him along, then pulled from her pocket the tablet and pencil and set to work on the article about the church social. Hopefully, she would have it written by the time Bonet returned. One less thing for him to fuss at her about. As for the article that she supposedly wrote when interviewing Ethan, she would simply tell him she hadn't finished transcribing her notes, and didn't want to show it to him until it was complete.

If she was still employed.

A man sat slumped on a bench outside the Western Union office, idly digging dried blood from under his nails with a hunting knife. He wore stained trousers with patches at the knees, a tattered jacket, and a slouch hat with so many holes in it the late morning sunlight left a spotty pattern across his bearded face.

Movement drew his head up.

The fellow he'd talked to earlier came out of the building across the street. Bowed under the weight of the big wooden box camera and tripod he carried over his shoulder, he hurried down the boardwalk to where people stood around a sheepherder's wagon parked outside the hotel.

Turning his head, the man checked the other direction, but the street was deserted. Seemed everyone who had been at the inquiry earlier was now either at the Red Eye or outside the hotel.

Which meant she was alone.

He straightened on the bench. Squinting, he tried to see through the window of the building the photographer had left, but the fancy writing on the glass made it hard. He slowly and carefully sounded out the newly painted letters. *Heartbreak Creek Herald.* He didn't know why they bothered with a newspaper. Half the people in town couldn't even read.

But she could. A woman. Reading. Made no sense to him.

Yet there she sat, a shadowy form in the dim office, writing at her desk. Busy, busy.

He'd been watching her a lot lately. Busy as a little bee, she was.

He thought he had run her off when he'd burned the cabin she'd moved into near his diggings. But now she was stepping out with the railroader—his next target. Maybe he should take her instead. It was too soon to kill her, but if he took her now, he could keep her awhile, have some fun before it was time. He could always do the railroader later.

He sat back, whistling through the gaps in his teeth and thinking about her in there. All alone. Ripe for the taking.

Buffalo gals won't you come out tonight . . .

He had never killed a woman before—squaws didn't count—and the thought of it made his palms sweat.

. . . come out tonight, come out tonight . . .

Images filled his mind. Pale skin. Soft, plump tits. Legs kicking and thrashing beneath him.

Would she scream? Beg? Try to please him?

Closing his eyes, he sucked in air through his nose, imagining the smell of her, the feel of that pale skin, the heat of her around him.

If she was good, he might let her live. If not . . .

He had never done a white woman before. Maybe it was time.

Buffalo gals won't you come out tonight . . .

Slipping the knife back into the sheath laced to his fur boot, he rose from the bench and hitched his sagging trousers. He would have to play it stupid. Put her at ease by pretending to be just another harmless, simpleminded prospector. Lure her over to the livery and the mule tied in the woods by the creek.

Then he'd have her. And they'd both get busy.

. . . and dance by the light of the moon.

He looked around one last time, saw no one headed his way, and stepped into the street.

Time for some fun.

Twenty-three

Audra was chewing on her pencil and thinking about Ethan's hands on her breasts when the door opened and a man came in. A prospector—big, dirty, bushy beard, maybe even simple, judging by the dull eyes and slack jaw.

"May I help you?" she asked.

He shuffled for a moment, looked around, then swiped a filthy sleeve over his mouth. "You the lady what owns the burned-out cabin yonder in the canyon?"

She rose, thinking this must be the man Mr. Tilly had mentioned. "I am."

"I think I found something what belongs to you."

She waited patiently as he dug in one pocket, then the other.

"Here somewhere," he mumbled, checking the same places he had already searched. "Unless . . ." He stopped pawing and frowned at the back wall.

"Unless . . . ?" She had decided it couldn't be the medallion. Curtis was quite certain he had put it in the box with Father's papers, and she was equally certain she had seen it since they had moved everything from storage into the Arlan house.

"Coulda left it in my pack, I suppose. Yeah. I remember now. Put it there to keep it safe 'cause of the hole in my pocket." To demonstrate, he stuck one grimy finger through a rip in the bottom of his ragged jacket pocket. Muttering, he shuffled toward the door.

Realizing he was about to leave, Audra stepped around her desk. "Do you remember what it was you found?"

He paused and combed his fingers through his beard, his mouth twisting from side to side as he thought it over. "A flat, round thing," he finally said. "Yeah, metal. Real pretty. Gold colored, but not real gold. Brass, maybe. Hard to tell with the soot. I'll bring it by next time I'm in town."

So it *was* Father's medallion. How odd. "Wait," she said when he put his hand on the knob. "You said it was in your pack. Didn't you bring that with you?"

He nodded.

"So where is it?"

"With Jenny." He smiled, showing broken, discolored teeth and red, swollen gums. The poor man was dreadfully neglected. "She's my mule. And a good one. I leave her tied in the shade behind the livery so she don't get too hot."

"Perhaps you could get it now?" Audra ventured.

"Get what?"

"Your pack. So you can see if the round thing is inside."

"I'm kinda busy. I need to get back." He opened the door.

Audra thought quickly. The man was obviously simple. The chances of him forgetting about the medallion altogether or failing to bring it back to town were high. If she wanted the award back, her best recourse would be to go with him to get it. She would go as far as the livery, and wait with the livery-man, Mr. Driscoll, while the prospector retrieved his pack. That should be safe enough. "Perhaps I should go with you."

"Go where?"

She plucked her bonnet from the peg. "To wherever Jenny is tied. To check your pack for the round thing."

"It's kinda far. All the way over by the livery."

"I don't mind." After settling the bonnet on her head, she looked around, wondering if she should leave the office unlocked. Then figuring there was little enough to steal, she motioned him on. "After you, sir."

She was just closing the door when a voice called her name. Looking around, she saw Lucinda and Edwina and an unfamiliar auburn-haired woman coming toward her.

"Thank goodness we caught you," Lucinda said, rushing up. "I have someone I want you to meet."

Audra glanced back at the prospector, but saw he was shuf-fling away. "Sir," she called after him. "If you can wait . . ."

But he had already stepped off the boardwalk and was dis-appearing into the narrow walkway between the *Herald* build-ing and the one that housed Hattie's Millinery.

Drat.

"Who was that?" Edwina asked.

"I'm not sure. He said he'd found something in my burned cabin, but he seemed confused."

Lucinda waved a hand in dismissal. "Never mind that. If it's important enough, I'm sure he'll be back. Do you remember my telling you about our friend who was off in Texas with her husband? Well, they've finally returned, and here she is!" Beaming broadly, she pulled the auburn-haired lady forward. "Audra Pearsall, meet Madeline Wallace."

"She's a famous photographer," Edwina gushed. "And trav-els around in the cutest little gypsy wagon with her husband, taking pictures. You probably saw it parked outside the hotel. And she's also a real countess! But you don't have to curtsy. Does she, Maddie?"

The woman gave a smile that involved her entire face and brought a sparkle to her beautiful brown eyes. "Of course not. I should be offended if she did." Taking the hand Audra offered, she gave a gentle squeeze, then released it. "I am delighted to meet you, Audra," she said in a cultured British accent. "These two have said such wonderful things about you, I feel I know you already."

The woman's warmth immediately put Audra at ease. "Like-wise, I'm sure."

"Come along," Lucinda said. "We can have lunch at the hotel and catch Maddie up on all the news."

Audra sighed. "I wish I could. But I'm alone here in the office and can't be gone for more than a few minutes. But if you have time and don't mind the smell of ink and being crowded by a bulky printing press, I'd be delighted if you came inside and kept me company until my employer returns. I've never been to Texas and would love to hear about your travels."

"Of course."

As the other two women filed through the door, Lucinda paused beside Audra, mischief dancing in her lovely green eyes.

"And after we hear about Maddie's expedition," she said in a voice that wouldn't carry to the others, "perhaps you'll explain why Ethan Hardesty spent the night at your house. And don't bother to tell me it was for an interview, Miss Pearsall."

"Four murders?" blustered the Scotsman—Angus Wallace, the Earl of Kirkwell, or Ash, to his friends. "Does everything fall apart the minute I turn my back?"

The rise in his voice brought up the head of the giant gray dog stretched beside their corner table in the Red Eye. Neither Sheriff Brodie nor Tait Rylander took notice of the animal, but Ethan found it a bit unnerving to have the dog peer over the table at him even though the animal was resting on its belly.

"An Irish wolfhound," Wallace said proudly, seeing the direction of Ethan's gaze. "And a fine war dog he is."

"He hasn't killed anyone, has he?" Ethan said it with a laugh, as if he was joking and the notion was too absurd to believe.

The earl didn't smile back. "Only the one. And he deserved it, so he did. But usually Tricks, here, is as gentle as a kitten, are you no', lad?"

Usually?

The hound grinned up at his master, long rows of sharp teeth glinting in the lamplight shining down from the dusty fixture overhead. Then with a sigh, he dropped his rough-coated head back onto his outstretched paws.

Ethan wasn't sure which made him more uneasy—the dog or the owner.

While the other three men talked, Ethan studied the newcomer. Tall and lanky, with the erect posture of a military man—British Cavalry, retired, Rylander had said when he'd introduced him—the Scotsman was younger than his graying hair would indicate, strongly built, and had the greenest eyes Ethan had ever seen.

The paragon returned.

Rifleman, brawler, owner of the fine Scotch whiskey Ethan had borrowed, and an earl, to boot. A man of authority and position. With a huge dog.

He could be in trouble.

"This calls for a drink," the Scotsman said, motioning to the bartender.

"It's barely noon, Ash," Rylander reminded him.

"Aye. And do you think our wee wives will let us come back later? I dinna think so. No' until they've talked us to death. So before we're called to muster, I'll be having my drink, so I will, and listening to all your sorry reasons why you've made a shambles of our fine town."

Ethan saw the bartender coming with the half-empty bottle he'd borrowed and braced himself. As the barkeep plunked it on the table, the Scotsman studied it for a moment, then poured a small amount into each glass. He took a sip, sighed, and looked at Ethan.

"I'm told before you turned railroader you were an architect, Mr. Hardesty. Perhaps you could take a look at the house I'm building." He aimed a glare at the sheriff. "And tell me why the foundation is so off-kilter."

"I told you to put rocks in the holes," Brodie defended. "Even cedar won't last long when it's buried in dirt."

Ethan started to explain that he didn't do that kind of work anymore, when the Scotsman turned to him again. Although his expression remained pleasant, there was steel in his green eyes. "I'll pay for your help, so I will." He slid the bottle of whiskey across the table. "I dinna realize this was already open, but if you'll settle for half a bottle . . ."

Aware he'd been offered a way out that wouldn't require the use of guns or fists, Ethan gave a wry smile. "Sure." Besides, he couldn't avoid construction forever, especially if he planned to build a house for Audra.

The Scotsman grinned and clapped Ethan on the back so hard it knocked his hat crooked. "There's a good lad. We'll go out to assess the damage tomorrow." As he spoke, his gaze moved toward the door where a man wearing a dusty Stetson and dark oiled duster stood scanning the room. "And here's another fine lad. Rafe, over here," he called, lifting a hand to motion the bartender for another glass.

"Rayford Jessup," Ash said, as the newcomer pulled a chair from an empty table, flipped it around, and straddled it. "A Texan, and my new wrangler for the herd I'm building, as well as the finest man with a horse as I've ever seen. And women."

He laughed. "I dinna understand it, myself, but the lad charms the fillies and lasses alike without even uttering a word."

Ethan studied the wrangler as the earl completed the introductions.

Another big fellow—probably early thirties—blond and clean-shaven, in contrast to the Scotsman's graying hair and dark stubble, and about half as talkative as his employer. Despite that reticence, he displayed great confidence, and a calm, unhurried manner that would win over even the most skittish horse. Or, apparently, any woman.

Ethan didn't understand it, either. Rayford Jessup wasn't particularly handsome, and looked older than he probably was, with those squint lines around his dark blue eyes and the deep brackets around his mouth. There was a kind of sadness in his expression, the same weary resignation Ethan had often seen in Thomas—as if he had seen more than he should and still carried those troubling images in his mind. He was certainly too rough and weathered for, say . . . a woman as refined as Audra.

Then he gave a slight smile at some remark the earl made, and Ethan saw the appeal.

Hell.

But despite his initial unease, as the talk continued, Ethan began to feel a grudging respect for the Texan. Especially when he took the Scotsman's teasing in stride, and gave back as good as he got. When he bothered to speak, at all. He and Brodie could fill a book with all the words they didn't use.

Ethan took heart in that. Audra was a talker. She was too curious and persistent to settle for silence. And a man as uncommunicative as Rayford Jessup would drive her crazy. God love her.

Balance restored, Ethan settled back and let the rapidly disappearing, smooth, smoky whiskey do its work. They talked horses for a while, then moved on to the fire, the new water tower, and progress on the railroad.

Then Ash asked about the murders.

No longer smiling, Brodie gave him the details, and told him how the deaths of the woodcutter and prospector might have been accidental, even though both men had items missing when they were found—the woodcutter's watch, and the prospector's nugget. "But the Chinaman's throat was slit, so that was no accident. And Gallagher's death was as brutal as any I've ever seen."

"Why do you think their deaths are related to the first two?" Ash asked.

"The Chinaman was missing something, too," Tait said. "His pigtail."

Ethan explained his theory that another Chinaman hadn't done it because he wouldn't have kept the pigtail. "And Gallagher was missing his whip."

Ash sipped and thought about that. "Two deaths made to look like accidents, followed by two that were obviously murder. Hard to see how they were done by the same man. Or for the same reason. What does Thomas say?"

"Ask him yourself." Brodie nodded toward the Indian crossing toward them.

Grinning, Ash turned. "Heathen," he called with a wave.

"*Va'ohtama, hovahe.*" Pulling another chair up to the crowded table, Thomas sat back, arms crossed over his wide chest. "So the man with too many names has found his way back to his teepee. Where is your dress, Scotsman?"

"'Tis a kilt, ye scalp-stealing savage. Meet my friend, Rafe. He has blond hair, which a black heathen such as yourself might find appealing. But be careful. He's handy with a gun, so he is."

Thomas nodded.

Rafe Jessup nodded back.

Neither smiled.

The earl poured more whiskey—although Thomas took his usual ginger beer—then they all settled back to hear what Thomas had learned about the Irishman's death.

"He was ambushed between this building and the one next door. I found blood. Broken teeth. Then he was dragged to the street and carried away, on a horse, I think, since I did not find wagon tracks. I followed a blood trail into the canyon to the place where he was killed. He did not die easy." Turning to Brodie, he added, "And I did not find the whip you told me to look for."

Ethan thought for a moment. "Gallagher was a big man. Which means the killer must be at least as big to be able to subdue him."

"The barkeep says he was drunk," Brodie put in, "so he might have been easy to overpower. But he fought hard enough to lose teeth and get bloodied, so he wasn't unconscious when he was attacked."

"But he might have been when he was dragged out of the alley," Ethan said. "At least a hundred and eighty pounds. Dead weight. Lifted onto the back of a horse. It would take a big man to do that."

"Unless he had help," Rafe offered—the first words he'd spoken beyond acknowledging introductions and a jab or two at his employer.

"Help?" Tait frowned, a thoughtful look in his gray eyes. "You mean there were two men? Thomas, did you see evidence of that?"

The Cheyenne shrugged. "I could not tell."

Brodie sat back, his face blank with surprise. "Two killers?"

Ethan didn't know why he hadn't thought of it. It made perfect sense. "Think about it, Sheriff. Two supposedly accidental deaths. Two obvious murders. Different ways of killing, but with one thing in common. Something was missing from each victim."

"Two killers." Brodie still looked stunned.

"Bluidy hell. We have to put an end to this." Switching from affable earl to hard-eyed commander, Ash started barking orders. "Rafe, since you and Tait have soldiering, you help me set a perimeter around the town. Tait, round up anyone who can help. Brodie and Hardesty, you question everyone, even the Chinese. And especially anyone new to the area. Thomas, keep tracking. We need to know everyone who moves in and out of this canyon. Particularly any newcomers. Anything to add, Sheriff?"

"Only that I wish I'd thought of all that," he said with a smirk. Then, sobering, he added, "We especially need to warn all the outlying homes and ranches. Make sure they stay alert and keep weapons handy."

Tait nodded. "The hotel will provide food for the sentries."

"And there are extra cots at the jail," the sheriff put in. "For those who won't mind sleeping in a barred cell."

"I'll go by the newspaper." Ethan hoped he could be civil to Bonet when he arrived to escort Audra home, especially after the son of a bitch's accusations at the inquiry earlier. "Ask if we can get something in the next edition." Not that Bonet would comply. In fact, he hadn't run a single article about the murders, other than to use the finding of each body as another opportunity to blast the railroads. Kind of odd, now that he thought about it.

"Well, gentlemen, if that's it . . . ?" The earl rose.

The others followed suit.

Ethan tucked the nearly empty whiskey bottle under his coat. No use tempting the locals.

"Let's meet in the hotel dining room at eight tomorrow morning," Tait suggested. "Give us a chance to talk over our plans and make any adjustments necessary."

As the others started toward the door, Tait grinned at Ethan. "If I need to get in touch with you, Ethan, will you be at the hotel, or at the Pearsall place?"

"We talked. That's all."

"Ah, yes. An interview, I believe she called it."

Brodie, who was walking directly in front of them, looked back with a scowl. "You watch your step, Hardesty. Ed would be upset if you treated her new friend badly. And when my wife's upset, she makes sure I'm upset, too. I don't like it. Besides, Audra's a good woman."

"I know that," Ethan shot back, his temper rising. "And if it makes you feel any better, I already asked her to marry me."

Brodie stopped in the doorway. "You did? What'd she say?"

Heat rose up Ethan's neck. "That she's thinking about it. Move on. You're blocking the door."

Tait clapped his shoulder. "Not to worry, friend. We'll set the ladies on it. They love nothing more than planning weddings, right, Declan? I predict they'll have you roped, branded, and prancing down the aisle of the Come All You Sinners Church of Heartbreak Creek in less than a month's time."

"You poor bastard," Declan Brodie said, and laughed.

Twenty-four

That afternoon, as Ethan rode toward the newspaper office to meet Audra and ask Bonet to put a warning about the killer in the next edition, he saw her come out the office door and walk briskly toward the edge of town.

"Stubborn, hardheaded woman," he muttered, angling Renny across the road to intercept her at the end of the boardwalk.

"You were supposed to wait for me," he scolded, swinging down. "You know I don't like you walking home alone."

"You fuss more than Lucinda." Taking the hand he offered, she stepped from the boardwalk to the street, then released it. "I decided to leave early since Mr. Bonet is still angry with me over the inquiry, and seeing you might have thrown him into a conniption fit." As he fell into step beside her, she glanced back at the bulging saddlebags and the bedroll and rectangular fiddle box tied on top. "Are you leaving town?"

"No. I'm going to your house."

"For the audition?" A spark lit up her hazel eyes, then quickly faded. "But what about Father and the Abrahams?"

"They won't be a problem, since there's not going to be an audition. I don't want you so far from town without protection, so I'll be staying on your *couch*," he said with emphasis, "until the killer is caught."

"There's an extra bed in Father's room."

"The couch will be fine. That way, between me and Curtis and Phe, no one will get into the house unannounced. What did Mr. Bonet do to send you running?"

"Actually, I was more concerned about what you would do. You're not very subtle in your dislike."

"I don't trust him." As they walked, he told her about the latest thinking that there might be two killers. "Other than the prospector who was caught in the rock slide, all the victims had something to do with our work here. And you know how Bonet feels about the railroad."

"He might be a bit shortsighted, but I doubt he's a killer. Besides, he wasn't even here when the prospector and woodcutter died. Nor was I, if you'll recall. So it makes no sense that I would be a target or he would be the killer."

"He could have snuck in early," Ethan argued, unwilling to give up the idea. But even he could hear how far-fetched it sounded. "I still don't like him."

She slanted a look at him. "Jealous?"

He forced a laugh. "Of a man you can barely tolerate? Not hardly."

"How about the Wallaces' new wrangler, then?"

He stopped so abruptly Renny almost clipped his heels. "How do you know Rayford Jessup?"

"I don't. But I met Maddie Wallace today, and she told me he came with them from Texas to help her husband start a horse herd. She says he's quite handsome." Seeing his expression, she laughed. "You needn't scowl," she teased, nudging him forward again. "Maddie also said he was even less talkative than Declan Brodie, and you know how well that would sit with me."

He allowed himself to relax. "You do like to argue."

"Not argue. Discuss."

"Like you're doing now?" He grinned down at her. The clear, sunny days had brought a faint sprinkling of freckles across her pert nose and a rosy glow to her cheeks. She looked like a country girl now, rather than a pale city dweller. And decidedly happier than when he'd first seen her beside the railroad tracks two and a half months ago. She was changing.

And changing him.

Already she had made a profound impact on his life. After telling her about the terrible events in California, his night terrors had stopped, and even that dark time with Eunice Eckhart had faded into distant memory.

He had hope again.

They walked without speaking past the last building and a stand of aspens that stretched along the creek. The fire hadn't reached this end of town, and the rustle of new leaves in the late afternoon breeze added to the sound of rushing water and the clomp of Renny's hooves on the hard-packed dirt. Off to the left, beyond the equipment yard, the new water tower squatted like a giant beetle with a single, dripping tentacle hanging over the tracks. And in the workers' camp nearby, the clang of sledgehammers on metal rails blended with the rhythmic *chuff* of the locomotive that carried supplies up and down the line that had already reached a mile into the canyon. The sound of progress. Finally.

"You know, Audra," he said once they'd left the noise behind, "if you married me you wouldn't have to go back."

She looked up at him. "Back to the newspaper?"

He nodded.

"But I like the work."

"Even though you have to deal with Bonet?"

"He's not so bad."

"Wouldn't you rather work on your own stories?"

"My lurid novels of romance and adventure?" With a shrug, she kicked a pinecone into the weeds. "Perhaps someday. Right now I need the income."

"I can support you. And your father and the Abrahams. Even Phe." He smiled to mask his growing uncertainty. Why was she being so hardheaded about this? Couldn't she see they belonged together?

She gave a crooked smile. "Trying to rescue me again, are you?"

"Trying to take care of you, Audra. That's all." Seeing that belligerent furrow form between her brows, he hastily added, "And not because I think you need taking care of, but because it's what I want to do."

"Oh, Ethan." Slipping her hand into the crook of his elbow, she leaned against his arm. "You're such a dear man. And I appreciate you so much."

He almost snorted. *Appreciate?* Hardly a stirring endorsement after what he'd gone through on her behalf. Why not love?

Lust for? Admire beyond measure? He'd seen her half-naked, for God's sake. What more did he have to do to win this stubborn woman?

Struggling to ignore the soft press of her breast against his arm, he looked down at her. "But . . . ?" With Audra, there was always a "but."

"But I appreciate my independence, too. Is that so difficult to understand?"

He gave up. "You're such a bluestocking."

"Thank you."

"That wasn't a compliment." But knowing he had come up against a stone wall, he tried a different tack. "All right. I'm not an unreasonable man. If you insist, I'll allow you to continue working after we're married. But not for Bonet."

"Allow?" That laugh again. Another hug on his arm. Another press of her breast.

His thoughts scattered.

"Let's get through the audition first," she said, the smile still in her voice. "Then we can negotiate."

Lovely. A command performance with his entire future at stake. Ethan wondered if this was how a stud horse felt when he was led to the breeding pen.

When they arrived at the house a few minutes later, Phe and Winnie came out onto the porch to meet them. Both looked worried.

"What's wrong?" Audra cried, releasing Ethan's arm and rushing up the path to the steps.

Winnie held up a staying hand. "Everything fine. Curtis took your daddy up awhile ago. But he's had a rough afternoon."

An obvious understatement. Her apron was splattered with food stains, and the white doily-thing pinned to her gray hair was crooked. She looked older than she had two days ago.

"But you might ought go to the doctor for more of that cough tonic that make him sleep," Winnie suggested. "When Mr. Percy don't get his afternoon nap, we all pay the price."

"But what if he needs me?"

"I'll go," Ethan offered. "You tend your father."

"Thank you." Flashing him a grateful smile, Audra hurried inside.

"How much tonic should I get?" he asked Winnie.

"Much as you can. Mr. Percy get worse as the day pass. By evening, he too upset to eat or sleep. If we could calm him down some, he feel better."

"I'll be back soon as I can," Ethan called as he walked toward Renny.

He arrived at the clinic just before Doc and his wife, Janet, sat down to supper. By the grateful look on Doc's face when he answered the door, she hadn't fixed his favorite.

As he followed the older man to the dispensary in his office, Ethan told him about Mr. Pearsall's agitation in late afternoon. "They can't get him to settle down enough to eat or go to sleep."

"That's not uncommon with folks suffering dementia," Doc said. "Getting through the day is difficult for them, and by evening they've worn out themselves and everyone else." Opening a cabinet filled with vials, brown bottles, tins, and paper packets, he bent to peer inside. "You can try taking him for an afternoon walk. Feed him a light supper, no coffee. Especially avoid loud noises and confusing situations. A hot footbath and a cup of warm milk before retiring might help. Got any hops?"

Ethan shrugged.

"Me, neither. These will probably work as well." He pulled out a tin and a lumpy packet.

"They were hoping for more of that cough syrup you gave him before."

Doc dusted the tin and squinted at the writing across the top. "Too strong. Depresses the whole body. Might as well give him some of that Chinese herb." He looked up with a frown. "Not that I'm suggesting opium. The pipe's addictive. The poor man has enough problems without rotting his lungs and further dulling his mind. Try this." He handed the tin to Ethan. "Lemon balm tea. Two pinches in a cup of hot water before he goes to bed. If that doesn't help, here's valerian root." He passed over the packet. "Pour hot water over it and steep for three minutes. Tastes like horse piss, but try to get him to take it three times a day." He closed the cabinet. "That's about all I can do. Best prepare yourself. And Miss Pearsall. Sounds like he's getting close."

Ethan rode thoughtfully back to Audra's home. He had hoped to give Curtis and Audra another shooting lesson after supper, but that would be too loud for the old man. He supposed he and Curtis could do a thorough examination of the house to make sure all the doors and windows had good locks. That would take care of any intruders. But he didn't know how to help Audra through the crisis ahead with her father, other than wait it out with her. That's all he could do for any of them.

When he walked into the kitchen a few minutes later, he found Winnie stirring a cup by the stove and Curtis slumped at the table. "How's Mr. Pearsall?" he asked, setting the items Doc had given him on the counter by the sink.

"Asleep." Winnie heaved a great sigh. "Plumb wore hisself out, carrying on. Never seen the like."

"And Audra?"

"Upstairs. Crying." She swiped a hand over her watery eyes. "Breaks her heart to see her daddy this way."

Ethan pointed at the teacup. "What's that?"

"Tea."

"Thanks." He picked it up and headed toward the stairs.

"Whoa," Winnie called after him. "Where you think you going?"

"She needs me."

"She an unmarried woman, Mr. Ethan. Last thing she need is some man barging into her bedroom."

He hesitated, wondering how much to say, then realized since this old Negro couple was part of her family, they had a right to know. "I'm not just some man," he told them. "I'm the one she's going to marry. And right now, she needs me." Without waiting for a response, he turned and continued up the stairs.

Audra lay curled on her bed, fully dressed, including shoes, a faded patchwork quilt pulled over her shoulders. He thought she might be asleep, but when he crossed to the table beside her bed, she rolled over.

"Ethan?"

He stopped, cup in hand. "Sorry. Did I wake you?"

"I wasn't asleep. What's that?"

"Tea."

"Oh." Sitting up, she propped her back against the headboard. After situating the quilt over her legs, she reached for the cup.

It shook in her hand, but she managed to drink without spilling. A few more sips, then she set it on the nightstand and flashed him a weary smile. "Thank you."

He stood for a moment, studying her. He could see she was struggling. "Is there anything I can do? Maybe bring you something to eat?"

She patted the covers beside her. "Just sit with me for a while."

"Sure." He sat facing her, his bent knee beside her hip, and took her hand in both of his. It felt small and cold. He wanted to say something, but didn't know what. As usual, when it was important, words deserted him. So he sat in silence, gently stroking the back of her hand with his thumb. Her eyes closed. He studied her as she dozed, marveling that such delicate beauty could hide her fearless nature.

Then his stomach rumbled.

She opened her eyes. "Apparently, you haven't eaten."

"I was waiting for you."

"No need." Releasing his hand, she shooed him away. "I'm not hungry. In fact, I think I'll turn in."

He glanced at the window. "It's barely dark."

"Dark enough."

"I don't want to leave you."

"Sweet Ethan." Eyes glistening, she sat up and put her arms around his neck. "As long as I know you're nearby, I'll be fine."

When she started to draw back, he pulled her closer, felt the ridges of her shoulder blades under his palm and wondered again how something so frail could shelter a heart so strong. "I wish there was something I could do for you. For your father."

"I know." Her arms tightened in a hug, then loosened as she drew back far enough to look into his face. "Things will look better in the morning. For all of us." She gave his cheek a gentle pat. "Now go eat. Otherwise, your noisy stomach will keep me awake all night."

He turned his head and kissed her palm. Then leaned down and kissed her lips. Tasted tea and the salt of her tears, and kissed her again. Straightening, he tucked a loose curl behind her ear and gave her as stern a look as he could manage, considering the thoughts in his head. "You'll call me if you need me."

"Of course."

One more kiss, then he rose and left the room.

The Abrahams were already eating when he entered the kitchen. Ethan took his usual chair, spooned a portion of stew onto the plate in front of him, and dug in.

No one spoke. Curtis wasn't much of a talker, anyway, but Winnie's reticence was unusual. Mostly she chewed and thought, her dark gaze aimed his way. But she held her silence until Ethan finished eating and pushed back his plate.

"You ask her yet?"

He didn't pretend ignorance. "Twice."

"What'd she say?"

"She's thinking about it."

"Humpf." Rising, the old woman began clearing the table. "Child does too much of that, you ask me. Needs to stop thinking and start doing. Get on with life before it pass her by."

"Given time, I think she'll come around."

"Time, she got in plenty. What she lacking is good sense."

Curtis nodded toward the porch. "I unsaddled your horse and put him in the paddock with Cricket. Fed him, too. Looks like rain, so I left a stall door open."

Ethan had wondered about the heavy stickiness in the air. He'd blamed it on nerves, but apparently a warm spring rain was on the way. "I appreciate that."

"Saddle was loaded up like you was leaving town. Didn't know whether to leave everything tied where it was, or bring it inside."

"I'm not leaving town. I'm staying here, instead."

Winnie turned from the sink to frown at him.

"On the couch," he added. "There's a killer running loose, and I'll be staying until he's caught." He looked from Winnie to Curtis, waiting for them to object.

Neither did.

Curtis pushed back his chair and rose. "Left your things on the porch. See you in the morning."

Winnie remained by the sink, drying dishes with more vigor than necessary.

"I'm here as added protection, Winnie. That's all."

Setting down her towel, she turned. "And why you think a

killer be coming after two worn-out Africans, a woman, and a sick old man? What we ever do to warrant that?"

"I don't know why he does what he does, Winnie. Maybe he doesn't have a reason, but kills because he likes it. Or picks victims randomly whenever they cross his path. I just want to keep all of you safe."

"Makes no sense." Winnie sucked on her bottom lip and thought for a moment. "From what I hear, he mostly after railroad folks."

Ethan didn't mention the dead prospector. "So it would seem."

"Then maybe he come after you next. Maybe by staying here, you bring him right to our door."

Ethan sat back, shocked that he hadn't thought of that. Could he be a target? Was his presence here putting them in more danger, instead of less? "Should I go?"

"No, you best stay. Either way, he crazy, and we better off with you around. But on the couch. Understand?"

Ethan nodded. "I understand." Rising, he went to get his belongings from the porch. When he returned, the kitchen was empty.

He stood for a moment, listening to the soft *whump* of distant thunder, then, calling Phe, went back out onto the porch as the first fat drops began to fall.

Twenty-five

Jarred from deep sleep, Audra bolted upright, her pulse pounding in her ears, fear clutching at her throat.

It was dark. Other than the tap of raindrops against the glass panes of her windows, all was quiet. Then what had awakened her?

Throwing back the covers, she rose and padded from the room. The plank floor felt cool and gritty beneath her feet. Cooking odors hung in the windowless hallway, along with the smell of urine from the linens she had left on the landing after changing Father's bed. Pausing outside his room, she listened. Heard nothing.

Alarmed, she pushed open the door.

He sucked in a deep gasping breath, panted several times as if starving for air, then finally settled into his usual snore.

Dear God. She sagged against the door frame, her legs wobbly with relief. Was he forgetting how to breathe, too? After a few minutes, once she had assured herself that he was breathing regularly, she pulled the door shut.

Darkness closed around her. The air felt thick. Hard to breathe. In the distance, thunder rumbled like heavy stones rolling across a wooden bridge. Too awake to go back to sleep, she returned to the bedroom for her robe. She put it on, tied the sash, then moved to the top of the stairs and looked down, thoughts racing through her head. No light showed, not even a flicker of firelight across the floor.

Was he asleep? Listening to the rain? Thinking of her?

She closed her eyes, imagined him in the dark. The need to see him rose inside her like a flood, drowning reason and filling her body with a nameless want.

Just a touch. A hand to hold on to. Something to tell her she wasn't alone.

She shouldn't go down there. A virtuous woman wouldn't. It was a violation of all the rules of decorum and everything she'd been taught.

She went down the stairs.

It was cooler at the bottom. Less stuffy. Quiet as a tomb.

She glanced toward the kitchen. It was dark except for the slightly paler square of the window over the sink. No coals glowed on the hearth. Phe didn't come to greet her as she usually did when Audra came down. Puzzled, she turned toward the other end of the long open room where the couch was. If Ethan snored, she couldn't hear him. Was he even there? Moving silently on bare feet, she crossed into the parlor, where she found a tangle of bedding strewn across the cushions, but no Ethan.

As she straightened, a breath of cool air swirled around her ankles and fluttered the hem of her robe. Realizing the front door was open, she moved silently toward its paler shadow in the blackness of the wall. At the threshold, she stopped and listened. Faint breathing. The rhythmic creak of the rocker.

"Ethan?"

"Jesus!" A clatter as he leaped from the rocker. Canine toenails scrabbling on wooden planks. "You scared the hell out of me!"

"Hush. You're frightening Phe." Bending, she held out a hand to the dog cowering at the end of the porch. "Come, sweetie. It's just me. You're all right."

The dog sidled warily closer, then relaxed against Audra's leg when she realized she'd been summoned for an ear-scratching, rather than a kick.

"What are you doing, creeping around in the dark?" Ethan asked, still standing beside the chair.

Now that she was here, all the reasons that had compelled her to come seemed foolish and immature. She was afraid? Lonely? Looking for someone to chase her night terrors away? She wasn't a child.

Giving Phe one last pat, she straightened and walked to the railing. Lifting her face to the cool night air, she closed her eyes and let the patter of slow rain soothe away the last remnants of whatever had awakened her.

"My father is dying."

She didn't realize Ethan had moved until she felt his breath in her hair. A moment later, his arms slid around her from behind and pulled her back against his warm, hard chest. "I'm sorry."

He felt so solid. Real. Strong enough to hold her if she fell. That awareness opened something inside her, released the fear and pain she'd held inside for so long. Folding her arms over his, she leaned against him and let his strength flow through her. "I thought I would have more time with him. I wanted that so badly. Prayed for it. But now . . ."

Her voice broke. Tears burned in her eyes. "He's suffering so much, Ethan. He's so angry, and bitter, and confused. I just want him to find peace."

"I know." His arms tightened. Warm breath swept past her ear.

Turning her head into the hollow of his throat, she felt the strong, steady beat of his pulse against her temple. "I'm glad you're here, Ethan."

"I wouldn't be anywhere else. This is where I belong."

For a long time they stood that way, his arms around her waist, her head turned and resting on his chest, the steady drip of rain matching the tempo of his heart against her back.

She loved this man. Needed him. Wanted him in ways she was only now beginning to understand.

But yet, that last niggling doubt remained. As persistent as a fly buzzing circles in her mind, it finally drove her to speak. "Do you love me, Ethan?"

His hesitation lasted less than a heartbeat, but still, she noted it.

"You really have to ask?"

Answer a question with a question. Which was no answer at all.

"Yes, I have to ask."

"Of course I do."

"Then say it."

Another hesitation. But this time, he moved his hands to her shoulders and turned her around to face him. "What's this about, Audra?"

"It's about everything, Ethan. The most important thing."

"I don't understand."

"I need to know that I'm not just another stray you feel you have to rescue. That this is more than duty or obligation. I want to know that you truly love me, Ethan. And I need to hear you say that."

"I do love you, Audra. And have, since the first day. To be precise," he added with a chuckle, "it was when you asked me to shoot you. I'd never had a request like that before."

"Don't make jokes about this, Ethan. I couldn't bear it."

"Sweetheart." He took her face in his hands and kissed her. "I'm not joking. When I saw you sitting there by your broken buggy, I expected tears, pleas, the whole helpless female act. Instead, you asked me to shoot you. Hell, you even instructed me where to put the bullet. I knew then that you were a woman with rare strength. And a bizarre sense of humor, which I admired even more."

She shrugged to hide how much his words had pleased her. "That's not very romantic."

"Oh. You want romance. Then how about the day you accused me of setting fire to your cabin? That was when I knew I had to have you for my wife."

"You're absurd."

"Maybe." Yet, his voice held no amusement, and there was a light tremble in his hands as he brushed back her hair. "But until that moment, I didn't realize how much your trust and respect meant to me."

"You were never truly in danger of losing it. I was wrong to accuse you."

"Thank you for that." Dipping his head, he gave her another quick kiss. "But the day I knew how much I needed you was when I found Gallagher whipping you. That was the worst moment in my life. Just the thought of losing you . . ."

Hearing the emotion in his voice brought a catch to hers. "But again, you came to my aid."

"And I always will, Audra. It's what I want to do. What I need to do. Because you're the woman I'll love all the rest of my life."

Unable to speak, she put her arms around his neck. "I love you, too, Ethan."

He hugged her hard and for a long time, then, keeping his hands on her hips, leaned back to look at her. "Since when?"

"Since the fire." Needing to touch him, she smoothed the shirt over his chest, learning the curves and hollows of his muscular frame. "When Father ran off and I found you sitting on the log beside him in the woods. You were so gentle and patient with him. So kind. How could I not love a man like that?" She rose on her toes to kiss him, then kissed him again because she liked doing it. He tasted like coffee and cinnamon and Ethan. When she finally settled back on her heels, that odd, delicious, shimmery feeling was surging through her again. "So when are we going to have that audition?"

His arms dropped away. "We're not," he said, and put space between them.

Undeterred, she stepped forward to fill it. "Ever?" She trailed a teasing fingertip up his chest to circle that deep hollow at the base of his throat.

"Audra, stop."

Leaning against him, she locked her arms around his neck. "Stop what?" she whispered into his ear.

"Teasing me." He was breathing faster now and heat was rolling off his tense body. "I'm trying to do the right thing here."

"Why? I want you. You want me, too." As she spoke, she pressed her pelvis against his. "I can feel it."

"Audra!"

But she noticed he didn't move away. She kissed his neck, ran the tip of her tongue around that hollow in his throat, felt muscles flex against her breasts. "Did you bring the preventatives?"

"Jesus." With a groan of defeat, he grabbed her at the waist and turned her around so that her back was against him. "I have another idea." One hand moved up to stroke her breast. The other turned her head back toward his. "Kiss me and I'll show you."

Twisting, she rose eagerly to meet him. It was a slow, lingering kiss that awakened that urgent, restless yearning again and sent heat pooling low and deep in her belly.

Then he was loosening the sash and sliding his hand inside her robe. He pulled down her shift. Cool air swept over her exposed breast before he covered it with his warm hand.

She shivered, feeling again the hot rush of desire. Arching into his hand, she rose for a deeper kiss. Less gentle now. Insistent. Hungry.

"You're so soft," he whispered against her mouth, his fingers tracing slow, teasing circles. "So perfect." He tugged at a hard peak.

Sensation flooded her body, robbed her of thought. Breaking the kiss, she leaned back against him, mouth open, her mind in shambles. *Don't stop.*

His other hand drifted down past her waist, lower, fingers pulling up her gown. "I want to touch you. Feel your heat."

She shivered, anticipation arcing through her as cool air reached her knees, her thighs. Then he was there. Touching her where no one ever had. Making her feel things she had never felt.

She was panting now, her legs trembling, her hands clutching at his arm.

"Shh," he whispered, his other hand still stroking her breast. "I've got you. Just let go."

She forgot how to breathe. How to think. Mindless with something she didn't understand, she reached up and grabbed his head, pulled it down to hers.

"Ethan," she gasped, her mouth open to his, her body straining, needing something . . . wanting . . .

Then suddenly it burst inside her. Rolling through her limbs in pulsing waves. Transporting her into white, hot light where she lost herself in pure delight.

It seemed forever before she found herself again. Her breathing slowed. Tiny sparks of pleasure danced along nerves that felt flayed, and her heart fluttered like wings against the walls of her chest. If he hadn't been holding her, her legs would have given way.

"Oh my Lord," she gasped.

Chuckling softly, he pulled her robe closed and wrapped his arms around her. "Now you'll marry me."

* * *

Audra slept late the next morning—Father, too, it seemed, judging by the snore on the other side of the wall. She dressed hurriedly, wavering between the need to rush down to see Ethan, and the urge to hide in her room until she was certain he'd left. Had she truly behaved in such a brazen manner? In front of the dog?

And yet, whenever she allowed herself to think about what Ethan had done, and how she had felt when he'd done it, she wanted to find him and do it again.

She was a brazen hussy. A true wanton. They had best marry soon or she would disgrace herself forever.

When she finally went downstairs, not only was Ethan still there, he was sitting at the table, gobbling food like a starving man and looking supremely pleased with himself.

"Good morning," she said, avoiding his eyes as he rose to pull out her chair.

"I told them," he said.

Knees buckling, she sank onto the seat. "You *what*?"

Curtis grinned and nodded.

"Congratulations," Winnie called from the stove. "When you finally doing it?"

"D-Doing it?"

Laughing at her look of horror, Ethan returned to his chair on the other side of the table. "Getting married."

Air rushed out of her. She glared at him, wanting to strike him. Hug him. Do that thing again. "I'm n-not sure," she stammered.

It pleased her that her answer wiped the smug look off his face, so just for spite, she added, "I wouldn't want to rush into anything, you see." Which—despite her lamentable lapse into wanton behavior—was true. But when she saw Ethan's look of disappointment and hurt, she let her annoyance go on a sigh.

"It's Father. I've always dreamed of him walking me down the aisle. But now . . ." She shrugged to cover the sudden tightness in her throat. "I don't know what to do. He wouldn't understand and it would only confuse him. But to marry without him at my side . . . it doesn't feel right." She looked to Ethan for understanding, but he said nothing, his mouth set in a grim line.

Curtis sighed and shook his head.

"You wrong." Winnie crossed to the table, plopped into the empty chair beside Audra, and put a wrinkled hand on her arm. "Mr. Percy not going to get no better. You know that. But right now, he still have his good days. Maybe he able to walk you down the aisle. Maybe he not. But you can't wait on him to start living, child. Was he able to, he tell you that hisself."

Avoiding the faces around her, Audra looked out the kitchen window, where the night's rain had given way to a crisp, clean sky so brightly blue it matched Ethan's eyes. Perhaps Winnie was right. Perhaps Father would have one of his good days and she could have the wedding she had always wanted. If not, she would still be surrounded by friends, and she would still be marrying the man she loved. That was what was most important, wasn't it?

Resolved, she smiled across the table at Ethan. "I'll check with the ladies. I'm certain they'll want to be involved in the planning. Perhaps a month?"

"Tomorrow would be better." Ethan's grin turned wicked. "I know how impatient you are."

"Tomorrow?" Winnie bounded to her feet. "Laws, no. We got a dress to make and cooking to do and the preacher to talk to and music—"

"Okay." Laughing, Ethan held up a hand. "Do what you need to. I'll cover any expenses as long as you get it done by the middle of June. That'll give me time to settle with the railroad."

"Settle what?" Audra asked.

"My employment. I have to give them some sort of notice."

"You're giving up your position?"

"Of course." He looked from one surprised face to the other. "I don't want to move from here. Do you?"

Head-shaking all around.

"Good. Then unless my employers at the Denver and Santa Fe want me to continue working here in Heartbreak Creek, I'll find something else to do."

"Praise the Lord." Winnie poked her husband's shoulder. "We staying."

But Audra wasn't convinced. "Like what?"

He shrugged. "Like architecture. My suspension ended over

a year ago. I still have my certification, although I may have to renew it. And both Tait and Angus, or Ash, or Wallace, or whatever that Scottish earl calls himself, want me to draw up building plans for them, so I should stay busy for a while."

Audra studied him, trying to read his expression. She remembered all the times she had seen him shy away from anything involving construction. She didn't want him to feel driven back into a profession he had seemed desperate to avoid. There were other ways to earn a wage.

"Is that what you want to do, Ethan? Go back into architecture?"

"Well . . ." Frowning, he scratched his chin and gave it some thought.

But Audra wasn't fooled. She had seen the laughter behind his blue eyes.

"If I can't live off widow ladies with lots of money," he finally said, "or the salacious novels of romance and adventure you have yet to write, I guess it'll do."

"Oh, you!" Winnie popped him with her dishrag. "Quit your teasing, Mr. Ethan. We got no time for it." Turning to her husband, she poked his shoulder again. "Curtis, first thing, you make sure that buggy clean, repaired, and ready to go. Then get a new shirt. And since Mr. Ethan paying, I'll get me a new dress, too. Lawd, Lawd, ain't it grand!"

Swinging the rag over her head, she danced a shuffling circle on the kitchen floor. "We finally got us a wedding to celebrate!"

Twenty-six

The next week passed in a blur for Audra as news of the engagement became the talk of the town. She knew the excitement wasn't solely because of her wedding. It was obvious, as seen in the large turnout at the church social, that country folk enjoyed any excuse to celebrate, and a wedding that promised food, music, and dancing was the best excuse of all.

Even Mr. Bonet offered his well wishes, although they were somewhat subdued. Audra had long suspected he held stronger feelings for her than friendship, and the disappointment she saw in his eyes when she told him the news momentarily damped her joy.

"I wish you all the best, Miss Pearsall. Mr. Hardesty is a lucky man."

"Thank you, sir."

"Will you continue to work after you marry?"

"I hope to. Mr. Hardesty knows how much I like being at the *Herald*, and has encouraged me to stay as long as you need me."

"Very generous of him, considering the things I said during the inquiry into the Irishman's murder."

Audra didn't know how to respond to that. Or how to react when he took her hand in his. There was something off about this entire conversation.

Staring down at her hand, he said, "I now know I was wrong

to accuse him of any involvement in Gallagher's death. Especially since my doing so created a difficult situation for you." He looked up, his dark brown gaze boring into her with that disturbing intensity that reminded her of Richard Villars. "For that I apologize, Miss Pearsall. And offer my heartfelt hope that we will always be friends."

"Of course, Mr. Bonet. I would have it no other way."

"Thank you." With one of his infrequent smiles, he released her hand. "Now let's get this edition out. I'm sure your neighbors are awaiting the official announcement so they can make plans to help you celebrate."

So much for her dream of a small, intimate ceremony. With only a few weeks to make all the arrangements, she might have felt overwhelmed if the ladies hadn't immediately stepped in.

"We have it all figured out," Lucinda had announced during tea with the ladies the Saturday afternoon after the announcement. She patted a tablet beside her plate. "Everything is right here. You're not to worry about a thing, Audra."

Edwina leaned forward, her blue eyes alight with enthusiasm. "Winnie and I are making your dress. I have a book of designs I want you to look over so we can get started as soon as possible." Turning to Maddie and Lucinda, she added, "Do you remember how much fun the fittings were when we were working on my dress for Declan's and my second wedding?"

Second wedding? Another secret to ferret out?

"Fun?" Maddie laughed. "What I recall most is how often you interrupted those fittings with trips to the necessary."

"And snacking," Lucinda added. "I never knew someone so skinny could eat so much."

"Oh, hush. I had reason. I was eating for two, remember. It's a shame, Lucinda, that you gave your wedding dress to that charity in Denver. You and Audra are near the same size. I could easily have altered it to fit."

Lucinda waved the suggestion aside. "Nonsense. Every bride deserves her own wedding dress. Even more so when the groom is covering all the bills. And get that worried look off your face, Audra. I assure you Ethan can afford it. Especially with that generous bonus the railroad paid him to stay on until the bridge line is completed. More tea or cookies, anyone?"

Getting no takers, she nodded to the server standing near

the door into the kitchen, then returned to her list. "Maddie, have you ordered the necessary photographic supplies?"

"I have. And that nice Mr. Tilly has consented to assist."

"Excellent. Audra, I'm assuming you'll be having the ceremony at Come All You Sinners."

Audra nodded.

"Good." Lucinda wrote on her tablet, then looked up with a worried frown. "I know Ethan set June fifteenth as the date, but that's a Thursday. Do you think you could convince him to wait until Saturday, June eighteenth?"

"Certainly." Although it wasn't Ethan who would suffer for the delay. Ever since that almost-audition the other evening, he had kept a distance between them, which had only increased her impatience for the full audition. She was utterly shameless.

"I'll have Pastor Rickman set aside the date. You may clear, Miriam. Thank you." While the efficient woman who handled everything from kitchen duties to housekeeping chores, and even some accounting tasks, cleared away the dirty dishes, Lucinda flipped through her tablet, making notations here and there.

Watching her, Audra understood why she was such a capable manager. The woman was a relentless organizer.

"Now let's settle the particulars of the ceremony, shall we?" Lucinda said, moving on to the next topic. "Weather permitting, we will begin the procession from the hotel to the church at one in the afternoon. Maddie, may I count on you to help decorate the Pearsall buggy?"

"Of course. Shall we drape it so Audra isn't seen before the ceremony?"

"A wonderful idea. Does Ash still intend to lead out with his bagpipes?"

"I'm afraid so. Audra, be sure to bring cotton for your ears."

"Then Ethan will come next," Lucinda went on, "followed by his attendants, Tait and Declan."

Edwina raised her hand. "If it's acceptable with you, can Thomas stand in for my husband? If Declan and I are both up front, who will watch the children?"

"Perhaps they might want to participate," Audra offered. "Brin could be the flower girl and her three older brothers could act as ushers."

A moment of silence as they all envisioned the disastrous results if the Brodie children were allowed to move freely about the church without strict supervision.

"We daren't," their stepmother finally said.

"You're right." Lucinda made a mark on her paper. "Audra, will Ethan mind if Thomas steps in?"

"More to the point," Maddie interrupted, "will Thomas mind?"

Another pause while they contemplated the likelihood of Thomas showing up at the church, much less taking part in the ceremony.

"Perhaps we should let Ethan pick his own attendants," Audra suggested.

Lucinda shook her head. "I've found the most efficient way to handle these things is to make all the arrangements, then tell the men what they're to do."

"I so agree. If I left such things to Declan, they'd never get done."

"How about Curtis?" Audra asked. He was as much a part of her life as Winnie. It was fitting that he should be part of her wedding day, too.

"Perfect!" Another mark on the paper. "So the order will be Ash with his pipes, then Ethan, followed by his attendants, Tait and Curtis. Then the female attendants, then the buggy carrying Audra and her father."

"Who will drive it, if Curtis is walking with Ethan?" Edwina asked.

They mulled that over for a moment, then Maddie said, "Rayford Jessup! Ash says he's very good with horses."

"And I'd like for Winnie to ride with me and Father," Audra put in. "That way if there are any issues . . ."

"Of course." Lucinda wrote that down then sat back. "And who will your attendants be?"

Audra beamed at the ladies gathered around the table. "Why, you three, of course. I wouldn't want anyone else standing beside me."

"Oh, dear." Maddie gave a regretful sigh. "I would love to, of course, but if I'm to take photographs . . ."

"Lucinda and Edwina, then."

"We'd be honored, won't we, Ed?" Without waiting for an answer, Lucinda asked Audra, "And who will give you away?"

That was a sticky one. What Audra wanted might not be possible. "My father, if he's up to it. If not . . ." She shrugged. "Is it permissible to walk down the aisle alone?"

"Whatever you want to do is permissible," Lucinda said firmly. "I had my guardian, Mrs. Throckmorton, walk with me. You must do what works best for you, Audra. It's your wedding."

"Pru walked with me." Edwina chuckled. "Caused a bit of a stir, but everyone got over it as soon as the food was served, bless their hearts."

"Then if Father isn't able, I'd like Winnie to take his place. She's been like a mother to me for the last twenty years."

"Done." More writing. "And now for decorations."

And on and on. But with Lucinda's direction, and Maddie's eye for composition, the details were quickly ironed out, except for the music selections, which Audra would discuss later with Biddy Rickman and the choir ladies.

Lucinda consulted her list. "Just to be clear before we put it in the *Herald* . . . June eighteenth, procession at one, ceremony at two. Weather permitting, a potluck picnic on the grounds around the church, followed by music and dancing until dark. It's an open invitation to all townspeople who want to attend. Anything else?"

When there were no more suggestions, Lucinda closed her tablet and smiled at Audra. "And as Tait's and my gift to you and Ethan, after the other guests have dispersed, the wedding party will retire to the hotel for a formal dinner and private celebration of our latest Heartbreak Creek wedding."

"Thomas found another body," Sheriff Brodie said as they took their seats at their usual corner table in the Red Eye—Brodie, the Scotsman, Rafe Jessup, Tait, and Ethan. "Thomas thinks it's the surveyor with the Southern Utah and Atlantic. There was a tripod and survey equipment nearby. He's still out there checking for anything else."

"Bluidy hell." The Scotsman signaled the bartender for a

bottle and glasses, then folded his arms on the scarred tabletop. "I canna believe anybody got past the sentry line."

"They didn't. This one died awhile ago."

"How?" Tait asked.

The sheriff waited until the bartender came and went. "Drowned in a foot of water." His expression showed how likely he thought that was. "But animals had been at him so it was hard to tell if he had been killed there or dragged into the water later."

Since it was the Scotsman's whiskey they were drinking, they waited for him to pour. They drank, gave silent tribute to the fine whiskey and sorry news, then Ethan asked if anything was missing from the dead man's body.

Brodie nodded. "That thing that goes on top of the tripod."

"The transit theodolite. It helps with triangulation. No surveyor would be without it. So now we have five dead, four of whom were railroad workers."

"Probably rules out anyone from a competing line," Tait said. "The only one who has shown real interest so far is the Southern Utah and Atlantic. And they'd be more likely to kill one of our surveyors, than one of their own."

"I think we can agree," Brodie said, "that it's someone who doesn't want *any* railroad coming through the canyon. Someone local, maybe."

"Most of the townspeople are glad we're here," Tait pointed out. "They're working again. More work and more money means they don't have to move elsewhere."

"So who would benefit most if the railroad dinna come through?"

They thought for a moment. "Peter Bonet hates the railroads," Tait said. "Blames them for his brother's death. But I don't think he'd be strong enough to do what was done to Gallagher."

"Unless he had help," Rafe Jessup suggested.

Ethan thought of the cold detachment Eunice had shown when he'd confronted her about the trinkets she had stolen from the patients she had killed. And the way she had laughed when she'd slashed at him with the knife. No anger or fear. None of the reactions one would expect during such a highly charged moment. Even during intercourse, she had shown little emotion.

A hunger to control him, perhaps . . . yet never any true passion.

But Peter Bonet was a passionate man. He showed all the emotions she lacked. Anger, resentment, jealousy, grief over his brother's death. He was incapable of being as coldly calculating as this killer seemed to be. "It's not Bonet," he said. "He arrived in town after the fire. And three of these deaths occurred before then. Quite a bit before, in the cases of the prospector and surveyor."

Brodie nodded. "And I doubt whoever is doing this would make his dislike of the railroads that obvious, anyway."

"Which brings us back to my question," Ash said. "Who would benefit most if the railroad dinna come through?"

After a long silence, Tait said, "It's got to be someone local. Someone who hates the railroad and is able to move freely through the canyon without rousing suspicion. Any thoughts on who that might be?"

An idea came to Ethan. One that he should have considered from the first. Voices faded as he played it through his mind, studying it from all angles until it finally made sense. "We're looking at this all wrong."

"How so?"

Ethan turned to the sheriff. "Did Thomas say how long the surveyor had been dead? Could he tell if he died before or after the prospector?"

Brodie shook his head. "His guess is they both died several months ago, but with the cooler weather back then, it's hard to tell."

"When was the woodcutter killed?"

Brodie thought a moment. "First week in March. A week before you came."

"And the Chinese worker?"

"During the fire. Early April. Maybe the fifth."

"And Gallagher?"

"The night of the church social. May fourth."

"So we know for sure the last three murders were a month apart." Ethan thought back to what he was doing the night Gallagher was killed. He had gone to Audra's to tell her about what happened in California. He remembered standing on the porch, watching her doze, seeing the tears tracks on her face . . .

in the dark? No, there was light. From the full moon barely showing above the trees.

"It's the lunar cycle," he blurted out, excitement surging through him. "That's what drives him. Like any predator, he hunts during the full moon."

"Bollocks." Ash sat back with a sigh. "We had a killer like this in India. A Punjabi soldier who said evil spirits made him rape and kill women in the villages. Verra brutal."

"Was anything taken from the victims?" Ethan asked, wondering if the habit of keeping mementos of their kills was something only Eunice and the Heartbreak Creek killer did.

"I dinna ken. The local tribesmen took care of it."

Tait swirled the whiskey in his glass. "We must be missing something."

"Aye. The killer. And we're no' getting any closer to catching the bluidy bastard sitting in here sucking down my whiskey. Come along, Rafe. Time to change the sentries."

"Hold on," Ethan said as they started to rise. "There's one more thing we need to consider."

They sank back down, but impatience showed in their faces. Ethan felt it, too. Six capable, intelligent men, including a skilled Cheyenne tracker, against one sloppy killer. This should have ended months ago.

"Of the five murders—assuming the prospector was first and there are no other bodies waiting to be found—only the last four involved a railroad worker. So why the prospector? What's different about him?"

"He's local," Tait said. "If the killer is local, too, it's probable that they knew each other."

"And what was missing from his body?" Ash asked.

"If you believe his partner, Weems," Brodie said, "a fair-sized nugget."

"Which probably means he had found a strike of some kind. So who would benefit most from his death?"

"His partner. But Weems was the one who reported him missing."

"*After* animals had dug him up and Thomas found his body in the rock slide."

Brodie sat back, a look of surprise on his face. "You think Weems killed him?"

Ethan shrugged. "Why not?"

"Then why kill the other four?"

"Maybe to deflect suspicion from himself. Think about it, Sheriff. If you'd found the prospector's body first, who would you have suspected? His partner, Weems. But now, after four more deaths, all seemingly related to the railroad, he's hardly a suspect."

"We need to think like a prospector," Rafe Jessup suggested.

All faces turned toward him. The Scotsman's wrangler might not speak often, but when he did, his words made sense.

"You've struck gold. You don't want to share, so you kill your partner. Then a surveyor comes snooping around, so you kill him, too. You try to make the deaths look accidental so no one else comes snooping around. But suddenly there's a bridge line going through and workers are wandering all over your canyon. The only way you know to keep them from stumbling onto your find is to do something to scare them off."

"He tried vandalism and fire," Brodie said. "When that didn't work, he turned to murder."

"Makes sense," Tait allowed. "We need to talk to Weems again."

"Even if he's not the killer, he might know of other prospectors in the area."

"There's something else," Ethan said. "The murders are getting more brutal each time. I think the killer is starting to enjoy it, and no longer cares whether his victim is with the railroad or not."

"So?"

"So now anyone could be his next target."

"Hell."

The Scotsman gave Ethan a studied look. "When did you say you were getting wed, lad?"

"June eighteenth. Why?" But he was already counting in his head.

The wizard with numbers got there first. "Let's hope he's no' after you, then. Since the next full moon is the third of June."

Twenty-seven

Hitching the bulky weight of the bedding higher on his shoulder, Ezra Weems carefully worked his way over the rocks and rubble strewn along the dark passage. In the confined space, sound was distorted. Sight was narrowed to the small circle of light cast by the lantern hanging from his other hand, and his shuffling steps became the whispered voices of the shadows dancing ahead of him along the rocky corridor.

He wasn't afraid. The voices didn't bother him anymore. He liked the dark. The closeness. The way light flashed on ribbons of water trickling down the walls and made them glisten like veins of ore.

But he knew there was no silver here. Or gold. Only bones and memories.

The deeper he went, the colder it became. The air grew damp and smelled faintly of piss and animal droppings and decay. He reminded himself to bring more blankets. He didn't want her taking sick and dying before it was time.

His foot rolled on a loose stone. He stumbled, and the chain hanging from the crook of his arm clanked against the rocks, startling him. He paused to listen as the echoes bounced along the stone walls. Would her screams last long enough to reach the entrance, or make it out of the airhole? If they did, would they give him away?

He laughed. Give him away to who? No one knew of these

old tunnels. He had hidden the entrance too well, and the air-hole was hidden under a bush. Besides, trespassers rarely came this far into the canyon, and if they did, he took care of them. He wasn't stupid. Which is why when the railroader came looking for her—which he knew he would—she'd be so deep underground he would never hear her. No one would know what had happened to her until he hung her up during the full moon.

Jiggety jig.

Two turns left, a dogleg right, then the third opening past the airhole. He was as familiar with this maze of tunnels as he was with the veins on the back of his hand, and knew this was the perfect place to put her. Deep and dark. Even if she somehow slipped her collar, she would never find her way out without a lantern. And he would make certain there were no lanterns within reach of her chain.

Home again, home again, jiggety jig.

Stepping through the opening, he let the bedding slide from his shoulder and set down the lantern. He stood for a moment, listening to the silence, imagining her in the dark, hearing nothing but her own breathing and waiting for the sound of his footsteps. Would she hope it was her railroader come to save her? If he told her he would trade her for him, would she save herself? Or stay here in the cold, dead, dark until her mind snapped?

He'd seen it happen before. It never took long.

Whistling through the stubs of his teeth, he bent and slipped the chain through the eyebolt anchored in the rock, then snapped the lock closed. He checked the collar on the other end of the chain and the lock that would secure it to her neck. Satisfied, he straightened.

The cow's in the barn and here comes the pig.

By his calculations it was four days until the next full moon. If everything went as planned, he would grab her tonight or in the morning, bring her back here and have at least four full days with her before it was time to kill her.

He would make that time last. Build up the anticipation. Get her accustomed to him before he took her. And when he finally did, he would wait until the last second before he used the knife, so that when he thrust inside her, he would feel her body convulse as the blood drained away and the light left her eyes.

It would be the best yet.
Jiggety jig.

Ethan was being decidedly difficult, Audra thought, watching him across the dining table. He had dodged every attempt she'd made to engage him in a repeat performance of that delicious almost-audition, and today, he wouldn't even sit beside her at the group's regular Sunday-after-services dinner at the hotel.

It was as if he didn't trust her.

Catching his eye, she winked and bit off the end of a green bean, then with slow deliberation, licked away every drop of butter sauce.

He froze, fork hanging in midair, his gaze pinned to her lips.

She watched that tiny muscle in his strong jaw tighten and release as she slowly chewed. "Mmm, these beans are delicious," she murmured, sliding another into her mouth.

"It's Sunday," Lucinda whispered beside her. "Show the man some mercy."

Audra dabbed the napkin at her lips, then turned to her friend with a bland smile. "I'm sure I don't know what you're talking about."

Green eyes twinkled with amusement. "I'm sure you do. Behave."

Before Audra could respond, Edwina leaned forward to see around her husband, who was glaring at the next table where Joe Bill had built a snowman with mashed potatoes and was catapulting peas into it with his spoon. "Have you time for a fitting this afternoon, Audra? I've basted the overskirt, but need to make certain it drapes correctly before I finish it."

Audra hesitated. Father had had another rough night, so he and the Abrahams had foregone services and dinner today. "If Winnie doesn't send word that she needs me, I'll try. But tomorrow is print day, and Mr. Bonet has asked me to check the typeset. Shall I come by after we finish?"

Edwina nodded. "If it would be easier, we could meet here at the hotel. It shouldn't take long. Lucinda, can we borrow your office?"

"Of course. With Tait off working on the Wallaces' new

house, Maddie and I are spending the afternoon together. Come by anytime. We'll have tea."

Audra glanced at Ethan, who was no longer watching, but was engaged in deep conversation with the other men. "Ethan will be out there, too. I'll tell him to meet me here rather than the *Herald* office." Seeing Lucinda's questioning look, she added, "He insists on walking me everywhere I go."

Edwina nodded. "Declan, too. I wish they would hurry and catch the killer, so we can get back to our normal lives."

"I thought we weren't going to ruin dinner by talking about him," Lucinda reminded her.

"Tell them that." Edwina tipped her head toward the men.

"That leaves us four days until he hunts again on the next full moon," Tait was saying. "Has Redstone found that prospector, Weems, yet?"

Brodie shook his head. "The man comes and goes as he pleases. Thomas is still looking." Turning to Ethan, he added, "But he did come across some recent diggings in a draw behind the burned Prendergast cabin. Not sure who they belong to, or if anyone is still working that area. But you know how protective those prospectors are. They hate anyone coming around their claims."

Audra looked at him in surprise. "You think that's why the cabin was set afire? To protect some prospector's mine?"

Brodie shrugged. "Four people and a dog moving into a cabin less than a mile away? Possible. Especially with your father's habit of wandering off."

Audra felt a shiver of unease.

Ethan gave her a reassuring smile. "You're safe at the Arlan place, Audra. All the locks have been repaired and the guns are loaded and ready. Between me and Curtis and Phe, no one can get in unannounced."

Tait smiled at her. "Those shooting lessons are going well, then?"

Before Audra could answer, Ethan cut in. "I wouldn't say 'well.' But at least now she keeps her eyes open half the time."

Audra narrowed those eyes at him.

He grinned back.

"Handling a gun is rather more complicated than you men make out," Lucinda said, defending her. "Remember, Tait?

When I tried to shoot Smythe with my new pepperbox pistol and forgot to load it?"

Audra gaped. "You tried to shoot a man?"

"In the groin, no less. What a mess that would have been." Ethan paled.

Lucinda laughed. "Don't worry, Ethan. He deserved it. But I never left my pistol unloaded after that. And a good thing, too. Later, when I went after his cohort, I was able to shoot him twice before Tait stopped me."

"In the groin?" Ethan choked out.

"Arm and leg, I think. I was rather distraught at the time and was shaking too much to aim well."

Audra looked at her in amazement. Serene, unflappable Lucinda? A shootist? What had the man done to break through her controlled reserve?

Not to be left out, Edwina leaned forward again. "I killed a vicious Indian with a shovel."

"You didn't kill him, Ed," her husband gently corrected. "It was the seventy-foot fall from the platform that killed him."

"Well, I knocked him off." She made a face. "Talk about a mess."

Appetite gone, Audra set down her fork. She looked at the beautiful faces around her and wondered what other dark secrets might rest behind those bright smiles. She felt she scarcely knew them, even though she now considered these ladies her best friends. Her own secrets seemed rather tame in comparison.

"I daresay I've never killed anyone." Maddie neatly folded her napkin, set it beside her plate, and smiled at Audra. "But I did shoot a man in the stomach right before Ash and his dog finished him off."

Sweet, gentle Maddie, too?

"Looking back," Lucinda said with a chuckle, "it was almost funny in a macabre sort of way. That poor lawman didn't know who to charge—Maddie or Ash or his dog, Tricks."

"He deserved it, too," Edwina put in. "He broke poor Maddie's nose."

"And shot at Ash." Maddie, Countess of Kirkwell and model of decorum, patted her husband's arm. "Naturally, I couldn't allow him to try again."

"Of course not," Lucinda agreed.

"And did I thank you properly for that, love?" the earl asked his wife.

She met his rakish smile with one of her own. "Several times, milord."

Stunned, Audra sat back. These ladies definitely had some explaining to do. They couldn't calmly mention over Sunday dinner that they had shot people, then let it go at that. As their friend, she deserved some sort of explanation. Especially when she could see by the hint of regret in their eyes that these events were not as casual as they made them seem.

"The point is, lass," Maddie's husband went on, "you do what you must to protect yourself and those you love. It isna pleasant, but 'tis necessary if you want to live. So mind your lessons. Keep your gun loaded and your cartridges dry."

Ethan pushed his plate aside, his expression bleak. "Hopefully it won't come to that. Not with me and Curtis looking out for her." Signaling an end to the subject, he turned to Tait. "Do you have an extra sledge? If we expect to fit the beams in the Wallaces' foundation this afternoon, we'd best head out there now."

As soon as the men left, Audra went to the newspaper office, where she found Mr. Bonet studying several papers at his desk. He scarcely acknowledged her arrival, which told her she was in trouble again. The man was as rigid as a headmaster in a Catholic school, ruling with glares and stares and pointed silences. Despite his fine words when she had told him of her impending marriage, he had been quite aloof since then, and his disapproval seemed more marked every day.

They worked in stony silence. He continued to read his correspondence, while she checked typeset as quickly as she could so she could return to the hotel for her fitting. To keep abreast of the news, he wrote regularly to several Eastern reporters and subscribed to a number of periodicals and newspapers. Audra admired his dedication, but thought today was too fine to spend cooped up inside reading or setting type.

As she worked, she let her mind wander. In less than three weeks she would be a married woman. A wife. Forever after, she would be Audra Hardesty. She liked the sound of that. Mrs. Ethan Hardesty. She liked that even more.

Smiling, she wondered if Ethan was thinking about her—if Lucinda and Edwina were waiting for her to come for her fitting—why Bonet wasn't helping her so they could finish sooner. Time seemed to creep by.

Beyond the front window, the street remained deserted—since this was Sunday and all the shops were closed—and the bright afternoon was beginning to fade. She hoped Winnie had taken Father outside to enjoy the beautiful day. He liked watching the birds flit through the trees.

The sun was slipping behind the high canyon wall when Mr. Bonet finally set aside his papers. She was aware of him studying her, one ink-stained finger impatiently tapping the arm of his chair. But as she was unable to think of a reason why he should be cross with her, she refused to be baited into asking him what was wrong, and continued checking the typeset for errors—a difficult undertaking when one's mind wandered, since they read backward when set into the slots.

"Miss Pearsall," he finally said. "Are you acquainted with a man named Richard Villars?"

She startled, then collected herself and continued studying the letters. "I am. Why do you ask?"

"I've been in correspondence with him."

"Have you?" She faced him, her fingers gripping her skirts. "About what?"

"Your father."

She waited, dread building, knowing he had more to say.

Abruptly, he rose and moved to look out the front window, hands clasped behind his back. "Percival Prendergast Pearsall. An unusual name. And vaguely familiar. I remembered you were from Baltimore, and checked with the newspaper there. Which led me to the Baltimore Society of Learned Historians. Which led me to Richard Villars." Turning, he gave her a tight smile, his face so flushed his freckles scarcely showed. "Another suitor, perhaps?"

"I'd rather not discuss it, Mr. Bonet."

His flush deepened. "Of course." He paced from the window to the desk, then slowly around the bulky printing press. "Still, you can imagine my surprise when he wrote that your father was supposed to be studying ancient Indian ruins in New Mexico, rather than here, in Heartbreak Creek."

"We altered our plans."

"Did you? I wonder why?"

"Because he became ill and needed rest and quiet."

He stopped pacing and faced her. "*Became* ill, Miss Pearsall? Or *was* ill? For over two years, it seems. Yet, miraculously, despite his failing health, he has continued to publish articles."

She let the pretense of ignorance drop. "Why is this important to you?"

"Why?" He gave a bitter laugh and ran a hand through his curly red hair. "Because I cared for you. Because I offered you my friendship and you've repaid me with lies."

"I was only trying to protect my father. To make his last years as pleasant as I could." She glanced past him through the front window, praying Ethan would suddenly arrive to walk her back to the hotel. But the street remained empty.

"How? By forging his signature?" He stalked the two steps to his desk, snatched up several periodicals and held them out. "On articles published under his name *since* he took ill?"

"I only transcribed the notes he had already written. A small deception. Who did it harm? The people eager to publish his work? The readers who clamored for more of it? Those dependent on me to put food on the table?"

"You collected money for papers he never wrote. That's dishonest, Miss Pearsall. Fraudulent. I'm quite disappointed in you."

She looked down at the floor, struggling to curb the angry words rising in her throat. He had no right to treat her like a recalcitrant child. She knew what she did was wrong. She had known it when she'd done it, and would do it again if she had to. If he thought to shame her, he'd failed. Certainly, she had regrets—that there had been no other recourse open to her, that her father had spent his money on travel and research rather than providing for his family, that sometimes hard choices had to be made—but not shame. "Have you told Mr. Villars?" she asked.

When he didn't answer, she looked up to find him studying her.

"Not yet."

"Will you?"

"I haven't decided. As a journalist, I'm honor-bound to print the truth."

He's enjoying this. Disgust curled her lips. She had thought they were friends. But now he threatened to expose her as punishment for her not returning his feelings and choosing Ethan over him. Vile creature. Masking her revulsion, she forced a conciliatory tone. "I understand that what I did was wrong, Mr. Bonet. What I don't understand is why you're so upset about it. It has nothing to do with you."

"It has everything to do with me!" He slapped the magazines so hard on the desktop, she flinched. "I hired you, taught you how to be a reporter, shared things with you I haven't spoken of in years. And how do you repay me? By making a fool of me." With every word, his face had grown redder, his expression more vicious.

For the first time, she began to feel afraid.

She should leave. Now. Before this went further. She glanced at the back door, wondering if it was unlocked.

He stalked toward her, his voice rising on every word. "And then you as good as called me a liar at the inquiry. Belittled me in front of half the town. Made a mockery of all that I've done for you. How could you do that to me?"

She edged toward the back. "I assure you such was not my intent, sir. I only meant to clear Mr. Hardesty's name. I'm sorry if you were hurt in the process."

"Hurt?" He laughed. "Disappointed, perhaps. Humiliated."

She continued to retreat. He continued to advance.

"In view of your feelings, sir, I think it best if I no longer work here."

"Of course it's best, Miss Pearsall. I have a reputation to uphold. The last person I need in my employ is a plagiarist and a woman who openly admits to a sordid liaison with a man who caused the deaths of three people. Count yourself fortunate I don't turn you in for fraud."

"Then I bid you good day, sir." Turning, she flung open the door, then drew back in surprise when she found a broad figure planted on the back step.

Ethan!
But when she looked up, it wasn't Ethan at all.

Dragging a sleeve over his sweating brow, Ethan looked toward the creek that bordered the Wallace property. It was later than he'd thought. Already the sun had dipped behind the aspens. By the time he stopped at the hotel to collect Audra, it would be dark. Bending, he began collecting his tools.

They had made good progress—Brodie and Ash lugging stones for the foundation blocks, while Ethan and Tait cut the posts to go on top of them. Once Ethan had checked with the water level to make certain everything was lined up correctly, they had started setting the beams that had been cut and left to season over the winter. Hopefully, by the time the plank flooring arrived next week from the mill in Pueblo, they would have the joists in. Then, once the flooring was nailed in place, they could begin framing the walls.

He looked around, pleased with their efforts. They made a good team.

It was a beautiful day to be outside, working on a project. It reminded him why he had been drawn to construction in the first place, and later, to architecture. He found it especially rewarding to create something with his own hands, to build a structure that would last through decades of use. He had missed the satisfaction that brought. While he'd worked, he'd drawn plans in his head for the home he would build for Audra. Out here would be a good spot. Plenty of sky and level ground, and a thirty-mile view to the taller peaks of the southern Rockies. She would like it here in the sun, with a creek nearby.

Suddenly anxious to see her again, he tossed the last of his tools into his saddlebag, then motioned to the three men notching beams so they would sit flush on the posts. "Better call it a day, fellows. It's getting late."

"And aboot time." Ash straightened. He had taken off his shirt, and was wiping a neckerchief across his unclothed torso. "Sweating like a Newmarket tart on race day, so I am." The man was a patchwork of scars, especially along the left side of his rib cage.

"A munitions explosion," he said when he saw Ethan staring.

He pointed to a puckered scar on his shoulder. "This was from a bullet in India. And these," he indicated two saber slashes, one near his neck and another on his arm, "I got in the Crimea." The man actually seemed proud of them. "Ever been shot, lad?" When Ethan shook his head, he added, "I dinna recommend it. Now Rafe there," he nodded toward the wrangler building a buck and rail fence atop the rocky soil between the foundation and the creek, "he's been shot several times. Once served as a Texas lawman, so he did, and got caught in a shoot-out over a woman."

"Did he win?" Brodie asked, walking up.

The Scotsman shrugged into his shirt. "Dinna say and I never asked. He may appear calm and mild-mannered, but I suspect he's holding a wealth of anger inside. Saw it often in my fellow soldiers. Probably why the lad prefers horses to people."

Brodie dropped his bucket of tools beside Ash's. "You want to see scars, Hardesty, you should see Thomas's chest. As a Dog Soldier, he participated in the Sun Dance Ceremony. Brutal tradition."

Ethan didn't want to see anybody's scars. He had enough of his own. Inside and out.

Brodie straightened to study the wrangler walking toward them. "Texas lawman, huh? Think he'd be interested in taking over the sheriff duties in town? Once we get this murderer out of the way, I'd like to get back to my ranch. The two cow chasers I've got working it are good men, but not that motivated."

"Hell, no, he wouldna be interested," the Scotsman blustered. "He's helping me with my herd, so he is."

Brodie snorted. "What herd? All I've seen is a deaf gelding and two fat mules. If you're expecting foals out of that bunch, you've got a long wait."

"I'll be getting prime English thoroughbreds, if ye must know."

"From where?"

"Kirkwell, of course."

"You're going back to Scotland?"

"Aye. For a while. As I've been reminded repeatedly by my Scottish solicitor and Maddie, I must return to complete the title transference." The earl sighed in disgust. "I hate the thought of making my bows before the Queen and all those bluidy English peers."

"Peers like you?" Brodie laughed. "Can't imagine you going down on your knees for anyone. Except your wife, maybe."

"Mind your tongue." Ash punched his shoulder. "But, aye. It'll require a lot of drink, I'm thinking. Luckily," he added as Jessup stopped beside him, "I'll have this fine lad to cover my back. Those English are a treacherous lot, so they are."

Tait walked up, his hat in hand and his coat thrown over his arm. Even after an afternoon of hard sawing, the man was hardly mussed. "What are you laggards standing around for? Let's go. I'm hungry."

Twenty-eight

A t first, she saw him as her savior, the ragged prospector
come to return the medallion he'd found in the ashes of
her cabin, his sudden appearance giving her a chance to escape
Bonet. Then in a move so sudden and shocking it froze her
where she stood, he reached out and grabbed her hair.

"What are you—"

He slapped her. Yanked her up on her tiptoes and slapped
her again. "Shut up."

She tasted blood and batted blindly at him, her scalp on fire.

Bonet rushed up behind her. "What do you think you're
doing?"

Ignoring him, the prospector lowered his face down to hers.
Soulless eyes. A matted beard brushing her cheek. Breath
so foul she could almost feel it slide over her skin. "Do what I
say, girlie, or I'll hurt you bad." Something pricked her neck,
then a warm trickle. "Understand?"

She panted in his face, dazed by pain and the suddenness
of the attack.

Another prick. Deeper. "Understand?"

"Y-Yes."

Releasing her so abruptly she almost fell, he looked past her
at Bonet. "Lock the front door."

"I will not! Leave now or I'll—"

The prospector's arm lashed out.

A cry. Bonet lurched back, one hand pressed to his bleeding face.

Audra stared in terror at the glistening blade in the prospector's hand. What was he doing? Why was he attacking them? Everything was happening so fast she couldn't think.

"Lock the door," he said again.

Bonet stumbled away.

Gripping her shoulder, the intruder steered Audra after him, past the press and toward the desks by the front window.

Go! she screamed silently at Bonet's back. *Run! Get help!*

But Bonet seemed barely able to walk. He looked back at them, his fingers still pressed against his bloody cheek. "Wh-What do you want? There's no m-money here. N-Nothing of value."

"Shut up."

Audra stumbled against a chair and almost fell when her attacker shoved her forward again. Swallowing back blood and bile, she staggered on. Why was he doing this? Where was Ethan?

Bonet reached the front door, locked it with shaking fingers, then leaned back against it, his legs wobbling. "T-Take whatever you want. Just let us go. Please."

"Sit." The prospector pointed the knife at the chair by Audra's desk.

"We won't tell anyone—"

Another slash.

Another scream.

More blood pouring down Bonet's face.

"Don't!" Audra cried. "We'll give you whatever you want."

"Sit. Now," he told Bonet.

Moaning, Bonet collapsed into the chair, blood coursing through his fingers.

Still gripping her shoulder, the prospector looked around, muttering softly to himself.

Audra tried to focus. She needed to find a way to stop him. To convince him to let them go. But how could she do that until she learned what he wanted? She wiped a shaking hand over her mouth, saw the blood on her sleeve and felt her mind start to spin. *No! Think! Do something!* But her thoughts were so scattered she couldn't make any sense of what was happening. Couldn't stop shaking. *Ethan, where are you?*

"Got any kerosene?"

Her heart lurched. Kerosene? Why did he want kerosene?

The knife poked her again. "Answer, girlie."

"N-No—only what's in the lamp."

Bonet watched them, his face dripping, realization dawning in his eyes. "You're him, aren't you? The killer. Weems."

The killer? Oh, God . . .

"I told you to shut up." Thrusting Audra aside, Weems stepped past her, his knife hand rising.

"Don't!" Audra grabbed his arm.

He jerked free.

"No! Wait!" Scrambling from the chair, Bonet flattened against the wall, hands raised in defense. "I'm on your side."

Weems stopped. "What side?"

Audra looked at the rear door. Unlocked. Her only chance. Watching the prospector's back, she sidled toward it, praying her shaking legs would hold her.

"I h-hate the railroads, too," Bonet pleaded behind her. "I want them g-gone as much as you do. I can help you get rid of them."

"I don't need no help."

Past the printing press. Eight more feet to the door. Six. Why wouldn't her legs move faster?

"Then wh-what do you want?" Bonet started sobbing, his voice broken and high-pitched. "I'll do anything you s-say. Just tell me what you want."

"Her."

Audra froze as Weems turned, his dark eyes pinning her where she stood. "I want her."

"Then take her! I won't tell. Take her and go."

What? Audra gaped, not believing what she'd heard.

Weems showed rotted teeth in a feral smile. "You run, girlie, I cut him. Your choice."

"No!" Bonet cried. "It's her you want, not me. I'm on your side. I can help you."

Weems continued to watch her, evil dancing in his eyes. "Decide now."

Shaking, her heart hammering against her ribs, she looked past him at the man cowering against the wall, his eyes wild, tears and blood dripping from his chin. Could she make it to the back door in time? If she stayed, would Weems let them live? "How do I know you won't—"

"Too late."

Another lightning movement. A cry that ended in a gurgle.

Audra watched in horror as Bonet slid down the wall, mouth open in a silent scream, fingers clawing at the bubbling wound in his neck. With a cry, she lunged for the door, yanked it open, then felt it torn from her fingers when a hand reached around her and slammed it shut.

"You shouldn't have done that," Weems snarled just before he gripped her head from behind and smashed her forehead into the wood.

Her knees folded.

Dimly, she heard him mumbling. Felt him grab her ankles and drag her across the floor.

She rose up, arms flailing. Then he hit her and everything went hazy again. She struggled to stay conscious as he gagged her and rolled her in a heavy canvas, pinning her arms against her sides. When he threw her over his shoulder and stepped out the back door, fear sent her into mindless struggles, but the canvas was wrapped so tight she couldn't move, could hardly breathe.

He walked faster, his shoulder digging into her stomach with every hurried step.

After a moment, she heard the sound of rushing water, and guessed he had taken her across the back lane and into the woods. He slowed, his stride uneven as he pushed through limbs and brush, until finally he stopped. With a grunt, he heaved her up and over the back of something that shifted beneath her.

His mule. *A good one. Named Jenny.*

She made futile attempts to slide free, but he quickly piled things on top of her, then lashed it all down tight. A moment later, the mule began to move back through the brush. The weight pressing on her back and ribs made every breath a desperate struggle. She began to fade. Like a cork floating on an endless black sea, her mind bobbed to the surface in occasional bursts of painful awareness, then sank into darkness again.

Once, she thought she heard voices. She tried to call out, but the gag and canvas muffled her voice, and by the time she worked the cloth out of her mouth, they were moving again. She stopped struggling and hung in helpless terror, aware of little beyond the throbbing in her head, the constant struggle to breathe, and the rolling nausea of being carried uphill and facedown on a moving animal.

Breathe, she chanted silently to herself. *Stay alive. Ethan will come.*

It was dark when Ethan followed the other four men into the lobby of the hotel. Looking through the door into the near-empty dining room, he saw Lucinda Rylander, Edwina Brodie, and the Scotsman's wife, Maddie, sitting at a table. The Brodie infant kicked his feet and waved his tiny fists in a basket by his mother's chair.

But no Audra.

"Anything left to eat?" Tait asked, walking toward them.

"The kitchen's closed," his wife said. "But I had Cook set aside leftovers."

It didn't seem that late to Ethan. Then he remembered the days were longer now, and by the time it was dark it was after nine. No wonder he was hungry. As the other men pulled out chairs at a nearby table, he looked around. "Audra here?"

Lucinda shook her head. "She went to the *Herald* right after you left and hasn't returned."

"She even missed her fitting," Edwina added.

"I sent Yancey to check," Lucinda went on, "but the office was dark and the door locked. My guess is she went home."

Ethan frowned. "She was supposed to wait for me."

"She might have been called away," Maddie Wallace said. "She said her father had a difficult night. Perhaps Winnie sent for her."

"I better check."

"Eat first," Tait suggested. "If anything's amiss, we would have heard."

But Ethan couldn't be sure of that. Not with Audra. She was both overly independent and prone to mishaps. A hazardous combination. For all he knew, she could be down at the Chinese camp, causing another riot.

"You go ahead," he told them. "I'll be back shortly. Save me a plate."

Winnie and Curtis were finishing a late supper when he arrived. He noticed there were only two plates at the table. "Have you seen Audra?" he asked.

Winnie looked at him in surprise. "Not since you two left for services this morning. Why?"

"I must have missed her."

"Maybe she went to have her dress fit." Rising, Winnie carried her empty plate to the sink. "Mrs. Edwina say yesterday the skirt was almost finished."

"That's probably it." Not wanting to alarm the old couple unnecessarily, he changed the subject. "How's Mr. Pearsall?"

"A good day after a bad night," Curtis said, bending to scrape his plate into Phe's bowl.

"Went to bed like a lamb," Winnie added. "Even the dog didn't wake him."

"The dog?"

Curtis patted Phe's head. She hardly flinched. A vast improvement since she'd arrived. "Couple of hours ago," he said, straightening, "she raised a ruckus. Thought it you and Miss Audra coming home, but she act more scared than happy. Ain't that so, Miss Phe?"

The dog continued to lick the plate.

"Did you look around?" Ethan asked.

Curtis nodded. "Didn't see nothing, though. Phe quieted down quick enough. Figure it was a coyote passing through."

Ethan thought for a moment. It could be coincidence. Or it could be something else. An uneasy, itchy feeling spread between his shoulder blades.

"Want me to help you look for Miss Audra?" Curtis asked.

"No need." Ethan smiled to hide his growing concern. He was probably overreacting, anyway. No doubt she was sitting in the hotel right now, eating the plate of leftovers set aside for him. "If she comes here before I catch up to her," he said, heading back out the door, "send word to the hotel."

The moon hung high in the sky as he turned Renny back toward town, reminding Ethan that in four more days, the killer would be hunting a new victim if they didn't figure out who he was and find a way to stop him. Unless he broke the cycle and hunted early.

That itchy feeling spread up the back of his neck. He should have brought Phe with him. She always seemed to know when her mistress was nearby. If he didn't find Audra in town, he'd go back for her and Curtis.

He rode slowly down Main Street, studying every storefront and shop along the way, but all the windows were dark except for those at the Red Eye and hotel. Reining in, he saw Yancey lounging on a bench outside the double doors, petting the hotel cat. "Audra show up yet?"

Yancey shook his head. "Been watching since you left. Ain't seen hide nor hair of her."

Damn. Ethan sat for a minute, wondering where to look next. The Chinese camp? Doctor Boyce's office?

The Chinese camp was settling in for the night, but he roused the Irish gang bosses to ask if any had seen her. None had.

He rode on to Doc's, but it was dark so he didn't stop and wake them. When he returned to the hotel, he saw Yancey wasn't on the bench, and took that as a good sign. Dismounting, he went inside, certain he would see her sitting at the table, chatting with her friends.

She wasn't.

Something was definitely wrong. A sense of dread, stronger than what he'd felt at Salty Point when he'd stood over the bleeding bodies of his workers, spread through his chest. His face must have shown it; before he'd crossed to the table, all four men had risen.

"You didn't find her?" Brodie asked.

"Not at home, or the Chinese camp, or anywhere in between. All the stores and shops are dark, including the paper. Doc's house, too. I don't know where else she would be."

Tait put a hand on his shoulder. "We'll keep looking. We'll find her."

Ethan struggled to bring his thoughts into focus as the sheriff began barking orders. Ash was to question the sentries—Rafe would ask Driscoll if he'd seen her and check the woods around the livery—Tait was to ride up to the old mine and along the creek behind the hotel. "Ethan and I will go back to the

Herald. Maybe she left a note or something. Anybody know where Bonet lives?"

Lucinda did, and offered to send Yancy to ask if Bonet knew where Audra had gone after she left the newspaper office.

"Have him check at the Red Eye, too," Tait called after her as she crossed toward the lobby. "Find out if anyone there has seen her since this afternoon."

Maddie and Edwina stepped forward, their faces showing concern. "What can we do?"

"Stay put," Brodie told them.

"Aye," Ash seconded. "She might show up here. Where's Thomas?"

"At our place," Lucinda said. "He was taking the children fishing this afternoon. Should we have him bring them here, so he'll be free to help you look for Audra?"

Her husband shook his head. "Let's not get ahead of ourselves. She could be visiting with a friend somewhere."

Ethan doubted it. All her friends were right here. So where could she be? And why would she walk away without telling someone where she was going?

"Has anyone checked with Pastor Rickman?" Maddie asked, her auburn brows drawn in a frown. "She might have gone to speak to Biddy about music for the wedding."

A long shot, but worth a try. Ethan was starting to feel desperate. This wasn't like her. Audra might be hardheaded, but she wasn't foolish. She wouldn't simply wander off in the dark.

"I'll send Billy, our bellboy, to the church," Tait offered.

Brodie took a lamp from a table and headed toward the door. "Meet back here in an hour. Come on, Hardesty."

Ethan tried to stay optimistic, but it was getting hard. Somehow, he knew. He could feel it, the same way he felt that prickle up his back before danger struck. She was in trouble. She needed him now, more than she ever had, and he didn't even know where she was. Fear was a vise around his throat. He could scarcely breathe. Every thought led to disaster.

"It's locked," Brodie said, a few minutes later, after checking the knob on the front door of the *Herald.* "Wait here. I'll go around back."

As the sheriff stepped into the narrow space between the

building that housed the newspaper office and the millinery shop next door, Ethan peered through the fancy new script on the front window. He made out the shapes of the desks, the printing press, boxes of supplies, and fat rolls of paper stacked against one wall, a mound of something—clothing?—below the window.

Light flashed. Squinting into the dimness, he saw Brodie come through the rear entrance, turn to pull the latch, then hesitate. He watched him lean close to the door, fingers tracing over the wood. What had he found?

Ethan tapped on the glass. "What is it?"

Brodie looked back at him, then turned and walked slowly toward the front, lamp held high, his head swiveling as he checked the narrow office.

Something about his posture. The tension in his shoulders. The way his hand rested on the butt of the gun holstered at his hip when he stopped and stared down at the mound of clothing on the floor below the front window. Then Ethan knew.

Oh, Jesus. It's not just clothing.

"Is it Audra?" When Brodie didn't answer, he raised his fist to break the glass just as the door opened. He shoved inside, then froze when he saw the shadowed form on the floor by the wall. "Is that . . ."

"Bonet. His throat's been cut."

Ethan stared at the body. A man's body. Not Audra's. The burnt, coppery smell of blood almost turned his stomach. But needing to see for himself, he took the lamp from Brodie and stepped closer—saw the gaping wound in Bonet's neck, the dark pool spreading across the plank floor, the wild-eyed terror in the dimming eyes.

Relief made him light-headed. *Not Audra. Thank God.*

Then where was she? He saw her spectacles sitting on her desk and knew she wouldn't have left them. Panic building, he looked around. "Where is she? Is she here? Did something happen to her, too?" Ethan saw the grimness in Brodie's face and that feeling of dread ballooned into gut-churning fear. "What did you find by the back door?"

"I'm not sure." Taking the lamp back, Brodie led him toward the rear of the office. When he reached the back door, he held the light high and pointed at a dark red stain on the wood. "What do you make of that?"

Ethan leaned closer. Touched it with his fingers. Damp. Sticky like blood. Not much of it and not high up on the door. Maybe as high as Audra's head would be. And beside it, caught in a splinter, several long, medium brown hairs.

Air rushed out of him. He went numb. His heart felt like it was trying to kick its way out of his chest.

Audra . . . no . . .

He turned to Brodie, his mind in chaos, the buzzing in his ears so loud he couldn't hear his own words.

"He's got her."

Twenty-nine

Audra didn't know how far they traveled before they finally stopped. He pulled her off and dumped her on the ground, unrolling her from the canvas as she fell. Cold jarred her awake. She struggled to her knees, spitting dirt and pine needles from her mouth, before a kick sent her down again.

She lay shivering, the pain in her body keeping time to the throbbing in her head.

No more, she cried silently. *Kill me or let me go.*

Something nudged her shoulder. "Get up."

She opened her eyes to see him standing over her, his bulky form silhouetted against the waxing moon. Something hung from his hand. Long and thin, the grip glinting in the moonlight.

She bolted upright, fear squeezing her throat, remembering the bite of the tasseled tip into her back.

He held it toward her. "Know what this is?"

She tried to speak, couldn't, and forced a nod.

"You can scream all you want. But if you run, I'll use it on you. Understand?"

"Why are you doing this?"

But he was leading the mule away. She thought about running, but before she could make her body move, he came back, picked up two bags and carried them into a sagging canvas tent with a stovepipe sticking out the top.

Lifting a hand to her face, she found a sticky lump above her brow where her head had hit the door. Her cheek felt swollen where he'd struck her, and her side hurt where he had kicked her, but nothing seemed seriously wrong.

She could run. Try to escape. But run where?

She looked sluggishly at the rough camp where he had brought her. With the moon directly overhead, she could see rusty cans littering the ground, tools and crates piled here and there. Other than the canvas tent, there were no structures. Beside a cold fire pit stood a rack of un-scraped animal hides, bits of drying flesh hanging from the curling undersides. The reek of it made her gag. On a line strung between two trees, the mule, bearing the white hairs of long-healed saddle sores, stood hock-deep in manure, watching her with disinterest as it slowly chewed a mouthful of hay. Closer by, amid scattered bones and piles of dried canine droppings, lay a chain with an empty collar.

If she could reach that chain or one of the tools . . .

Head swimming, she crawled onto her hands and knees then hung there as sparks flared and dimmed behind her eyes. She tried to push herself up to her feet, but her legs kept tangling in her skirts.

"What are you doing?"

She glared up at him through a tangle of hair. "Vomiting," she said hoarsely. "Want to see?"

He studied her for a minute, his small dark eyes moving over her in a way that made her shudder. Then he patted the whip tied to his belt. "Remember what I said." Picking up another bag, he walked back to the tent.

Despair defeated her. Weeping, she slumped onto her side, then flinched when something sharp gouged into her hip. She reached down to pull it away, and found a hard thing half-buried in the dirt. She dug it loose.

A piece of tubular metal. Thin but solid. Probably a broken tine from a pitchfork. Hands trembling with excitement, she slipped it into her skirt pocket just as Weems came back out of the tent.

Now she had a weapon. She could fight back.

*   *   *

Ethan had read somewhere that pain was God's gift to a wounded heart because it gave the mind a focus and the body an enemy to fight.

But God gave him numbness instead.

From the moment he saw the blood on the door and realized the worst had happened, he stopped feeling. His body functioned, but his mind went numb. The shaking stopped. His heart ceased its erratic rhythm. His breathing slowed.

That was a good thing. A necessary thing. Because he knew emotion wouldn't help him now. He had to set aside the fear, ignore all the terrible imaginings of what might be happening, and curb the crippling panic that stole his will. He knew those thoughts were still there, like demons dancing along the periphery of his mind, looking for a way in. But he couldn't allow them into his head. In some way he didn't question or understand, he knew if he stayed strong, Audra would stay strong. If he believed, she would believe. And that would keep her alive.

Faith and hope. Little of either remained after Salty Point, but he called up what he had left. He would find her. Audra was all the good he had lost in his life, and all the promise in his future. He would not let her die.

Four days. That's all he had until the full moon.

"Let's get the others."

"Stand up."

Do what he says. Stay alive.

She forced herself to her feet, praying he hadn't seen her slip the piece of metal into her pocket. Hoping to distract him, she asked where his dog was.

"With you. Start walking."

That collar belonged to Phe? No wonder she was so frightened of men.

A shove sent her stumbling toward a moonlit trail winding up the slope behind his camp. She struggled to keep her footing. Whenever she faltered, he gave her a kick, twice knocking her to her knees. Both times, she was able to pick up a rock and slip it into the pocket with the piece of metal.

When they reached the top, she sank to the ground, gasping for air, her skirts ripped and her petticoats stuck to her bleeding knees. The pain in her head had settled into a constant pounding, and she was so thirsty her tongue felt swollen and dry. "I have to rest," she choked out. She expected to be yanked up again, but he wandered a few feet away into a jumble of boulders.

She looked dully around.

They must be high, because the trees here were shorter and less branchy than those in town. The wind that had stunted them along one side now cut through her dress, making her teeth chatter. Lifting her face to the sky, she watched stars wink to life in its wake as the moon slipped to the west, and wondered if she would ever see them again after this night.

Would Ethan be able to find her in time? Would he even know who had her and where to look?

Tears dimmed the stars. If she knew why Weems had chosen her, or what he intended to do with her, maybe she could find a way to stop him. But stop him how? With a tiny piece of metal? A feeling of utter hopelessness gripped her, and for a moment she considered ending this terror by throwing herself back down the slope.

But her father needed her. Ethan needed her. And she wouldn't leave them this way.

God . . . please help me. I'm so afraid.

With a hitching breath, she reached into her pocket and wrapped her fingers around the cold, hard metal. She didn't know what she would do with it, but feeling it in her hand gave her hope.

Ethan would come. He always had, whenever she had needed him. And if not, she had this. She ran her thumb over the sharp, jagged point. Imagined plunging it into Weems's throat. All she had to do was stay alive until she found her chance.

How long did she have?

She struggled to remember what she had heard at Sunday luncheon—was it only a few hours ago? Tait had said the killer only hunted on the full moon, four days from now. Did that mean he would keep her alive until then? Why? What was he going to do to her?

"Get up."

She blinked up at him, saw the unfurled whip hanging from his hand and renewed terror surged through her. "Why are you—"

"You want this?" He wiggled the whip, made it snake along the ground like a living thing.

"N-No."

"Then get up."

"I'm just trying to underst—"

A whistling sound, then something bit into her arm. Pain exploded. She doubled over, gasping, awaiting the next lash.

"Want more?"

"N-No . . ."

"Then stand up."

She tried, tangled her feet in her skirts, and fell again.

"Stupid woman." He bent down and slapped her. Slapped her again.

Darkness sucked her down. When next she awoke, she was being dragged again, this time by her arm down a long stone corridor. Light cast by the lantern swinging from his other hand flickered on the rocky ceiling overhead.

When had he gotten a lantern? Where was he taking her? Into a tunnel? A mine shaft?

She hadn't the strength to fight him, but allowed herself to be dragged along, rocks digging into her back, her shoulder burning from the strain.

She tried to memorize every change in direction, every unusual rock or outcropping along the way, but before they had gone a hundred feet, she was hopelessly turned around. All she knew for certain was that they were steadily descending. She tried not to think about the tons of rock overhead, or the suffocating closeness pressing around her, or what Weems would do to her once they reached their destination.

Ethan would come. God wouldn't let her die like this.

After several more twists and turns, he stopped and yanked her onto her feet.

She struggled to stay upright, hugging her aching arm to her side.

"In there." Weems pointed to a narrow opening in the stone. She saw only darkness. A bottomless pit? A living grave?

Courage deserted her as a lifelong fear of dark, closed spaces flooded her mind. "No . . . please. I'll do whatever—"

He shoved her through the opening. She fell against a rocky wall, then blundered into another, so disoriented by the darkness she didn't know where to step next. "I c-can't see."

He stepped in behind her, holding the lantern as high as he could in the low-ceilinged cavern. "Home again, home again, jiggety jig."

Home? Here? In growing horror, she looked around.

It was a space barely ten feet square, hewn from solid rock. A chain hung from a bolt drilled into the rocky wall. On the loose end was a collar with a lock—too big for her ankle or wrist, too small for her waist. Perfect for her neck. A pallet of dirty blankets lay against the wall beside it, and on the floor nearby, a bucket, a pitcher, and a plate of dried meat over which scurried a dozen flat-backed beetles. There were no candles, no lamps other than the one he had brought, and nothing that could be used as a weapon . . . except for the piece of metal and two stones in her pocket.

He set the lamp on a high rock jutting from the wall and picked up the chain. "Come here."

"Why are you doing this?" she asked, struggling not to cry.

He jiggled the chain. "Now."

"You won't get away with this. They'll come searching for me."

"They won't find you."

Fury engulfed her. "What have I ever done to you?" she burst out, her voice ricocheting off the walls. She hated that she couldn't stop the tears, that her voice wobbled. She hated letting him see her fear and weakness. "If you intend to kill me, why don't you just do it?" Maybe if she lured him closer, she could use the piece of metal. Go for an eye, the vein in his neck.

"In time. Come here."

When she still didn't move, he grabbed her arm and threw her facedown on the pallet. Before she could roll over or strike him, he had a knee in her back and the collar around her neck. He snapped the lock closed, rose, and stepped back.

She jumped up and lunged after him, hands raised to claw out his eyes, but was jerked violently backward when she reached the end of the chain. Choking and coughing, she fell in a sprawl on the pallet, while his laughter boomed off the walls.

"You're a fighter. I like that." He picked up the lantern. "There's water in that pitcher by your bed, and if the bugs left you some, there's dried buffalo strips on the plate. Best look around and see where everything is. Don't want you mistaking the water pitcher for the waste bucket in the dark. Sweet dreams."

Laughing, he slipped into the corridor, taking the lantern with him.

"You bastard," she screamed, pounding the covers with her fists. By the time her voice faded, all light was gone. She closed her eyes. Opened them. There was no change. The blackness was total, the silence so complete she could hear the beetles tearing at her dinner.

Dimly, she heard a high-pitched whimper—a terrible, animal sound—then realized it came from her own throat. With a sob, she clasped her hands over her mouth and began to rock back and forth, driven to needless motion to assure herself she was still alive.

She had descended into hell.

Thirty

By the time Ethan and the sheriff arrived back at the hotel, Yancey, Billy, and the other three men had returned.

"Get Thomas," Brodie told the bellboy when he walked into the lobby. "Have him bring the children here. Yancey, get someone to help carry Bonet's body to Doc's clinic."

"Bonet's body?" Tait looked at him in surprise. "He's dead?"

"And Audra's gone."

Ash dragged a hand through his graying hair. "Bluidy hell."

After assuring the women they would keep them apprised of any changes, Brodie took the men back to his office so they could organize the search for Audra without them hovering nearby.

They now knew the killer was Ezra Weems. Ash reported he was the only person to cross the sentry line that afternoon. "They let him pass because he's a regular traveler in and out of town. They dinna see anything suspicious."

"Driscoll said he saw him earlier," Rafe Jessup added, "leading his mule down the back road behind the hotel. Could have been headed to the newspaper office."

"Then let's go after him," Ethan said, impatiently. "The longer we wait, the more danger she's in."

"Better to wait for Thomas," Brodie advised. "He knows exactly where Weems's camp is, and how best to approach it unseen. If we go barging in, no telling how he'll react."

"Aye. A surprise attack would be best, lad."

It made sense, but the thought of sitting and doing nothing while Audra was out there . . .

Ash rested a hand on Ethan's shoulder. "Ten minutes, lad. That'll give Thomas time to get here, and time for us to come up with a battle plan. If Weems stays true to form, she'll be safe until the full moon."

If . . .

Ethan let out an explosive breath. "Then I'm going to the Arlan place for my heavy jacket and rifle and bedroll. I'll be staying out until I find her, no matter how long it takes."

"Good idea." Tait followed him to the door. "I'll tell Lucinda to have Cook pack food to take with us."

A few minutes later, Ethan walked into the kitchen at the Arlan house. A lamp sat on the table, but the main room was empty except for Phe, who came to greet him with a wagging tail. Ethan gathered what he would need, and was rolling up his bedding when Curtis came out of the downstairs bedroom.

Winnie came behind him, tightening the belt on her robe. "You find her?"

"No." He finished tying the bedroll then turned to the old couple. "He's got her." Admitting that aloud for the second time sucked the strength from his legs. He sagged onto the couch, suddenly dizzy. "He killed Bonet and took her. I don't know why. It makes no sense."

"The killer got our Audra?"

"Laws a 'mercy, my poor baby."

Ethan looked up, his eyes burning. "We'll find her. We'll bring her back."

At a sound, he looked over to see Mr. Pearsall standing on the stair in his nightclothes. Seeing how the old man's hand shook as he clutched at the handrail, Ethan rose to go help him.

Palsied fingers gripped his arm. Faded brown eyes bore into Ethan's with fierce intensity. "My Audie is in trouble?"

Ethan nodded.

The fingers tightened, dug into his arm with surprising strength. "Then you find her, boy. You find my girl and bring her home."

"I will, sir."

* * *

The other men were mounting up when he returned to the sheriff's office. Thomas was there, sitting calmly on his spotted horse, weapons strung all over him; a sheathed knife, a rifle, a bow and quiver of arrows strapped across his back, and a long-handled war ax hanging from a low belt over his leather tunic. Every inch the Cheyenne warrior.

"You're not bringing your dog?" Ethan asked the Scotsman when he reined in beside him.

"I wouldna want Tricks killing the bluidy bastard before we learned the lass's whereabouts. He's an impatient sort, so he is."

"There will only be the six of us," Brodie said as he swung up on his leggy sorrel. "We'll move faster and quieter that way. Hold up your right hands."

The sheriff rattled off the deputy oath so fast Ethan scarcely made sense of the words, but he said, "I do," with the others at the appropriate time.

"Thomas says Weems's camp is on a high, open ledge about seven miles up the left fork." The sheriff explained that since they wouldn't be able to approach unannounced, they would have to split up. He and Tait would ride into the camp like they were doing a general sweep and Weems wasn't their target, while the other four moved into hidden positions.

"Thomas and Ethan will go north and watch the camp from the top of the slope above his camp. Ash will be watching from the west, and Rafe from the east. On the south is a hundred-foot drop, so we don't have to worry about that. Since we're boxing him in, if there's shooting, be careful where you aim so we don't get each other in a cross fire."

"He'll want to keep her hidden until the full moon," Tait added, "so be patient. After the sheriff and I talk to him, we'll ride out while you four remain to see what he does. Eventually, if he feels he's safe, he'll go to wherever he has her hidden. Then we'll have him."

Unless it's already too late.

Ethan blocked the thought and fought to bring the panic back down. He took a deep breath and let it out, then saw Thomas studying him. No expression showed on the Indian's swarthy face, but he gave a single, curt nod, and Ethan saw the resolve in those hard, black eyes.

Somehow, Audra had made it onto the warrior's protected list. Thank God.

It was full dark when they rode single-file into the canyon. Since the south side of Weems's camp was a sheer drop, the only way Ash could get to his position on the west was to loop north, so he followed Thomas and Ethan up the right fork along the sluice. The other three would ride past Audra's burned cabin, then Brodie and Tait would leave Rafe to cover their backs, and ride in alone.

After following the sluice for a couple of miles, Thomas angled off onto a higher trail. They rode through tall pines that soon dwindled into the stunted growth of alpine firs, and finally broke into the open above the timberline. The moon was still high enough to cast enough light for them to see a long way in the treeless terrain.

Ethan was glad he had gone back for his shearling jacket; the wind was sharp and steady, sweeping through the low scrub with a keening moan. The silvery light leached the world of color, and the black-and-white landscape seemed alien and barren.

After about two miles of picking their way over rocky trails and broad open stretches, Thomas reined in. When Ethan and Ash stopped beside him, he pointed down to a stand of wind-bent firs. "Ethan and I will leave our horses there and go the rest of the way on foot. Scotsman, you continue to that outcrop ahead, then cut south. The wind is against us, so that will help hide the sound of our passage. Go now, *nesene*, my friend."

As Ash rode off, the Cheyenne glanced down at Ethan's sturdy boots. "If you make noise, *ve'ho'e*, you will take those off. From now on, we do not speak." Without waiting for a response, he rode down toward the trees.

Ethan followed.

Minutes later, they were moving on foot through the stunted trees. Ethan tested every step so he wouldn't tread on a downed branch or kick up loose stones. When he caught the scent of wood smoke, it was a struggle to keep from racing ahead to see if Audra was there. The deeper they went into the trees, the less wind there was, and by the time Thomas signaled for him to stop, Ethan was sweating under his heavy jacket.

"Hatahaoe," the Cheyenne whispered and pointed down the slope. "There."

Ethan crept to the edge and peered down.

Thirty yards below was a wide ledge that was bordered by trees on the east and west, the slope where Thomas and Ethan waited on the north, and a sheer drop on the south. At the edge of the camp, a mule stood under a line stretched between two stunted trees. Nearby sat a sagging tent with a stovepipe sticking out the top, and behind it, in a group of boulders at the base of the bluff, a small spring dribbled water into a rocky pool. In the center of the clearing, a fading campfire sent up lazy tendrils of smoke, and on a rock beside it, scraping a hide by the light of a sooty lantern, sat Ezra Weems.

But no Audra.

Ethan looked at Thomas.

The Cheyenne shook his head.

Hell.

Looking back at the moonlit camp, Ethan searched for any sign of movement other than Weems working by the fire, or the mule moving restlessly on his tether. He saw nothing. The night was so still, he could hear the prospector muttering and singing. It sounded like "Buffalo Gals."

Where was she? Was she even down there?

Frustration drumming through him, he stretched out beside Thomas to watch for Brodie and Tait, careful not to send loose pebbles bouncing down the slope. If she was being held nearby, at least Weems was sitting outside alone, rather than off hurting her in his tent or somewhere else. Ethan strained to listen, but heard only the singing and mumbling of the man by the fire.

A few minutes later, the mule snorted and lifted its head. Ethan froze, hoping the animal hadn't caught their scent, but it was looking off to the east.

Weems dropped the hide and rose. Picking up the rifle leaning against the rock he had used as a seat, he scanned the edge of the clearing, then hurried over to duck behind a big boulder near the spring directly below Ethan and Thomas.

Ethan heard them then, the clatter of shod hooves on rock announcing two riders making no effort to hide their progress. A moment later, the sheriff and Rylander rode out of the trees and into the clearing.

"Hallo the camp," Brodie called as they reined in.

Ethan brought up his rifle in case the prospector came out shooting.

"That you, Sheriff?" Weems shouted from behind the boulder.

"It is," Brodie called back. "And Tait Rylander from the hotel."

The prospector stepped into view, his rifle ready but not at his shoulder.

Ethan relaxed. Flattening on the ground beside Thomas, he watched the men below.

Weems walked down toward the fire. "Out kinda late, ain't you, Sheriff?"

"We're looking for somebody. A woman."

Weems snickered. "Then you come to the right place. Got a whole passel of them yonder in the tent. Take yer pick. Damn whores won't leave me alone." Pleased with his wit, he broke into a belly laugh that ended in a coughing and spitting fit.

Ethan's fingers itched to close around his neck.

"We're looking for the woman who works in the newspaper office," Brodie went on once Weems caught his breath. "Miss Pearsall. Somebody carried her off. You see anyone ride by here this evening?"

"Nobody rides by here, Sheriff. I'm so far off the beaten path, not even the badgers visit. She the one marrying the railroader?"

"How'd you hear about that?"

"I get to town now and again. Today, in fact."

"Did you notice anything out of the ordinary while you were there?"

"Like a woman getting carried off?" Another laugh. Another cough. More spit. "Can't say's I did," he said, wiping a jacket sleeve over his mouth. "'Spect I mighta noticed that."

"Anybody else farther up the canyon?"

The prospector shook his head. "Trail ends here. Too steep beyond. Until the railroad blasts it out, I suppose." He made a show of looking around. "And speaking of railroads, why ain't her *fi-an-say* here looking for her?"

"He is. Over on the other side of the ravine."

Tait shifted in the saddle, one hand reaching down to rub his bad knee. "The man who owns the newspaper was found dead in the office. Last she was seen, Miss Pearsall was headed that way."

"Maybe she killed him and run off."

"I doubt it."

"Then maybe the railroader killed him."

"He was with us all afternoon," Brodie said.

"Then I guess you wasted your day."

"Probably." Brodie swung down and handed his reins to Tait. "But just to be sure, I'll take a look in your tent before we head back to town."

Weems waved him to it, and settled again on his rock, the rifle across his bent knees. "Tell the ladies I'll be in shortly," he called and laughed.

Ten minutes later, Brodie and Tait rode out.

Weems continued to sit by the fire until the sound of their progress back down the trail faded, then he laughed, put the rifle away, and dug out the fixings for supper. While it cooked, he puttered around camp, turning the hides on the drying rack, throwing hay to his mule, carting buckets of water from the pool in the rocks. Then he sat on his seat by the fire and ate his meal straight from the pan.

Apparently, he wasn't saving anything for Audra—if she was even there. Once he licked the pan clean, he dropped it on a stack of firewood by the fire, picked up his lantern, and started up the slope where Thomas and Ethan waited.

Expecting to be discovered, Ethan grabbed his rifle again. But before he could work the lever, Thomas put out a hand to stop him.

"Not yet," he whispered.

Weems continued up the slope, humming softly to himself. Halfway up, he stepped off the trail and disappeared behind several big boulders. Not even the glow from his lantern showed in the darkness.

Ethan looked at Thomas. "What's he doing?"

Thomas shrugged.

"I'm going down." Ethan started to rise.

"Patience," Thomas said, and pulled him back down. "If he does not show himself soon, we will both go down."

"'Soon' better not be more than a few minutes."

Thirty-one

Audra didn't know how long she sat in the dark. Minutes? Hours? Without light, she had no way to mark the passage of time. As if to compensate, her other senses seemed to grow stronger, adding fuel to her overworked imagination.

She heard things crawling, smelled the rankness of the decaying meat on the plate, tasted acid from her own churning stomach. Trapped in blackness, she jumped at every furtive rustling, not knowing what was coming at her and from which direction. She wondered how the blind could bear it.

She tried to combat the terror with thoughts of Ethan, Father, all her new friends in Heartbreak Creek. Did they know now that she was missing? Were they looking for her yet?

Earlier, she imagined she'd heard hushed voices, but they were gone in a moment. They sounded like they had come from just outside in the corridor, or from somewhere overhead. But that was impossible. She had seen the stone walls of the passageway and this small cavern. If someone had been walking on the ground above her, she couldn't have heard them this far underground.

Time passed. And as she huddled fearfully in the dark, arms locked around her knees and skirts tucked so the bugs couldn't crawl up her legs, a horrible realization had come to her. They wouldn't find her in time. Even if Ethan came to Weems's camp, he would never think to look for her in this black pit. She would die here unless she found a way to escape.

But to do that, she would need light.

She knew Weems wouldn't simply give her a candle or lantern. She would have to bargain for it. But all she had to bargain with was herself. The notion was so repugnant she almost vomited. There had to be another way.

Forcing the fear aside, she tried to think. What did Weems want most?

To kill me.

So why didn't he?

He's waiting for the full moon.

And what would spoil his plans?

If I killed myself first.

A horrifying thought. Yet, it might work if she could bluff him into thinking she would actually do it.

How?

I could tell him I'll fling myself against the collar so hard it will break my neck.

Improbable that it would work, and doubtful that he would believe her capable of doing it.

I could hang myself.

From what? There was no convenient hook in the ceiling or a chair from which to take that final fatal step.

I could refuse to eat or drink.

Too long. She only had four days. Or was it three now?

I could swallow my tongue.

Was that even possible? What if he dared her to try it?

I could use the piece of metal in my pocket. Threaten to open a vein in my wrist.

And what if he called her bluff? Could she stick the tine in her arm? More likely, as soon as he saw what she intended to do, he would take it away from her, leaving her with nothing to use against him later.

So it would have to be something she could demonstrate if necessary, without doing permanent damage to herself. Something so believable he would give her a candle or lantern rather than miss out on the fun of killing her.

Like what?

For a long time, she played different scenarios through her mind. Most were implausible at best. All of it was implausible, in fact. Absurdly macabre—horrifying—that she would be sitting here in a living tomb, at the mercy of a madman, devising ways to end her life.

Perhaps she was trapped in a terrible dream.

Perhaps she was insane.

Either way, she wouldn't allow Weems to defeat her. She would keep thinking and plotting, and as long as she didn't let fear and despair take over her mind, a workable idea would come to her.

And finally it did. She remembered that several of her father's papers on ancient cultures had dealt with ritual human sacrifice. She recalled one involving self-strangulation. The victim put a noose around his neck, tied the other end to a stationary object behind him, then knelt down at the end of the tether and leaned into the noose until he slowly ran out of air. Because the spine couldn't bend backward, even if the victim fainted, he would hang there against the noose until eventually he died.

She sat up, hope building. She had the noose—her collar. And she had the stationary object—the wall to which the chain was bolted. All that was missing was the will to do it. Or, at least the ability to convince Weems she had the will.

It could work.

A faint glow of light showed through the opening. Shuffling footsteps.

Terror engulfed her, sent irrational thoughts careening through her head. What if it was already the full moon? What if he was coming to kill her early? What if he intended to force himself on her, torture her, beat her with Gallagher's whip just for fun?

She buried her face in her knees, almost choking on fear. Then that voice of reason screamed through her mind. *No! You can do this!*

She had to. Or go insane. Or give up and die.

On trembling legs, she stood, smoothed back her tangled hair, and clasped her shaking hands at her waist. Hiking her chin, she stared at the opening and watched the light grow brighter with each shuffling step.

Then suddenly he was there, a hulking form in the opening, his rank odor wafting through the small space like a poisonous cloud. Breathing through her mouth, she squinted against the sudden brightness.

"Still alive, I see." His laughter boomed off the walls. "The little buggies didn't get you yet?"

"I want a lamp."

He set the lantern on the high rock, then faced her, hands on hips. "Not a chance."

"A candle then. Or I kill myself."

He tensed. "Kill yourself how?"

"Self-strangulation. It was a practice among ancient cultures that indulged in human sacrifice." Seeing he had difficulty following, she explained how she would go about it. "It's really quite painless," she concluded. "And most effective."

"Why would you do that?"

"To ruin your fun. And because I'm afraid of the dark."

She watched speculation flash in his pig-like eyes, and realized she would have no trouble driving the jagged point of the piece of metal into one of them. But he was too crafty to come within reach of her tether.

"I ain't giving you no lantern."

She didn't respond.

"But I guess a candle wouldn't hurt." Reaching up to the shelf where he had set the lantern, he retrieved a candle and a small box of friction matches. When he saw her expression of surprise, he snickered. "Poor little girlie. Spent all that time crying in the dark when she had a candle right above her head." He tossed the candle and matches at her, laughing as she fell to her knees, scrambling to find them in the tangled blankets.

"They came looking for you today."

She rose, the precious candle and box of matches in her hands.

"Didn't stay long. Looked around some, then left. They'll never find you, girl, not in this old mine shaft, so you can get that hope out of your head. You're here to do with as I please. Or at least until the full moon." He laughed and rubbed his crotch. "Now for some fun."

Horrified, she sidled away.

He grabbed the chain and hauled her back. "Relax. I ain't

gonna hurt you. Not this time. Just want to see the goods. Take off your shirt."

"N-No."

Another yank almost pulled her off her feet. "Do it, girl. Or I will. In fact, you keep defying me and I may do more than look. Now take it off." Grinning, he stepped back out of reach and slid a hand into his trousers.

Do what he says. Stay alive.

Shaking so much she feared she'd drop them, she slipped the candle and matches into her skirt pocket, then unbuttoned her blouse.

"Open it," he said, hoarsely. "And pull down that underthing so I can see your titties."

She did, her tear-blurred gaze fixed on the far wall, bile rising in her throat.

"Nice. I like 'em plump and round."

Shivering with revulsion, she waited for him to touch her. He didn't.

But she heard his breathing change and the rustle of fabric grow louder as he fondled himself, and imagined the vile thoughts circling his maggot brain.

A few minutes later, he let out a deep groaning breath. More rustling as he righted his clothing. "Next time I'll have a taste." Picking up the lantern, he turned and walked through the opening.

With trembling fingers, she buttoned her blouse, then sank down onto the pallet. Nausea rolled through her stomach. She couldn't stop shaking.

Yet, as the light and his footsteps faded, despite the loathing and fear, she felt a thrilling sense of triumph.

"I'll kill you!" she screamed into the darkness, then cringed when her voice ricocheted back at her from all directions, building into a thousand angry voices. But instead of frightening her, they filled her with hope.

Now she had a weapon. And a light. She could win this.

Impatience ate at Ethan. Weems had been out of sight for too long. What was he doing? Where had he gone? Did he have Audra hidden in those rocks?

"I'm not waiting any longer." He rose, then immediately dropped down when the prospector stepped back into sight. After pausing to do up his trousers, he headed down to his camp, the lantern swinging from his hand.

Apparently, the boulders were his latrine. *Son of a bitch.*

Beside him, Thomas muttered something in Cheyenne and shook his head.

So where was Audra? If she was here, why hadn't Weems gone to her?

Unless she wasn't here. Or someone else had her. Or Weems had no more use for her.

No. She's alive. He could feel it.

Weems went into his tent. Before long, a thin wisp of smoke drifted up from the stovepipe, reminding Ethan that he'd left his bedroll tied to Renny's saddle, and that the night would get colder. A few minutes later, the tent went dark and silence settled over the camp.

He had been so sure the killer would lead them to Audra. Now they would have to wait until dawn. If the bastard didn't go to her then, Ethan vowed to go down and confront Weems himself. His only comfort was that Weems wasn't with her now.

With a weary sigh, he lay back and watched the moon slide toward the western peaks. In the trees nearby, an owl hooted, and farther away, the howl of a wolf cut through the stillness. Lonely sounds on a cold, lonely night that conjured up thoughts of Audra, and another night not too long in the past when he'd held her in his arms and felt her shiver beneath his stroking hands.

Would he ever touch her again?

The waiting was agony—not knowing what was happening to her or what he should do. She could be within feet of where he sat, waiting for him to come. Not even those chaotic hours after the walls fell at Salty Point had been this bad.

He glanced over at the man dozing beside him, his hands folded over his belly, his chin tucked to his chest. The waiting didn't seem to bother Thomas. Either the Cheyenne was made of stone, or he was unconscious. Ethan had never seen a man sit so long without moving. He wished he could doze like that, but somebody had to keep watch. Maybe if he closed his eyes just for a minute . . .

When next he opened them, the moon had disappeared, the sky was the color of pewter, and Thomas was sitting nearby on a downed log, eating from one of the packets of food Tait had given them.

Ethan sat up when a second packet landed on his chest. "Canteen?" he whispered.

The Indian smirked. "White people."

Even though he had no appetite and his stomach was a mass of knots, Ethan made himself eat so he could keep up his strength. He was finishing off a slightly stale biscuit when Thomas suddenly appeared beside him—how did the man move so silently?

Bending, the Cheyenne whispered, "I will go now to check with the others. You will stay here and make no sound."

"Tell them that as soon as it's full light, I'm going down there."

"Wait until I return. I will go with you."

After Weems left, Audra lit the candle and studied her prison. Knowing she wouldn't have light for long if she burned the candle continuously, she mapped every inch of the cavern in her mind so she would still be able to find her bearings in the dark.

Now that she knew searchers had come and gone, she gave up any hope of being found in time. And as much as she might want to kill her captor, she knew if Weems died, she would remain chained to the wall in this hole forever.

Her only hope of survival was escape. And her only hope of escape was to break her tether.

Working as quickly as she could in the flickering candle-light, she examined the chain. Rusty but still solid. The collar was too thick to cut through with her piece of metal, and the lock on it wouldn't budge. If there was any weakness, it was where the chain attached to the wall.

Wishing she had her spectacles, she studied it intently. A screw with an open, looped top had been drilled into the stone. The chain was then passed through the loop and secured with another lock.

She yanked on the chain. Nothing. She tried to pick the lock, but the metal tine was too big to fit into the keyhole. Using her rocks, she struck the bolt again and again, trying to snap it off, but the rocks broke apart first. Sobbing in frustration, she sank down against the wall, trembling from lack of food and sleep, her mind dulled by hours of unrelenting fear.

I can't do this anymore. I want it over.

How? A brutal death at the hands of Weems? Or a slow, agonizing death by starvation? Or . . .

Tears streaming down her face, she pulled out the piece of metal.

Or . . . end it herself.

The idea was abhorrent. An affront to everything she believed. But what choice did she have? They weren't coming back. And if they did, they would never find her down here. Better to die on her own terms, rather than those of a madman.

Tipping her head back against the wall, she watched candle-light play across the rocky ceiling and thought of Ethan's lop-sided smile, his beautiful blue eyes, and those strong, gentle hands. It wasn't fair that all her dreams should end like this. It wasn't right. There had to be a better way.

Weeping, she looked down at the sharp metal in her shaking hand, wondering if she could stick it into her own flesh.

Then it came to her. A solution so simple it might actually work. Sitting upright, she swiped tears from her eyes as thoughts raced through her mind. Anything that could be screwed in could also be screwed out, right? The looped bolt was the key. And her piece of metal was the leverage.

Hope soaring again, she bounded to her feet, then staggered for balance as sparks flashed behind her eyes. Once the spinning stopped, she slipped the piece of metal into the loop and wrapped a wad of her skirt around it to protect her hands. Then, praying the tine wouldn't break off, she pushed against it with all of her might.

At first, nothing. Then something gave—she was sure of it.

She pushed again. Harder. Slowly, in tiny increments, the bolt began to turn.

A sob broke from her throat. "Thank you, God."

With renewed energy, she blew out the flame so the candle would last longer, then wrapped her hands around the bolt and set to work.

Thirty-two

Dawn came and went without Thomas.

Ethan's nerves hummed like stretched wire. They had been watching all night, and still no sign of her. What if they were watching the wrong man?

Weems came out of his tent, stretched, scratched, coughed, and spit, then wandered over to piss in the bushes. After he buttoned up, he stoked the fire and set a pot to boil. Soon the smell of coffee and frying bacon drifted up the slope.

Ethan thought about going down there and working the bastard over with Gallagher's whip. That would get him talking. Assuming Weems was the killer and he had Audra.

Damnit, where was Thomas?

He would wait just a little longer, then confront Weems on his own. He wouldn't let Audra go through another day with this man.

After finishing his breakfast, Weems set out a bucket of water and grain for the mule, then headed up the slope toward the latrine.

Ethan sat back, indecision gnawing at him. Wait for the other men? Or go down alone? He was sick of waiting. They had been doing that for eight hours, and Weems had never once taken her food, or water, or done anything to give away Audra's whereabouts. Either somebody else had her, or the prospector had no need to take her anything because she was already dead.

Dead.

His mind reeling at the thought, Ethan bent over and sucked in air, one hand pressed to his churning stomach. When the cramps eased, he straightened, determined to find out the truth. If she was alive, she needed him. If not . . .

He peered over the edge.

Weems was almost halfway up the slope. It was time to make his move. Deciding on the pistol rather than the rifle, he checked the load, then rose.

A hand clamped over his wrist and yanked him back down. "Not yet," Thomas whispered.

Ethan rounded on him. "Where the hell have you been?" he whispered back.

Instead of answering, the Cheyenne pointed to the camp as Ash, Rafe, Brodie, and Tait rode into the clearing.

Weems saw them, too. He stopped on the trail, glanced up at the boulders, then down at the mounted men below. "What do you want?" he called.

Brodie motioned the others to dismount. "The newspaper lady."

"I told you I ain't got her."

"Mind if we look around just to be sure?"

"Suit yourself." Weems started up the slope again, faster than before. Escaping.

"Now," Thomas said.

But Ethan was already up and moving to the edge of the slope, his Colt hanging in the hand by his side. "Going somewhere, Weems?"

The prospector stumbled to a stop. He blinked at Ethan, a look of panic widening his eyes. "What you doing up there?"

"Watching you."

The look of panic increased when Thomas started down behind Ethan, the war ax in one hand, his rifle in the other.

"Don't do anything stupid, Weems," Brodie called. "Just come down and let us look around, then we'll be out of your hair."

The prospector's head swiveled as he looked at the men in the clearing, then up at Ethan, who had already drawn level with the boulders. Muttering under his breath, Weems headed back down to his camp. "Don't know what you expect to find, Sheriff. Already told you she ain't here."

"Then you won't mind us checking for ourselves." When the prospector reached level ground, Brodie motioned to the rock by the fire. "Have a seat. And keep your hands where we can see them."

Ethan came to stand beside the prisoner, gun in hand, while Brodie went into the tent and the other four men spread through the camp and into the trees where the mule stood watching.

He wished Weems would try something. Wished for any excuse to get his hands around the man's throat. But until they found out where he had hidden Audra, they had to keep the bastard alive.

Brodie came out of the tent, a burlap bag in his hand and a look of triumph on his face. "Come look what I found, fellows." As the men gathered around, he dumped the contents of the bag on the ground by the fire.

A long black pigtail. A beaded pouch. A pocket watch. A faded tintype of two children. A gold medallion. A couple of crumpled envelopes addressed to someone other than Weems, and several other items Ethan had never seen before. "I also found Gallagher's whip and that thing that goes on top of a survey tripod. The gold nugget is probably in there, too."

Rylander studied the man watching them with dark, darting eyes. "Looks like you've been at this for a long time, Weems."

"I found that stuff. In a trapper's cache other side of the canyon."

"And this?" Ethan picked up the brass disc. "This belongs to Audra's father. How'd you get it, Weems?"

"Found it," the prospector said with a nasty laugh. "At the Arlan place. Right there beside your *fi-an-say*'s lacy underthings in the bureau drawer."

Ethan's fingers closed so tightly around the medallion, the hard edge dug into his still-sore palms. "You were in her house?"

"Maybe. Maybe she invited me in. Maybe she even spread her legs for me."

Ethan cocked his pistol. It took monumental effort not to ram it into that rotten mouth and pull the trigger. Instead, he hunkered on his heels in front of the sweating man. "Where is she?"

"Who?"

"Audra Pearsall."

"The little newspaper whore?"

Ethan jammed the barrel of the Colt against the top of the prospector's fur boot and squeezed the trigger.

Noise exploded. Weems screamed. The stench of blood and singed fur mingled with the acrid odor of spent powder as the injured prospector rocked back and forth, clutching his foot.

"Damnit, Hardesty!" Brodie stomped forward, but Ash held him back.

"You can tell me now, Weems," Ethan said, ignoring the others. "And face a judge. Or you can delay and face another bullet. Either way, you'll be telling me where she is."

"I don't know where she is!" Weeping, the prospector slipped a hand into his boot to staunch the blood seeping through the hole.

Ethan lifted the gun again.

"Stop it, Hardesty!" Brodie shouted. "You're a duly sworn deputy. You can't go around shooting people."

"He's right," Ash said. "Waste of bullets. Thomas, you bring that skinning knife with you?"

In a move so fast it caught them all unawares, Weems lurched to his feet, his arm slashing out.

Pain shot down Ethan's arm. The gun fell from his grip. He looked in astonishment at blood welling from a cut in the sleeve of his jacket. Then Weems was on him, throwing an arm around his neck from behind, knocking off his hat and jerking him off-balance.

"I'll cut him," Weems shouted in a panicky voice, hopping on one foot as he pulled Ethan away from the others. "I swear it!"

Gulping for air, Ethan reached up to pull Weems's arm from his throat. Another slash, another searing pain across his arm. His fingers went numb. Dimly, he heard hammers cock. "No!" he gasped. "Don't shoot!" If they killed Weems, they would never find where he'd hidden Audra.

"Let him go," Brodie ordered the prospector.

"So you can kill me?"

"We won't shoot, I give you my word."

"Yeah. Right."

Ethan struggled to breathe. Darkness pressed against the edges of his vision. *Where is she?* he cried, but no sound came out.

The men advanced, coming from three sides, driving Weems and Ethan back toward the edge of the drop-off. Dimly, Ethan saw that the only one not holding a weapon was Thomas.

"Stay back!" Weems shouted, pressing the knife against Ethan's chest. "I'll gut him like a trout. I swear it!"

The others stopped, but Thomas continued on, his steps calm and measured, forcing Weems steadily back. "Where is the woman?"

"Dead and buried."

Ethan went cold. An icy fear spread through his chest.

"Where?" Thomas asked.

"You'll never know."

Another step back. Warmer air swept up the cliff face from the jagged rocks below, cracking the ice that numbed Ethan's mind. "She's dead?" he choked out.

"As a stone." Weems laughed in his ear. "And a lively little virgin, she was. Tight as a banker's fist."

Fury exploded. Ethan slammed his head back. Heard bone and cartilage snap. Weems staggered, his arm still locked around Ethan's throat.

Ethan grabbed the prospector's knife hand, and using all the strength he had left, shoved it up and into the face of the man behind him.

A scream. Weems lurched backward, dragging Ethan with him. The ground gave way. Locked together, they started to slide.

Thomas lunged, caught Ethan's ankles. Others grabbed his belt, his legs. For a moment he hung stretched between the hands that kept him from falling, and the arm dragging him down. Then just when he thought his head would come off and his lungs would collapse, the arm around his throat fell away and he was free.

Coughing and choking, he felt himself pulled back up onto solid ground, where he lay gasping, air whistling through his bruised throat. After a moment, he looked over at Thomas, stretched on the ground beside him. "Is he dead?"

Thomas nodded, his own chest heaving.

Jesus, no . . . Audra.

The realization that she was lost to him forever sent his mind spiraling away.

He became vaguely aware of someone working on his cuts. His jacket was off, and he started to shiver as cold from the ground seeped into his back. Voices warbled around him—someone saying he had lost a lot of blood and they needed to get him to Doc—Brodie telling Rafe to untie the mule and Thomas to get the horses.

"No!" he rasped, struggling upright. "We have to find her!"

"Lad." Ash hunkered beside him. "It's too late."

"No . . . she's here. She's . . ." He looked around, his mind starting to spiral again. "She's here . . . somewhere." He looked up at the men standing over him, their faces grim. "I can't . . . I can't just leave her."

"We'll come back," Brodie promised. "As soon as we get you to Doc, we'll gather searchers and find her and bring her home."

Tears clogged Ethan's aching throat. He could make no sense of it—the madness that had driven Weems—Audra's suffering—why God had taken her and not him. Better if he had gone over the cliff with Weems.

Audra . . . I'm so sorry . . .

Time passed in a haze of pain and despair. Somehow, he kept breathing despite the emptiness inside. Moving by rote, he did what he was told to do—mounted Renny, fell into line when the others started back down the canyon—held on with one hand to keep from sliding off.

But with every step away from Audra's resting place, a voice in his mind whispered that it was wrong, he shouldn't leave her, she still needed him.

The candle guttered out. Clutching the broken pieces of metal in her bleeding hand, Audra watched the lingering halo of the flame fade from her vision.

Hope dimmed with it. With the tine broken, she had no leverage to turn the bolt, and her fingers weren't strong enough to unscrew it from the stone. Using the last of her light, she had searched every inch of the cavern that her tether would allow her to reach, but she had found nothing else she could use.

She had failed. Soon Weems would come. He would humiliate her again, force her to do things that would degrade her to the point that she no longer cared whether she lived or died. And then it would be done.

Three—or was it now two?—days of torture and abuse, followed by a brutal death. That was her future. All she had left.

In some distant, detached part of her mind, she wondered how she should use her remaining hours. Relive memories? Pray to the God who had abandoned her? Devise a way to end her life before Weems could, even if it meant eternal damnation?

A wobbly laugh broke from her throat. *No use burning bridges, old girl. God might still be out there somewhere.* Pulling the foul blanket over her shivering body, she closed her eyes and began the prayer her mother had taught her so long ago.

"Now I lay me down to sleep . . ."

By the time they rode past Audra's burned-out cabin, Ethan's numbness had faded and the whispered voice in his head had risen to a shout.

He shouldn't be riding away. He shouldn't give up so easily. What if Weems was lying, and saying she was dead had been the final cruelty of a brutal, deranged mind? What if she was still alive?

"No." He pulled Renny to a stop. "I'm going back."

Horses bunched up behind him. Ahead, Brodie reined in his sorrel and turned in the saddle. "What's wrong?"

"Weems was lying. She isn't dead." Saying the words aloud destroyed any lingering doubt. Audra was alive. He was certain of it. He looked from face to face as the other men reined in beside him. "Weems only kills on the full moon. That's three days away. He wouldn't break his cycle now."

"Maybe he didn't intend to," Tait argued. "Knowing Audra, she would have fought hard. It could have been an accident."

"Or maybe he was lying," Ethan insisted.

"If you want, lad. We'll bring Tricks back with us. He has a verra keen nose, so he does."

"There's another reason I think he was lying." Ethan hesitated, then realized disloyalty to Audra was secondary now. "She's not a virgin. She told me she wasn't, and I believe her. Why would Weems lie about that?"

"Maybe just to goad you," Rafe said. "The man was demented."

"Exactly. So why would we believe anything he said?"

No one responded. The horses moved restlessly, apparently as ready to head home as their riders were. The men had been out all night and half the day. They were tired, hungry, disheartened. And Ethan could tell by the way they avoided looking at him that they thought he was speaking now from emotion, rather than logic.

It didn't matter. She was alive and he would find her. "I'm going back." He started to turn Renny.

Ash grabbed his reins. "I know this is hard, lad. If something had happened to my Maddie—"

"There is something else," Thomas cut in. "I thought it was another foolish thing that white people did. Now I am not so sure." Turning to Ethan, he asked, "When is the only time Weems was out of our sight?"

Ethan curbed his impatience. "When he was at the latrine or in his tent." But then a sudden image flashed through his mind—Weems pissing into the bushes by his tent. Why hadn't he gone up to the boulders like before? The buzzing started again, almost drowning out Thomas's voice.

"And would a man—even a white man—put his latrine above the source of his water?"

"No." Jerking the reins free, Ethan spun Renny around. "Bollocks."

"Rafe, take the mule on to the livery," Brodie ordered. "Tell the ladies . . ."

There was more, but Ethan already was racing back up the trail to the camp.

Thirty-three

A voice called her name. She lurched up, not knowing if she was awake or dreaming. It was so dark she couldn't even tell if her eyes were open. Holding a hand before her face, she blinked and felt her lashes brush against her fingers. Awake. Or dreaming she was awake.

The voice came again. Distorted. Hollow-sounding. Like an echo.

She scrambled to her feet and looked in the direction where she knew the opening to be. Was it growing lighter? Was someone coming? Weems?

Or maybe help had come at last. The thought made her heart pound so hard it made her dizzy.

Please God.

She stared into the darkness.

Again. Closer now. "Audra!"

Ethan? "Ethan! I'm here!"

Footsteps. Voices. Not Weems.

"In here!" she cried.

Light burst through the opening, blinding her.

"Oh, Jesus—Audra!"

An arm closed around her, pulled her hard against a solid chest. His whole body shook with his ragged breathing. "God . . . you're alive . . ."

"Ethan . . ." She clung to him, her legs trembling beneath her. "You found me, you came . . ."

"Are you all right?"

She couldn't answer, couldn't stop crying, didn't want to let him go. Other voices rose around her, but she was weeping so hard she couldn't make out the words. "Weems said—"

"He's dead. He'll never hurt you again. Let me look at you." He drew back, then stiffened when he saw the collar around her neck. "Somebody get this off of her," he said hoarsely, his voice unsteady. "Now!"

Thomas appeared beside her. She saw the knife in his hand and shrank away.

"Do not fear me, *katse'e*—little one. I will not hurt you. You know this."

Ethan turned her face into his chest. "Let him, sweetheart. It will only take a moment."

She felt the blade slip between the collar and her neck, but Ethan's heart drummed so loudly beneath her ear she couldn't hear the sawing of the knife on the thick leather. A moment later, she was free.

Free. Alive. Whole.

If Ethan hadn't been holding her, she might have fallen. "T-Take me out of here."

He bent to peer into her face. "Can you walk?"

She gave a choked laugh. "I can run. Hurry. I want to see the sun."

They seemed to weave forever through the rocky passageways. It was a miracle they'd found her with all the twists and turns. The uphill slant left her winded and unsteady in the knees, but when she saw the sunlit opening ahead of Declan, who held the lantern, she wanted to push him aside and run the rest of the way. Yet, at the last moment, she had to slow, blinded by the brightness after so many hours in the dark. She stumbled forward, one hand shading her eyes, then felt Ethan's hand on her shoulder.

"Keep going," he said at her back. "I've got you."

Tears streaming from beneath her closed lids, she let him guide her out of the mine shaft. Once everyone came through the entrance behind her, she stopped and waited for her eyes to adjust.

She felt the heat of the sun on her face—smelled juniper and pine as a gentle breeze swept away the dank mustiness of her prison—heard the distant cry of a hawk circling on updrafts rising off of the sun-warmed earth.

Life.

A hand gently brushed the tangled curls off her face. "Now let me see how badly you're hurt."

Blinking fast in the glare, she squinted at the slits in Ethan's jacket. "Why are you bleeding?"

"It's nothing. A couple of cuts. Ash put on a field dressing until I can see Doc. What about you? That bump on your head looks nasty, and your face is bruised, and I can see you're favoring your arm. How bad?"

She forced a smile. "Not bad. Just sore."

"And those cuts on your hands?"

"I found a piece of metal and tried to use it to loosen the bolt on the chain, but it broke. They're only scrapes."

Noticing that the other four men were clustered around her, faces grim, she gave them a tremulous smile. "Thank you . . . all of you . . . for finding me. I-I . . ." Her voice cracked.

A moment of awkward silence as she struggled with tears, then Maddie's husband said, "When Weems told us you were dead, lass, we almost lost hope. But the lad wouldna give up. Thank him."

"Will you be able to make it down the hill?" Sheriff Brodie asked. "Or would you like one of us to carry you?"

She glanced at Ethan's bloody sleeve, and decided if he couldn't carry her, she would make it on her own. "I'll walk." But when the others headed down toward the slope, Ethan held her back.

"Are you all right?"

She saw the pain and worry in his beautiful blue eyes, and some of the fear that had locked her in its grip began to crack. "You mean did Weems force me?" She shivered as the memory of that humiliating moment in the cave swept through her. "No. He never touched me . . . not that way."

"Thank God." His arm came around her again, so tight she could hardly breathe.

And suddenly she was crying again. "I love you . . . I love you . . ."

He held her for several minutes, his body trembling, his breath harsh in her ear. "Audra, I'm so sorry you got caught up in this," he said in a broken voice. "I should have protected you better. I should have—"

"You couldn't have foreseen this any more than I." When he started to protest, she pulled back and pressed trembling fingers over his lips. "You didn't give up. You found me. That's what's important." Taking her hand away, she gave him a hard, fast kiss then stepped back. "Now please . . . take me home."

"After we go to Doc's."

Even though Ethan's arm was barely functional, and his neck and shoulders were so sore he could hardly turn his head, he insisted on having Audra ride back with him rather than with one of the other men. He didn't want her out of his sight or his reach for a single moment. Even so, Thomas stayed close by, as if expecting him to let her slide off or something.

When they reached town, Brodie reined in. "I'll stop by your house, Audra, and tell the Abrahams you're safe and will be home after Doc checks you over."

Tait offered to ride ahead to the hotel. "The ladies have been very worried."

"Why don't you go there after you see Doc," Ethan suggested to her. "It'll be awhile before he's finished with me, and you could take a long bath in the hotel washroom. I'm sure Lucinda will lend you clean clothing. I'll come take you home as soon as I finish at the clinic."

Tait read her hesitation as assent. "I'll tell them to start heating the water."

When the other three men rode ahead, Thomas stayed behind. "I will go with you to your healer. And take her to the hotel when she is ready."

They arrived at the clinic a few minutes later. Thomas hung back when Ethan and Audra went up the walk.

Doc Boyce took one look at the two of them and started shaking his head. "If you two aren't the most pitiful pair I've ever seen. What have you done to yourselves this time?"

Ethan explained about Weems as he followed Doc and Audra down the hallway. But when he tried to go with them

into the examination room with them, Doc put out a hand.
"You're still not married, son. Best wait out here."

Too weary to argue, Ethan did as he was told. As soon as
the door closed behind them, weakness overcame him. Sliding
down the wall, he sat on the floor, arms braced across his bent
knees. He couldn't stop shaking. Couldn't seem to catch his
breath. Couldn't clear the fear from his mind.

I didn't lose her, he told himself over and over. *She's safe.
She's going to be all right.*

Emotion constricted his throat. Dropping his head onto his
folded arms, he gave into shuddering relief as tears he never
thought to shed again mingled with the blood on his sleeve.

By the time Audra came out, he had himself in hand again.
Rising, he looked her over—ointment on her forehead, her
hands, a cut on her neck, and who knows where else. She looked
like a battered and dirty china doll. "How is she, Doc?"

"Bruises, abrasions, a bump on the head, and plumb worn
out. She told me what happened. Glad you killed the bastard,
Hardesty, so I wouldn't have to go against my oath. Don't forget
this, Miss Pearsall." He held out gauze, sticking plaster, and a
small brown jar. "After your bath, put more ointment on your
cuts, then cover them with gauze. They should heal quickly.
Your turn, Hardesty."

Thomas stepped out of the shadows at the end of the hallway, startling them. How long had he been standing there? "I
will take her to the hotel now," he told Ethan. "And will guard
her until you come."

Ethan's visit took a lot longer . . . and required fifteen
stitches. Luckily, he had been wearing his thick shearling
jacket, or the blade would have cut to the bone. As it was, he
would be sore for a while, but unless infection set in, he should
heal without a problem. More of that stinking salve, horse liniment for his neck and shoulders, a thick linen wrapping and a
sling for his arm, and firm instructions to stay the hell out of
trouble for a while, then Doc sent him on his way.

He rode slowly back to the hotel, drained in body and spirit,
feeling like he'd been gone for weeks, rather than a night and
a day.

Audra was still in the washroom with the ladies, so he went
through the lobby and around into the door of the Red Eye

where he found the men seated in their usual corner. A bottle of the earl's fine Scotch whiskey sat in the middle of the table. When Ash saw him, he motioned the barkeep to bring another glass. Ethan pulled up a chair between Thomas, who was sipping ginger beer, and Rafe Jessup, who was scratching Ash's wolfhound behind the ear.

Brodie nodded toward Ethan's sling. "Serious damage?"

"Just a few stitches." Ethan glanced around the table at the men who had become like brothers to him. That knot of emotion clogged his throat again, and it was a moment before he trusted his voice enough to speak. "Thank you. For going back and helping me find her. For saving my life. I owe you."

"Aye, you do," Ash said, and they all laughed in that embarrassed way men have when things are on the verge of getting too emotional. "And I'll take my debt in construction help."

"I'd like your expertise on the depot plans," Tait added.

So much for avoiding architecture. "Rafe?" Ethan asked.

Giving Tricks a final pat, he looked up with a half smile. "I'll keep the mule. Poor animal's had a rough life."

Ethan turned to Brodie. "And you, Sheriff?"

"I'm thinking on it."

"Thomas?"

"You will build me a school."

They all looked at him in surprise. "What do you want with a school?" Brodie asked.

"When Prudence Lincoln comes back, she will want to teach. She must have a school to do that."

Ethan wondered if the others were thinking what he was: that Prudence Lincoln might never come back.

"An excellent idea, Redstone," Tait said. "Heartbreak Creek needs a real school. I'll talk to Mayor Gebbers about funding it. And now that Bonet is gone, we need a publisher for the *Herald*, too. Do you think Audra would be interested, Ethan?"

Maybe if they moved the paper to another building. After seeing her employer butchered beside her desk, Ethan doubted she would ever want to go into the *Herald* office again. "I'll ask her." Figuring she would be finished with her bath by now, and probably hungry after going so long without food, he rose. "Dining room still open?"

"Mrs. Abraham is waiting dinner." Brodie tossed back the

last of his drink, then stood. "Thomas, if you'll take Ed and the children home, I need to return a widow-lady's watch and a Chinaman's pigtail, then fill out all sorts of troublesome paperwork for the judge."

After the group broke up, Ethan walked with Tait and Ash back to the hotel, where they found the ladies having tea in Lucinda's office. Audra looked exhausted, huddled on the couch in a thick woolen robe, shearling slippers, and a patchwork of plaster bandages. At least the dirt was gone and the tangles had been brushed from her damp hair—but the warm water had brought out the color in her bruises. She was so weary she looked like she was about to nod off.

"We better go," Ethan told her. "Winnie's waiting supper."

"How's your arm?" she asked when he helped her to her feet.

"A few stitches, that's all." Remembering, he reached into his pocket and pulled out her father's medallion. "We found this among the prospector's things," he said and handed it to her.

Tears filled her eyes, even though she was smiling. "I thought it was lost forever. He said he'd found it in the ashes of the cabin, but I wasn't sure I believed him."

He didn't tell her what Weems had said about finding it at the Arlan house in her dresser drawer. She didn't need to know a killer had been going through her things.

They said their good-byes, then Tait came out to help her up on Renny and wave them on their way. Several people stopped on the boardwalk to watch them, calling, "Glad you're back," and "Welcome home, Audra," as they rode by, but Ethan didn't stop to chat.

Winnie and Curtis came out onto the porch when they rode up, Mr. Pearsall in tow. When Curtis saw Ethan's sling, he stepped up to help Audra down, gave her a bear hug, then offered to take Renny to the paddock out back.

Winnie couldn't stop crying. Mr. Pearsall just looked bewildered.

They had a late family dinner at the worn dining table, and even though Audra could hardly keep her eyes open, she managed to eat a fair amount. When Curtis took her father up to bed, she trailed behind them with Winnie, almost stumbling, she was so tired. After the Abrahams tucked the two of them in bed, they came back downstairs and sat at the table while Ethan told them about Audra's ordeal.

"Oh, my poor baby." Winnie dabbed at her eyes with a tattered dish towel. "What kind of man would do such a thing? And why?"

Ethan had a fleeting memory of Eunice, then quickly shoved it away. "There's no accounting for how some people think, Winnie. They're just not right in the head. It's like something is missing."

"Praise the Lord you found her, Mistuh Ethan."

It was late by the time he finished answering their questions and helped clean up the dishes. When the old couple went on to bed, he heated a pot of water and washed by the hearth, then pulled fresh clothes from the saddlebag Curtis had left by the couch. Not bothering with boots, he slowly climbed the stairs to Audra's room.

She lay curled in the middle of the bed, bathed in shadows and silver moonlight. He stood for a long time, looking at her, his chest tight with emotion.

What if he hadn't insisted on going back to Weems's camp? What if they had never found her and she'd suffered a slow, agonizing death chained in that cold, dark hole? How could he have gone on if he'd lost her?

More tears burned in his eyes, but he blinked them away.

It's over. She's alive.

He moved the chair by the window next to the bed, and with a deep sigh, settled in to watch over her while she slept.

Audra awoke to darkness and a hand holding her down. With a cry, she lashed out, twisting and kicking, until Ethan's voice broke through the terror.

"It's all right. I'm here. You're safe."

She slumped back, her mind in tatters, her body shivering so hard her teeth chattered. "L-Light the lamp. It's too dark."

Once the lamp was lit, she looked fearfully into all the corners, half-expecting Weems to come bounding out, that evil grin on his face.

But the only one there was Ethan—beloved Ethan, her

savior and hero. How he would laugh if she called him that. Sitting up, she reached out for him, felt his good arm close around her in a tight embrace. "Don't leave me," she whispered against his neck.

"I won't."

Wrinkling her nose, she drew back. "What's that smell?"

"Probably the horse liniment."

"It better work," she muttered, moving into his embrace again.

For a long time, she lay cuddled against his chest, his heartbeat a soothing rhythm beneath her ear. But when weariness claimed her again, she lay back, yawning. "Stay with me," she said, patting the bed beside her hip. "I don't want to be alone."

She didn't have to ask twice. Without removing anything but the thick belt in his trousers, he stretched out on top of the covers, his injured arm on the outside, his good arm wrapped around her, holding her close. "How's this?"

She snuggled closer, and tried to ignore the smell of the liniment. "Perfect."

He pressed his lips to her silky hair. "I love you, Audra."

"I love you, too, Ethan."

Safely anchored against his warmth, she finally drifted into a deep, dreamless sleep.

Thirty-four

Audra spent most of the next two days in bed, her body so sore she could scarcely roll over, much less go up and down the stairs. Despite Winnie's hard looks, Ethan stayed the nights with her, sleeping fully dressed except for boots and belt, on top of the covers, his good arm wrapped around her, ready to comfort her when the night terrors came.

And they came often.

Their scrapes and cuts improved rapidly. By the end of the third day, Ethan dispensed with the horse liniment and sling, but their bruises remained livid, fading from bluish-purple to greenish-yellow. Audra fretted endlessly over whether they would be gone by the wedding in just over two weeks.

Ethan didn't care. He was just grateful that she was safe, and anxious for the waiting to end so they could start their lives together without all the artificial barriers between them. In his heart and mind, they were already married.

One or other of the ladies came by every afternoon for the first three days, either to discuss the wedding plans, or to bring pastries for an afternoon cup of tea, or simply to sit and chat about nonsensical things. Between their visits and Winnie's fussing and her time spent with her father, her days seemed to pass fairly easily.

But the nights dragged.

Stretched out beside her, Ethan knew how restlessly she

slept, and when she lay awake, staring at the lamp she insisted remain lit all night. He tried to coax her into talking about what had happened, hoping that might help her sleep better. But she wouldn't say much beyond what she had already told him—that Weems only came to her a few times, and all the other hours she either spent huddled in the cold dark, or working on the bolt in the wall once she had the candle.

"I thought I was going to die," she tearfully told him after one especially fearful dream. "I even planned it, wanting to end it myself, rather than give Weems the satisfaction of killing me. But I couldn't."

"Thank God," he'd murmured, holding her close. "I don't know what I would have done without you." He couldn't bear thinking of her waiting in that cold cell, dying a little more each minute he didn't come. What if he had believed Weems, and had never come back? That thought haunted him, sent him into gasping wakefulness at least once every night.

He didn't know what to do for her—or for him—or what he could say that would help them push these fears from their minds.

The third night after he brought her home, he awoke to find her standing at the window in her gown, her slim form backlit by the rising full moon. He wondered what was going through her mind. If it was another night terror, or if her ordeal had planted fears in her mind about their impending marriage.

He rose and moved up behind her. Sliding his arms around her, he bent down and kissed her neck. "What's wrong? More bad dreams?"

"It's the full moon. This was the night he was going to kill me."

He felt a shudder run through her, and held her tighter. "But he didn't."

"Thanks to you." After a bit, she turned in his arms to face him. With the moonlight behind her, and the lamp burning low, he couldn't see her expression, but he knew she was crying.

"Talk to me, sweetheart. Tell me what's wrong. Maybe I can help."

She looked away. "No . . . it's too . . . I can't."

"Audra." When she still wouldn't look at him, he brought his hands up to cup her face, felt her tears on his fingers, and leaned in to kiss them away. "I love you. You can tell me anything. Just talk to me. Please."

It was awhile before she spoke and when she did, the words were disjointed and hesitant, her eyes downcast rather than meeting his. "He made me unbutton my blouse and pull down my shift so he could look at me while he touched himself. It made me feel filthy. Like spiders were crawling across my skin."

Ethan tried to keep his voice even. "It's his shame. Not yours."

"I know, but . . ." She took a deep hitching breath and closed her eyes. "But that memory keeps circling in my mind. I can't make it go away."

"When we marry, we'll make new memories. Good memories."

"Will we?" Her eyes opened, finally met his. "What if this fear never leaves me? What if it comes between the two of us and I can't . . . can't . . ."

That was his fear, too. He remembered how responsive she had been during his almost-audition. Had this terrible experience robbed her of the unbridled joy and enthusiasm she'd shown when he'd touched her? Taking his hands from her face, he pushed back the hair from her brow and kissed the furrow between her eyes. "Give it time, sweetheart."

"And if that doesn't help?"

"It will. I won't let Weems come between us. Trust me."

"I do trust you, Ethan. But I don't want to wait. I need to know now if I can get past this. I want to make new memories tonight while the moon is full, so that in the years ahead, whenever I see it above me, I'll think of you and not him."

How could he resist that? Or her? Or his own need for assurance? Sleeping beside her every night had tested his resolve to keep his hands to himself, and when she looked at him the way she did now, he could deny her nothing. Bending lower, he kissed her, and felt that simmering desire he always felt whenever he was around her boil over inside him. "You're sure?"

"I've been sure." Her fingers fumbled with the three buttons on the placket of his collarless shirt. When he tried to help, she brushed his hands away. "No, let me."

He forced himself to stand still, his body humming with anticipation, his heart beating so hard he wondered if she could hear it. After she loosened the last button, she pulled the shirt free of his trousers, then slid her hands underneath the fabric. "You're so warm."

Not warm. Burning up, his skin prickling, his muscles quivering beneath her trailing fingers. "Maybe your hands are cold."

"Or maybe you're ticklish." She slid her hands around his waist to his back, slowly pushing up the fabric until her fingers brushed over the first long scar Eunice had given him. "What's this?"

"An old injury."

Her fingers found the second scar below his shoulder. "From when the glass fell?"

"Yes."

"I'm sorry. It must have hurt dreadfully." She pushed the shirt up to his shoulders. "Lean down so I can pull it over your head."

He did.

Mindful of the thick bandage over the cuts that Doc had stitched, she carefully pulled the shirt down his arms, then tossed it onto the seat of a straight chair near the window. She studied him in the slant of moonlight coming through the window, her face softened by the faint glow of the lamp on the other side of the room. "You're so beautiful. All rounded muscle and coiled strength. Like the perfect gift I always wanted, but never realized how badly I needed until you came into my life."

As happened so often when he was with Audra, glib words deserted him and emotion took over. It was all he could do not to sweep her up in his arms and carry her to the bed. But he knew he had to go slow. Let her set the pace. Allow time for her fears to fade.

But he almost forgot that noble intent when her hand slid up his chest to his neck.

"Kiss me," she whispered, rising on tiptoe.

He did, gently at first, then with more feeling when his control began to fray. He needed this woman in ways he had never imagined, and with a depth he had never known was within him. Cradling her head in his trembling hands, he put into that kiss all the love he felt for this kind, fearless, confounding woman . . . and hoped it would be enough.

When he felt her start to draw back, he instantly took his hands away. "I'm sorry. Did I—"

Her soft laughter cut him off. "I ran out of air."

He drew in a relieved breath. "I don't want to rush you."

"You're not. But you can take off your own trousers. I am a lady, after all."

"You're sure?"

"That I'm a lady? Of course."

Despite the quip, he heard the tension in her voice, and knew she was struggling.

"Do stop giving me chances to back out, Ethan. Of course I'm nervous. And a little afraid. And worried that that horrid feeling when Weems made me expose myself will come back. Then I remind myself it's you, not him, and you love me as much as I love you. So . . ." With a deep breath, she loosened the bows on her long nightgown, and slipped it off her shoulders. It floated to the floor in a whisper of fabric.

And there she was. Bathed in moonlight and bared to him as she had never been, her body even more beautiful than he had imagined. Her breasts were high and round as he remembered them. Her waist was so small he could span it with his hands. Her legs were long and firm.

And shaking.

"Look at me," he said when she turned her face away.

Reluctantly, she did, her eyes wide and reflecting the yellowish glow of the lamp. That small furrow between her brows told him she was worried.

"It's me, sweetheart. The man who loves you so much it's like a fire inside him. The one who will never hurt you, and who will always protect you and keep you safe. Tell me you believe that."

She smiled, even though tears rolled down her cheeks. "I do."

He opened his arms. "Then come here."

Knowing there would be only one first joining, and even if it wasn't perfect, it would matter more than all the next times they came together, he went slow, calming her with gentle touches and whispered praise. She was as fragile as a bird in his arms, her heart drumming like frantic wing-beats beneath her breast. He didn't know if it was from fear or desire, but she didn't retreat or tell him to stop.

After laying her out on the bed, he kissed her for a long time, learning again the taste and texture of her lips, and skin, and flower-scented hair. He kissed her breasts, nibbled her neck, traced the shape of her ear with his tongue, all the while keeping his hands gentle as he learned what she liked and where she wanted him to touch her.

When she began to shift restlessly, and grew more insistent when she pulled him down for a kiss, he allowed himself to become bolder. Slowly running his hand down her belly, he found her warmth, and stroked her there until her breathing grew rapid and her movements became more frantic.

"Now, Ethan," she whispered against his lips. "I want you now."

Rising up on his good arm, he looked down at her. "Open your eyes."

She did.

"Think only of me." He positioned himself over her, kissed her again, and said, "Remember how much I love you. That I'm yours until the day I die. And there's nothing I would ever do to hurt you."

"I know."

He pushed inside, heard her gasp, but kept moving. She bit his shoulder. But soon she was rising to meet him stroke for stroke, her legs tight around him, her head thrown back. Then she stiffened and cried out his name, and the world exploded in such heart-stuttering splendor he didn't know where he ended and she began.

It was the best it had ever been.

Collapsing beside her, he pulled her tight against him, his chest pumping as he struggled to catch his breath. "God," he finally choked out. "You're amazing. Perfect. I had no idea . . ."

She pinched him. "You lied."

Startled, he lifted his head to look down at her, and was relieved to see her smile.

"You said you would never hurt me. And that hurt."

"It did?"

"At first."

"And later?"

Her smile widened into that saucy grin. "And later, it didn't."

Chuckling, he let his head fall back to the pillow. "You're a liar, too. You said you weren't a virgin."

"I said *maybe* I wasn't a virgin. I was only trying to ease your worries about the audition."

"Did I pass?"

"Oh, you're definitely the man for the task. As I knew you would be all along."

He grinned, relieved. And proud. "No regrets?"

"And no fears. Weems is gone. There's only you, now and forever." She trailed a fingertip up to the hollow at the base of his throat. "I'm game for anything now."

"Oh?" Laughing, he pulled her on top of him. "Then how about this?"

Epilogue

Through shimmering tears, Lucinda watched Ethan lean down and kiss his bride. The wedding had gone perfectly, even to the point that Mr. Pearsall—with Winnie at his side—was able to walk his daughter down the aisle. Edwina had cried only slightly louder than her infant son, and the other Brodie children had behaved themselves. Thomas had even put in an appearance, stepping inside for the exchange of vows before disappearing again, and Lucinda's guardian, Mrs. Throckmorton—newly returned from Denver with her two chaperones, Mrs. Bradshaw and Buster Quinn—hadn't caused a single ruckus. Yet.

Now, as she and Tait followed the bride and groom from the church, Lucinda felt the prick of more tears, ones that were both happy and sad.

She was delighted to add these two new friends to her Heartbreak Creek family, and was overjoyed to have her guardian back. But she was upset that most of them would soon be leaving her again.

Within a few months, Mrs. Throckmorton and her escorts would accompany Maddie and Ash and Rayford Jessup to New York. When the Wallaces and Jessup went on to Scotland to complete the transference of the earl's title and purchase breeding stock for Ash's horse herd, her guardian would stay behind in Manhattan to close up her house and settle her affairs before returning to Heartbreak Creek permanently.

She would miss them dreadfully. Even Thomas, who would accompany the travelers as far as Indiana, where he would stop off to visit Pru. Hopefully they would all return in spring. By then, the depot would be up and running and the trains would be coming through regularly. Ethan would have the Wallace house finished, and would be nearing completion on the one nearby that he was building for himself, his bride, and her three charges.

And her Heartbreak Creek family would be all together again.

But it would be lonely with everyone gone—especially after Declan found a temporary replacement for his sheriff duties, and took his family to the ranch until fall. It seemed just when she was getting everything set up the way it should be, everybody was leaving.

"It's only a few months," Tait whispered in her ear.

She gave him a look, wondering when he had become so adept at discerning her thoughts.

"And maybe without everyone to fuss over," he added, "you'll spend more time tending yourself."

She swatted his shoulder with her hanky. "I don't need tending."

"Not you, perhaps." His eyes glowed with that fierce protectiveness he had adopted of late. "But the baby might."

"Rothschild is fine," she teased.

"Uthred," he teased back.

The tip of a walking cane poked Tait's calf. "It's rude to whisper," a querulous voice behind him chided. "Especially in front of the partially deaf."

"You're not deaf in the least," Lucinda said, slowing to loop an arm through her guardian's. "You're just overburdened with a surfeit of curiosity."

"She means nosy, doesn't she?" Mrs. Throckmorton asked Tait.

He simply smiled, and offered a hand to help her down the church steps.

They had told no one about the child she and Tait were

expecting. Lucinda felt it would encroach on the wedding cel-
ebrations. This was Audra's day. Hers would come later in
December—God help her. Besides, she wanted to wait a few
more weeks just to be sure.

"After you close up the house in Manhattan," she said to
Mrs. Throckmorton in an effort to change the subject, "what
are you going to do about Pringle?"

Pringle was her guardian's irascible butler—a testy old cur-
mudgeon Mrs. Throckmorton put up with out of pity since she
was convinced he had been in love with her for years—a con-
viction based on what, Lucinda had no idea. Still, he was part
of the family, and if let go, would have a difficult time finding
another position at his advanced age.

"I'm giving him to that foreign person."

"Ash?" Lucinda looked at her in surprise. "You're sending
Pringle to Scotland?"

"It's the perfect solution. Despite his strenuous objections,
I have convinced Mr. Wallace that no self-respecting aristocrat
should be without a manservant."

Lucinda smiled, imagining that conversation. "And what if
Pringle doesn't want to go?"

The old woman waved a hand in dismissal. "It's either that, or
Heartbreak Creek, or the streets. At least this way, he can continue
to harbor hopes of being reunited with me in the future."

Tait started to laugh.

Lucinda scowled at him.

He laughed harder . . . until a cane bounced off his shin.
"What are you carrying on about, you ruffian?"

"Your innate wisdom, madam," he said with a light bow. "I
can think of no greater amusement than watching Pringle bring
Lord Kirkwell up to snuff. An inspired move."

The crafty old woman smiled, her faded blue eyes twinkling
with merriment. "I thought so myself. Almost makes me want
to go with them simply to see how they get on."

"Shall I book you passage?" he asked, hopefully.

"You shall not. But I will certainly be interested in seeing
the changes in that Scottish rogue when they all return. Yoo-
hoo," she called, advancing on Buster Quinn, her man of all
tasks, ex-Pinkerton watchdog, and today, chair carrier. "Take
it over into the shade, if you will, Mr. Quinn."

When they all return, Lucinda thought. That could be in months. Perhaps an entire year. All sorts of things could delay them.

A feeling of panic gripped her. What if Maddie and Ash decided to stay in Scotland?

"We could go with them, you know," Tait said by her ear.

She reared back. "To Scotland?"

Tucking her hand into the crook of his arm, he led her away from the well-wishers crowding around the newlyweds, and steered her past the little cemetery beside the church.

"Maybe not that far," he said, once they were out of earshot of the others. "Not in your condition. But we could visit Pru, then go on to New York to help Mrs. Throckmorton with her move. Wouldn't you like to visit our old haunts in Manhattan?"

A chill seeped into her heart. "You miss it. You want to go back."

"Back?" He swept his free hand at the distant mountains, the aspens crowding the creek, the children playing kickball behind the church. "And give this up for sooty air? Trade peace and quiet for the constant noise and bustle of the city?" Smiling, he shook his head. "No, Luce. I love Heartbreak Creek. It's my home—*our* home. This is where I want our children to grow up. But I wouldn't mind seeing a play or two and visiting a museum, or dining in some of our favorite restaurants, or standing at the rail of a ferry on the Hudson and watching the city lights come on."

"But who would watch over Heartbreak Creek if we left?"

He laughed. "You're such a worrier." Leaning down, he gave her a quick kiss. "You're going to be a wonderful mother. Especially with me there to rein you in."

"You." She poked his arm. "But really, Tait. With so many of us gone, who will oversee the bridge line, and start the new school, and run the hotel, and—"

"Ethan can handle the railroad part of it," he cut in. "And it's time you trained Miriam to run the hotel. And with Audra available when she's not busy at the newspaper, and Edwina there to help once the Brodies come back from the ranch in the fall, everything will be fine."

"As long as Ed stays out of the hotel kitchen," she murmured.

They walked in silence while she considered the idea. It did have appeal. She could visit Pru on the way. And Mrs. Throckmorton could certainly use her help with all those knickknacks in her rambling Sixty-ninth Street brownstone. And it would be amusing to see how Ash and Pringle got along. Perhaps while she was in New York, she could refresh her wardrobe, buy some things for the baby, even pick up a few items for the hotel.

"We could be gone for only a couple of months," she said after a while. "I want to have Uthred here, not in some boxcar in Missouri."

"Rothschild."

"In fact, we should have our own railcar. One large enough to accommodate Mrs. Throckmorton and Mrs. Bradshaw and Mr. Quinn, too. With a lavatory. And a decent cook. I hate those dime box lunches."

"I'll see what the Denver and Santa Fe has available."

"Perhaps you should get one for Maddie and Ash, too. They are titled, after all."

"Yes, dear."

She stopped and faced him. "You must promise me we'll come back, Tait. This is my home."

"Mine, too, Luce. I would live nowhere else."

She let out a deep breath and patted his arm. "All right, then. We'll go. But only as far as New York. And we'll be back by the first snow."

"By the first snow. I promise."

She lifted her face for a kiss, then looked past him at the musicians setting up on the church steps. "We'd best get back. Declan will be dancing soon, and that's a treat not to be missed."

Smiling, she watched the people she had grown to love gathering to celebrate the latest Heartbreak Creek wedding. Yes, this was where she belonged. With her family. In the town she had helped build.

But a short vacation before she took on the exhausting role of motherhood might be just the thing. And surely the town could survive without her . . . just for a month or two.

Read on for a sneak peek of the next
Heroes of Heartbreak Creek novel

SOMETHING IN HIS SMILE

Available July 2014 from Berkley Sensation

Prologue

Rayford Jessup was still a quarter of a mile away from the Hendricks place when he heard the screaming.

He nudged his horse into a run. Fifty yards closer and he could tell the sound was animal, not human.

A horse.

By the time he splashed across the small creek running beside the house and barn, the noise had escalated to loud bangs and shouted cries. His own horse snorted, head up, ears pricked, his steps sidling and hesitant. Feeling the beginnings of a shy, Rafe murmured softly and reached down to run a hand along the chestnut's neck, reminding the young gelding he wasn't alone, and that he needed to pay attention to his rider, not what was going on in the barn.

Stopping in front of the house near an odd sheepherder's-style wagon, Rafe sat for a moment, keeping his hands and legs calm, his voice even and unhurried. While he waited for the gelding to settle, he looked around.

Like most of the scattered holdings in the dry mesquite and cactus country along the Texas–Mexico border, the Hendricks place was a grit-scoured collection of warped wood corrals, rough outbuildings, and sagging lean-tos bleached by the sun to the color of pitted pewter. That it survived at all was due to the narrow muddy creek that fed the single, wind-damaged cottonwood shading the wood-and-adobe house. Rafe supposed there was some appeal in the endless expanse of open sky, but he much preferred the rolling grass and cedar-dotted hills farther north, or the bluebonnet fields in central Texas.

Sensing no immediate danger, his horse began to relax, though he remained alert to the shouts and whinnies that continued to come from the barn. Rafe praised him with more pats, then dismounted as two men came out of the double barn doors.

One was tall—probably as tall as Rafe, but leaner—with graying hair, and the rolling loose-hipped gait of a lifelong horseman. The other man was older, short and stocky. James Hendricks, the man who had sent word for Rafe to come.

"Glad you made it, Jessup," Hendricks called, angling toward him. "Got a real mess going here."

Rafe didn't give a response, since none was required. After looping the reins around the hitching rail in front of the house, he turned and studied the stranger.

Despite the gray hair, the man wasn't as old as Rafe had first thought—not much older than his own thirty-two. And probably ex-cavalry. In addition to the tight buff-colored trousers tucked in to knee-high, polished boots, and the small military-style case attached to his belt, he had a confident, commanding way about him and a directness in his green gaze that hinted at either a background as a military officer, or one in the law. Having been a U.S. marshal for several years, Rafe recognized the probing look, and knew when he was being assessed.

"This here's Angus Wallace," Hendricks said, stopping before him. "Although he says most call him Ash because of his hair. Ash, meet Rayford Jessup, the man I told you about."

"The wizard with horses." Wallace spoke with a strong Scottish accent, offering a firm handshake and a broad smile. "You'll be needing magic, so you will, to deal with the lad tearing up the barn."

"Ash is looking to start a horse breeding ranch up in Colorado," Hendricks explained. "Heard at the fort I had mustangs, so he and his wife came by to see what was available."

Rafe didn't have much admiration for Hendricks's horses. Mostly scrubs. The decent mustangs had been rounded up years ago, except for a few small herds that roamed back and forth across the border between Texas and Mexico. If the Scotsman was thinking to build a stable with these pickings, he wasn't as knowledgeable about horses as Rafe had surmised.

Hendricks flinched when he heard a guttural whinny followed by a series of loud thuds and men yelling. "Well, come along," he said, waving them toward the barn. "Best see if there's anything you can do."

As they walked, Hendricks explained that two sage rats had brought in the mustang several days ago. "Nice-looking stud horse. Or was, before they got ahold of him. Animal was tore up good, and mad at the world. We barely got him locked in the stall before all hell broke loose. For two days he kicked and screamed and snapped at anyone who dared open the stall door to throw him some food. Wouldn't eat or drink. Still won't eat. Quieted down some yesterday, so I figured we'd try again. But you can hear how well that's going."

As they moved out of the glare of the midday sun and into the barn, the air cooled and grew thick with the odors of hay and sweet feed and manure. Comforting, familiar smells that reminded Rafe of his early years on the farm in Missouri. When his eyes adjusted to the gloom, he saw two men standing well back from a stall at the other end of the open center aisle. The stall had a divided door, but as they approached, Rafe could see splintered wood in the bottom half, and blood smears on the upper half where the door hung by a broken hinge.

Another shriek, more thuds rattling the timbers and sending puffs of hay dust sifting down through the gaps in the planked loft floor overhead.

"Don't go too close," Hendricks warned. "He's already taken a bite out of one of my men. *Vamoos,*" he said to the two Mexican watchers. "See if any more new foals dropped today."

As the ranch workers left, Rafe stepped up to the broken door. Staying out of kicking or biting range, he peered into the darkened stall.

Crazed eyes stared back.

The animal was a mess. Blood on his mouth where he had bitten chunks out of the door. Scraped knees, hind legs skinned, pasterns red with blood. It was a wonder the horse hadn't shattered a hoof kicking holes in the walls. Rafe stepped back, almost bumping into the Scotsman who had moved up beside him to study the mustang.

"Bollocks," Wallace muttered. "I dinna think the puir beast will make it much longer."

Rafe didn't either. "What were your plans for him?" he asked, turning to Hendricks.

"Figured to breed him to my mares. Or sell him, if I can get a good price. But can't do either unless he's at least broke to halter. That's why I sent for you." He met Rafe's frown with a shrug. "Heard you could break a green colt without raising a hand. Thought maybe you could settle this one."

Rafe doubted it. The mustang was too mature, too accustomed to running wild, to ever be biddable. And as for breeding, neither his conformation nor his attitude would make him a decent stud. Some horses were best left alone. This was one of them. Reaching into his vest pocket, he fingered the few coins he'd brought with him. "How much you want for him?"

Hendricks named a price that was double what the mustang was worth, even if he could be broken, although broke or not, Rafe doubted the animal would live long enough to attract any buyers.

"I'll pay you half that," Wallace broke in.

Rafe looked at him in surprise, wondering if the man knew he was offering good money for a bad animal. He had thought the Scotsman had horse savvy, but apparently he didn't. Frowning, Rafe stepped back as the two men negotiated.

A wasted trip. He had hoped to pick up enough money to head north, maybe sign on with one of the big ranches along the Chisholm Trail, or find work at the stockyards in Abilene, Kansas. Then once he had enough set by, he'd look for a patch of land in Wyoming Territory where he could plant his stake and start over. Now that he was recovered and strong enough to do hard labor again, he was anxious to put Texas and all the bad memories behind him.

"You'll stay for supper?" Hendricks called back to Rafe as he walked toward the front doors, several eagles and half-eagles clinking in his palm.

Rafe shook his head. "Thanks anyway."

"Tell my wife we'll be leaving, too," the Scotsman called after him. "I'll be in directly to help her pack her equipment."

Seeing Rafe's curious look, he grinned. "She's a famous

photographer," he said proudly. "A.M. Wallace. And verra good, so she is. You've heard of her, no doubt."

Rafe hadn't, but rather than admit it, he gave a noncommittal smile. "What are you going to do with the mustang? I doubt he'll go calmly."

"Aye. He's a wild one, puir lad." Moving closer to the stall, the Scotsman watched the horse warily as he reached for the slide bar on the lower door. "Mind your feet, Jessup," he warned in a calm voice. "He'll be coming out fast."

"You're turning him loose?"

"He's too proud to bend, and I'll no' break a horse I dinna need any more than you would. He'll find his way home. Best stand back now."

Rafe stepped out of the horse's pathway to escape.

Wallace slid the bolt and eased back the stall door. Holding it open, he stood against the wall and waited.

At first, nothing. Then a snort.

And suddenly, the mustang burst out of the stall at a dead run. Tufts of hay and dirt clods flew as he raced toward the light at the open end of the barn. A second later, he was tearing across the field, tail up, head raised in a triumphant whinny. Free. Unencumbered. As he was meant to be.

It was a moving sight. One that made Rafe want to race along with him, just to feel the wind in his face and see what was over the next rise. He watched in silent envy until the horse topped the ridge and disappeared from view. Then Wallace startled him with a hard clap on his shoulder.

"So, lad. Where you headed? Back to the family?"

"No family. North, probably."

Looping an arm over Rafe's shoulder, the Scotsman steered him back through the barn. "As free as the wind, are ye?"

Wallace made it sound exciting and purposeful, rather than the aimless flight of a man trying to outrun a past too painful to face. "Mostly looking for work."

"If it's work you seek, I can offer it. As Hendricks said, I'm putting together a herd."

"Of mustangs?"

"Thoroughbreds."

Rafe stopped so abruptly the Scotsman's arm slid off his

shoulder. "In Colorado?" Pure thoroughbreds were magnificent animals. He'd seen less than a handful of them this side of the Mississippi.

"Eventually." That broad grin again. "But first, I need a wrangler to go with me to get them."

"Go where?"

"To God's own heaven." A rumble of laughter, and a flash of pure delight in those moss green eyes. "Northbridge, in the highlands of Scotland."

One

"You sure?" Rafe asked.

Thomas Redstone nodded.

"But not all of it."

"It is only hair."

Crossing his arms over his chest, Rafe shook his head. "It's more than that, Thomas. It's part of your identity. Like Wallace's kilt. Or a priest's robes. It's part of who you are."

"And who am I, *nesene*?"

"An Indian warrior."

"I am also white. And to honor my grandfather, I choose now to go the white way."

"You're only white when it suits you, Thomas, and you know it. You're a Cheyenne Dog Soldier. Which is a lot harder to be than white."

"I know this." Thomas flashed that rare and startling smile that always caught people off guard. "And I did not earn that name because of my hair."

Rafe threw his hands up in frustration. "Why are you doing this? Because of whatever happened in Indiana?"

A chill crept into the barbershop. "We will not speak of Prudence Lincoln."

"Hell." Rafe knew he treaded dangerous ground. Thomas and the beautiful mulatto had a long history together, only some of which Rafe knew. But something had happened between the two of them in Indiana that had made Thomas decide to continue on to New York, rather than stay for a longer visit with Miss Lincoln, or return home to his mountains in Colorado Territory.

The others traveling with them from Heartbreak Creek to Manhattan had wondered about it, too, but Thomas had rebuffed all questions.

Tait Rylander and his pregnant wife, Lucinda, had made the trip to help Lucinda's guardian, Mrs. Throckmorton, close up the Manhattan brownstone where they were all staying now; then they would return to Heartbreak Creek. Meanwhile, Ash—or the Earl of Kirkwell, as he was known in Britain— and his countess wife, Maddie, would go on to Scotland to check on the earl's estate and purchase thoroughbreds for Ash's horse ranch in Colorado. Rafe had agreed to go with them—as Ash's wrangler, not Thomas's nursemaid.

But upon arrival in New York, the Scotsman had asked him to keep an eye on Thomas until their steamer sailed . . . a more difficult task than Rafe had anticipated, since the Cheyenne had a tiresome habit of wandering off whenever the mood struck him.

Like this morning. Luckily, Rafe had tracked him to this barbershop before any damage was done. But now, seeing how adamant Thomas was to cut off the long black hair and feathered topknot that had marked him a Cheyenne warrior, Rafe wasn't sure what to do.

"What is this really about, Thomas?"

The Indian sat in stony silence for a moment, then sighed. "People stare."

A laugh burst out before Rafe could stop it. "Hell, Redstone. They'll always stare. And not because of your hair." He glanced over at the barber, who watched them with wary curiosity. "Am I right?"

The barber nodded, shook his head, and shrugged all at the same time. An indecisive fellow, it seemed.

"Then why?" Thomas asked.

Rafe couldn't find the words. There was something about Thomas Redstone—perhaps the utter confidence in the way he spoke and moved and looked at the world. Heads would always turn when he came into a room because without saying a word, he dominated it. Like Tait and Ash and the other men from Heartbreak Creek, he was a strong, resourceful, intelligent man. But with Thomas, there was something more. An unknown factor. None of his friends was quite sure what he would do if pushed too far, or if someone he cared about was threatened.

Rafe had heard the rumors about the leather pouch Thomas had once worn beneath his war shirt. It had purportedly contained the blunted bullet that had killed his wife and son, and the Cheyenne had vowed to return it to the trapper who had fired it—by shoving the piece of metal into the man's beating heart.

Vengeance. Rafe understood that. It was something they had in common.

No one knew if Thomas had actually carried out that threat, but one day the pouch was gone. When questioned about it, he had simply said, "It is over."

The Cheyenne warrior was a law unto himself, and because of that, he was a man to reckon with. Even without the topknot and eagle feather, anyone who looked into those dark eyes knew it. "Ash and Tait aren't going to like it."

"Ho. You think that will stop me?"

Rafe gave up. "But only to your shoulders. And keep the temple braids. Women love them."

Thomas smirked. "As do you, it seems."

Rafe ignored that and waved the barber in.

But as the long black strands fell to the floor, he wondered what had brought Thomas to this decision, and once the change was complete, if it would accomplish all that he had hoped.

A half hour later, they were back on the streets.

And heads were still turning.

"I think it is you they look at," Thomas teased when a trio of women standing at the window of a dry goods store stopped speaking to stare at them when they walked by. "Women like big men, and your gold hair is prettier."

"It's probably the gun." Realizing the wind that whistled around the buildings had blown open his jacket to expose the six-shooter holstered on his hip, Rafe quickly buttoned the coat, not wanting to draw undue attention. But after the riots in this area two months earlier between Irish Protestants and

Catholics, he wasn't about to go without protection, especially considering the high crime rate with the corrupt Boss Tweed and his Tammany Hall gang in control of the city.

"Not many in this place wear guns," Thomas noted. "Yet you do."

"Habit." But having as little interest in discussing his painful past as a Texas lawman as Thomas did in discussing Prudence Lincoln, Rafe changed the subject. "Ash is making me get a suit. You'll need one, too, if you expect to eat in the dining room at the castle."

"What is this castle?"

"Northbridge. A big stone house that the Wallaces have in Scotland. You do know Ash is the Earl of Kirkwell, don't you?"

"I know he has many names and one is earl."

"Earl is more of a title. Like chief."

"He still has too many names. And he likes to wear a skirt."

"Kilt." Rafe grinned down at the Cheyenne. "And maybe as payment for taking you with us to Scotland, he'll expect you to wear one, too."

"Ho. I will not do it."

Rafe laughed. "We'll see. Let's start with a suit first. And real shoes."

Although Thomas had set aside his war shirt and leggings in favor of denim trousers, a collarless work shirt, and a blue cavalry jacket with the sleeves cut off—God knows where he got that—he still wore knee-high fringed moccasins with a long, sheathed knife laced on the outside. Even with the shorter hair, he stood out like a two-headed wonder among these city dwellers.

Opening the door of a tailor's shop, he ushered the Indian into the dark-paneled store with bolts of fabric stacked on shelves. Several headless, life-sized, wirework figures modeled fine suits of clothing, including boots.

Thomas stopped inside the door and glared at the figures. "I do not like this place," he announced, and turning, left the shop.

With a sigh, Rafe followed him. "I know someplace you will like," he said, falling in beside the Cheyenne as they walked up Fifth Avenue toward the Central Park project. "They have lakes and bridges and even a sheep meadow."

"Good hunting, then?"

Rafe looked at him in alarm. "No. No hunting. Not any-where in the city."

"Then why do they keep sheep there?"

"For show."

"Like Pringle."

"Exactly."

Pringle was the ancient butler at the Sixty-ninth Street brownstone owned by their hostess, Mrs. Throckmorton. He and Thomas had gotten off on the wrong foot upon their arrival the previous night when Pringle had answered their knock, saw the Indian on the steps, shrieked, and tried to slam the heavy front door in his face.

Then this morning, Ash had informed them that the old codger would be going with them to Scotland as his manser-vant, which amused Tait Rylander no end. Apparently he had dealt with Pringle before. Rafe figured it was only a matter of time before something dire happened. And not to Thomas.

After a long traipse through the park, he and Thomas were back at Mrs. Throckmorton's brownstone, waiting impatiently for Pringle to answer their knock. The haughty butler was as slow as Christmas.

When the door finally opened, the old man glowered at Thomas, then hiked his pointed nose. "Yes?"

"Just open the door," Rafe snapped.

"And who may I say is calling?"

"The man who's keeping this Indian from slitting your throat."

With an affronted glare, Pringle opened the door.

Ash was crossing the entry as they stepped inside. When he caught sight of Thomas, he stopped dead. "You cut your hair."

"But I will not wear a skirt." Elbowing Pringle aside, the Cheyenne stalked toward the kitchen at the back of the house.

"Kilt," the Scotsman called after him. "And I dinna ask you to." Turning back to Rafe, he asked what that was about.

"He wants to look white. Says he's tired of being stared at." Rafe unbuckled his gun belt, and ignoring Pringle's sniff of disapproval, hung it on the hall tree by the door. "He wouldn't let the tailor fit him for a suit, either."

"Bluidy hell." Realizing the butler was listening to their conversation, Ash waved him away. "Dismissed, Pringle."

The butler made a deep, sneering bow. "Thank you, your lordship. Should you have need of me, I shall be in the back, scraping manure off your boots."

Ash rounded on him. "The old lady is making me take you to Scotland, you simpering sod, but that doesna mean you'll arrive there safely. Do ye ken?"

Pringle's nostrils flared. His faded blue eyes narrowed mutinously below his bushy white brows. "I do, indeed, sir. Your lordship." Another smirking bow.

As the muttering butler shuffled down the hall, Ash grimaced and dragged a hand through his gray hair. "This is becoming a bluidy circus, Rafe. I'm saddled with that bumbling ass, my wife's acting strange, and now Thomas wants to be white. By the bones of Saint Andrew, I've a mind to go by myself."

Rafe didn't respond.

"Aye, well, too late for that. The vouchers from the White Star Line came this morning. We leave in a week on the *Oceanic*. Since I dinna want Thomas—white or not—prowling about in steerage, you and he will be sharing a cabin next to ours. But if he expects to eat with the other first-class saloon passengers, he'll need a proper suit of clothes, including neckwear, and real boots."

"Have your wife and Mrs. Rylander tell him. He responds better to ladies."

"Aye." Ash flashed a broad grin. "They'll bring him to heel in no time."

A week later, Rafe stood in the cabin he would be sharing with Thomas and looked around at the luxurious accommodations. Two tidy beds, a private lavatory with a tub that boasted hot and cold running water, an electric bell to summon the steward, bureaus, a built-in closet with a mirror, and a promenade deck right outside their window. Impressive. Rafe had read the brochure that came with the tickets, and knew the *Oceanic* was the latest design in oceangoing steamships. In addition to the hot and cold water and promenade deck, it also carried four masts for auxiliary sails, twelve boilers, a four-cylinder compound engine, and had an iron hull. They were traveling in class.

Thomas was less impressed. "Is that the only window?"

"Better than belowdecks in steerage with Pringle and the other single men. They don't have any windows." Opening his trunk, Rafe began transferring clothing and books to the bureau built into the wall beside his bed.

Thomas peered through the small window at the chairs lined up along the open deck. "I will sleep out there."

"Not allowed." As he unpacked, Rafe watched the Cheyenne pace the small cabin. He knew it was difficult for the Indian to give up the freedom he was accustomed to, and could only guess at how difficult it must be to straddle two cultures. But Thomas had chosen this path, so Rafe would try to make the transition as painless as possible—mostly for himself. He didn't want to listen to him pace all night. "I thought you wanted to act white."

Thomas turned to look at him.

"Then you'd best get used to sleeping indoors, and wearing proper clothes, and following the rules. Can you do that?"

Muttering in Cheyenne, Thomas slouched onto the bed against the far wall.

Ignoring the glare in those dark eyes, Rafe resumed unpacking. He respected Thomas. Liked the man's steadfast loyalty and assured manner. But he sensed this whole "white" thing was destined for failure. What would happen to Thomas then?

After he emptied the trunk, he set it in the closet, then stretched out on his bed with one of the books he had borrowed from Mrs. Throckmorton's library—*Rob Roy,* a historical adventure novel by Sir Walter Scott. It was hard reading because a lot of the dialogue was in Scottish, and he had to flip to the glossary for the meaning of the words. But since he would be visiting Scotland for a month or two, he wanted to get a feel for the people.

"You brought many books," Thomas said after a while.

Rafe nodded absently. Then an idea came to him and he lowered the book. "Can you read, Thomas?"

There was a long pause before the Indian answered. "When Black Kettle was my chief, white missionaries came to our village with a book about your Christian god. They offered to teach us to read it. I tried. But I was young, and found the lessons boring, so I stopped going. Later, the bluecoats came with the papers they called 'treaties'. I could not read them, but I wanted to believe they would keep the People safe. We soon learned the words written there were false.

"Then Prudence Lincoln came." He looked toward the window, a small smile tugging at his lips. "I was a much better student with her." The smile faded. "But none of her books spoke of the People. So I have not read since she left."

"But you did learn your letters?" Rafe persisted.

"And numbers. But because I have no interest, I am slow."

Rafe rose from the bed and went to the bureau. After studying the titles, he pulled one from the stack—*The Last of the Mohicans* by James Fenimore Cooper. "You might like this one." He handed the book to Thomas. "It's about an Indian and a white scout who fought together against the French many years ago."

"Did they win?"

"Read it and see."